By Laura Kinsale

FLOWERS FROM THE STORM
THE HIDDEN HEART
THE SHADOW AND THE STAR
UNCERTAIN MAGIC

LAURA KINSALE

THE HIDDEN HEART

AVON BOOKS
An Imprint of HarperCollinsPublishers

This is a work of fiction. Names, characters, places, and incidents are products of the author's imagination or are used fictitiously and are not to be construed as real. Any resemblance to actual events, locales, organizations, or persons, living or dead, is entirely coincidental.

AVON BOOKS
An Imprint of HarperCollins*Publishers*
10 East 53rd Street
New York, New York 10022-5299

Copyright © 1986 by Laura Kinsale
ISBN: 0-380-75008-2
www.avonromance.com

First Avon Books paperback printing: April 1986

Avon Trademark Reg. U.S. Pat. Off. and in Other Countries, Marca Registrada, Hecho en U.S.A.
HarperCollins ® is a trademark of HarperCollins Publishers Inc.

Printed in the U.S.A.

10 9

THE
HIDDEN
HEART

Prologue

Standing amid a bedraggled group of nearly naked Indians, Lady Tess Collier was aware she didn't look much like a lady. She didn't need the peculiar glances of the genteel European residents of Pará to tell her that after a six-month odyssey down the Amazon she presented a most unprepossessing figure. Skirt torn and heavy with water and sand from landing the pirogues on the beach; hair unkempt and trailing down from the knot at her neck; fingernails blunted or broken by the efforts of unloading her precious collection of plants and animals—no, she didn't look much like the only daughter of the Earl of Morrow.

She pushed back a loose strand of ebony hair and generously informed the Indians that the jungle monsters with holes for faces were no longer in pursuit, and now that the boats had been unloaded, the men could return home in perfect safety. The relief on their faces was sadly comical. They had escorted the white woman out of Barra do Río Negro in order to save themselves from the supernatural beasts that she had said would surely descend upon them if they hadn't. All the way down the river, they had cast worried looks over their shoulders.

At her words of dismissal, they wandered off, looking as lost and disconsolate in the unfamiliar urban surroundings as she felt herself. Six months. Six months and a thousand miles downriver, and she still had not completely accepted her father's death. He had succumbed to yellow fever on New Year's Day, in a village upstream from Barra. January 1, 1863—ten years to the day since he had packed up his motherless eleven-year-old daughter and left his rich estate in West Sussex to wander the world as a natural scientist.

"Go home," he had told her, lying sweating and faint in an Indian's hut. She had not cried. She had smiled at him as he slipped away, and told him not to worry for her. She buried him in the shallow soil of the jungle, beneath the towering trees he had loved, with only herself and a Portuguese priest and one naked little Negro boy to mourn his passing. Go home, his soundless voice had whispered under the silent trees. Go home.

An ill-tempered squawk sounded at her ear as she stood musing in the sandy street. Tess turned a little, speaking soothingly to the tiny, bright-plumed parrot perched on her shoulder. The small bird looked at her with a bleak, suspicious eye, and then began to pull at her dark hair with its yellow beak. She leaned away with a smile. "You aren't having second thoughts about coming home with me, are you, Isidora?"

Isidora regarded Tess solemnly. Tess had tried to free the friendly parrot before leaving Barra, but when the door of the bird's woven cage had been opened, all Isidora had done was hop onto Tess's shoulder and settle comfortably. With no more coercion than a ready supply of nuts, the parrot had accompanied Tess down the river, and showed every intention of following her all the way to England. Tess had grumbled aloud at the bird's unabashed begging, but she was secretly glad to have even so small a friend along. The thought of returning to her old home filled her with far more trepidation than this journey alone on the Amazon. Natives and mosquitoes and river flood were troubles she understood. It was the life of a wealthy English heiress that was the mystery.

Go home. How simple that sounded, and how frightening. It had been as if her father had suddenly realized, on his sickbed, just how alone and unprotected his only surviving daughter would be without him. Through all those years of adventure, he had never seemed to worry about her future, and with the faith of a child, Tess had not either. She had let herself believe that their traveling life could continue indefinitely, that her father would be with her forever.

She lifted her chin. No use to dwell on that now. It was nearly two miles from the beach to the country house of Abraham Taylor, the British consul in Pará. She knew from what her father had told her of the papers she was to deliver to his old Eton friend that Mr. Taylor was to be the trustee of her estate. It was a comforting thought, one of the few in a sea of discomforting ones. In the lengthening shadows of late afternoon, she stumbled across rough stone paving and through the deep sandy stretches of unpaved road, lifting her bedraggled skirt and perspiring in the wet heat.

As she left the main city, a wild tangle of vegetation closed around her. Brilliant green-and-blue-striped lizards stood high on four legs and scampered out of her path with their tails held like spikes in the air. She walked up the quiet lane, followed by sleepy birdcalls and the flutter of a spectacular metallic-blue butterfly which she identified automatically as the genus *Morphos*. When the Taylors' weathered gate appeared, she trudged up the steps onto the wide veranda of the rambling *rosinha*.

A Negro maid answered the knocker. Tess followed the woman into a central hall, where the evening air was touched with a welcome coolness, fragrant with foliage smells. A vampire bat fluttered high in the shadowed timbers of the roof—out early, as it was not quite twilight. The large rooms of the stuccoed home were still well-lit by the orange and gold shafts of sunset that poured through the tall windows and doors. Tess was escorted through the bare hall into a sparsely furnished parlor, where a slender, gray-haired woman sat reading to her husband.

Mrs. Taylor laid aside her Bible, rising from her seat with a surprised cry. Mr. Taylor started forward, a smile on his stalwart, generously whiskered face, while his wife stretched out both hands. "Lady Tess—thank the Lord!" she cried. "We've been so worried; we heard nothing for so long! Your dress—what's happened? Where's your father?"

Tess took a deep breath and walked to Mrs. Taylor, steadying the older woman's trembling hands in her own young and supple fingers. "Papa is gone, Mrs. Taylor," she said gently. "The fever took him."

Mrs. Taylor's face changed. Tess felt the shaking in her hands increase and pressed them. "Please, ma'am, sit down," she urged. "I'm sorry—it was cruel, not to prepare you, but there was no way to send word."

Mrs. Taylor sank into her chair. Tess knelt beside her and looked up through the blur that swam suddenly in her own eyes. To give this news to her father's oldest and truest friends somehow made it fully real. She would never again see her father, never again hear his beloved voice describing some botanical wonder he had found. The demands of the journey had obscured the magnitude of that loss; while she had fought her way through adversity, she had felt him always at her shoulder. Now, when she had reached her goal, her lower lip began to quiver.

"When?" Mr. Taylor asked quietly.

Tess strove to keep her voice steady. "New Year's Day. Upriver from Barra."

"New Year's Day—" his wife said weakly. "So long—"

"You've been alone since then?" Mr. Taylor interrupted. His tone was harsh, but Tess recognized the pain beneath. She could see him counting days and miles, and all the dangers on the river.

She nodded slowly. "It—took a long time to come back."

He made a rough sound and turned away. Mrs. Taylor laid her trembling hands on Tess's hair. "Oh, my poor love!" she whispered.

"I'm all right," Tess mumbled through the rising lump in her throat. She brushed absently at Isidora, who was determined to destroy what little was left of Tess's chignon.

"You are—" Mr. Taylor stopped, and then said, "I believe you are the bravest young woman I have ever met, Lady Tess."

"Oh, no," she said faintly. "I'm not brave at all."

Mrs. Taylor stroked Tess's hair, ignoring Isidora's rasping complaint. "Never mind. You're safe now, safe with us."

"But I can't stay." Tess looked up. "I have to go to England—I promised him."

Mrs. Taylor touched Tess's cheek with fingers that shook softly, the effect of the wasting disease that was slowly consuming the older woman. "Don't you want to go home now?"

"No." Tess bit her lip. "I don't."

"But darling, why not?"

"B-because—" To her horror, Tess heard her voice break childishly. She tried to stop herself, but all the tension and weariness and grief of the past six months welled up into a sudden, violent sob. "Because," she cried miserably, burying her face in Mrs. Taylor's skirt, "all those English people—they'll expect me to be a lady! They'll laugh at me, and think badly of Papa for bringing me up, and I'm— It's so stupid, I know, I'm such a coward . . ." She stood up, and dashed the tears angrily away. "Oh, blast—I *won't* cry! But he made me promise I would *marry!*" Her voice rose unhappily as she spread her hands to take in her ruined skirt and disheveled hair and the parrot that had hopped brazenly to the top of her head. "Oh, look at me, Mrs. Taylor— what gentleman will want a yahoo like *me* for a wife?"

Chapter 1

*I*n the warm December downpour, Gryphon Meridon rubbed rain off his aristocratic nose with a gesture that spoke less of aristocracy than of common disgust. If he neglected to slam the flimsy door of the Santa María de Belém do Gran Pará customhouse behind him, it was more from a fear that the rotting barrier would fall off its hinges in his hand than from any gentler sensibilities. He doffed a shapeless and dripping hat and shook his head, flinging sparkling droplets from a wild cut of curls that were tarnished to a wet bronze and plastered to his forehead.

With the aid of a liberal dose of Mexican silver, he'd just finished registering his ship in port—the *Arcanum,* out of Liverpool, owned and commanded by Captain G. Frost. No matter that each of those facts was a bald-faced lie, as long as they agreed with the papers. Captain Frost he was to the world at the moment, and the name passed off his tongue as if it were completely his own.

He avoided a yawning puddle at the foot of the steps, straddling it in one easy stride that took him into the waterlogged, unpaved street. His ship was not even visible through the misting rain, though she was docked at the end of the wharf just in front of him. He swore morosely, hoping his chief mate was coping with the new crew. Grady would be doing his tyrannical best to keep the unfamiliar men working, but they were a damned sorry lot.

"Normal" was not a term Gryf or anyone else would have applied to *Arcanum*'s typical operations; but the ship's current situation was certainly far from her standard. Well above it, most would say, but Gryf wasn't so sure of that. True, they were running with a full crew of twenty-three this time, instead of the usual ten that included Gryf himself and Grady, but the jailbait that made up the difference had turned out to be worse than nothing.

It was all, of course, for Her Delicate Highness, Lady Terese Collier. In the space of two months, Gryf had found his clipper transformed from a hired blockade-runner into a vessel that resembled nothing so much as an elegant floating nursery.

Up until this quixotic mission, he had been reasonably happy working for the eccentric Earl of Morrow. The earl's charter had been a lucky break for Gryf. Instead of the *Arcanum,* Morrow could have hired one of the needle-fast steamers that were being specially built to run the Yankee gauntlet; he probably would have, except what the earl had in mind amounted to mercy calls. He wasn't interested in quadrupled profits. He simply wanted to *give* the cargo away, to make sure his Rebel friends didn't starve behind the line. There weren't many takers for a deal like that, when there was real money to be made at the same degree of risk.

But that particular enterprise was over now. Gryf had made his appointed port in Nassau, looking for further instructions, hungry for more work even though the blockade was beginning to tighten dangerously. In the back of his mind had been the hope that the earl might even keep him on after the war. It would have been the answer to half a lifetime of prayer, to find a permanent charter. A miracle, to know where their next mouthful would come from. At twenty-five, Gryf had forgotten what that kind of security felt like—could not even imagine it anymore, so that he was not really disappointed, he told himself, that it hadn't worked out.

The earl's Nassau agent had offered Gryf one last job. No, that was perhaps too gentle a term. He had *insisted*. A letter had arrived from Brazil—the earl was dead; the earl's daughter wanted to go home. The agent had looked over the *Arcanum* and pronounced her a perfectly satisfactory conveyance, with a few improvements. Gryf had been willing, until he heard the going rate, and who was getting the bill for the "improvements."

So they'd simply blackmailed him. It was easy enough: a known blockade-runner, a discreet word to the Yanks, and he was nothing but floating cinders. Lord Morrow had paid fair and not threatened. He had been a gentleman. His solicitors and agents were another matter.

As was his daughter.

Gryf hunched deeper into his oilskins. He was uneasy, out of his depth in this new scenario, with a crew that seemed ludicrously huge and useless and a ship he hardly recognized himself, with all the new decoration. They would put Lady Collier in the captain's cabin, a thought which made Gryf ache inside, with an old and barely perceptible pain. It was stupid, that pain, and pointless. The *Arcanum* had been fast and new and sailed under her true name once, years ago, before pirates had lured her into ambush and left her a floating hulk mainly filled with dead. On that fatal voyage the captain's cabin had been given up to Gryf's mother and father, and his two pretty sisters. In Gryf's mind it would always be theirs. Just as the *Arcanum* or *Aurora* or *Antiope* would always be the *Arcturus* to him. He slept forward with Grady, away from those ghosts, and kept his charts on the mess table.

Stupid, too, how that name still could pull at his heart, make it swell a little in foolish pride. *Arcturus.* He kicked at a puddle in self-disgust. Sentimental tripe. His weakness, his damnable softness, was that he needed something to love and all he had left were Grady and the ship. What he would be now, without his old friend and the *Arcturus,* Gryf could not imagine. And he never intended to find out.

He quickened his pace, thinking of wet baggage and reduced profits and what they might look for next, after this delivery was complete. No one legitimate would trust him with a charter in an undermanned, outdated clipper of questionable registry, so he either bought his own cargo or took the occasional smuggling job, spinning in a never-ending circle, making enough to pay for cargo, wearing the ship down delivering it, and then pouring all the pathetic profits down the greedy maw of maintenance, so that the ship was at least seaworthy enough to let him scrounge again for a cargo stake to start the cycle over.

He'd hoped the blockade work would end all that. It should have, until the agent had ordered the overhaul and extra crew, and Gryf had seen his precious savings vanish like a morning mist. Worse than that, he was getting a reputation, which meant time for another name change, because the last thing he needed was a reputation in the kind of places where he already had one under older aliases. He was small fry, unimportant and unnoticed, and he wanted to stay that way. Too much time, too many names and faked papers and unpaid debts stood between him and that distant afternoon adrift in the Indian Ocean, when a scared and weeping boy had stood by and watched his dying uncle, the last of his own blood kin, sign a thin scrawl to the paper that made twelve-year-old Gryphon Meridon into captain, owner, and most of crew of the *Arcturus*. Too many years of running and skimping and scraping by with whatever cargoes, legitimate or illegal, that he could find to carry. He was not a criminal by nature—he was not even very good at it—but the demands of his ship had no end. He did not know how else to live.

Grady materialized out of the mists in front of Gryf, the gray-streaked hair and red beard unmistakable even through the soup. "Cap'n!" The mate's voice was gritty with more than usual emphasis, as if the dismay which widened his milky-blue eyes had found a way down his throat to choke him. "Cap'n, we've done bought us some trouble dear!"

A familiar twist went through Gryf's stomach, a surge of the constant and ingrained anxiety that had colored all his adult life. "What?" he demanded. If there was trouble . . . if there was trouble . . . His mind went blank and then raced, panning a whole unpleasant vista of possibilities. "What in the name of God is it?"

Grady flung out his free hand, waving toward the forecastle, which was barely visible through the haze. "Up over, Cap'n," he ground out. "Divil take her, I be stymied."

Gryf followed the gesture, seeing nothing on deck but a green tangle that looked to be a few square yards lifted right out of the jungle itself, and an oilskinned crew member tugging ineffectually at one of the larger plants.

He relaxed a degree, not identifying any immediate threat. "They told us to expect that, Grady," he said, puzzled by his chief mate's agitation. "Those are the earl's specimens. Just secure them in the hold amidships the best you can."

Grady set his feet and turned to Gryf with a look that was mutinous. "*You* do 'er, then, by God. I'm right busy." He nodded vigorously, shoring up his rebellion. "I done told you, Cap'n, what I thinks about this trip. Plain folly, 'tis. I said that. You see to the bloomin' plants."

Grady's captain looked after his friend in bafflement, feeling decidedly at a loss as the older man stalked away. Chewing on his lower lip, Gryf looked up again toward the ship. The same crewman, or another—they were unrecognizable in the ubiquitous oilskins—was still doggedly rearranging plants. Gryf considered a moment, came up with no particular explanation for Grady's behavior, and started for the plank.

"You there," he hailed the persistent crewman as he gained the deck. "Forget those plants. You'll be needed on dockside to dolly the baggage."

The man remained bent over a specimen, ignoring Gryf's orders. Gryf hesitated, swearing under his breath, cursing himself as much as the seaman for his own ineffectiveness. He was a captain, yes, but captain of a crew of ten, running an embarrassingly democratic ship.

This new crew intimidated Gryf. Once, he had accidentally let slip a "please," and gotten such a queer look in return that he'd added "sir" in confusion, and then realized the ridiculousness of it himself: the captain calling the steward "sir." He felt hot blood go to his face at the humiliating memory, and snapped "You!" at the recalcitrant seaman, using the impetus of irritation to carry him across the deck in three strides. His hand came down roughly on the bent crewman's shoulder, and he whirled the man around to face him.

In the moment of action, he already regretted it. The flash of anger, directed toward himself, would not see him through a confrontation. He searched madly for the righteous bullying indignation of authority, failed to summon it, and glanced down at his captive with a chagrin that metamorphosed rapidly into shock.

His seaman was a woman.

The suspended second of discovery passed like infinity; Gryf stood paralyzed, open to a thousand minute details that came too fast to catalogue. She was tall for a woman, but not nearly as tall as he was, with dark hair and ivory skin, high cheekbones, a delicate chin, and eyes of blue-green or gray or some color too complex to comprehend, their brilliance outlined with a bold thick fringe of sooty lashes.

He felt his mouth go slack, his hand dropped, and the details came together in a thunderclap. She was beautiful. Unquestionably, painfully, soul-searingly beautiful, even in a set of baggy, bedraggled foul-weather gear. He blinked and felt his heart contract as it did when the official questions got too sharp and suspicious. The rush of blood should have saved him: in that state of mental panic he could usually summon his best and smoothest lies. Instead, his dockside eloquence vanished. All he could find to say was "Um."

Her dark eyebrows arched, managing offense and amusement at the same time. She looked up at him with an absolute lack of fear or modesty. Gryf had a sudden suspicion, a horrible vision of possibilities that solidified into numb certainty. He bit his tongue and tasted blood before he had his voice under control. "Lady Collier?" he ventured, a hoarse whisper of dismay, while he hoped with a forlorn and futile hope that he might be wrong.

She nodded, with a smile that went through him like light through clear water. He smiled back, the reflex of total desperation. A long moment of painful silence dragged past before Gryf said, "Oh."

"And you are . . . ?"

For an agonized split second, Gryf forgot the name he was using. But the survival habit of years was strong; he focused on a point near her right ear that was a degree less hypnotic than a head-on gaze into those level, sea-colored eyes, and made his tongue form words. "Gryphon Frost."

He had the feeling that he should bow, or offer to kiss her hand; the bald statement of his name seemed too abrupt.

"Of course," she said calmly. "The captain."

Her voice was smooth and melodic, as lovely as her face. Gryf observed a damp black curl that peeked out from behind her delicate earlobe, and wondered if he would ever again in his life see anything as beautiful. He felt the idiotic smile creep back onto his face, remembered how he had laid a threatening hand on her, and wished himself decently buried under eighty tons of ballast.

"Forgive me," he blundered. "I thought you were . . . I mistook you for one of my crew."

She laughed then, showing small white teeth, and touched her hand to the floppy brim of her hat. "I can't imagine why!"

Gryf wished he could think of some further expression of contrition, something more appropriate to his degree of mortification: throwing himself off the poop deck and drowning might suit. He remembered his own hat, pulled it quickly off his head, and stood there with rain running down his face. "Lady Collier—"

"Put your hat back on," she cried. "Or you'll certainly catch a fever!"

He obeyed her. The gesture of common sense gave him courage. It was conceivable that she was human, in spite of being an heiress. "Lady Collier, surely you don't need to concern yourself with stowage, especially on a day like this. We'll have the plants below shortly."

This was not quite true; the plants were last on his list of priorities. Foodstores came first, along with finishing out his cargo with a small purchase of india rubber that he'd managed on his own. Jerome Gould, the earl's Nassau agent, had loaded the ship with smuggled Southern cotton in the islands, infinitely pleased in the notion that he'd badgered Gryf into going past the safe draft limit again. Gryf had neglected to tell the man that in the process of the new outfitting and paint job, he had arranged to have the load lines placed five inches lower on the hull than the original marks. There was room for another twenty tons of cargo without danger.

Tess herself was oblivious to the proper loading order of ship's stores, and she had no intention of being put off again on the subject of the plants. She had dealt with stubborn ship's officers before. Whatever it took, coaxing or ordering or throwing an unladylike tantrum, she was ready to do battle for her specimens.

Captain Frost was obviously still embarrassed by the perfectly natural mistake of taking her for a crewman; he kept glancing down and up and anywhere but at her. His diffidence gave Tess ample opportunity for observation. He looked exactly as a blockade-runner should, she decided, with his sou'wester tilted at a rakish angle above strong, well-formed features, and his face clean-shaven and deeply tanned. No softness, except in his smoky-gray eyes, where an unexpected youthfulness contrasted with the hard lines etched around his mouth. Tess found herself warming to him, even as she ruthlessly prepared to take advantage of his discomfort. She raised her chin and smiled persuasively. "But Captain, the specimens will be on deck."

"Not for long," he vowed. "I promise you, ma'am, we'll have those plants out of the rain within the hour."

"You will do nothing of the sort," she retorted, changing tactics smoothly. "I want the pots lashed securely just aft of the forecastle deck. Your mate wouldn't do it, so I was trying to get on myself, but I can't seem to manage the larger ones."

Gryf looked down at his premier passenger in consternation, and found that Grady's rebellion suddenly made sense. "You were trying to move them yourself?"

"Since your crew didn't seem inclined to help. Something about the plants being a hazard on deck, which is nonsense. If we put them here, just between the anchor deck and the windlass, they won't be in the way at all."

The idea that Lady Collier would even know port from starboard, much less recognize the windlass, made Gryf's eyebrows go up in dubious surprise. He absently wiped a rivulet of rainwater from his cheek. "I'm sure Grady meant that the plants themselves wouldn't be safe here," he temporized. "The hold—"

"—will be too dark," she finished for him. "Captain, several of these specimens have already traveled halfway around the globe on deck. I'm certain they will be fine."

He took a breath. "On a steamer, I'm sure they were. But the *Arcanum* is a clipper under full sail, ma— uh, Your Ladyship. We'll have water across the bow if we get into heavy weather."

"If the weather threatens, then we'll move them below, of course. But my father and I sailed from New Guinea to San Francisco on an American clipper, and even in foul weather, there was never any problem with salt water this far forward. That's one reason why I would like to have the specimens here."

Gryf glanced away, unable to look into her lovely face and argue deck sheer and freeboard heights and the difference between his Aberdeen-built ship and a Yankee design. Driving into rising seas, there would be plenty of salt water on the foredeck; enough to wash a man overboard, and certainly enough to damage the plants. But the answer was simple enough. Let the plants stay where they were for now. He'd have them moved after the *Arcanum* was under way.

"As you wish," he said at last. "I'll see that they're secured on deck."

He was rewarded for his surrender with a smile so bright it made him blink.

"Thank you. You're very reasonable, Captain Frost. I shall take myself out of your way, then—I know you won't fail me. And you had my note? The Taylors would like you to dine with us this evening."

All Gryf could manage was an awkward nod. There was a pressure building inside of him, a knot of hopeless yearning that he wanted to hide and was afraid he could not. He bowed to her, followed her to the rail, was turned down with a laugh when he offered to escort her home. She left him standing on the deck like an adoring puppy told to stay. He had that kind of worship on his face; he knew it, because when Grady came on board a moment later there was a disapproving scowl in the older man's glance.

It made no difference. Gryf watched her walk away, determined and graceful in her ill-fitting oilskins, and nothing in his life but his ship and his dreams had ever made him ache that way before.

Chapter 2

$\mathcal{T}$he small group that gathered for dinner on the Taylors' veranda was not exactly the cream of English society, but Tess was nervous all the same. It wasn't the Taylors who made her ill at ease. It wasn't the Campbells, either, for the Methodist missionary couple who were to accompany her back on the ship as chaperones were a delightful pair, with their dour Scots' expressions and absurd wit. It was, Tess thought resentfully, entirely Captain Frost's fault.

She had dressed so carefully, in a white linen gown sashed with pale gray to indicate half-mourning. With an excited anticipation that she saw now as childish, she had intended to elicit that same look of stunned admiration from everyone that she had seen on Captain Frost's face that morning. It was a new and heady sensation, to put a gentleman ill at ease with her mere presence. Captain Frost didn't actually count as a gentleman, of course, but he was the best she could do at the moment. She and the maid had worked for three hours to smooth her hair into a glossy, blue-black roll just like in the old issue of the *Illustrated London News* that she had discovered behind a dictionary in Mr. Taylor's study. When she walked into the parlor before dinner to greet their guests, she had felt quite regally self-assured, ready to impress them all with her polish.

Unfortunately, it was Captain Frost who had done the impressing. The shipboard figure in wet and well-worn oil skins was transformed; a tall, golden-haired stranger stood in his place and kissed her hand with a touch so brief and reserved she hardly felt it. He was extraordinarily handsome—far more so than Tess had realized initially. Well-tailored clothes emphasized his patrician features; in place of foul-weather gear there was a fine white cravat and gold tie pin, a spotless blue coat, and an aura of severe elegance that was as intimidating to Tess as it was unexpected. She looked up as he released her hand, hoping to find the appreciation she had seen in his eyes that morning, but he turned away without meeting her shy smile, and afterwards never once looked directly at her.

Tess sat now at the table across from him, slowly sipping her pumpkin soup and trying not to glance up too often. In the wavering candlelight his face was beautiful and remote: a golden, gloomy Lucifer after the Fall. She wished she were someone else. Someone graceful and pretty and full of teasing gossip, like the daughter of the new bank director just arrived in Pará. Someone who knew all the news of England, the scandals and the politics, and could tell them with such droll lightness that everyone would laugh. Perhaps then Captain Frost would not sit so impossibly silent and detached. Perhaps then Tess would make him smile, and look at her, and . . .

And what?

Tess sighed over her soup. She did not care; she *refused* to care what Captain Frost thought of her. If he was bored to tears, as he gave every appearance of being in his wordless preoccupation with his meal, it was nothing to her. He was a blockade-runner, for pity's sake, not the Prince of Wales.

It occurred to her that she would probably be meeting the Prince of Wales before the next year was out. Her father had said something about it, rambling on about balls and drums and being presented at one of the Queen's Drawing Rooms. The thought was appalling. If she had so little success in pleasing a blockade-runner, whatever would royalty think? Obviously, she had been wrong that morning when she had thought that Captain Frost admired her—he had just been surprised, that was all—surprised and probably offended by the appearance of a mannerless girl who took the liberty of prowling the docks in a man's foul-weather gear.

A renewed surge of resentment flowed through her. What right did he have to be offended? Captain Frost was hardly a scion of respectability himself, considering his occupation. If she hadn't gone to the dock when she'd heard his ship had arrived, his crew would have stowed her plants in the hold! She would have to go back again tomorrow, to make sure they took care of the live animals properly—no doubt the elegant Captain Frost was so ignorant of the poor creatures' needs that he would put the baby sloth in a cage with a boa constrictor.

The cheerful conversation between the Taylors and the Campbells lagged while the soup bowls were cleared and a large platter of fish offered round. Tess stared at the table in front of her, folding and refolding a corner of her napkin restlessly. After a moment, she stole another look toward Captain Frost, and her heart gave a quick squeeze of alarm as she realized he was watching her.

It was not an obvious perusal, only a fortuitous tilt of

his head, so that he might have been watching the Negro footman serve Mrs. Campbell's fish. But he seemed instead to be fascinated by the cut of Tess's gown, for he stared at her bodice with a hooded, dreamy expression, not even aware that she had looked up.

She felt her face warm, certain that he saw some flaw in her outfitting. His gaze traveled upward with painful leisure, so that she was sure he must be finding fault with her white lace collar and the styling of her hair. It must be years out of date, she thought miserably. That magazine was so old . . . and the banker's daughter doesn't dress her hair like this at all.

Shamed, Tess bowed her head. But the suspense was too much; she raised her lashes surreptitiously to see what he was judging next. His ash-gray eyes met hers in a direct encounter, and in the instant of contact there was communication, an intensity revealed beneath those half-closed lids that shocked her. His look held hidden wildness, and more: for a moment there was romance and adventure and a kind of madness there, a frustration, held in check and then banished by the flick of his gilded lashes as he looked away.

It was startling—and rather frightening—as if she had narrowly escaped the claws of a tiger and saw the beast still, transformed to a house cat and curled near the fire. The vague unease that had plagued her seemed to crystallize into something solid: a queer, pleasant tightening at the base of her throat, an awareness of the pressing softness of her shift across her breasts. For the first time in her life, she had a strong sense of herself as *female*, and of Captain Frost as . . . something else.

As soon as the feeling took shape in her mind, she knew that it was wrong. Sinful. Tess was fully informed on sex and reproduction; she had seen and studied things that she knew were unmentionable, which would have made most young ladies of her own class swoon. She had approached the subject with the rationality her father had taught her, maintaining a disengaged, clinical interest, compiling facts which were part of the study of nature.

But here, in the shuttered glance of a silent man, was mystery. Here was something dangerous and dark: a torrent she could drown in. She felt her immortal soul hang in the balance and flung herself back from the cliff, looking down at her poached fish as if it were the gateway into Hell itself.

A heartbeat more, and the feeling passed. The fish was only fish again, and a good deal safer to contemplate than the face across the table from her. What Captain Frost had thought of the instant of encounter she could not tell; she was afraid to look at him again. Mrs. Campbell said something to him, but it might as well have been the gabble of a goose for all Tess understood it. The only thing she comprehended was the sound of the captain's answer: not the words, but the rhythm and the timbre of his voice, the reserve that lay like a thin shield over deeper things.

Tess drew that same cloak over her own feelings, though it seemed in her case pathetically transparent. She sat through the meal subdued, the food like dust in her mouth. Dim appetites moved in her that had nothing to do with hunger. She saw the captain's hand rest against his wine goblet and wished to touch him; saw the tousle of sun-colored curls and wished to smooth them. She wanted to be held, to press her cheek against his coat and feel the living warmth beneath. And with each temptation, she became more of a stranger to herself, someone new and mystifying within her own skin.

It was a relief when Mrs. Taylor stood up from the

table. A relief, and a new frustration, for the men stayed on the veranda with their port as the ladies went inside. Tess was angry at her own disappointment—and angry at herself for joining the ladies in urging the men not to tarry long. She had other things to think of, she reminded herself firmly. Important things. Arrangements had to be made to catalogue all her father's specimens when they arrived in England; Mr. Darwin would want to see some of the orchids, and there were several of her father's monographs that might, with a little editing, be presented at a meeting of the Linnean Society if Tess could find a member who would read them. There were a hundred things she had to consider, all of them more interesting than a blockade-running sea captain.

Sitting in the drawing room, she tried to keep her mind on those interesting things, but whenever the sound of male laughter drifted to her through the open windows, she found herself glancing toward the door. Mrs. Taylor and Mrs. Campbell remained deep in a conversation about the price of Irish butter, a subject to which Tess had nothing to add, and which hardly seemed to warrant the amount of time they were spending on it.

She stared morosely at the needle and undarned stocking in her lap. This is how it will be when I'm married, she thought. Waiting on men and talking of butter. Or worse, talking of fashion and scandal and money, like the banker's daughter.

Such a future loomed utterly bleak before Tess. From her aborted attempts at friendship with the newly arrived young lady, Tess had already found out that amusing stories about the vagaries of trying to trap live monkeys were anathema. Similar tales of encounters with elusive snakes and lizards had elicited shrieks of alarm instead of laughter, and a tentative mention of the beauties of Brazilian forests had brought nothing but a look of polite boredom. Tess had given up in despair after one visit, and she had not received an invitation to further the acquaintance.

She dropped the stocking in her lap and interlaced her fingers, gripping them tightly. How she wished to go back to Tahiti, instead of to England. She'd had a friend there, a real friend: Mahina, with her dark and laughing eyes and adventurous spirit. The two of them had climbed green-swathed mountains right up into the mists; they had swum in the lagoons, and sailed to their own special small island to camp and play and giggle over nonsense, living on the fish they caught until their supply of fresh water ran out and they had to return to Papeete.

The carefree, girlish Tess of those days seemed far away now. It had been five years since she had left Tahiti—harder years than her idyllic time in the islands, but still full of excitement and challenge. As she matured, she had absorbed her father's fascination with the natural world. She had learned from him, and under his encouraging guidance had developed habits of logical thought and discipline. Gradually, she had taken over the practical portion of their journeys: the supplies and logistics, things that her father had managed with impatience and not always very well. Under Tess's supervision, they had not necessarily traveled in great comfort, but they had seldom run short of salt or sugar or glass jars to preserve their collections.

Footsteps sounded on the veranda. Tess looked up, realized that she had done so, and quickly looked down again. She tried to cover the sudden quickening of her heartbeat with several deliberate stabs at her stocking until she realized that she had not threaded the needle.

No gentlemen appeared at the door. Mrs. Taylor and

Mrs. Campbell chatted on. Between anticipation that the men were coming in and disappointment that they seemed only to be moving to another spot on the porch, Tess found it hard to keep her hands still. She twisted the stocking, wondering what she might say to Captain Frost when he did come inside. Then she pressed her lips together in exasperation, asking herself what earthly difference it made. Her mind bounced back and forth between fretting over the captain and scorning herself for doing so, until she threw down the stocking with a violent motion of self-disgust.

The other two women looked up at her in surprise. Reddening, Tess cast about and seized on the first excuse for her action that she could find. She picked up the large Bible from the table next to her chair and asked brightly, "Shall I read to you?"

Mrs. Taylor smiled. "I'm sorry, love—we old women have been maundering on, haven't we? Please do. Mrs. Campbell, would you suggest a passage?"

Mrs. Campbell obligingly did so. Tess turned up the oil lamp on the table to supplement the pale yellow light from the gas lamp that hissed softly overhead. She found the recommended place, took a deep breath to gather her scattered wits, and began to read.

Outside, Gryf stood on the veranda near the open window. He tensed a little at the first sound of Lady Collier's clear voice, and then relaxed as it began to play over biblical passages like the sweet tones of a flute. He was faintly dizzy, from the dinner wine and the port and the soft, heady perfume that seemed to him to have lingered since she had left the table. The conversation of the two other men was an annoying undertone; he wished they would be quiet, so that he could listen to her.

His mother had done that when he was a child, read

the Bible of an evening, after dinner, and he had sat on the veranda of their bungalow in Calcutta and listened. It had always made him feel secure, feel that life was at rights and unchangeable . . . the small safe world of a boy, seeing the future as nothing but endless days and hours of delight.

His real future had come all too quickly: one day he had been a child, well-loved, and the next he'd been alone and terrified. Gryf's family had never made it home to England on his Uncle Alexander's proud new ship, betrayed instead by their own decency. A burning vessel, a plea for help—they had all been false, cunning lures into a pirate trap. Only Gryf had lived, and Grady, who was the second officer, and Gryf's uncle, for a little while.

Gryf rotated the glass of port in his fingers and took a sip, letting the nightmarish memory slide away as he concentrated on the soothing voice from inside. It touched a chord in him, a lonely echo in the emptiness, so that he hurt for things he could not have. He should be taking his leave, he knew, going back to where he belonged, but he could not bring himself to break the spell that wove its siren arms around him.

So he stood, drifting in his mind and soul, until Mr. Campbell excused himself to go inside, and their host addressed Gryf.

"You're quiet, Captain. Will you have another port?"

Gryf looked through the darkness toward Taylor, who was seated in a wicker chair, visible only as a silhouette with a glowing pipe bowl. "Thank you, no."

"I fear that we're boring you with local politics."

"Not at all," Gryf said honestly. He was not paying enough attention to them to be bored.

The older man was silent for a moment. Gryf labored to bring himself out of his trance, not wishing to appear impolite. He had taken a cautious liking to Taylor. The consul seemed to have assumed control of the late earl's affairs with a competent hand, and to Gryf's surprise and relief had evidenced no curiosity about the *Arcanum* and her questionable British registration. He could only wish that the earl's Nassau agent had been as easy to deal with.

As if the consul followed Gryf's thoughts, Taylor said suddenly, "Tell me, Captain Frost, what did you think of Jerome Gould?"

Gryf wet his lips, brought back to reality with a jolt. He tried to read the disembodied voice for nuance, unsure whether the question was rhetorical or serious. If Gould had been playing games with the earl's accounts, Gryf had no desire to be implicated. Nor was he in a position to be making accusations. Even though he had done an honest job for Morrow, Gryf's own reputation was not exactly spotless. Stirring up the water around somebody else was a good way to get muddier himself.

"We didn't always see things from the same point of view," he said finally. There was no use pretending peaches and cream; the man had only to question Gould to find the truth of that.

"Is that so?" Taylor said, with no emotion that Gryf could discern. "And you're loaded with cotton now?"

Gryf's hand tightened a little around his glass. That was indeed a rhetorical question. Taylor knew exactly what the *Arcanum* was loaded with, and how much of it, except for rubber. "Yes, sir."

"I've been impressed with the job you've done for the earl, Captain."

"Thank you, sir." What the devil was the man getting at? "We've been lucky."

The pipe glowed brighter for a moment. "Perhaps. Come over here and sit down, away from the window. I have a favor to ask of you."

Damn, Gryf thought. He obeyed uneasily, seating himself on the edge of a chair and waiting.

"In my capacity as Lady Collier's trustee, I'd like to keep you on for a while. Would you be willing?"

Gryf hesitated. He didn't want any more blockade work, and he'd certainly had enough of Jerome Gould, but after this trip, Gryf would be without cargo and beyond the edge on cash. Stranded. The problem had been haunting him from Nassau: here was the answer.

"Yes, sir, I would."

"Without even knowing what I'd like you to do?"

"Try the blockade again, I assume, Mr. Taylor."

"You are either a very brave man or a desperate one, as the saying goes."

That cut a little too close. Gryf was left without a plausible answer, and so kept an uncomfortable silence.

"I don't want you to risk your ship again at that, Captain. The earl is gone, and his estate has been left to his daughter in my trust. But I must act exclusively within her wishes, and she has expressed no interest in continuing the blockade work."

Gryf looked into the darkness at his feet. Easy come, easy go, he thought wryly.

"I would like you to stay in England for a time. Do you have relatives there?"

Gryf looked up, startled, and hoped that his voice did not shake. "Not any longer."

"No? Well, you may have to manufacture some."

"I'm afraid I don't follow you."

The consul sighed audibly, and the pipe faded to a barely perceptible glow. "I knew Robert Collier a long time, Captain. Since Eton. He was not a . . . conventional man. I don't suppose he really thought like the rest of us. He loved his daughter; he took care of her, in his own way. But until the end, I don't think it had ever occurred to him that he had done her a grave disservice by taking her away from her home, and from any chance at a life of her own, without making serious provisions for her future."

Gryf waited. He had no idea what this explanation had to do with him.

"When Morrow fell ill," Taylor continued after a moment, "he apparently realized his mistake. He did what he thought he could; he wrote something of a will, leaving his estate to Lady Tess as her separate property, and naming me as the trustee. And he made her promise, on his deathbed, that she would marry as soon as possible." Taylor stood up abruptly, and rapped his pipe on the railing. Tiny sparks flared and fell down into the shadows below. "Unfortunately, an unwitnessed will made under such peculiar circumstances does not give Lady Tess much protection. A husband could easily find grounds to contest the trust. If it was held invalid, the estate would still be hers, but under the common law of England, her husband would control it."

Gryf was beginning to wish he were somewhere in the moonless dark off Charleston, running into port dodging Yankee gunfire. There was no reason for Taylor to discuss the legalities of Lady Collier's inheritance with an outsider, unless he planned to get that outsider seriously involved.

Taylor turned away from the rail, and took a step closer to Gryf. The consul's voice lowered earnestly. "In deference to my old friend, to the charge he put upon me with this trusteeship, and also to my own deep affection for his daughter, I must do my utmost to see that she does not marry a man who will take advantage of her."

Gryf cleared his throat. "You'd better explain just what it is you want me for."

"I need your help, Captain," Taylor said. "Your experience and judgment. In spite of her station and inheritance, Lady Tess will be virtually unprotected when she returns to England. She has naught but her mother's sister and her husband—a stiff-necked pair with more respectability than common sense—and a brood of brainless young cousins. She'll be a fish out of water, and an extremely plump and juicy one to every gazetted fortune hunter east of Land's End. She's rich, beautiful, intelligent, and utterly naive. It's a fatal combination."

A slow horror crept over Gryf as he pieced the plan together. "Surely you're not asking me to—"

"Indeed I am, Captain Frost. I want someone to look after her, to make sure she doesn't fall into the wrong hands, so to speak. I'll pay all your expenses; give you letters of introduction, so that you can move in the right circles. Until she becomes properly engaged, I'd like you there to look over any prospective suitors."

"I can't believe you're serious," Gryf stammered.

"Quite serious. I would go myself, but my wife . . ." Taylor stopped and then went on. "Unfortunately, with her illness, it is impossible for me to travel. I can handle the financial aspects of this trust from a distance, but I cannot give Lady Tess the guidance she will need. I'm willing to pay you double what we paid for each blockade run, on a monthly basis, and dry-dock charges for the ship as long as she's in port. Or wages for a substitute captain if you'd like to keep her working."

Gryf took a deep breath, trying to steady his fingers around the glass of port. "Mr. Taylor," he said softly. "I don't know why you're offering me this job, but I can assure you that you have the wrong man."

"Hearing you say that only strengthens my opinion."

"But—"

"Captain. Please. I need someone whom Lady Tess

can trust, someone she can think of as a friend. She's not to know of this agreement, of course."

Gryf clutched at that straw. "I thought you were obliged to act within her wishes."

"Or her father's. It was the earl who suggested you. Lady Tess brought the letter to me still sealed."

Gryf's mind had begun working again; he thought of the money, and his other gloomy prospects. Twice the blockade pay would buy him cargo—put Grady at the helm and keep the ship moving on top of what Gryf made. Two months of that and he would be even; four months and he would have a stake to work with; six, and he could buy into one of the China tea routes if he kept his purse strings tight.

He thought of the *Arcanum* as she had been just three months ago: hard-driven and shabby, her teak decks unvarnished, and leakage rotting the woodwork. She was in perfect condition, for once. Barring catastrophe, she wouldn't need any major maintenance for over a year. The offer was beginning to sound appealing.

"Why me?" he asked finally, slowly, because he was afraid he was going to say yes to this insane idea instead.

Taylor did not answer immediately. Instead, he walked back to the rail, where a faint light from the waning moon glazed his shoulders with silver. "For one thing, I haven't many choices. I need a man who can conduct himself in society, can befriend Lady Tess with some degree of sincerity and offer sensible advice . . . most importantly, I need someone who can be objective about Lady Collier and her inevitable suitors. Call it intuition. The earl liked you . . . I find that I like you. I believe that you can do it."

Gryf had the urge to laugh—or weep—at a description that seemed to fit anyone but him. Objective he could not be: he suspected he was half in love with Lady Collier already. His store of sensible advice for a young gentlewoman was extremely slim, consisting mainly of the firm conviction that she ought to stay clear of people like himself, and his half-forgotten knowledge of conduct in polite society was so shaky that he had hardly dared open his mouth since stepping inside the Taylors' door for fear of making a fool of himself.

"You really are my last hope, Captain," Taylor went on. "When Lady Tess sails with you, she'll be beyond my protection. I have written several friends in England to ask them to watch over her, but of course they'll not be in a position to dispense advice, or to—shall we say—make the intimate acquaintance of any young man she seems seriously interested in."

"You place a great deal of trust in someone you hardly know," Gryf stalled.

"Actually, I feel I know you rather well, Captain. For instance, I'm aware of the fact that you're carrying twenty tons of india rubber which is not on the cargo list."

It knocked Gryf off-balance, made his heart speed a little. Another blackmail? No . . . there was nothing really illegal about carrying off-list cargo: the worst they could do would be to fine him. Which was bad enough, considering his cash reserves. "Yes, sir," he said faintly. "I am. Would you like me to take it off?"

Taylor did not answer directly. "When I looked back over some of the previous reports, I found a curious discrepancy between the capacity of the *Arcanum* on her blockade runs and her capacity now."

Gryf sat silent, trapped, and ashamed he was trapped, stripped of his meager disguise as a gentleman and shown to be dishonorable before a decent man.

"Is the rubber yours or Mr. Gould's, Captain?"

"Mine."

"You changed the load lines on the ship."

"Yes."

"Why?"

Gryf swallowed, and then suddenly felt angry. He was tired of being taken, and doubly tired of taking the blame for every circumstance that drove him to the wall. "Mr. Gould overloaded me every run," he said evenly. "I knew he would do it again. I could risk it on those shorter legs, but not transatlantic."

"So you saw your chance when overhauling your ship to do something about it? Assuming rational discussion with Mr. Gould would not solve the problem?"

"Mr. Gould and I seldom had rational discussions."

"But he understood that he was overloading your ship?"

Gryf allowed himself a humorless smile in the dark. "Oh, yes. He knew it."

"Even on this latest voyage, when the marks had been changed, he overloaded the ship according to the bogus marks?"

"The load lines show we took on a quarter too much."

"Is the ship overloaded now, Captain?"

"No."

"Then I think you are the kind of man I want looking after Lady Collier."

Gryf blinked. "Because I duped your agent about the load lines?"

"Because you are a pragmatist. A more honest man might have come running to tell—a more dishonest one might have risked his ship and split the profits. Lady Collier must have someone close by with a realistic view of the world, who knows that people are not always what they seem and knows how to deal with them."

Taylor paused, and took a long puff of his pipe. "If it helps you to make your decision, please recall the considerable sum that Collier put out to refurbish your ship."

Gryf turned sharply, staring toward Taylor through the darkness. "Pardon me?"

"Come now, Captain, I'm not a man to mince words. You've come out of this deal quite handsomely, with the blockade pay and an overhauled ship besides. Surely you would like to continue to do business with us?"

Gryf was hardly listening. He sat back in his chair and swore softly, consigning Jerome Gould to the deepest, darkest, hottest pit in Hell. A sham, a cheap trick, all Gould's talk about the Yankees—and Gryf had fallen for it! Lord, his stupidity, his utter gullible imbecility, to have believed a word of the Nassau agent's chicanery. All Gryf's precious, hard-earned cargo stake—given away like candy to a dirty lying cheat.

"Captain?" Taylor prompted.

"Sir." Gryf took a deep breath to keep the quiver of rage from his voice. "*I* paid for that overhaul."

A silence heavy with significance stretched between them. Taylor pulled at his pipe, then grunted and said, "So one of us has been misled."

"You might say that," Gryf answered dryly. "And I suspect it was me."

"You're understandably angry."

Gryf gave a short, flat laugh. "Or just unbelievably stupid, to let Gould deduct the expenses from my account. Apparently I'm not as clever as you thought."

"I should reimburse you for your loss."

Gryf took note of that: the offer, and the implication that it was indeed himself who was out the money. He knew what was coming next.

"I will reimburse you," Taylor said, and paused. Gryf

smiled sourly at the accuracy of his own prediction. He would have given ten to one odds that Taylor's next word would be "after."

". . . after Lady Tess is safely married."

"Thank you, sir," Gryf acknowledged, making no attempt to hide his sarcasm. "You're more than generous."

"Call it an incentive, Captain. I don't ask questions about you, or about your ship—though we both know that I could if I wished. You've done the devil of a job for the earl, and I owe you that much, whatever you decide. I understand you have no personal feelings for her, having only met this evening, but I hope you will give the proposition serious consideration. She has need of you. Think on it tonight. I'll be on the dock in the morning with a contract, if you care to sign it."

Chapter 3

$\mathcal{T}$ess finished the last line of a long passage from the Sermon on the Mount. She had fully absorbed herself in the reading, successfully blocking out her surroundings and the unwelcome thoughts that had accompanied them. She was glad to have read; she felt much more relaxed than she had earlier, and the lines Mrs. Campbell had chosen brought a pleasant peacefulness to Tess's agitated soul. "Consider the lilies of the field . . ." What better guidance could be offered? She was too worried about the future. Let it come; she would open her heart to newer joys.

As her voice trailed into silence, she closed the book and looked up. She started slightly, realizing that the men had come quietly into the room while she had been reading. Captain Frost stood nearest the door with the ghost of a smile on his lips. It disappeared so quickly that Tess might have imagined it.

"Lovely, my dear," Mr. Taylor said heartily, amid a general murmur of agreement. "Will you continue?"

Seized by a sudden shyness, Tess demurred. Mr. Taylor did not seem at all disappointed, but immediately suggested a game of whist pitting the Campbells against the Taylors. No one but Tess appeared to realize that this scheme left the captain and herself with no entertainment but each other. She looked toward Mrs. Taylor in appeal, but the consul's wife was already engaged in hunting a pack of cards from a drawer in the credenza.

As the four players gathered at the card table, Mr. Taylor said carelessly, "Didn't you mention an interest in Lady Collier's animal collection, Captain? Perhaps she would be so kind as to show you her little zoo."

Tess saw the brief surprise in the captain's countenance. He recovered rapidly, but a glance that seemed oddly intense passed between the two men before Captain Frost turned to Tess and said he hoped she would do him the favor.

She swallowed down the anxiety that leaped into her throat. It was impossible to deny such a request, made by her host and reinforced by a guest. She realized that she was clasping her hands together in a nervous rhythm; she forced herself to still them and said, "Of course. Will you wait a moment, while I find a lamp?"

"Take this one, dear," Mrs. Taylor said, with a small wave of her trembling hand. "The gas is just over the card table, and we won't need more light."

Tess stood, lifting the oil lamp from the table next to her chair. She gave the captain a brief, nervous smile and led him into the hallway, acutely aware of the sound of his footsteps close behind her.

The animals were housed in a small shed in the rear of the garden. The term "garden" was more hopeful than realistic, for the space was a chaotic growth of vigorous plants and trees which refused to follow any order or reason but their own. Tess loved it. The fragrance of frangipani lay heavy on the still night air, and little rustlings and insect noises greeted them as they stepped outside. The light from the oil lamp was a small

spark in the black tangle, and the shed loomed up unexpectedly from the shadows.

Tess heard the low whining from inside the building
even before she lifted the latch. Frowning, she stood
back to let the captain enter and followed him inside.
The lamp threw grotesque shadows on the walls, and a
monkey gave a startled screech, setting off a jumble of
croaks and frightened calls. Tess touched the captain's
arm and raised her voice above the din. "They'll settle
down in a moment. Is there anything in particular you
would like to see?"

The question seemed to leave him at a loss. As the
menagerie quieted, he glanced around randomly and
asked, "What's that?"

On the near wall, above the stacked cages, Tess had
hung a smooth-sanded board. Stretched on the wood
was a brightly banded snakeskin.

"*Micrurus,*" she said. "A coral snake. One of the
neighborhood children brought it yesterday. He wanted
me to mount it." She realized suddenly how strange
such an explanation would seem and shrugged self-
consciously. "I know skinning snakes isn't a very . . .
ladylike talent, but I suppose I'm rather good at it."

He looked at her with a peculiar expression. "I'm
sure you are."

Tess blushed hotly. He must think her barbaric. She
bit her lip and turned away quickly, setting the lamp on
a crate before she bent to open a cage. She spoke quietly
to the hissing jaguar kit inside. The small black animal
pressed backward in fright, but Tess waited with hand
outstretched until the kitten nosed her suspiciously.
Recognizing his adopted mother, the kitten squeaked
happily and began a hoarse purr as Tess carefully lifted
the little ball of sleek fur into the light. Tiny claws
pricked at her fingers.

"This is Victoria," she said. "A planter shot her mother for raiding his pigs. I really don't want to take her home, but she's too young to be released."

The captain looked at the wriggling animal with interest. Despite herself, Tess was pleased to see a smile curve his lips as he reached out one careful finger to stroke the kitten's silken head. The grin was appealingly boyish, all the more so in contrast to his earlier severity, and she felt her own lips turn upward in automatic response.

"Victoria," he said pensively. "She's beautiful. Such black hair, and green eyes . . . like—"

Tess looked up curiously at the half-finished sentence, but he did not go on. He seemed very intent on scratching behind the kitten's ears. They stood without speaking, and Tess became aware again of the low, unhappy whine which emanated from the far corner of the hut.

"Now, who is that in trouble?" she wondered, and bent to return the jaguar to its cage before she turned back to the captain. "Please—may I have the lamp?"

He followed her as she carried the lamp toward the source of the sound. Tess knelt, frowning into the cage where the baby sloth usually hung contentedly upside down from its perch, munching on leaves. At first she could not see the animal, though its plaintive whimpers were clear enough. She finally recognized it cowering among a pile of fresh vegetation at the far corner of the small cage.

"I hope he isn't ill," she said fretfully. "He seemed perfectly all right this evening, when I checked." She held the lamp closer, trying to see the sloth. It blinked slowly in the light and ceased its whine. Tess reached with her free hand to open the cage.

"Lady Collier." Something in the captain's quiet voice made her stop. She turned to look at him, her arm still outstretched, and found herself staring down the barrel of a Colt revolver.

She froze. The ominous click of the cocking mechanism was loud in the unnatural silence. She opened her mouth, but his deadly calm words silenced her. "Set down the lamp."

Her glance flicked downward. Her hand was unsteady, and the light threw weird, dancing shadows on the walls. Close by her side, something moved, a thin, vertical shape that didn't belong among the familiar objects inside the shed. She looked at the moving apparition from the corner of her eye. Something in the shadow gleamed, as cold as the metal of the captain's gun. Horror rose in her throat like a sudden, choking hand.

"*Jararaca,*" she whispered, naming the deadly snake that seemed to sway with awful leisure inches from her arm. She was trapped, as helpless as the baby sloth, too close to escape before the serpent could strike. As she looked, the snake's movement quickened into jerky spasms. She drew in a sobbing breath of anticipation.

"The lamp," Captain Frost repeated.

With the numbing clarity of terror, Tess realized it was the movement of her own hand that caused the snake to seem active. Its shadow vibrated on the wall behind; the dark serpent itself was perfectly still, poised to strike in macabre silence. She could even see its eyes, glittering like unholy stars in the lamplight. Her breath and heart seemed to stop. From some unknown place inside of her came the ability to move: she lowered the lamp with painful slowness until it rested firmly on the dirt floor. The shadows ceased to dance, and the snake stood out from the background with sinister reality.

"Thank you," the captain said. Tess could not suppress a hysterical giggle at the incongruous politeness.

The wild sound burst out of her in a startled cry as the revolver erupted, filling the hut with a thunderous crash. In the same instant, Tess was aware of a flipping motion where the snake had been. She stumbled backward, brushing frantically at the headless reptilian body that landed across her arm. The snake fell to the ground, thrashing convulsively amid a riot of animal noise.

Tess stood gasping, unable to tear her eyes from the writhing shape. She was vaguely aware of the captain's arm around her, pulling her against him in an embrace that seemed intoxicatingly safe. She turned into his shoulder and hid her face for a long, blank minute, not thinking, not feeling, aware of nothing but the solid warmth of him, until voices rose above the sound of the animals as the Taylors and Campbells crashed through the dark garden to the hut.

Mr. Taylor reached the shed first. Tess looked up as the door slammed open and his hoarse voice demanded to know what had happened. She saw him take in the twisted body of the snake, and then his eyes went to the revolver still in Captain Frost's hand. The consul's whiskered face broke into a fierce grin. He whooped, adding to the general tumult, and turned to pull Mr. Campbell into the hut.

"Look at that, my man!" Mr. Taylor bellowed. "Good God, what a shot." He kicked at the snake. "Right in the head, and in this light. You couldn't have done better yourself, Lady Tess!"

Tess straightened, suddenly embarrassed by her weakness. She stepped away from the captain and looked down at the dead reptile. The two older ladies and a Negro gardener had crowded inside. More voices chattered in excitement beyond the door. The noise of animals and humans rose to deafening proportions.

Tess had a vision of the silent moment before the gun-shot, that instant of pure terror: the black shadows dancing, the snake poised above her offered arm and the revolver aimed at her head. As she thought of it, the noise seemed to roll over her like a wave, and the dark confines of the hut closed in. She felt oddly weightless, a peculiar, dreamlike sensation. The snake lost importance, the voices faded. She turned instinctively back toward the haven of the captain's arms.

It felt like a blink, but when she opened her eyes, everything had changed. She was no longer in the dim-lit hut; a gas lamp gave a cool, bright light to the white-washed walls that moved past in the rhythmic bounce. Her arm hurt, and she slowly understood that she was being carried: the pain came from the tight grip around her shoulders. She looked up at Captain Frost's face, at his mouth set in a firm line against the effort of holding her, and began to struggle.

He gave her a sideways glance, and hefted her into a more secure position. "Almost there," he said, as if that explained everything.

"What are you— Why are you carrying me?" she demanded. She arched, trying to wriggle out of his arms. "Put me down."

He ignored her, pausing to look over his shoulder. Mrs. Taylor's voice came from close behind him. "To the right, Captain. The first door."

The ceiling spun above Tess, and she recognized her own room. The captain deposited her gently on the large suspended hammock that served as a bed and pushed her back firmly when she started to rise. She protested vigorously. He leaned close to her ear and said in a soft voice, "You'll ruin my heroic image if you stand up so soon from a faint."

Tess looked up in confusion and saw his lurking smile. "I didn't faint!" she exclaimed. "I never faint!"

"Oh." The smile deepened perceptibly. "My mistake."

Tess struggled to a sitting position, but this time it was Mrs. Taylor who restrained her. "Rest a moment, dear. You've had a shock."

"I have not." Tess flushed crimson with shame at the captain's evident amusement. She rolled away from him, curling herself into a ball. In a muffled voice, she cried, "I'm not afraid of a snake, so you needn't laugh at me, Captain Frost!"

"Lady Tess!" Mrs. Taylor protested.

In her mortification, Tess curled tighter. She could not face the captain's derisive laughter at her weakness. When no laughter came, she snapped, "Leave me alone. I'm quite all right. I thought it was all the fashion in England, to swoon over nothing. I'm sorry you find it so funny when I do it."

There was a disconcerted silence behind her. Tess felt hot, unreasonable tears leak from beneath her lids. She rolled over and bounced to her feet, facing them defiantly. Mrs. Taylor looked upset. Her hands were trembling visibly, which made Tess feel even worse. She turned on the captain, ready to blame him for everything, including her own perversity. "I know I'm ridiculous," she cried. "I'm sure you think I'm an unmannerly clod, and I am. I don't know how to dress my hair, and I don't know any clever gossip, and I'm sure that I bore you exceedingly, but I'm not afraid of snakes, and I *don't faint!*"

"Lady Tess!" Mrs. Taylor said again. Tess heard the note of accusation in the older woman's voice. "Captain Frost may well have saved your life!"

"So," Tess said wildly, "perhaps he shouldn't have

bothered! I'm sure polite society would have muddled along quite well without me."

"Oh, don't say such things!" Mrs. Taylor was near tears herself.

"It's true." The words tumbled from Tess before she could control them. "I might as well be a naked Indian. That's what everyone will think of me. Ask the captain what he thinks of a lady who skins snakes for a past-time!" She bit her trembling lip, remembering the feel of him, the way he had held her close. She longed to throw herself into his arms again and beg him not to despise her for this stupid tantrum, for her ingratitude, for her clumsy manners and unfeminine ways.

"I was hoping," he said slowly, "that the lady would skin my snake. I'd like to hang it in my cabin."

The quiet words took Tess by surprise. She looked up at him with wide, questioning eyes.

"I've never shot one before, you see," he added.

"Oh," Tess said. She had the strange desire to giggle through her tears at the expression on his handsome face.

"I suppose you wouldn't think it was anything," he went on, as if compelled to justify himself. "They tell me you've shot thousands."

Her lips curled upward. She could see the captain's mouth twitch in an effort to control an answering smile. He was not laughing at her, she realized; he was laughing at himself. "Not thousands," she said, struggling to keep her voice steady.

"Hundreds?" he asked hopefully.

"Maybe fifty. And not all as cleanly as you hit that one."

He looked pleased, whether at the compliment or at her sudden return of good humor she could not tell. "Then you'll mount mine?"

"Of course I will," she said shyly. "I'm rather good at it, you know."

His smile warmed her. "Oh, yes," he agreed, so softly that she barely heard. "I know."

The smooth black hull of *Arcanum-Arcturus* rose above Gryf, a solid shadow cast on the night itself. He secured the dinghy with a practiced ease and swung himself up the boarding ladder, tossing his coat and hat ahead across the rail before he dropped lightly onto the deck.

The night was still, a heavy silence broken only by the hollow sound of his boots and the occasional slap of an errant wave. He'd given all the new crew shore leave, half-hoping that a few of the worst would jump ship; only four of his own crew stayed on board at a relaxed watch, playing cards in the forecastle deckhouse. The windows cast a golden friendly glow, but Gryf turned away toward the stem and the darkness, wanting nothing of camaraderie tonight.

Grady was sitting on the poop deck, near the wheel, as Gryf had known he would be. Gryf threw himself down on a bench, without comment, stretched his long legs out before him, and rested his head against the deckhouse.

A vast melancholy filled him, a weight that started somewhere behind his throat and spread outward. It had begun on the Taylors' veranda with the sound of a feminine voice, and now it drugged him like a subtle poison, so that he wanted to move, and could not; wanted to speak and found himself dumb. He simply sat, with his eyes closed, and listened to the collection of tiny creaks and moans that made up the soul of his ship.

"Fine evenin'," Grady said at last.

Gryf let out a long breath. He opened his eyes and looked at the stars without answering.

At length, Grady hazarded, "Maybe it ain't, then."

"Maybe not."

"I tol' ye not to go."

"So you did."

Silence fell again. Gryf roused himself, sat up a little straighter, shifting his gaze from the sky to the occasional flicker of lights onshore.

"They treat ye proper, Cap'n?"

The question was slightly belligerent, an invitation: if Gryf wanted to bare his wounded pride, Grady was there to salve it with suitably derogatory remarks about the gentry. It was loyalty, and a way of gathering Gryf back into the fold, reaffirming his place among the outcasts of the world who had to stick together.

"They were very kind," he said, hearing the weariness in his own voice.

Grady harumphed, knowing his young captain as no other human being did. "Yer hurtin' for their ways, ain't you?"

Gryf stood suddenly and walked to the rail, ran his hands along the wood that was varnished to a new and silken polish. She's beautiful, he thought, and in his mind the ship was a living thing, a lovely image wound around and tangled with the memory of a satin-smooth cheek under a lock of hair as dark as midnight. He grasped the rough hemp of a shroud, feeling the taut vibration beneath his fingers, the life that ran like a heartbeat from the deck rigging to the lofty tip of the mizzenmast a hundred feet above. He rubbed his cheek against the twisted hemp, taking comfort in the scratchy reality of it. She was his. She was his, and he thought in that moment that he would have sold himself into Hell to keep her.

"It'll do yer no good to envy," Grady warned, not without a rough kindness that blunted the edge of his words.

"Envy." Gryf gave a morose chuckle. "Is that all this is?"

"Less ye fancy yer in love."

Do I fancy that? Gryf asked himself. The question was answered by a flush of misery that seemed to well up from his toes and settle around his heart like lead. He thought of blue-green eyes, brimming with feisty tears. He thought of the heart-deep fear that had seized him when the snake materialized from the shadows so near her. His shot had not been lucky; it had been aimed with the precision of pure terror. One chance. One chance to shoot four inches past her beautiful, frightened face into near-darkness. He remembered how she turned to him, how she let him hold her. He had not been able to do more than stand and feel the press of her slender form, the silken brush of raven-black hair against his jaw. Every other capacity had deserted him, every thought but the will to hold her safe and alive in his arms forever.

The space of silence was not lost on Grady. Absence of words was proof enough.

"Who is she then, Cap'n?"

Gryf leaned against the shroud, letting the hemp rake a harsh path across his cheek with the movement. He stared at the black water below, half-hypnotized by the restless rise and fall of silvered swells. "Lady Collier," he whispered, and knew as he said it that the admission might as well have been a death sentence, for all the happiness it would bring him.

Grady sighed resignedly. "I be feared o'that." There was a faint click of flint as he lit his pipe. "Ye know she ain't for the likes o' thee."

Gryf's jaw tightened. "That's not true, Grady." The shroud bit into his palm. "You know that isn't true."

"Ah, Gryphon, what else be there to say? Ye be cryin'

that yer a markee, that yer oughter be rich, when there be none to listen to ye but me an' this old ship."

But I am, Gryf thought desperately. His Lordship Gryphon Arthur Meridon, the Sixth Marquess of Ashland.

I actually outrank her.

It seemed the final irony, the punchline of some colossal joke played on him years ago. If the world had run on its usual course, he might have been one of the prospective bridegrooms, sizing up Lady Collier for her fortune and breeding, instead of bleeding himself weak on the very thought of her.

The bleak humor of it restored his equilibrium a little, made him see the difference between reality and dream. He turned back to Grady. "You'll never guess what they want me to do."

"Sell 'em your ship," Grady speculated, in the same tone of voice he might have used to say, "Sell them your firstborn son."

Gryf smiled grimly and left the rail to sit down again. "Taylor wants me to stay in England to keep the riffraff from Lady Collier's doorstep, until she finds a husband to take over."

"I don' fathom that," Grady snorted. "Does he think yer a bloomin' butler?"

"He's afraid she'll fall for a fortune hunter. He wants me to protect her, to root out the skeletons in every prospective suitor's cupboard." Gryf shook his head and laughed sadly. "He seems to think I know something about dark secrets and the people who have them."

"The man's a demmed lunatic!"

Gryf shrugged. "One who offers to pay rather well for his lunacy."

"Yer not thinkin' of it?" Grady asked in dismay.

"Have you looked at the books lately? By the time we make London and pay off this mob of good-for-nothing half-wits that Gould saddled us with, we'll be distinctly short of the ready. Even with that measly load of rubber. Which Taylor knows about, by the by."

"Does he now?" The words were a growl. "It's that sneakin' second mate what tol' him then. Him and Gould was thick as thieves in Nassau."

Gryf sighed glumly at this mention of the most troublesome of a sullen lot. "Did you have any problems with him on the docks today?"

"Aye, we did. I warrant more's to come, for 'ee been't too happy with lockin' up below."

"He's down there now?"

"He is. Eatin' up all our stores and doin' nothing for it."

"Was that necessary, to lock him up?"

Grady made a sound of long-suffering patience. "Sure, an' it was. Ye don' treat that kind man-like. Ye do 'em like an animal, an' then they get the sense of it."

Gryf took the short lecture to the heart. Grady always knew these things. Shipboard discipline, chain of command; for all that Gryf had captained a ship for thirteen years, he had not really had to face them, because his own crew was small and loyal and chose to respect his judgment without question. And that, too, could be laid at Grady's door.

"Hang ye, Gryphon," Grady added good-naturedly, calling Gryf by his first name as the older man did when he meant to make a point. "You know no more of men than you do of wemminfolk."

"I suppose not."

" 'Tain't be thought of as a failin', though. It's a strength in you, that after all the world's done to ye, losin' yer family and yer home when you be nought but a boy, you ain't turned hard. It's why yer own crew stays. You keep on that way, an' let ol' Grady lock up them what needs lockin'."

Gryf could not help but smile. "You have a bargain there."

"Same follows for wemminfolk."

"Does it? I won't be having much fun, if you handle women for me, too."

"Pah! You shoulda done what I tol' yer to do tonight, 'stead of eating fancy food with a silver spoon. There be nice girls, safe and clean, over at that Hulia's. I checked 'em for you."

Gryf laughed aloud at this evidence of solicitude. "That was a rough job, I imagine."

"Gryphon," Grady said seriously. "Ye laugh, but I warrant it's the itch that makes yer look to Lady Collier."

All the amusement went out of Gryf like water from a broken vase. "Grady," he said tautly, "don't."

Perhaps because Gryf had never really disputed his old friend before, had never questioned the value of advice from the man who had been as good as a father, Grady missed the warning. " 'Tain't but sense," he said doggedly. "Yev been too long. 'Fore two days out, you'll be after yer lady like a ruttin' goat, and eatin' yer heart out for it."

Gryf was up and two strides toward Grady before he controlled the surge of violence that shot through him. He froze, within arm's reach of the black shape that was his chief mate and his friend. When Gryf found his voice it was low, and savage in its softness. "You will not speak her that way."

Grady held his ground, his only sign of startlement a certain wary stillness. "I be speakin' o' *thee*," he said, equally softly. "Sir."

Gryf took a deep breath. A sense of trapped frustration swelled inside him, a silent howl of pent-up fury. His jaw clenched, and his fists poised to smash at shadows. He said no more to Grady, not trusting his own voice to speak, but spun around and headed below, where he could be alone with his personal madness.

He found his way down by feel, stumbling once on the ladder because he was angry and careless. He groped for a lamp and tinderbox, managed to get a light, and took it with him to the first officer's cabin, where he locked it into a gimballed wall bracket. Slamming the door behind him with an ill-tempered crash, he sat down on the bunk and pulled off his boots.

Halfway through unbuttoning his shirt he realized he had left his coat and the silly hat on deck. That discovery was deflating, reminding him as it did of the trepidation with which he had dressed for the evening, the stupid worry over whether he had tied his neckcloth properly and whether the coat fit. It was an all new uniform, another clever idea of Gould's, because Gryf had owned nothing acceptable to wear before a lady even on board ship.

He dismissed the finery as unimportant, in the mood to let it rot all night in the tropical dew. Barefoot and shirtless, he poured himself a measure of Nassau rum and stretched out on the bunk, propping his shoulders on the bulkhead and balancing his drink on one knee.

The brief rage had all drained out of him, leaving nothing but a fatigue that seemed infinite, a weariness down to his bones. His life stretched before and behind him like a desolate plain, promising nothing, offering nothing of remembered happiness. He lived from day to day, one hour to the next, not thinking. He had the ship; he and Grady kept her going. It had been enough, till now, to make him want to see another sunrise.

But as he lay there in the cabin which had been his own thirteen years before, the ghosts of buried memory came back to him. In the silence of the night, he could almost hear their voices: his father and his uncle, talking quietly together in the saloon over a late smoke, discussing his grandfather's health, the bad spring weather at Ashland, things that might have worried a young Gryf, if he had known the meaning of worry then.

He had not. His grandfather's illness, the reason Uncle Alex had fetched them all from Calcutta, had been only another adult concern to Gryf. He'd never met his grandfather, the Fifth Marquess of Ashland. The only way that the impending death had touched Gryf was with the news that his Uncle Alexander, Viscount Lyndley, would not go to sea anymore when he became marquess. It had been implicit in the low, earnest tones: Gryf's father urging his elder brother to marry, to settle down.

Gryf had seethed at that, the taming of his adolescent idol, his dashing Uncle Alex. He'd envisioned marriage as a sort of execution by smothering in petticoats, the same yards of flounced material that his mother and older sister wore. To think that his uncle would even consider giving up the *Arcturus*, give up the glorious life of the sea, for something as dull and muddy as ten thousand acres in Hampshire and an income of a hundred thousand pounds a year was outrageous.

Gryf, in his boyish fantasies, had planned to offer his own services as captain of the *Arcturus*, should his uncle succumb to those satanic wiles. To that end, he had made it a point to befriend the second mate, questioning till a lesser man would have thrown him overboard, but Grady had been as patient then as he was now. Gryf had even been allowed to climb to the top of the foremast, over the protests of his mother, so that he had been one of the first to see the smoke from the burning ship.

It was the single clear memory Gryf had of that day. Standing with Grady, holding on for dear life with the amplified surge and sway of the ship, Gryf had felt himself as close to heaven as a mortal could come. The sea had been a bright blue featureless plain, the wind a living force. Off to the north, he had seen the sails of the navy brig that came in tandem with *Arcturus,* a twenty-gun man-of-war commanded by Captain Nathaniel Eliot.

The instant hate that poured through Gryf at the thought of Eliot was old—old enough to have cooled, but after all the years, it had not. The bitterness and grief were still there, still locked away, walled off in a corner of Gryf's mind. It was Eliot who had murdered Gryf's family, as surely as if he had boarded the ship with the pirates. It was Eliot who had kept his guns at a distance, just long enough to be sure the killing was done. And it was an Eliot who held Ashland now.

Captain Eliot was related to the Meridons, having married the niece of the old marquess, but until one week before the family left Calcutta, Cousins Grace and Nathaniel had been just one more set of faceless names to Gryf. Cousin Grace had died in England when Gryf was no more than a baby and her widowed husband had been kept out of sight and mind by an active naval command. There was a son, Stephen, near Gryphon's age, a troublemaker who lived at Ashland while his father sailed—Gryf had known this because each time there was a letter from the marquess bemoaning his great-nephew's antics, Gryf's mother used that "unfortunate child" as an example of how boys needed maternal care.

Then, so short a time before they left for England,

Captain Eliot's warship had put in to Calcutta, and of course he had paid a call on his late wife's family. Gryf had been anxious to meet him, ready to admit another hero to his temple, but the navy commander was nothing like Gryf's beloved Uncle Alex. The difference between them had made a certain childish sense to Gryf: a military man would of course be stiff and taciturn and have little time for amusement, and less still for a pesky boy of twelve who asked too many questions.

How unbelievably fortunate, his mother had exclaimed, when the departure of Captain Eliot's ship from Calcutta had coincided with that of the *Arcturus*, though Gryf's father and uncle had scoffed at the rumors that new pirates out of the China Sea had been seen as far east as Ceylon. So of course Gryf had scoffed, too, because his uncle did, and considered it rather an embarrassment to be escorted by the Royal Navy.

He had thought, in his naiveté, that it would be more heroic to battle pirates alone.

The *Arcturus* had been newly built then, on the return leg of her maiden voyage. She'd been one of the first of the new British tea clippers, a beautiful, expensive aristocrat's toy with a purpose, made to compete with the fast American ships on the run from Shanghai to Liverpool. It was just one of the many ironies of her career that she had never yet carried a crate of tea. That first voyage had been empty, so that she went light and fast carrying only passengers.

They would never have caught her, the pirates, without their trick of the burning ship. It had seemed a true conflagration, a cleverly faked horror that turned into a real one for the *Arcturus*. When the first "survivors" had come aboard, a mixture of races and language, filthy beneath their disguise of Western dress, only Grady and Uncle Alex had guessed. In those few critical moments, the crew and passengers of the *Arcturus* had not questioned, and so had doomed themselves.

The memory of the slaughter was a jumbled kaleidoscope of brutal images, things Gryf could not forget: his sister's screams, his father's blood, the wild whites of a man's eyes in the instant before his club smashed against Gryf's skull. He had lived because they left in a hurry, left him for dead among the others. He knew that, although he did not remember it; remembered nothing else, in fact, but waking up to pain, and the aftermath of nightmare.

How Grady had survived Gryf never knew, never wanted to ask. The mate was there, nursing a shoulder wound, when Gryf regained consciousness. His family and the crew were already gone, buried at sea; the decks were clean of blood and Uncle Alex was dying. He lived long enough to dictate a will to Gryf, leaving whatever in the world was his to Gryphon Arthur Meridon, the last direct heir to Ashland. Signed by his uncle and witnessed by Grady. Gryf still had the pathetic, scribbled document in the safe, along with Uncle Alex's signet ring and the true title to the ship, which had been made over to him also. He kept the papers from sentiment alone. No court of law would hold them valid, and even if one did, Gryf had no proof that he was who he was. The ship and the white-gold ring with the emerald crest of Ashland could be identified, but a boy who had grown to a man could not. There was only Grady's word and Gryf's own, which would amount to precisely nothing.

Probitas Fortis, the ring proclaimed.

Undaunted Honor.

Gryf remembered little of the days after the attack. They had limped along under the lower course of sails only, and Gryf had learned to handle a ship in a hurry, standing terrified at the wheel while Grady managed the lines single-handed—a feat which Gryf had only later come to understand as nearly superhuman. A storm carried them south; they were two months drifting in the Indian Ocean, staying alive on plentiful provisions originally stocked for thirty souls.

It had been a week after the blow to his head before Gryf's eyes had ceased to blur. It took him two weeks to wonder about Captain Eliot's ship, and another several days before the question found a focus, and he asked Grady why the warship hadn't rescued them.

The answer was a shrug. Gryf had thought on it, and did not ask again.

On the day Uncle Alex had died, after they buried him, Grady had asked Gryf where he wanted to go.

"Home," he had said, the extent of his plans for the future.

"England or India?"

He'd thought of his pony, left behind in Calcutta, and a pet mongoose named Sebastian. He'd thought of his family and the bungalow and rooms that would be empty, rooms that his mother and sisters would not laugh in again. In the space of a breath, the moment between a question and answer, he had begun to understand what life was going to be.

"Ashland," he said.

So Grady took him.

They had made landfall off the southeastern coast of Africa. Grady had gone ashore alone, come back with two men, and they had left again, with Gryf never setting foot on land. They headed south, for the Cape, stopped again four times, and ended with a crew of eight—a motley crowd: himself, Grady, three Americans, one Dutchman, a Frenchman, and an African.

Grady's obsession with secrecy had confused Gryf, whose first instinct would have been to find the authorities and cast himself upon their mercy. He realized now what the *Arcturus* and her strange crew had been: an easy plum, ripe for picking, too few men on a valuable ship. Now, Gryf understood about authority. He knew, from hard experience, just how much justice weighed against power. Or how little. The authorities would have been only too happy to take the *Arcturus* under protection, and send her young owner packing to whatever fate might befall him.

Gryf took a stiff swig of rum and let his head drop back against the unyielding bulkhead. He would dream tonight, thinking of these things. He dreaded it, wished himself blind drunk instead. A measuring glance at what remained in the bottle told him that he didn't have enough. He had to be up in four hours anyway. His nights were mercifully short.

He finished the glass and stood, his eyes sweeping over the pile of book-filled boxes stacked in the shadows against the opposite wall. They were Uncle Alex's books, removed from the captain's cabin in preparation for Lady Collier's comfort, and also because Gryf did not want to leave them where he could not reach. Well-read, they were all the higher education Gryf had known—a mongrel collection, Plato and Chaucer, Jonathan Swift, *The 1849 Register of British Merchant Ships*. There was poetry by A. H. Clough and an entire set of Jane Austen, which Gryf had glanced through that afternoon to refresh himself on correct behavior in gentle society. He had added to the selection: Voltaire and Virgil, Dante and Dumas, Bentham and Poe and Ralph Waldo Emerson—whatever struck his fancy, until the boxes overflowed and he could never find the volume that he wanted at any given time.

He had a sudden recollection of the library at Ashland, that great book-lined room that he had seen only once in his life, for perhaps a total of thirty seconds. Imprinted indelibly with the mental picture was a clear memory of Nathaniel Eliot's face, in the first stunned moment of recognition, when Gryf had presented himself at Ashland sixteen months after the attack on the *Arcturus*.

For the space of a heartbeat, the two of them had stood facing each other: a ragged boy and the naval commander, the only man at Ashland who could know who that boy was. Then Eliot's face had closed on the truth, narrowed and hardened, and he had called Gryf a beggar and a thief, ordered him imprisoned, ordered him chased down when he ran. Finally he torched the old barn where Gryf took refuge.

Gryf remembered that chase too clearly, the smell of smoky pitch, and the voices of the men outside waiting for him to flee the fire. But he would not, because he had finally comprehended, almost too late, what Grady had never quite said in words: that Gryf's cousin, Nathaniel Eliot, was a mortal enemy.

The noise and flames had sent rats scuttling, and it was only desperation that had sent Gryf after them, so that he found the clogged entrance to an old cellar and squeezed himself below into a space too small for movement. He'd cringed there, choking and crying while the inferno raged above him, as mindless with fright as the rats themselves. And ever afterward, he'd felt a kinship for such creatures, who knew what it was to be hunted like vermin.

So Gryphon Meridon had died twice, once in a pirate raid in the Indian Ocean, and once a nameless beggar-thief in an abandoned, burned-out hayrack. There was no one to dispute it when the old marquess died and

Nathaniel Eliot took control of Ashland in the name of his own son.

There was no one left named Gryphon Meridon.

In his place, Gryphon Frost poured himself another drink and sat down heavily on the bunk. It felt stiff and unfamiliar, unused as it had been for over a decade. He wished, rather sullenly, that he could sleep where he usually did. He stared at the ceiling and felt sorry for himself on that account, knowing better than to feel sorry for himself on any other. There were some things better left locked away, some currents that ran too deep and strong to dare.

He tossed back the rest of the rum and snuffed the lamp. In the sudden, smoke-scented darkness, he felt his way to the bunk, lay down without pulling back the musty bedclothes, and shut his eyes. With a determination learned from years of watches that were too long and sleep that was too uncertain, he concentrated on nothing. After a long time of nothing, he let go, and fell over the brink into troubled sleep.

Chapter 4

$\mathscr{T}$ess took a surprised gulp of the soft April breeze that fluttered through her open boudoir window. She emitted a faint squeak as her maid pulled the corset strings taut. An echoing squeal drifted up from some carriage braking suddenly in the bustle on Park Lane, but the sounds of London, interesting as they were, did not penetrate far into Tess's beleaguered awareness at that moment. She had other, more immediate, concerns.

"Oh, no," she panted. "That's much too tight!"

"Not at all, mum," the woman said briskly. "The gown wouldn't fit, else. If you'll 'old your breath 'twill be a sight easier."

"But I was measured—" Tess began, and then squeaked again as another notch was taken on the corset. Tears sprang to her eyes, so that the last pull and tie was accomplished as she took in a great gasp of air and stared at the blurred gold-leaf decoration on the ceiling. "How will I—breathe?"

"You'll soon get used to it, mum," the maid said confidently." 'Ere now, 'old the arms up."

Tess, too weak from lack of air to protest, closed her eyes and raised her arms. There was a rustle of silk, and the gown dropped down over her head. She opened her eyes as a cascade of emerald-green slid past her nose, then the room reappeared again. The dress formed a generous puddle around her waist, resting on the wide cage of her crinoline and petticoats. The maid began to fluff and smooth, and guided Tess's hands through the tiny dropped sleeves. The low-cut bodice, which exposed all of Tess's smooth white shoulders and arms, fitted precisely to the artificial shape that the corset forced on her. There was not one fraction of an inch to spare.

The quick, shallow breaths she had been taking made her dizzy, and she concentrated with great effort on slowing them. The maid continued to fuss and adjust, buttoning buttons and fastening hooks. At her instruction, Tess sat, a slow and intricate process in the stiff corset. The woman tucked back a stray curl that had escaped the smooth coil of Tess's hair and placed a crown of white flowers on her head, cheerfully ignoring Tess's protest that the wires hidden in the greenery pricked her severely.

The maid's persistence had its effects; Tess finally submitted to the adornment with an impatient sigh. She sat still while various pins and combs were placed with utmost care, trying not to dwell on the evening ahead. It would be her first taste of London society, and the prospect made her feel dizzy again. She took a deep breath to clear her head, chiding herself for developing a case of nerves that would do any young London miss proud.

I've faced alligators, she thought. Jaguars. Indians. Typhoons.

But somehow, none of those dangers equaled the terror of facing Fashionable Society. She wished longingly to be back aboard ship, standing at the rail and watching the spray spin past in a shower of rainbow colors, with an honor guard of dolphins cavorting on the *Arcanum*'s bow wave. A faint smile traced her lips as she remembered how Captain Frost had sometimes joined her there, and they had talked of places they had been, of islands and cities and wild empty coasts. He had been a different person at those times, not the taciturn gentleman at the dinner table. He laughed with her, and teased her for letting her hair fly free in the breeze, and once he had even reached out to brush a dark strand from across her cheek. The memory of that touch brought a flush of warmth to her face; she should have stopped him, moved away. It was unwise to associate with Captain Frost at all. A blockade-runner, an adventurer; he was not what her father would have called "suitable," by any stretch of reason or imagination.

But the queer excitement that took over her when he was near was addictive. Everything seemed to come clearer; her senses sharpened and life seemed sweeter. Seen through his eyes, the sky and the sea became ever-changing wonders; he knew their moods and lived by their rhythm, understood them, in the same way Tess understood the complex life of a tropical jungle—by instinct, and by a lifetime of watching and listening.

But he had always changed when one of the Campbells appeared on deck. Whenever one of her chaperones was near, his mask of wary reserve fell into place, and he would not speak to her. She had been hurt at first, thinking she had made some blunder and offended him. But like a hesitant, wild animal drawn to a sweet in her hand, he would come again, and she learned to be patient with him as she had been with the creatures of the forests. She went every afternoon to stand alone by the rail, and her patience was rewarded; the day would come when she looked up to find him at her side. He never spoke of why he sought her out, but Tess thought there was a shadow behind the ready smile in his gray eyes, and she drew her own conclusions. He was lonely, as she was, and so they had been friends.

It was probably just a sign of her general vulgarity and lack of taste that she counted a blockade-runner fairly high on her short list of friends and acquaintances. But at least with Captain Frost, she had not had to weigh every word before she said it. He had listened to her tales without criticism, with respect, even, and when she was finished, he had smiled and shaken his head and asked her if she cared to join his crew and shame them into showing some spirit. It was joking praise, but the look in his eyes when he said it had warmed her inside.

But that pleasant interlude was over, and now she had to apply herself to the business of finding a proper husband, which seemed to have nothing to do with friendship or respect, and everything to do with title and fortune. Her aunt had already made up a list of eligible gentlemen, and tonight Her Ladyship Terese Collier, the fabulously wealthy heiress of Morrow, would be presented for their perusal.

With a last pat and a wish for a pleasant evening, the maid declared Tess ready for inspection. Formidable Aunt Katherine—no: dear, kind Aunt Katherine, Tess recited firmly to herself—was waiting in her room for the troops to be assembled. Several of Tess's cousins were already there: tall, long-nosed Charles and his twin sister Anne, who might have been identical in everything except dress; dreamy Francis, the despair of his parents for his poetical aspirations, and pert Judith, who was exactly Tess's age and already married and widowed for over a year. Judith would appear at dinner, but not at the ball afterwards, in deference to her situation.

Tess's entry caused a well-bred sensation. Francis, the

one friend she had made since her arrival in England, professed himself overwhelmed, and even solemn Charles agreed with his twin that Tess looked particularly well this evening. Aunt Katherine nodded a terse approval, in keeping with her square-jawed, militant face and iron-gray hair. She was satisfied that the heathen had been tamed into a lady, or at least the image of one.

"But I hope, Terese dear," Aunt Katherine warned, "that you will *not mention* that distressing trip down the Amazon *alone*."

"I wasn't alone, Aunt," Tess said, pricked into speaking when she knew she should have kept her peace.

Aunt Katherine fanned herself. "Most *particularly* do not say that you have traveled with a troop of naked savages, if you please. This ball is being given for the sole purpose of introducing you into good society. It has been a great deal of trouble to arrange. Pray do not disappoint your uncle and me."

Since Tess knew very well that it was herself, or her estate, that had paid for the ball, the dinner, all the clothes, and the very house they were standing in, this comment provoked a stinging mental reply. Outwardly, she only smiled politely and said, "I shall try my best, Aunt Katherine, but—"

Tess had been about to say that she could hardly lie if she were asked a direct question, when a new and strident voice interrupted. "Oh, Cousin Tess, if you *dare* speak of that horrid place you came from, I shall faint, I know it. What will Sir Walter think of us? Mama, you must make her promise!"

The late arrival, Larice, was engaged to Sir Walter Sitwell. She fixed Tess with a pinched glare from near-sighted blue eyes, her pretty heart-shaped face reddening with emotion at the thought of such a breach. Tess, seeing that the reinforcements had arrived and she was outnumbered, promised faithfully not to mention the Amazon, Brazil, naked savages, or anything remotely connected to them. What she would talk about in their place did not seem to worry anyone but herself.

Aunt Katherine was calling Tess to task on another point before she had any time to think of suitable topics of conversation. "Terese dear, who is this Mr. Everett that your guardian so high-handedly instructed me to invite? I declare, I cannot understand why your uncle was not appointed trustee; it would have been so much more suitable. People will think it very *odd*. Your poor dear papa was so unpredictable, God rest his soul."

That lament had become increasingly familiar to Tess in the past three months. It was useless to debate the subject, and she addressed herself to the first question. "I don't believe I've ever met a Mr. Everett, Aunt, but I'm certain that if Mr. Taylor recommended him to you, then Mr. Everett is a person of merit."

"Well," said her aunt, "he is invited, whomever he may be. I only hope he is presentable. Some protégé of your guardian's, no doubt, who hopes to climb in political circles. The letter said he was attached to the governor in Trinidad, or some such place." She waved the matter away with a snap of her fan and stood up. "Come now, it's time to go down. Larice, you look charming. Do straighten your sash, Anne dear. Take shorter steps, please, Terese—do *try* to show some delicacy."

The ballroom at Morrow House was two stories tall, with a barrel-vaulted ceiling and a riot of plasterwork by the Francini brothers. Pristine white garlands of flowers, swags, and smiling, unclad cherubs cavorted across the arch and down the walls, outlined on a background of crimson and gold. Larice had complained of the house's rococo dowdiness, and said that all the fashionable families had remodeled to the Gothic style, adding turrets and crenellations to their simple Georgian manors. Tess kept her opinion of that to herself, and resisted the advice on updating with what she considered to be admirable restraint.

Now, the ceiling, the sparkling chandeliers, and the grand staircase made a splendid setting for the multitude of aristocratic guests. By her own admission, Lady Katherine Wynthrop, daughter of an earl and married to a baron of impeccable reputation, could command the attendance of the highest in the land. The guest list had mounted to five hundred before a limit was called, and the only reason the newlywed prince and his princess had not been invited was because Tess had not yet been presented at court.

Tess's feet ached horribly in her tight slippers, but she maintained a frozen smile as guest after guest was announced and brought to her for introductions. It seemed that the world consisted of nothing but viscounts and dukes and their ladies. She remembered none of their names, and little more of their faces. When the dancing began she was immediately dragged into a quadrille of thirty-two people with a young man whom she vaguely recalled was a distant relative. She missed many of the steps, and was quizzed and pitied by several elegant and self-possessed matrons of at least eighteen years, who made sure to tell her how they had suffered at their first ball, and how long ago it all seemed. Tess nodded and smiled, and nodded and smiled, and was glad that at least she did not have to worry about saying the wrong thing, for she seldom had the chance to say anything at all. A veil seemed to have come down over her eyes, making her surroundings a bright confusion of sound and color.

Lord Thaxton, Lord Welborn, Lord This and Lord That; she was surrounded constantly by a suffocating crowd of punctilious gentlemen, most of them young and a few so old that they creaked in corsets as tight as the one she wore. Her card was completely filled with the hastily scratched names of her future dance partners and she glanced at it often to try to keep their names straight. Aunt Katherine had warned Tess, on pain of instant ostracism, not to dance more than once with the same partner. It had not sounded difficult at the time, but now, with all the faces a blur, she thought she might have been dancing with the same one over and over and never known the difference. She formed the habit of glancing toward Aunt Katherine at each request, and quickly learned from the degree of tilt of that haughty chin just how desirable a particular partner might be.

That was how Tess knew the slender, dark-haired man introduced as Mr. Eliot was a prime candidate. The name, she remembered, had been at the top of Aunt Katherine's list, but it was the angle of chin tilt that truly distinguished Stephen Eliot from all the other aspirants. When his number came, Tess thought that her feet were beyond supporting her any longer, but one look at Aunt Katherine's chin made Tess accept the invitation with as much cheerfulness as she could manage.

Thankfully, Mr. Eliot was a forgiving partner. When Tess missed a step, he recovered smoothly for them both, and shook his head deprecatingly at her apology.

"Never mind," he said simply. "Dancing is nothing. Your natural grace outshines them all, mademoiselle."

Tess looked up at him in surprise, focusing clearly on his face for the first time. He smiled and raised his eyebrows, returning her look with one of sharp, icy blue. There was something in his eyes she could not interpret, something that made her question the smile, and she

lowered her lashes again as color sprang to her cheeks.
"I have all the natural grace of a water buffalo tonight."

"Ah," he said calmly. "Now you are fishing for compliments, for you know I have to deny it."

"I'm not!" Tess protested, and then, before she realized how it would sound, added, "My feet hurt."

He stopped dancing instantly. "That would explain
it. I had wondered why the brilliant Lady Collier found
nothing at all pleasing about her first ball. Come then,
and sit down."

Tess followed him gratefully off the floor, only a little
worried about the acceptability of cutting off a dance in
the middle. Mr. Eliot, she presumed, would know the
rules much better than she. She sank into the chair, and
nodded to his offer of champagne. She had learned that
holding a glass discouraged would-be dancers, several
of whom began to converge on her as soon as Mr. Eliot
left to fetch her drink. She held them off with difficulty
until he returned, and then listened in amazement as he
dispatched them deftly elsewhere. When he turned to
her again, she said, "I should like to learn to do that."

"What, send your admirers packing?"

Tess laughed. "I would hardly call them admirers."

"Would you not? You're very wrong, then, my lady."

She slanted a questioning look toward him, again unsure of his sincerity. There was a certain intent in his
cool expression; he smiled, but the smile never reached
his eyes. And yet she felt oddly comfortable with him.
He was handsome and charming and totally at ease in
this alien environment—exactly the things that intimidated her in other people. But his compliments, though
extravagant, were delivered with a cynical solemnity
that put her at ease. He couldn't possibly mean them.
She sipped at the last of her champagne, and accepted
another that he procured from a passing footman.

"I must leave you now, I'm afraid," he said as she took the glass.

"Oh, dear," Tess said unthinkingly, seeing her short respite at an end. "So quickly?"

"It's too soon to set the tongues wagging." He smiled his enigmatic smile. "We shall do that soon enough."

Tess gave him a startled glance, but he was already reaching out to bring an aged baroness into their circle, and by the time the introductions were complete, he had disappeared. Tess conversed stiffly with the baroness, managing to offend the woman almost immediately by mentioning Morrow's Whig affiliations. She was rescued from further blunders by Larice. "Cousin Tess," that plump and rosy beauty bubbled, "may I present my very special friend, Miss Louisa Grant-Hastings? And this is my fiancé Sir Walter Sitwell, and oh, yes, here is Miss Grant-Hastings's cousin, ah, Mr. Everett, am I right?"

Tess rose and managed to curve her mouth once again into a smile. Her eyes went first to Sir Walter, and she had the impression of a very ruddy face and blue eyes much like Larice's before Miss Grant-Hastings stepped forward in a rustle of glaring magenta skirts and clasped Tess's hand. Tess began a sentence, but the mechanical words of greeting froze on her lips as she focused on the tall figure behind Miss Grant-Hastings. "Why, Cap—" she began, and then suddenly shut her mouth.

Captain Frost stood watching her, without a trace of recognition on his face. An instant surge of pleasure went through Tess, but she caught back the words of greeting. Whatever had Larice called him? Mr. Everett . . .

Comprehension dawned. Captain Frost! Captain Frost was the mysterious Mr. Everett, so highly recommended by Mr. Taylor! And to Tess, the reason was immediately obvious—young English gentlemen might go into blockade-running for adventure and profit, but they carefully concealed their family names if they did so. Frost, indeed. She set her own face into the same mask of indifference, and was rewarded by a barely perceptible quirk of his lips.

Miss Grant-Hastings was waiting with a cool lift to her delicate brows for Tess's reply to some question. She was several inches shorter than Tess, but the proud set of Miss Grant-Hastings's shoulders and elaborate coil of golden-brown hair beneath her garland made her seem equal in height. Larice had told Tess about her friend; Miss Grant-Hastings was the celebrated beauty of the season, not overly rich, but from a fine family and lovely enough to capture the heart of any eldest son she might choose, if not the heart of his mother. From Francis, Tess had learned that Miss Grant-Hastings was an accomplished flirt, but that she had set her sights too high on Lord Falken, heir to the dukedom of Alderly. Falken, Francis said meaningfully, was no fool, but he would be glad to take advantage of any young chit who was.

Looking into Miss Grant-Hastings's beautiful cold eyes, Tess thought that perhaps Lord Falken had met his match. She managed some small inanity in reply, and then thankfully let Larice carry the conversation. The unexpected appearance of Captain Frost—Mr. Everett, she reminded herself—had surprised Tess into breathlessness. It was good to see him, tall and strong and visibly tanned in comparison to the lily-white hands and faces of the London gentlemen. Even dressed in the same long black coat and white cravat and waistcoat of every other male in the room, he seemed to Tess to be different. The sight of him brought back all the joy of sun-filled days in the tropics, and she imagined when he took her hand and murmured some stock phrase that she could smell the salt-sea air.

Tess waited impatiently for Larice and Sir Walter to wander away, and was gratified when Miss Grant-Hastings was taken out to dance by an elegant, sleepy-eyed, blond gentleman whom Tess suspected was Lord Falken. Sir Walter offered for Larice, which pleased everyone and left Tess at last with Captain Frost.

She turned on him with a pointed smile. "You, Mr. *Everett,* are a scoundrel and a liar. And you look very fine tonight."

Gryf, who had been fighting since he arrived to keep his eyes from straying to her too often, managed a reasonable smile in return, despite the thumping of the pulse in his neck. The compliment was not what he expected. He had prepared himself with reasons and rationalizations and a whole made-up history, only to find that she had accepted his new identity with perfect calm. The moment when she recognized him had been one of the worst in a long career of bad moments; from the astonished look on her face, he had been sure she would protest aloud and have him unceremoniously ejected from the premises. But she had recovered herself, and suddenly, from the sly smile that curved her soft lips, he realized that he had a ready coconspirator in deceit.

"Thank you," he said softly. "And you are . . . lovely." Which was the understatement of a lifetime.

She surprised him by blushing profusely; he would have thought the endless stream of besotted mashers he had watched with her all evening would have inured her to such simple praise. She looked down and then up again, and the emerald of her gown made her eyes very green. He swallowed, and they stood together like a pair of shy children. Finally, with monumental stupidity, he asked, "Are you enjoying your ball?"

She smiled suddenly, that same smile that always set the blood hammering in his veins. "Not at all. I rather preferred fighting mosquitos in Barra, but I'm told not to mention it. I presume you have given up your career for the time being?"

"Career?"

"The block—" She paused, and looked like a child caught with a hand in a jam jar. "I'm sorry, I'm sure you won't want to discuss it here, Mr. Everett."

"I can't imagine what you're talking of," he said. "I am the perfect idle gentleman, as you can see."

She raised her eyebrows. "No, I don't think so. You'll have to stay out of the sun if you want to be recognized as truly idle. What becomes of your ship now?"

"I suppose you mean my yacht," he corrected gravely.

"Oh yes, of course," she said, and he could see the twinkle in her eyes. "Your yacht."

"I imagine she'll have to work for her living under someone else, since I'm busy staying out of the sun."

She shook her head. "Are you really going to give up that life by choice? For this?"

He followed the quick sweep of her hand that took in the glittering crowd. "Not exactly by choice," he said carefully. "It was necessary. A family concern."

"Oh. I hope no one is ill?"

He shook his head, not wanting to create a more complex story than he could easily support. With a wry smile, he thought the truth would do as well. "Shall we say I'm under a certain . . . pressure to remain in England a while?"

"Oh," she said again.

So he let her make up her own plot, figuring she would assume Yankees hot in pursuit or something like it, because it was certainly plausible enough. But her next comment threw him.

"So we're in the same predicament," she said sympathetically.

"Predicament?" Uncertainty sounded too clearly in his voice and he smiled again to cover it. "Are we in a predicament?"

"It seems like one to me. I don't see how I'm going to choose a husband when I can hardly tell all these gentlemen apart. I wish you better luck with the ladies." She paused, and then glanced up at him with chagrin. "I beg your pardon. Now I'm sure I've been vulgar, but it *is* a problem, and I wondered if I was the only one who had it."

Gryf cleared his throat. There was only one lady that meant anything at all to him, and she was as far out of his reach as the moon, though she stood not a foot away. If she chose to think that he was in England searching for a bride, then perhaps it was better that way. Maybe he would not lose himself so hopelessly in the sea-green depths of her eyes if he concentrated on other women.

Maybe.

"I'm sure you'll recognize anyone who goes so far as to ask for your hand," he said, and was glad to make her laugh.

"I suppose so, but— Oh, pooh, here is my aunt, and she will send you away because I've said more than three words in a row to you."

Gryf cast one look at the frowning matron descending upon them, and saw that Lady Collier's assessment was correct. He stood his ground long enough to be introduced. Lady Wynthrop thawed slightly when she understood that he was supposedly related to the Grant-Hastings. Not for the first time, Gryf silently appreciated the cleverness of Taylor in attaching Gryf to that particular family. Since the letters of introduction he had brought from Brazil had carried relief from certain burdensome loans that the Grant-Hastings labored under, and considerably enhanced the eligibility of Miss Louisa with a substantial contribution to her marriage portion, the family had welcomed their counterfeit cousin with open arms. They were also the kind of people Gryf was used to dealing with. Gentlefolk or not, they lived on the edge of their means, which was pretty much the same struggle at any level of society. When money was on the line, they would cooperate. Particularly Louisa. He had seen women like Louisa Grant-Hastings before. They ran bordellos and bars and gaming houses, and when they looked at a man, all they saw was what he might be worth to them.

Mr. Everett should come to call at Morrow House with his cousin, Lady Wynthrop was saying, which suited Gryf's purposes well enough. He trusted Louisa to identify Lady Collier's serious admirers for him, but if he ended up in the unlikely and unpleasant position of trying to discourage an attachment, he would need to be on familiar terms with the household.

The thought made him bemoan once again the impossibility of this ridiculous mission. He asked himself, for the thousandth time, what the devil he was doing here. His motives for accepting Taylor's offer were shaky: the money would be a godsend, but he had managed without it before. A full crew, a tight ship, a cottage with a housekeeper for Grady, and a chance at a China run: those were dreams, things he had lived without for so long that they hardly had any meaning. Deep inside, he knew that he was here for something else, something that was far more dangerous than unfulfilled dreams. He looked at Lady Collier, at her eyes and her hair like deep midnight, and a cold despair crept into his heart. Another guest joined the group, some rich and titled gentleman, with smooth manners and money oozing out of every pore, and the cold turned into ice. Gryf bowed and took his leave, wanting air, wanting freedom, wanting this spell off his heart and his mind.

He found no escape in the crowded ballroom. Louisa Grant-Hastings caught up with him before he could ease out, drawing him back for some scheme of her own which became clear when she led him to a pair of young men lounging in the empty card room. One of them he recognized as Falken, Louisa's unabashed quarry. He gathered that he was expected to disengage the other from the prize, leaving Louisa and Falken to a comfortable tête-à-tête. Gryf was willing to go along, in order to keep Louisa in debt to him rather than the other way around. He summoned an easy smile as she began the introductions.

A moment later, the smile faded. His wits deserted him; the hand he held out in greeting faltered, and he had to make a conscious effort to raise it again. Stephen Eliot. Gryf heard the rest of the name through a loud drumming in his ears. Stephen Eliot of Ashland Court.

The slender hand that grasped his own was smooth and unblemished, white against his brown and work-hardened fingers. The shock was too great for rage: there was none of the hatred that Gryf had thought he would feel, only a pounding in his chest and a suffocating tightness. Stephen Eliot. Nathaniel Eliot's son. He had the look of Eliot, a neat figure not overly tall, with well-trimmed Dundreary whiskers and dark brows over blue eyes that penetrated. The old antagonism began to creep into Gryf's blood. It wasn't Stephen who had killed Gryf's family, but now it was Stephen who profited. The strong desire to wipe the cool confidence from those finely modeled features surged through Gryf. Instead he disengaged his hand with calculated gentleness from the other man's grasp.

". . . my cousin," Louisa droned prettily. "Just come from the West Indies."

"Indeed," Eliot said, casting an assessing glance at Gryf. "And how are the pesky plantation slaves? Still restless?"

"Cousin Gryphon was attached to the governor of Trinidad," Louisa said encouragingly.

The blue eyes suddenly focused into a sharper look at Gryf. "What an unusual Christian name. How do you spell it?"

"Like the mythical beast," Gryf lied smoothly. "Two *f*'s and two *i*'s."

"Ah. I had a cousin myself by the name, Miss Grant-Hastings. He spelled it differently. I haven't heard it for years."

Louisa smiled serenely. "Yes, it is unusual. I suppose I've never met your cousin?"

"Very unlikely. I'm sure you know of the tragedy. That fellow came to a sad end, I fear."

Louisa had a good grace to look startled, and then uncomfortable. "I'm so sorry—I had forgotten. It must not be something you like to talk of, Mr. Eliot. A very unfortunate accident."

He lounged against the back of a chair and smiled. "You needn't turn pale with embarrassment, my girl. It was rather fortunate for me, as the world well knows. I never laid eyes on that part of the Meridon family. Considering how things turned out, I can't say that I mourned them with any great passion."

Like I wouldn't mourn you, you bastard, Gryf thought, if I found the chance to commit murder.

"Go away, Eliot," Falken said calmly. "You're upsetting Louisa."

Stephen Eliot turned, and gave a short bark of laughter. "Oh, it's Louisa, is it? Things have got farther than I thought. Forgive me, I had no idea you were so highstrung, Miss Grant-Hastings. Come along, Everett, we're entirely extraneous here."

Gryf saw no choice but to follow Eliot out of the room. He choked back the growing knot of antagonism in his throat and nodded at Louisa and Falken. Outside the card room, Eliot showed no inclination to leave Gryf alone.

"What do you think of that?" Eliot asked, indicating the couple they had just left with a casual jerk of his head.

"Nothing," Gryf said shortly. "It isn't my business."

"Oh, you scoff at a connection with Alderly? Or maybe just at the kind of connection that it is likely to be?"

Gryf stopped, willing Eliot to walk on without him. But the other man stopped too, and leaned against a pillar, fixing Gryf with that cool gaze. "Your cousin will never catch Falken. Especially now that the lovely and impossibly rich Lady Collier is in our midst."

Gryf cut short the excuse he had formed to escape. He slanted a look toward Eliot. "Will Falken be dangling after Lady Collier?"

"To be sure. He's in a bit of pinch, but all the sufficiently wealthy girls are regrettably plain this year, and so he amuses himself with Miss Grant-Hastings. But now—now there is a more appealing prospect available. Have you met her?"

"Lady Collier? Yes."

"Through that little cow Larice, I assume. The real beauty of Lady Collier, you see, is that she is not only rich and ravishing, but she's of age and has no immediate family. The sharks are circling. But I predict, this time, that they'll not have the juicy morsel."

Gryf felt his jaw stiffen, but he schooled his voice to calm interest. "You think not?"

"I know not." Eliot straightened, and brushed an imaginary crumb from his coat. "I plan to have her myself, dear boy. She suits me perfectly."

Gryf wasn't surprised at this admission. His hands tightened behind his back, but he only said, mildly enough, "Good luck."

Eliot smiled. "Thank you." His blue eyes swept over Gryf with an unsettling intensity. "Are you tired of this little bash, Everett? Care to join me in a tour of the town?"

Gryf could guess at the itinerary of the proposed tour. A nocturnal visit to Haymarket was hardly a black mark against an unmarried man, but strong drink and lowered inhibitions would encourage confidences that might otherwise be impossible to obtain. He smiled darkly at his new acquaintance. "I've been looking for a guide."

Chapter 5

In the soft April darkness outside Morrow House, a pale glow from the gas lamps barely illuminated the long line of waiting carriages. Eliot waved away the footman who stepped forward, and strolled down the steps and along the wide promenade. Gryf followed in silence; they walked together past the patient horses, with Eliot whistling a tuneless ditty that Gryf recognized from the docks. The smell of budding foliage mingled with the horse scent, and faint strains of music rose and fell behind them. If he had been with anyone else, Gryf might have enjoyed the spring night. With Eliot, he simply walked, and tried to shut out all the savage memories that clamored at the fringes of his mind.

"So," Eliot said casually, "you've just arrived in town?"

"A few weeks ago." Gryf hesitated, and then added, "I've never been in London before," figuring that his practiced persona of naive mediocrity was appropriate. He set his thoughts into that mold, careful not to appear too stupid. Eliot was a man who would be easily bored.

"Really? Where on earth have you been? Not in a backwater like Trinidad all your life, poor fellow?"

"India."

"Ah. Father in the army?"

"Diplomatic service." Once again, Gryf kept with the truth, and hoped Eliot had few acquaintances among the British Indians.

"Your family is still there?"

"No." Gryf searched for some bombshell that would stop this line of questioning. He found it, and said slowly, "They were at Cawnpore."

It had the needed effect. Eliot stopped, and turned toward Gryf. "The devil—not during the Mutiny?"

Gryf let silence answer the question. The lie was even fairly close to reality—the reports of the horrible massacre of men, women, and children at Cawnpore seven years earlier had not been so different from the slaughter of his own family. Let him believe it, Gryf thought ferociously. Let him imagine what it was like, the "accident" that gave him what he has.

"I'm sorry, Everett," Eliot said softly, and took Gryf's arm. "Damned ghastly business."

They walked on without speaking. Eliot leaned on Gryf's shoulder a little, which made him wonder if his cousin had had more to drink than his self-possession indicated. But Eliot seemed to have no trouble recognizing the carriage with the green and silver arms of Ashland emblazoned on its side; he spotted it sooner than Gryf did, and led the way without releasing his arm.

The coachman, seeing their approach, leaped down and held open the door. Eliot shook his head. "Fetch my purse, Barron, and hail a hansom for us. You may take the horses home."

The cab was signaled, and Gryf climbed after his companion into the padded leather seat. It was a tight space. Eliot called up some direction to the driver and leaned into his corner as the hansom jolted into motion. He lowered the window shade nearest him and stretched his other arm across the seat behind Gryf. "Put your side down too, my friend. We're going anonymous tonight."

Gryf dropped the shade, cutting off the view from the street, though the space above the door in front of them remained open to admit some light. Eliot tossed the purse into Gryf's lap. "Look in there. I've a present for you."

Gryf worked the bag open, and pulled out something silken and black. He held it up, and looked curiously at Eliot. "A mask?"

The other man smiled without warmth. "I told you we're going incognito, dear boy. You may call me Pygmalion, and you shall be my statue come to life. Living clay in my hands. I'll show you all you need to see of London."

Gryf gave him one long, hard look through the darkness, and then shrugged. "It's your party."

"Here, let me tie." Without waiting for permission, Eliot grasped the black silk and swept it around Gryf's head. He took a long time to secure the ends, his hands extraordinarily gentle as they moved in Gryf's hair. When the task was finished, Gryf had to turn full face to see his cousin, in compensation for diminished peripheral vision.

"It's fortunate you're not well-known here," Eliot said, reaching for the purse still in Gryf's lap. "Anyone who saw that crop of gilded curls more than once would recognize it in a moment, mask or no. Will you tie mine?"

Gryf accepted the offered mask and tied it, without much ceremony. He was growing uneasy with Eliot's quick assumption of intimacy, and a chilly, unreasonable suspicion that Eliot knew who Gryf was tugged annoyingly at his consciousness. When the mask was tied, Eliot smiled and gave Gryf's hair a patronizing stroke, curling one lock around his forefinger. "Lovely," he said. "I wonder how you come by it."

"I was born with it," Gryf said, on a barely veiled note of irritation.

Eliot laughed in his short, cold bark. "Of course. You'd never stoop to bleach, I'm sure. God knows, no bleach would ever result in that superb golden color."

"Where are we going?" Gryf asked, to change the topic.

"To see the abbess, my colonial innocent."

Gryf, who was as innocent as any boy who had grown to manhood on docks from Shanghai to San Francisco, only hoped that "the abbess" kept girls who were free from the pox.

The streets that the cab rattled along began to narrow, and the spring smell of horses and foliage changed. The odor of horses remained, but the waft of spring became the smell of sewage. Ahead, through the opening of the cab, Gryf could see women standing about under the lamps; they called to the hansom as it hurried past. Eliot appeared unaware of the bawdy invitations. He lounged back in the seat, his mouth and jaw a pale contrast to the black mask. He seemed to be watching Gryf, although it was impossible through the mask and the dimness to tell for certain. Gryf turned deliberately away and raised the window shade, which brought renewed calls from the street nymphs.

The scene began to change again as they jolted through a cleaner section. The simple, well-swept front of the house where the hansom stopped was a relief to Gryf; his concerns about Eliot's tastes eased a little. Two men, young and strong-looking, stepped forward as the cab pulled up, and one moved to peer inside without speaking.

"We're come to see Madame Birchini," Eliot said. "She's at home?"

This statement seemed to satisfy the suspicious doorman, and he stepped back, nodding. "She is. Come in, sirs, and welcome."

Gryf disembarked, feeling a little silly in the black mask. But he had drunk deeply at the ball, in preparation to face Lady Collier, and that blunted the edge of self-consciousness. The two fancy men appeared to think nothing of his appearance, merely leading the way up the steps. Inside, he and Eliot were greeted by a surprisingly motherly figure in purple silk, not at all the kind of abbess Gryf had expected, and taken to a well-appointed parlor.

They were left alone there. Waiting for the girls to appear, Gryf assumed. He would have liked to take off his mask; it was unsettling to have his vision narrowed down to a third its normal field. But Eliot retained his, and so Gryf did likewise, sipping sherry from a glass he could not see.

"Do you come here often?" Gryf asked, breaking the quiet.

"On occasion." Eliot downed his sherry and poured himself another glass. At that rate, Gryf thought, he would have the man's life story out of him within an hour. Eliot topped off Gryf's glass before sitting again. "Drink up, man," Eliot urged. "You're far too sober for this night's work."

Gryf took an obliging swig of his drink. The sherry burned a little going down. He turned his head to look for the door. "Are we expecting someone?"

"Later," Eliot said. "I thought we might relax a bit—acquaint ourselves better. Have you been in a house like this before?"

Gryf thought that was carrying the joke of provincial naiveté a little too far. "On occasion," he said shortly.

Eliot chuckled. "What a prickly fellow." He stood up, and came to sit on the couch where Gryf had settled. "I had hoped we could be friends, but you seem disinclined."

Gryf turned to look at his cousin in surprise. He thought he had been conducting himself amiably enough. "I imagine we can be friends," he said, choosing his words. "Maybe you mistake my unpolished colonial manners for prickliness."

Eliot laughed, and reached across for the decanter, refilling both glasses and replacing it. He made no effort to avoid touching Gryf, leaning instead for a long moment with one hand on Gryf's thigh. It was not something that Gryf was used to, this casual and constant physical contact, but he supposed he would have to accustom himself to genteel mannerisms, if he planned to associate with gentlemen.

He was not finding out much about Eliot, except that the man appeared to have a weakness for sherry and held his drink well. The decanter was emptied rapidly, with no noticeable change in Eliot's demeanor. Gryf tried to drink slower, but Eliot laughed and made a pointed remark about it, so that Gryf had to keep up and hope that he could retain his wits.

"Where are the girls?" he asked after a time, and heard the thickness in his own voice. He shook his head, to clear it, and focused again on Eliot. The other man was still smiling.

"Patience, my friend. Finish your drink."

Remembering his mission, Gryf tried to think of a question that might reveal Eliot's weaknesses, but the accumulating level of sherry in his brain made thoughts come more and more sluggishly. He frowned hard at the man next to him and struggled with phrasing the only question that occurred. At last, with the bluntness of alcohol reasoning, he asked, "Do you get drunk?"

Eliot laughed, a pleased and giddy sound. He squeezed Gryf's shoulder affectionately. "Yes, I believe I do. In fact, I think I am. And I know you are, my provincial potboy. Come now, don't let yourself get dry."

Gryf watched Eliot fill the glass. The decanter of sherry seemed to have gone from empty to full without Gryf's noticing. It was already half-empty again, and when it was dry for the second time—or was it the third?—he caught a blur of movement at the edge of his restricted vision and turned in time to see the abbess refilling the decanter. She disappeared noiselessly, a trick which seemed to Gryf inordinately clever.

He became quieter and quieter as the sherry dwindled again, answering Eliot's questions and comments with infinite care. Gryf had forgotten what he was or was not supposed to say, and so it seemed safer to say nothing. He sat staring down at his lap, thinking about Lady Collier's alabaster-smooth shoulders above a gown of emerald-green. The vision fascinated him; he felt himself responding physically, a hot glow that seemed to spread outward to his fingers and toes. In a confused dream she came, leaned close and whispered—then suddenly, the abbess was in front of him with her hands on her waist, grinning broadly. The image of Lady Collier vanished like a swirl of smoke. He stared at the proprietress and then turned, remembering Eliot, but the other man was gone. The abbess held out her hand.

"Come on, now, he wants you."

"Who?" Gryf blinked, his eyelashes brushing the soft silk of the mask.

But she only took him by the hands and pulled him

bodily to his feet. He stood, swaying a little, and looked around for Eliot, rubbing at the mask which blocked his vision. His efforts only made the trouble worse, and he yanked the annoyance off with a grunt.

"There now," said the abbess. "You're a fine-looking trick. But I'll wager your friend wants you to wear it."

She took the mask from his fingers and replaced it with the swift efficiency of an executioner. Gryf, concentrating on standing, made no objection. He was even glad of her support as she led him out of the room. He had a vague impression of a dark hallway with stairs, of many doors, and then one opening to a room hardly better lit than the hall.

With a light shove from the abbess, he stepped inside, stumbling only slightly. The mask still interfered with his vision, and he swung his head to see the room. His eyes fell first on a girl, wearing a volunteer uniform coat and nothing else. She held a birch rod, and when she moved, the coat fell open, revealing the flash of white breasts and belly. There was another woman, entirely naked except for boots and stockings, and a young, blond boy, not more than five or six, in a loose white flannel gown.

Gryf closed his eyes and opened them again. He took a step backward, but the abbess blocked his movement. From somewhere, she had procured a birch, and she pointed with it, drawing his attention back into the room. "There's your naughty boy," she said, giving him another little push as she pressed the rod into his hand.

Gryf's fingers closed autothatically around the birch, then dropped it as his eyes focused on the silent silhouette standing in the shadows beyond the foot of the large bed. The figure held another rod, thicker and more menacing than the rest. The face was hidden beneath the eerie blankness of a full white mask; only the eyeholes glittered, inhuman wells of darkness.

With a terrible clarity that penetrated the alcohol haze, Gryf knew exactly who that specter was. He made a sound, an incoherent protest that was all his numbed tongue could manage.

"Another pretty gentleman," the figure whispered. "Come in."

The abbess pushed at Gryf again. He set his feet against her. "No."

"Come in," came the whisper again. "I have a bad boy here for you." One black-gloved hand gestured toward the child, and the volunteer shoved him forward.

The boy made a small sound that might have been excitement or distress. He cast an apprehensive glance at the stick which the volunteer brandished; she wriggled it at him, and he climbed quickly onto the bed. The other stepped forward with a length of cord and began to tie his hands to the bedpost.

Gryf felt nausea rise in his throat. The dark spell that had bound him broke; he shut his eyes on the picture and turned, stumbling blindly for the door. He blundered into the corridor, tore off the mask, and strode down the hall, bewildered by the maze of stairs and doors, unable to bring himself to open one for fear of finding another such scene. When at last he broke into the parlor where Eliot had left him, it was to come face to face with the two fancy toughs who had first escorted him inside.

They arranged themselves meaningfully in front of the door to the central hall. Gryf looked at them, weighed probabilities, and sat down with a groan. He buried his face in his hands, fighting sickness. A long interval passed, silent except for the ringing in his ears. The turmoil in his belly subsided slowly, leaving him drained and sobered. When there was a movement at the door and Eliot's cold voice spoke to Gryf, he was able to stand and look without wavering into those icy blue eyes.

"Don't be an ass, Everett."

Gryf glanced past him. The toughs had left. Eliot stood alone by the door, adjusting his cuff with cool meticulousness. "Are you quite scandalized, my country puppy?"

Gryf waited, without answering, his mouth taut.

Eliot sighed. "My mistake, dear boy. I had hoped you might enjoy the more . . . sophisticated pleasures." He cocked his head, and looked at Gryf with a peculiar, predatory narrowing of his eyes. "I see that my own predilections misled me. I have a treacherous weakness for golden hair." He pursed his lips. "My lamented cousin Lord Alexander had hair just the color of yours. I doted on that man as a child—God knows why, for he turned out to be a fool. Left me." He gave a short laugh. "Went off and got himself murdered."

Gryf's hands closed into fists.

"I needn't remind you not to mention this little episode to your acquaintances?" Eliot strolled farther into the room. He stood out of Gryf's path and motioned toward the door. "You had better go home—I'm sure it's past your bedtime."

Gryf cast him a level glance, answering the veiled sneer with stony silence. Eliot's smile faltered slightly, and Gryf strode past, heading gladly for the door and his own kind of freedom.

The line outside the Throne Room at Buckingham Palace was long, a weary eternity of young ladies holding the elaborate trains of their court dresses over one arm and chattering nervously. Tess was grateful for the talk; two months after her first ball, she was as ill at ease as ever in London society, and the high-pitched voices reassured her that every other girl was as self-conscious as she. Perhaps they would not have been so agitated if word had not gone down the line earlier that Queen Victoria herself was presiding over the presentations. For the past two years since Prince Albert's death, the Queen had remained in seclusion, leaving the four obligatory Drawing Room ceremonies given each year for the season's debutantes to her son Edward, who stood now beside his beautiful new bride Alexandra. No one could explain why the Queen had chosen to appear today, as she had refused to attend any other public functions despite the growing dissatisfaction of her subjects regarding her reticence.

Tess's heart beat faster as she moved forward in the line, out of the hall and into the Throne Room itself. She had expected the space to be dominated by Her Majesty; instead, it was the huge room that dwarfed everyone in it. Even in late June, its stone walls held a chill. Tess's eyes were drawn upward to the distant, vaulted ceiling hung with banners, and only after several moments did she focus on the trio at the head of the line.

Prince Edward was immediately recognizable, a solid, scant-haired figure in red, with a beribboned golden sash across his chest. The new princess beside him seemed to float above an enormous, pale-cream crinoline skirt, which sparkled with jewels and delicate lacework. She smiled at each debutante with a bashful friendliness which won Tess's heart immediately.

Queen Victoria dominated the group by her very severity of dress. As Tess moved closer, she could see that there was no ornamentation at all on the black silk of Her Majesty's bodice, and plain widow's weeds were all that graced her head. She was a small, plump woman with a round face and protruding lower lip, impossible to call attractive beside her lovely daughter-in-law. Tess smiled to herself, thinking of how she had named the little black jaguar kitten after the Queen. The name hardly seemed appropriate now, though the stubborn temper evidenced by Her Majesty's pouting lip was something the Queen held in common with the jaguar. Tess thought she would not like to be on the wrong side in an argument with either.

The line moved slowly forward, each young lady curtsying to Victoria and her children and then contriving to back out of the room without tripping on her own train or turning her back on the Queen. It was this procedure that intimidated Tess; she was sure she would never manage, though Aunt Katherine had spent hours coaching her niece on the technique.

Inexorably, the moment arrived. Tess stepped forward as she was announced, sinking into a curtsy so deep that her knees quivered. She lightly kissed the Queen's hand and hoped that the slight bounce that was necessary to reverse the curtsy and rise was not noticeable. She raised her eyelashes to smile at the Queen, and found Victoria smiling warmly back.

The obvious affection in the Queen's expression was unexpected. Tess had been told that there was no need to speak, that royalty would not have time for more than a nod before the next debutante was introduced. The Queen retained Tess's hand, halting her retreat. "Robert's daughter," Victoria said, and the smile changed her face from dowdy to pleasantly motherly. "It is you I hoped to see today. I am so very glad to know you, child. Our dearest Albert thought highly of your father, God rest both their souls."

Tess was barely aware of the faint buzz of curiosity from the crowd. The Queen's kind words and sad smile brought a mist to Tess's eyes; it was the first time since she had come to England that anyone had spoken of her father with real affection. "Your Majesty," she said in a small voice. "Thank you. I—I grieve for your own loss, as I still grieve for my father."

The Queen's pouting lip trembled a little, all trace of stubbornness gone. "Yes, child. You do understand, don't you? It seems at times that no one does."

Her look of wistful sorrow made Tess want to abandon all ceremony and reach out to comfort this woman who was a queen, and still a human being, a wife who loved and missed her husband. Tess saw suddenly how hard it was, how much the pressure to return to public life without her beloved Albert had hurt Victoria. "Your Majesty," she said impulsively, "everyone understands your feelings. They must. And if I find someone who does not, I will *make* them understand."

Victoria smiled again. "You're very young still, Lady Collier. The world does not listen so easily as you may think, but we thank you for your sympathy. You may come to us freely if you ever have need."

With that formal dismissal, she released Tess's hand. Tess curtsied again, gave her obeisance to Prince Edward and Princess Alexandra in turn, and began to back away. She tripped, as she had known she would, but the Queen nodded encouragingly, easing the sting of mortification that colored Tess's cheeks. When she had finally reached the exit, she turned with a sigh of relief and joined her aunt and Larice, who insisted on a full interrogation to make sure that Tess had said nothing barbaric to disgrace the family.

Chapter 6

"*I* have had another proposal," Tess said with mock gravity. She glanced expectantly toward her companion as their horses ambled slowly through the long morning shadows of Hyde Park. She had come to depend on Captain Frost's company each Tuesday and Thursday in the park; if he had not been there, to ride and talk and race with her until she was breathless, she was sure she would have long since given up trying to cope with Fashionable Society. Their first meeting in the park had been happenstance, but Tess had made sure that the morning ride soon became a steady appointment. It was the only time she felt that she could be herself, alone with him except for the groom who always trailed behind just out of earshot.

He turned to her, and a stray beam of early sunlight flashed in his bright hair. "Who's the hopeful fellow this time?"

"Mr. Jeremiah Bottomshaw."

He smiled wryly. "Ah, yes. One of my favorites."

"I suppose you will say you told me so."

"I did indeed. He has only been working on his nerve."

"Well, he might better have been working on his address," Tess said mournfully. "He read me a *poem*."

Captain Frost laughed, a sound that seemed to echo through the empty park and bring it alive.

"It's very well for you to think it funny," she said with calm indignation, "but I was quite sorry for him. It was an awful verse, and I believe he wrote it himself. Something about 'music on the waters.'"

At that, the captain's face took on a peculiar shade of pink. His lips thinned and quivered. "I don't suppose it began, 'There be none of Beauty's daughters . . .'?" he asked as he drew an unsteady breath.

Tess felt an answering flush begin at the base of her throat. "Oh, dear—do you mean Mr. Bottomshaw didn't write it?"

The captain pulled his rawboned black mount to a halt and looked at her with an odd expression. Barely controlled laughter strained his features, but his voice was low and solemn as he recited:

> *"There be none of Beauty's daughters*
> *   With a magic like thee;*
> *And like music on the waters*
> *   Is thy sweet voice to me:*
> *When, as if its sound were causing*
> *The charmed ocean's pausing,*
> *The waves lie still and gleaming,*
> *And the lulled winds seem dreaming;*
>
> *And the midnight moon is weaving*
> *   Her bright chain o'er the deep;*
> *Whose breast is gently heaving,*
> *   As an infant's asleep:*
> *So the spirit bows before thee,*
> *To listen and adore thee;*
> *With a full but soft emotion,*
> *Like the swell of summer's ocean."*

Tess listened in wonder to the melodic words. He had begun with amusement in his face, but after the first line, the poem seemed to spring to life of itself; Tess could see the ocean, and the moonlight: the scene touched her with the gentleness of a caress. When he had finished, she was silent as they resumed their easy progress, sure that wishful thinking had made her imagine the way he had looked at her as he spoke. At length, she said lamely, "It sounds much better from you."

"Perhaps because you recognize it as Lord Byron, instead of Mr. Bottomshaw."

"Perhaps," Tess said, although she was not at all sure that discovering the true author of the poem was what had made it sound so sweet.

"And what did you tell him?"

"Tell who?"

"Mr. Bottomshaw."

"Oh." She sighed. "I said I must think about it."

A significant pause stretched between them. Tess dared a brief glance at the captain. His handsome face was closed; he rode along without any sign that he had even heard her.

"You don't approve," she said finally.

"I think if you are going to say no, then you should say it."

Tess shrugged unhappily. "I know. It isn't at all fair."

"He's a good man."

"Oh, yes," she said wistfully, accepting the judgment without reservation. "Very good. I just wish—"

She broke off, catching herself before she said the unthinkable. It would hardly do to admit that Captain Frost himself had become the standard by which she measured all her suitors. In her opinion, no one else was as handsome or amusing or easy to talk to—and no one else kindled that strange, hot pleasure that weakened her knees whenever he smiled at her.

She hung her head in embarrassment, not wanting him to see the foolish hope in her eyes. He was her friend; what more did she wish for? She had begun telling him of her numerous offers of marriage out of the silly idea that he might—just might—come to see her as desirable himself. But he acted always like a brother, like a friend, nothing more.

She should be satisfied with that, she told herself. He did not have to spend any time with her at all. He had been an instant success among the London ladies, with his elegant features and his sweetly old-fashioned etiquette. Even Miss Grant-Hastings seemed suddenly torn between spending time with her attractive cousin and chasing Lord Falken. Everyone had speculated on it: had Miss Grant-Hastings developed an affection for her cousin, or was she just trying to make Falken jealous? Tess was inclined to believe the latter. She simply could not imagine Miss Grant-Hastings allowing herself to fall in love with anything less than a baronet.

That did not mean, though, that the captain might not have fallen in love with Miss Grant-Hastings.

This thought was so unpleasant that Tess immediately tried to banish it for something more appealing. "You haven't asked me about my presentation at court," she said.

"A clever change of subject. Allow me to ask you about your presentation at court, since you are determined to leave Mr. Bottomshaw dangling."

Tess rolled her eyes in exasperation. "Has Mr. Bottomshaw hired you as an advocate, Captain Frost, or do you simply want to make me feel as guilty as possible about that poor man?"

"My name is Everett," he reminded her. "And he isn't at all poor."

"Aunt Katherine has made me fully aware of the Bottomshaw fortune, you may be sure." With a gloved hand, she plucked at the hem of her burgundy riding jacket. "I'm sorry, but it's very difficult to remember you are not Captain Frost anymore."

"Is it?" He sounded surprised. "Call me Gryf, then."

Tess raised her eyes, pleased. "Gryf. It's really Gryphon, isn't it? I like that name. I saw it on one of your letters to Papa once. You may call me Tess, of course. It will give Aunt Katherine a chance to have the vapors."

Her wickedly innocent smile made it impossible for Gryf to continue in the role of fatherly adviser. He had tried to maintain his objectivity—dear God, he had tried—but to argue the cause of a gudgeon like Bottomshaw was hopeless. The image of the plump and earnest Mr. Bottomshaw reciting Byron while Tess fidgeted made Gryf's mouth curl in silent mockery.

He should have known that the man would make himself ridiculous. It was Gryf who had suggested the poem; like a latter-day Cyrano de Bergerac, he orchestrated the courtship of another, encouraging the timid Bottomshaw to woo Lady Collier with enthusiasm. Gryf could tell himself that he was fulfilling his contract—the man was exactly what Gryf was sure Taylor and the late earl had been hoping for: rich, steady, serious-minded, and as dull as a doormat. It was less comforting for Gryf to admit to himself that he had known from the beginning he was championing a man who had no hope of winning favor, particularly not by reciting romantic poems.

The obvious contradiction in his own actions annoyed him. He took a deep breath of the cool morning air and invited Tess to a canter down the wide green, even though his hired hack had a jarring gait, no aid to relearning the equestrian skills he had not practiced since his childhood. Gryf's first morning ride in the park had left him painfully sore; his leg muscles had been stiff for days, and he still had bruises where the ill-tempered black had pitched him twice.

Tess readily agreed to a run, but even that small relief seemed about to be denied when the groom's mount tripped after two strides and pulled up dead lame.

"Botheration," Tess muttered, just loud enough for Gryf to hear. She rode up to the dismounting groom. "Is it badly pulled?"

"Aw, no, mum," the groom said apologetically. "I shoulda told you, mum—old Ralph 'ere; 'ee can't go a stroke above a fast trot wi'out gettin' bolluxed up wi' his own front feet." He bent and ran a hand down the horse's lower leg. " 'Tain't nothing' much, is it, old man? No more hot-footin' it today, but I wager you won't even remember it tomorrow."

Tess glanced up, disappointment clear in her face. Gryf resisted that look of appeal for all of ten seconds. He heard himself say, "It's a shame Lady Collier should have to go in so early. Would you trust me to see her home after her ride?"

The groom looked up. "Oh—I couldn't go 'ome wi'out 'Er Ladyship. I'm sorry, sir. Indeed I couldn't. Missus ud 'ave me skin for it."

"But you could wait for me at the park gate," Tess said quickly. "I won't be above a half-hour, I promise you."

The servant hesitated, looking doubtful, but Tess wasted no time in argument. As if it were settled, she wheeled and put her chestnut gelding forward into an easy run down the green. Gryf exchanged a helpless look with the groom, controlling the restive black with one hand as the horse circled and danced in its anxiety to join the chestnut. "Wait at the gate," Gryf said, and fished a sovereign from his pocket. The groom caught it with a quick fist as the gleaming coin arched in the morning light.

He grinned. "As long as you like, sir," he said, as Gryf let the black have its head.

The chestnut was already halfway down the green, but the black was surprisingly swift in spite of his bony frame. He stretched his neck and laid his ears back evilly as he lengthened stride in pursuit. They caught up with Tess well before the woods, but Gryf hung just a little behind her, giving himself the illicit pleasure of watching her slim body move easily with the rhythm of the horse.

Familiar torture. The morning rides had not been part of his original plan, but they had become the chief bittersweet pleasure of his existence. He'd taken the horse out the first time from boredom alone. The years of living on a few hours' sleep every night had ingrained the habit in him; he found he could attend balls till two and go drinking till five, and still he was awake and restless by nine the next morning, while society lay abed till noon. Fortunately for his pride and his cover as a gentleman, he had not met Tess in the park that first day. He had brought the beast under control and was working on his seat by his second ride, when Lady Collier and her groom trotted unexpectedly out of the mist.

The absurd happiness that had swept over him on seeing her should have been a warning. He had chosen instead to take Tess's appearance as a piece of luck, furthered by her suggestion that they meet regularly and her ready willingness to confide in him. Just what Taylor would have wanted, Gryf had told himself, and known it in his heart for the lying excuse that it was.

He was paying for his weakness. He had to listen as she told him of her admirers: what they said, what she thought of them. It was misery, a just damnation, restitution for the pleasure he took in seeing her smile. The full extent of his folly was apparent each time she reined up, flushed and sparkling from a hard gallop across the green, and laughed at how her hat had fallen free and loosed her shining hair.

In the absence of Grady, there was no one in London whose company Gryf could enjoy besides Tess's. He'd had one letter from his friend—a note, really, short and full of misspellings and grammatical errors that had brought a vision of the mate so clear and familiar that he might have been standing in front of Gryf. The letter had been posted in Madeira; the ship would be long gone from there and halfway back from the Río Plata by now, carrying a cargo that Taylor had commissioned. An aching surge of homesickness had gone through Gryf as he read. He missed the ship. He missed Grady. He hated London, hated the soot and the crowds and the smells. By the end of a day, even the parks held the odor of too many humans and horses; it was why he rode in the mornings, after the night dew had settled the stench. He despised what he was doing, and he fell more hopelessly in love with Tess Collier every passing day.

Ahead of him, Tess reached the end of the open ground and pulled her horse to a walk, turning to see if the captain was close behind. Gryf, she reminded herself with a happy little sigh. His homely mount came down to a walk beside her, and she allowed herself a lingering glance at his hands, gloveless, relaxed and masculine on the reins. The look drifted downward, taking in the long, muscular line of his thigh outlined by riding breeches. A familiar spurt of warmth touched her breasts and spread upward and down. She looked away.

"Will you help me dismount?" she asked, for no reason other than that she wished for him to touch her.

He swung easily off his horse and came toward her. As she slid into his arms, it was easy to imagine that he might pull her close, and her heart did a flip of anticipation. But he did not. He set her lightly down and let her go. Tess, shamed by her own thoughts, turned quickly away and led her horse into the shade of the trees. She pursed her lips, unreasonably petulant. In a mood of frustration, she said what she knew he would not like.

"I go tomorrow to an archery club at Tonbridge." She paused artfully, and then added, "Mr. Eliot formed the party."

The immediate tightening of Gryf's jaw rewarded her. He said in a flat voice, "I'm sure you'll do very well."

That was true enough. Tess's skill as an archeress was already renowned. She had learned it not as a sport, but as another method of obtaining specimens for her father. It had been a severe blow to the myopic Larice to find that her cousin could pin a target at fifty yards, for Sir Walter had been quite audibly impressed. But it was not Sir Walter that Tess wanted to impress.

"Mr. Eliot has been very attentive," she commented, a nonchalant twist of the knife.

Gryf said nothing.

She played with her horse's reins as they walked down the shade-dappled path. "I really think he will offer for me soon."

She thought a sound came from the man beside her; she looked toward him quickly, but his face was a set mask.

"I wish I knew why you object to him," she said.

"I wouldn't like to see you hurt."

Tess stopped, tilting her head in puzzlement. Gryf

turned toward her. Without their riders, the horses went immediately for grass, their bodies blocking the path and enclosing Tess and Gryf in the narrow space between them.

"How can he hurt me? He doesn't gamble—you've told me that yourself. He's been very kind to me, and he certainly can't stand in need of money."

He hesitated a long moment, his mouth compressed. "There are other faults a man can have."

Tess stared into his eyes, closer than she had ever been. They were light-gray, like smoke, with a darker rim. She wished very much to reach out and touch the hard plane of his cheek, to soften the set of his jaw.

He looked away.

"What are these awful faults?" she asked.

His frowning gaze swung back to her, startling in its intensity. His hands came up in a quick motion, as if he would shake her. "I don't want him to hurt you," he repeated roughly.

"Would you care?" she murmured.

He stopped in midmove, dropping his arms awkwardly. "Of course." There was an edge in his voice that thrilled her. "Of course I care."

The words made her brave. She met his eyes. "Why?"

He seemed to have no answer for that.

Tess touched her upper lip with her tongue, excited and a little afraid of the peculiar intimacy of the moment. She saw his eyes flicker to her mouth at the movement and linger there. It came to her suddenly that he wanted to kiss her; he was very close, so close that she could see the pulse at his throat. Her own heart fluttered painfully. A bird in the wood behind her took up loud song, filling the air around them. After a moment, the wild melody ceased. Tess hesitated; it was all her imagination: the way he looked at her, the tension, the desire that seemed to vibrate in the air between them as loudly as the birdsong. It seemed to Tess to be another girl, in some different world, who lifted her face with a timid smile and offered her lips to be kissed.

"Oh, God," he said woodenly.

He stared down at her upturned face. She waited. The silence was tangible around them, like the dappled shade, the horses, broken only by the occasional jingle of a bridle and the swish of her gelding's tail. Then slowly, so slowly that her knees weakened with anticipation, he raised his hand to touch her cheek. He still held the rein of his grazing horse; she felt the warm, supple leather brush against her skin as his fingers slid downward and cupped her chin.

He bent his head. With a sudden motion, he sought her mouth, dropping the rein as his palms spread across her cheeks, pressing her face upward. It wasn't what she had anticipated; it wasn't gentle or soft or tentative. There was a fierceness to his kiss, the taste of him, the heat. He wrapped his fingers behind her neck; his mouth moved hard against hers, forcing her lips open under the assault. It hurt her, a sweeter pain than any she had ever imagined. She felt his firm male shape all down her body through the thick folds of her riding habit. It was what she had never known, and yet always known; what she had wanted—this fire in her limbs, this wild rush of joy. Her arms came up to twine around his neck. He tasted of salt and horse and the lemony tang of shaving lather; his palms were hot against the flushed skin of her throat. She leaned into him and clung with a faint whimper of excitement as his tongue touched hers and his hold on her tightened convulsively.

Her eager response rocked through Gryf like a cannonade. He caught her waist and pulled her closer, deepening the kiss greedily. He could not breathe and didn't care. If he died like this, he wouldn't care. The last remnant of control gave way, hopelessly vanquished by the yielding curve of her back and waist and hips as his hands slid downward. His fingers worked beneath the heavy hem of her jacket with their own will. Somehow they found buttons and velvety clasps and flicked them open, until nothing but the thin, white crispness of finely woven silk lay between his palms and her skin.

The touch made Tess's eyes fly open. She could not see his face as he pressed a hungry kiss to the tender place below her ear, but his breath came hot and uneven against her skin, and he made a sound low in his throat as his fingers drifted upward. He cupped her breasts. His thumbs passed over her tautened nipples, setting off sparks that made her body twitch and arch toward him in answer. She buried her face against his shoulder, embarrassed, delighted, trying to stem the little sobs of pleasure that rose unbidden to her lips.

He said her name, a harsh whisper, and raised a hand to plunge his fingers into the rich coil of her hair. Her plumed hat fell free, and hairpins strained and prickled as he forced her head back to seek her mouth again. She felt fragile and small, as helpless as a doll pressed against his heated strength. His lips raked like fire across her cheek and he took her mouth again urgently, holding her hard against him.

In some back corner of her mind, Tess knew that she should stop him. Dear God, the park—right here in the public park—and he was fumbling with the buttons of her blouse and sliding his hand into the recess, and her body seemed to react of its own will, pushing upward to give him more freedom to touch her. The brush of his fingers across the tender swell of her breast sapped all modesty and reason. No one had ever told her . . . she had never guessed it would be like *this,* all hurtling flame and exhilaration as his lips slanted across hers and his tongue delved for the warmth within. Her head sagged back, exposing her throat to his kisses; her legs felt so quivery that she thought she could not even stand alone. She did not want him to stop. She wanted it to go on forever. It was too soon, far too soon, that she felt his withdrawal in the stiffening of his back and shoulders.

"Damn," he groaned against her skin. "Ah, damn, damn . . . I can't . . ."

His hold on her loosened. With a little whimper, Tess sought to renew the kiss, unwilling to have it end so soon. But he turned his head, breathing hard and unsteadily. Slowly, as if he had to will each tiny move, he let her go.

Tess looked up into his face. The raw disgust that hardened his features brought reality back with a jolt. She took a deep breath, realizing suddenly just how far she had compromised herself.

With a bitter curse, he turned away. Tess stood still, clasping and unclasping her hands in an agitated rhythm. There was nothing she wanted more than to forget all scruples and cast herself into his arms again. But the moment was gone, and all magic with it. He yanked his horse's head up from grazing with unnecessary force, then stood with his back to her, staring rigidly at the horse's shoulder.

Tess bit her lips in mortification. What had been exhilarating became suddenly something else, something wicked and depraved. But, oh, God, it had felt so good—could anything that wonderful be wrong? She clutched at her gaping blouse and did the buttons with quick, shaking fingers. She could hardly command her trembling knees to support her as she bent to catch up her fallen hat.

She straightened, and watched in distraught silence as he led her chestnut forward. The expression on his face was set. He did not meet her eyes as he mutely offered his cupped hands and boosted her into the sidesaddle. When she turned to thank him, he was already mounting his own horse. They rode out of the thin woods together, heading by unspoken consent to the park gate.

"Will I see you on Thursday?" she asked, a ritual question at the end of each ride.

"I think not," he said.

She gave him a stricken look. He added without emotion, "You'll be tired from your visit to Tonbridge."

"No," she said in a small voice. "I won't be. I'm not going to go."

It was meant as a peace offering, a truce. She saw him hesitate, and her heart rose. The hope lasted only a moment. He said coolly, "I'm sorry. I have another engagement."

If he had slapped her face, it could not have stung more. "Of course," she whispered. "Perhaps some other day."

"Some other day." He gave her a nod, obviously meant for parting. "Good morning to you."

"Good morning," Tess said dully as he turned his horse away, back into the park. She could not help watching as he trotted off. He kept up a steady post until he was almost out of sight, and then the rawboned black broke into a hard gallop and disappeared from view.

Aunt Katherine was "at home" that afternoon, and Tess was obliged to sit with Larice and Judith and Anne in the drawing room to help entertain visitors. It was understood that the younger ladies all talked together, so that Tess was spared the need to make conversation with the Mayfair matrons themselves. She had only to deal with their daughters.

The girls were grouped around the fireplace, where coldblooded Anne always insisted on keeping a small pile of coals glowing, even in the spring and summer. Tess was glad of that, for the chilly mists of England often seemed to reach all the way to her tropical bones. She held a sketchbook in her lap, idly tracing the outline of a violet and listening to Louisa Grant-Hastings talk about Princess Alexandra's couturiere.

The older women were deep in conversation on the far side of the room when Larice said, in an excited undertone, "Louisa, you must tell us what happened last night at the Gosfords'!"

A giggle arose from Judith and the two other young visitors. Anne said quellingly, "Hush, now. Mama—"

"Oh, don't be a gooseberry, Anne," Larice whispered loudly. "They won't hear us."

"It was Zoe Mayland." One of the visiting girls swept them all with a knowing look. "And Colonel Perry."

"What happened?" Larice demanded. "Lady Mary said that for certain he would be going this morning to speak to Mr. Mayland."

"That wouldn't be a bad match," Judith said. "Even if the colonel is a younger son. Mama says he has over forty thousand pounds."

"But what *happened?*" Larice's voice was a pleading whisper. "Oh, if only Judith and I hadn't been home with the headache last night. We can't get a thing out of Mama or Anne or Cousin Tess about it!"

Since Tess hadn't had any idea that anything unusual had happened at the Gosfords' dinner party the night before, she returned Larice's scathing look with an apologetic shrug.

"Lady Gosford found them after dinner," Louisa said

portentously. All eyes in the group went to her. "Upstairs in her boudoir."

There were gasps of horror, quickly squelched by Anne.

Louisa smiled ironically, looking suddenly much older than her nineteen years. "He was kissing—"

"Oh, my heavens!" Larice's mouth had fallen open, and Louisa narrowed her eyes at her friend.

"—her hand, Larice dear."

"Well," said Larice, "that is shocking enough! And of course now he must offer for her—poor Zoe, do you think she really wants him?"

"She let him take her upstairs," Louisa said calmly. "I suppose she likes him well enough, or she is quite a little ninny."

"Can you imagine?" Judith sighed. "He kissed her hand in the boudoir. How romantic."

"Romantic!" Larice squealed. "The boudoir? I think it most disgusting. Sir Walter would never be so bold!"

Her sentiment was echoed vigorously by the others. Tess stared down at her sketchbook, hoping no one noticed the heat that had risen to her cheeks.

"That is because you are still a child, Larice," Judith said stiffly, taking on the tone of the experienced widow. "You don't know what you're speaking of."

"Well," Larice bridled, "I never thought you liked old Quince's embraces so much!"

"Please!" Anne said sharply. "Watch your tongue, miss. Judith is quite right. You're not of an age to discuss such things."

Larice turned on Anne with a pointed smile. "And have you ever been kissed by a man, Anne dear?"

"Of course not."

"Has anyone?" Larice looked around the tittering group with an avid eye.

Amid the general denial, Tess found herself blushing furiously. She pretended to drop her pencil and bent down to pick it up, but Larice, though shortsighted, could see color well enough. "Cousin Tess," she said wickedly, "you've turned quite pink!"

Tess took a deep breath and straightened her blue and white muslin morning dress. "I dropped my lead," she said hastily.

"Has anyone ever kissed you, Cousin?" Larice persisted. "You mustn't fib to us, you know! Look at her blushing, I believe she *has* been kissed!"

"No—" Tess said helplessly. "No, never."

"Perhaps the very thought makes her color," Louisa said in a cool tone.

Tess forced herself to smile. "I assure you, I've never yet been invited to anyone's boudoir."

"That's true," Larice said. "Mama has kept a special eye on Cousin Tess, so that she won't embarrass us all with some nonsense about monkeys. I don't believe she is ever out of Mama's sight."

"Only in the morning," Judith said matter-of-factly. "She rides in the mornings, you know, Larice."

"At nine o'clock!" Larice scoffed. "There wouldn't be anyone in the park to kiss her at that hour!" Her eyes grew very round. "Was it Mr. Bottomshaw, Cousin Tess? Did he try to kiss you?"

Tess shook her head, and pretended to concentrate on her drawing. "No. He read me a poem by Lord Byron."

"How romantic!" Judith said.

Larice giggled. "I think she's fibbing. I think it was Mr. Bottomshaw who kissed her! Now you *must* marry him, Cousin, for the truth is out."

"No," Tess said, growing desperate. "He didn't!"

Strangely, it was Louisa who came to Tess's aid. "Nonsense, Larice. I can tell you for certain that Bottomshaw would dare no such thing. Do you ride often in the park in the morning, Lady Tess?"

"Every Tuesday and Thursday without fail," Anne said wearily. "We must always hold luncheon for her."

Louisa gave Tess an odd little smile. "Tuesdays and Thursdays. How invigorating. Perhaps some morning I will join you."

Tess bit back the quick protest that sprang to her lips. "Please do," she said. What difference would it make now? Gryf would never come back to meet her again. She had forfeited his friendship by showing herself the most brazen creature alive. Innocent Zoe Mayland's crime was nothing compared to the rush of passion Tess had shown in the park. Nothing to what she still felt, for the imprint of his body against hers was yet vivid, the place where his fingers had touched her still warm.

In the midst of the covey of gentle young ladies, Tess felt suddenly so alone that she had to look quickly down at her sketchbook to hide the tears that sprang to her eyes. The others shrank in horror from a man's caress, while she had found an incalculable joy in it. What was more, she knew that she would find that same joy again, if she were given the chance.

However, it was not likely that the man who could bring her such pleasure would ever want to see her again.

Chapter 7

Thursday morning, Tess went to the park, even though a chilly, misting rain clung to the trees and made the scene miserable. The dismal tone of the day echoed the misery she'd felt herself, tossing in her bed at night or sitting primly with her cousins while her mind played over and over those moments on the shady path and the cold parting afterward. On this gray morning, the park was a different place: the new leaves hung dull and limp, and the open green was a stretch of foggy desolation.

He will not be there, she told herself. He said that he would not come.

But still, she looked for him.

Her heart leaped into her throat as she neared their meeting place. A figure on horseback waited, shrouded by mist. With a little cry of gladness, Tess urged her mount into a canter. "Good morning," she called, in a voice breathless with delighted relief. "Hullo!"

The outline of the waiting figure solidified. Tess hesitated, slowing instinctively as she realized the other's horse was not black, but dappled gray. In her enthusiasm, she put the color change down to an illusion caused by the mist, until a calm, feminine voice floated over the dewy ground.

"Lady Tess? It is Louisa Grant-Hastings. I've come to ride with you."

Tess reined up. Louisa! Bitter disappointment swept over her. Tess had never for a moment expected the other girl to act on her polite offer, and particularly not on a dreary day such as this. Her horse dropped to a walk, and she covered the last yards to Miss Grant-Hastings reluctantly.

"Good morning," Tess said again, with considerably less hospitality. "I wasn't expecting you to come so soon."

"Weren't you?" Louisa asked, tilting her head so that her plumed cap of green velvet nodded curiously. "It seems you were expecting *someone*."

"Oh no," Tess lied. "It's just that so few people are out on a day like this—I was glad to see anyone."

Louisa turned her horse to walk down the wide green.

"Then you won't mind if I accompany you. Are there usually more people out at this time of day?"

Tess, out of civility, was forced to follow and answer the question. "Not many."

"You always ride alone?"

"With my groom," Tess said quickly.

Louisa half-turned, showing a sly smile. "My cousin Gryphon asked me to give you a message."

Tess looked up, her insides twisting.

"Oh yes," Louisa said calmly. "I'm well-aware that you meet him here. It is a very foolish thing to do, Lady Collier. I'm sure your aunt would not approve."

"Thank you for your concern." Tess allowed the coldness that she felt toward Miss Grant-Hastings to creep into her voice. "I've done nothing of which my aunt would disapprove."

"I don't agree, Lady Tess. I may call you Lady Tess, may I not?"

"It seems that you already do," Tess said.

"How gracious you are," the other girl said pleasantly. "Please call me Louisa. Perhaps I can ride with you regularly, for I really do feel that Lady Wynthrop would think it most inappropriate for you to be riding with my cousin without a proper female attendant."

Tess pressed her lips together, holding back a sharp reply.

"In fact," Louisa went on, "I have convinced my cousin of that very thing. He is new to London, you know—as you are—and he isn't quite clear on exactly what is acceptable. He is now in complete agreement with me that these clandestine meetings are most unwise."

"Clandestine!" Tess protested. "I never met your cousin in secret! We have always—" She stopped, encountering Louisa's interested gaze. "My groom is always with me when I ride," Tess finished lamely.

They went along in silence for a moment, before Louisa said, almost timidly, "Perhaps there is something you should know, Lady Tess."

Tess looked at her, surprised by the uncharacteristic hesitation. Louisa's beautiful face was angelic—a little too angelic, Tess thought acidly.

"My cousin—dear Gryphon—has declared himself to me."

The shock almost betrayed Tess. Her whole heart and lungs seemed to constrict, making it hard to breathe. She swallowed, and said the first thing that came into her head. "But I thought—Lord Falken . . ."

"Oh, my dear, you don't think I ever set my sights to *that* dizzy height, do you? Lord Falken is a great one for the ladies, you know. I would be too foolish if I were to think anything of *his* attentions. I think I shall be very happy with my own sweet cousin, though Lord Falken may have all the rank and wealth in the world."

These sentiments ran so counter to Tess's every conclusion about Miss Grant-Hastings that she could not even summon a response. Gryf and Louisa . . . the anguished impossibility of it whirled in her head. Surely it had been only two nights ago at the Gosfords' party that she had seen Louisa clinging to Lord Falken. They had held a long, low conversation in the privacy of a secluded corner; Tess had noticed, because Mr. Eliot made one of his caustic remarks about them. When the couple broke up, Falken came away with a thunderous frown, which darkened his face and was gone almost instantly as he approached Tess, smiling his usual lazy smile.

Suppose that was when Louisa had told him this news? Suppose that was why he had looked so angry with her, and Louisa so white and unnaturally controlled. They had stayed apart the rest of the evening. Tess had noticed that, too, because Falken had spent the entire time being excessively solicitous toward her. She had not liked it, because she did not like Falken, with his languid air and hard eyes. She remembered wishing that he would patch up his quarrel with Louisa and go away.

It seemed that they would never patch it up now.

"Wouldn't you like to know the message my dear Gryphon sent you?" Louisa asked sweetly. "He is so kind, he thinks of everyone but himself . . . he said to tell you that he regrets he cannot see you again, and that he wished you every happiness in your future life."

Tess summoned all her courage, and said in a numbed voice, "Tell him . . . thank you. I hope you will be very happy."

"Oh, I know we shall!" Louisa said with a sigh. "He

is all I've ever dreamed about . . . I have loved him since I was a child. We pledged ourselves when I was nine, and he fourteen—a silly thing, as children will do. I hardly dared hope that he would truly wait for me—he's been in the West Indies for so long. When I saw him again, I knew at once that I loved him still."

"I-I see," Tess said. "How wonderful for you."

So he had been pledged all along. A stab of pain tore at her heart. She had never had a chance! It had not been her rank; it hadn't been her money, as she had been so sure. He had simply loved someone else for years. She couldn't even say she had been deceived; he had never offered more than friendship; he had even encouraged her to accept another man's proposal. It was not his fault if she had been so stupid as to let that friendship grow into something more in her own mind.

Now that she looked back, all the pieces fell into place—his blockade running, his sudden appearance in London, everything made sense. He must have been accumulating money, so that he would have something to offer his chosen bride. Anyone could see that Louisa would not be inexpensive in her needs. He had cared enough for her to risk his life at the blockade, over and over again, so that he could dress Louisa in the silk and satin that she loved. Tess felt a sudden surge of rage at Louisa, who would let him do such a thing. But then, perhaps she hadn't known. She had said the West Indies: perhaps she believed that. He would have wanted to save her the anxiety of knowing the truth.

And his kiss . . . the very thought of it made Tess cringe inwardly. She had all but forced him to kiss her, offering herself in the park like a street girl. All the time, he had been thinking of Louisa.

All the time, he had loved someone else.

A little hiccough, almost a sob, escaped Tess. She covered it with an awkward cough and turned to her companion. "I'm sorry, I think it's too damp for me to stay out longer. I must go home."

"Oh, of course!" Louisa was all concern. "Go at once. Please don't let me detain you. I thank you for allowing me to accompany you, Lady Tess. Despite the weather, it has been a *very* pleasant ride."

It was two days later when Stephen Eliot proposed to Tess. She sat and listened to him in the same dull dream that she had walked in since she had met Louisa in the park. He read her no poems, though he did kiss her hand, very gently, as if she might break beneath his touch. There was no trace of the cynic in him, none of the acerbic wit that had grown familiar over the past months. He was quiet, and earnest, and infinitely more serious than she had ever seen him before.

She said that she must think about it.

Larice was full of the news. She was certain that Tess would accept—who would not? Tess heard her cousin whisper it to old friends and new, to mild acquaintances. To Miss Grant-Hastings. Louisa took Tess aside and wished her all the best. Tess did not bother to say that she had not yet accepted the proposal. She was sure that she would, eventually. It was a minor delay; just that she had not quite been able to say yes to him, so soon after losing what she had never had.

And then Gryf came to call.

He came alone in the morning, when Tess was the only one awake. She sat up from picking listlessly at her breakfast and looked in shock at the butler who brought the news.

"Shall I say you are not risen yet, my lady?"

Tess set down her teacup. "No," she said slowly. "No. I will see him in the library."

She rose from the table with care, her heart thundering in miserable excitement. He had come. Louisa would have told him, and he would be offering his good wishes. He must. On what grounds could he object to Stephen Eliot now, when he never had any solid accusations before? What a child she had been, to hope that it was jealousy that had prompted his dislike of the other man.

What a fool.

He was standing by the window, his back turned to her as she entered. Sunlight caught golden fire in his hair as he looked up. She could not see his face for the glare from the window. With feigned calm, she crossed the room and sat down.

"Hullo," he said softly, keeping his silhouetted position near the window.

"Good morning." Tess was surprised at how naturally the words came out.

He seemed at a loss then; he stood without speaking. Finally he shifted, and took a step toward her. "I want to apologize."

She said evenly, "You have nothing to apologize for."

"In the park . . ." He hesitated, turned suddenly back to face the window. "I wronged you very much."

His choice of subject was confusing. Tess stared down at her hands in her lap. "It doesn't matter," she said. A long silence fell between them, and at last she added, "I understand that you are to be congratulated."

He swung around, and she saw his face clearly for the first time. "Congratulated?"

His surprise was patent. Tess suddenly felt the ground fall away from beneath her feet. "Are you not—engaged?"

He made a sound of incredulity. "Of course not. Engaged to whom?"

"To—your cousin," Tess said, in a very small voice.

"Louisa?"

Tess nodded.

"Did she tell you that?"

"She said you had declared yourself."

"Declared myself . . ." He spun on his heel and strode to the window, then whirled and came back, much closer than before. "Damn her. What the devil does she think she'll gain with a story like that?"

A tendril of warmth had begun to curl in Tess's middle. It grew, and became a steady flame. "You're not engaged."

"Certainly not. It's *your* intentions that I've come to talk about."

"Are you speaking of Mr. Eliot?" she asked cheerfully.

"Yes," he said, and the grim look in his gray eyes washed the newfound gaiety from hers. "Louisa said you would marry him."

Tess knew not why—perhaps to have revenge for the misery of the past few days—but she said, "Perhaps I shall."

"You cannot."

The blunt command brought an instinctive resistance. "I don't see why I can't, if I please. He has offered for me."

He took a deep breath, and let it slowly out again. "I know you think it none of my affair, but I can't stand by and let you do this."

Tess smiled, thoroughly enjoying his frustration. He had to care—he must, at least a little. "Then you will have to tell me exactly why I shouldn't marry Mr. Eliot," she said, with a trace of smugness.

"There are . . . reasons."

"What are they?"

He strode back to the window and looked down on the street below. Tess watched his profile lovingly, taking pleasure in every line and plane, every movement of his tall, well-muscled form. He frowned, then shook his head. His lips curved into a sour smile, as if some secret irony had occurred to him. "I don't believe this."

"It shouldn't be so hard to believe. I must marry; I promised my father, and I rather like Mr. Eliot."

He leaned against the windowsill. "That's hardly reason enough to live with the man the rest of your life."

Tess stood up indignantly. His tastes were obviously very different from hers: he urged her to accept the most preposterous clodpole, disliked a perfectly acceptable gentleman, and dismissed her own judgment out of hand. "I suppose you think I should have accepted Mr. Bottomshaw on no firmer grounds?" she asked haughtily.

He reacted to her coolness with a quick burst of anger. "He'd certainly be better than Stephen Eliot!"

"I don't agree."

"You don't know what you're talking about."

Tess narrowed her eyes. "Oh, I think I do, Captain—or Mr. Everett, or whatever you'd like to call yourself. I will marry whomever I please, whenever I choose to do it, and if I choose to become Mrs. Stephen Eliot, then I most certainly shall."

"No."

Just like that. No. Tess sputtered, and her voice rose threateningly. "How dare you?" At his stubborn frown, her voice gained more furious volume. "How dare you? Who in the world do you suggest I marry, then? I have to marry someone, and I won't have Jeremiah Bottomshaw!"

"I don't care!" he shouted. "I don't give a damn who you marry! As long as it isn't Eliot." He turned away, and braced his hands on the windowsill. In a tone that sounded perilously near desperation, he spat, "Good God, if you're so set on marriage, you'd be better off marrying *me!*"

A fraught silence followed his outburst. To Tess it seemed to spin into a small eternity. A slow, joyous comprehension spread through her, a woman's certainty. His deep, uneven breathing was audible from where he stood again by the window, staring blindly out, his hands balled into white fists behind his back. She sat down, to keep her legs from buckling under her, and said quietly, "Was that a proposal?"

His whole body stiffened. "No."

"Then I shall marry Stephen Eliot."

She had said it as a gamble, but it came out with a ring of dreadful finality. Gryf bent his head and pressed his fists against his forehead. "I won't let you," he said dully.

Very gently, she answered, "You have no right to stop me."

He dropped his hands and stared at the ceiling. She sat still, so afraid that he would walk out the door that she had to make a conscious effort to take each breath. He crossed the room and fell onto his knees before her, gathered her cold hands in his and bent over them, holding her so hard that her fingers ached. "Damn you," he whispered harshly. "I love you. Does that give me the right?"

A burst of happiness exploded inside of her. "Then this *is* a proposal," she said, in a voice of unnatural calm.

His grip tightened; he made a wordless sound of misery. "No. I can't."

She leaned down and pressed her lips to his burnished hair. "I love you too."

"It won't work," he said, muffled. "It would never work."

He seemed to her like a small boy, badly in need of comfort. She pulled one of her hands free and rested it on his shoulder. "I love you," she repeated softly.

He groaned, but his fingers sought hers again, intertwining with them. He raised his head. "You don't know what you're saying."

Tess smiled into his anguished eyes, those smoky hawk's eyes lined with sun and distance. "You've already tried that one."

"I don't have any money."

She shook her head. "That won't do either. I have quite a lot."

"You don't—I can't—" His mouth curved in a grimace and he shook his head. "I'm not what you think I am."

She gazed down with loving amusement. "What are you, then?"

"It doesn't matter. You wouldn't believe me. I can't marry you."

Tess sighed. "Then I shall have to become Mrs. Eliot."

His face darkened. He pulled away from her, and began to prowl the room. Tess pretended to gaze at her lap, but her eyes never left him as he paced a gilded cage with the powerful, unconscious grace of a wild animal. Her experience with such creatures gave her the sure knowledge of what to do. She sat silent and still, schooling herself to wait, though her pulse fluttered erratically. Let him think; let him overcome his fear. The bait was there, and the hunger. She knew it, had seen it in his eyes. He wanted her. The thought made her tremble with anticipation. Oh yes. He wanted her.

He stopped, and Tess turned to look at him openly.

The painful doubt in his expression tore her heart. She forgot patience, forgot tactics, forgot everything but the need to ease the hopeless despair that lined his features. "I don't care," she said firmly. "I don't care what you are, or what you have been, or what you think you might become. I don't care if you have no money. I don't care what your name is. I love you. I will marry Mr. Eliot if you won't have me, but I will still love you. I'm sorry if it hurts you. It hurts me, too, but I can't change it, and I don't want to."

He stared at her for a long moment.

"All right." His voice shook. "All right. God help us both, but I'll marry you if that's what you want."

By the time he returned to his rented flat on Mount Street, Gryf was no less dazed than he had been when he left Morrow House. He had walked an indeterminate distance through the city, hoping this incredible delusion would vanish into the depths of his imagination where it belonged. But when he had walked for thirty blocks through the London chaos, he was still just as much engaged to be married as he had been when he started.

He threw his hat and stick on the entry table, and got a frown from his valet for not waiting to transfer them in a more civilized manner directly into the man's hands. "A brandy," Gryf ordered, feeling himself in bad need of one. He went up the stairs into the sitting room and flung himself into an overstuffed red velvet armchair. He stared at a faded landscape painting that hung on the opposite wall, not seeing it or the room around him. The heavy mahogany furnishings had nothing to do with him anyway: the place, like the valet, was one that Taylor had recommended, and it had never felt like home.

After a while, he let out an explosive sigh, and rubbed his face with his palms. The valet entered the door Gryf had left open, placed a silver tray and a snifter on the table next to Gryf, and asked if there would be anything else.

"No," Gryf said wearily, and tapped at the crystal. "Just keep this full. I'm planning to become excessively drunk."

The valet, a middle-aged cockney who had done his share in making Gryf acceptable in London society, gave his temporary master a sympathetic look. "A dog's day, then, Mr. Gryphon?"

Gryf smiled humorlessly. "That doesn't begin to describe it."

"Afore you finds yerself hindisposed, sir, you might be wantin' to know . . . 'twas a lady 'ere to see you. She wouldn't leave no card, but says she'll be back, an' she's come once or twice since."

"A lady." Gryf thought immediately of Tess. A mingled misery and joy gripped him. "A dark-haired lady?"

"No sir. She wouldn't 'ave 'ad dark 'air, I don't fancy."

"Oh." Gryf frowned. "Is it all right for me to have a lady caller here?"

The valet was used to such questions; Gryf had made no secret of his social ignorance.

"I don't 'spect hit says much for 'er, Mr. Gryphon."

Gryf picked up the glass and twirled it. "I don't suppose I can turn her off the doorstep. Whoever she may be."

"No, sir. I don't think she'd take that, seein' as 'ow she's so wild to see you."

"Well," Gryf said, "I'm mystified."

A bell tinkled, and the valet turned. "I 'spect that'll be 'er, Mr. Gryphon."

Gryf took a stiff mouthful of brandy and swallowed it. He stood. "See her up, then. I can't see how my life could possibly get any worse."

He realized how wrong he had been in that happy sentiment a few minutes later when Louisa stepped into the room with a pleasant smile. "Cousin Gryphon," she said musically, as the valet closed the door behind her. "I'm so glad to find you at home."

He eyed her warily, and gave a brief nod. "Louisa."

"That's right. Louisa. Your favorite cousin. May I sit down? Thank you so much; you're such a kind host. Tell me, Gryphon dear, are we first cousins, or is the connection more distant?"

"It's as distant as you care to make it," Gryf said blandly.

"Really? Suppose I care to make it rather close?"

Gryf sat down. "Could this sudden closeness have anything to do with my purported 'declaration' to you?"

Louisa's sharp blue eyes probed him. "You have spoken to Tess Collier."

"I have."

"I asked you not to." She began industriously to pull off her gloves. "That business of meeting in the park, Gryphon—a little too much, don't you think? If Lady Wynthrop knew of it, you would be run out of town. It would have been best to stay away from Lady Tess until her engagement is announced. Stephen Eliot wouldn't care for any hint of scandal."

"I don't give a damn for what Stephen Eliot thinks," Gryf said calmly. "And I don't care for you telling lies about me."

She gave him a small smile. "Why, lies are all I've told about you, Gryphon dear. Is there any reason to change the pattern now?"

He matched her smile with a hard one of his own. "You're being paid for those particular lies, Louisa. I'd prefer it if you didn't extemporize."

"Is that a brandy, Gryphon?" she asked airily. "Would you mind if I finished it for you?"

He shrugged. She waited a moment, then rose to retrieve the glass herself. She sipped it with a greediness that caught his attention. He suddenly realized that she was nervous.

She was silent until she had finished the drink, then set the glass aside and ran her tongue delicately over her upper lip. "Actually, Gryphon dear, I haven't really been telling lies about you and myself."

"Haven't you?" His tone was dangerously polite.

"No. I expect you to marry me."

By dint of old and ingrained conditioning, he managed to keep himself from jumping out of his chair. "May I ask for what reason you expect me to marry you?"

She fluttered her lashes downward. "I'm carrying your child."

"Pardon me?"

Her lashes flicked open. "A baby, Gryphon dear. Yours. I'm sure you'll do the right thing."

For a moment, breath failed him, and then he found his tongue. "Louisa," he said in a dead neutral voice. "I've never touched you."

She drew herself up. "Never touched me! But here I am, lured to your apartments. Totally alone. My good name is ruined."

"How sad for you."

"Oh, no. I've put it about that we're childhood sweethearts. Secretly engaged for years. That should damp any notion that the marriage is rushed."

He stood up, crossed the room, and looked down at her. "Is this Falken's child?"

Her face stiffened, but she recovered quickly. "It's yours, my love. Don't try to deny it."

"I can help you, Louisa. I'll find a doctor—"

"No!" She leaped to her feet. "I'll not submit to some filthy knife! I'd likely die of it!"

"All right, calm down. I have a little money—my ship will be docking soon. You could take a passage to France—"

"No!" she wailed. "I'd be ruined; I could never come back! Not a soul in England would receive me!"

"It appears to me that you're already in that position."

"Not if you marry me." There was a rising note of hysteria in her voice. "I don't care what you do afterwards—you may take yourself off to perdition if you please, but we must wed! It's the only way."

With a sense of disbelief, Gryf found himself saying for the second time in one day, "I can't marry you."

Her pretty eyes gleamed. "Oh, yes, you can. And you will. Because if I go down, *Cousin,* I'll make sure I bring you down with me!"

An old and familiar chill touched his spine. "Would you care to make that threat more clear?"

"I'll make sure they all know it's yours," she sneered. "I'll drag your name through the mud. No one will speak to you. You'll be a pariah! I'll see that you never step in a decent drawing room again!"

The tirade confused him at first, until he realized that Louisa was threatening him with what she was most afraid of herself. It had not occurred to her that Gryf could care less if he ever saw a decent drawing room again for the rest of his natural life.

He sat down, pretending to look worried. "What if I deny it? I'll simply say it's Falken's child."

"No one will believe you," she said, recovering herself a little. She too resumed her seat. "I'll make sure they don't, and I imagine Lord Falken would be a little put out."

Gryf couldn't restrain a short laugh. "Yes, I suppose he would be. Have you told him, Louisa?"

Color sprang into her face. She had, Gryf concluded from her silence. And Falken had probably politely instructed her to go to Hell.

"I think we should set an early date," she said matter-of-factly. "It will save speculation."

"Louisa," Gryf said gently. "I cannot marry you."

"You mean you don't want to."

"I mean I can't."

Her hands fluttered. "Why ever not?"

"Because I'm engaged to Lady Collier."

The motion of her hands ceased. "I see."

At the frozen expression on her face, Gryf felt a wave of disgust for Falken's callousness. "Will you let me help you in any other way?"

"No." She grasped her gloves and stood up suddenly. "No, thank you. I must take my leave now. Good-bye, Gryphon dear. Will your man see me out? Good-bye."

The door closed behind her before Gryf even had the chance to rise. He heard her footsteps, drumming down the stairs, and then the slam of the door, much too soon and loud for his valet to have had any hand in the matter. After a few moments, the man opened the sitting room door tentatively.

"Is the lady gone for good, then, sir?"

Gryf looked at him in bemusement. "It would appear so."

"I 'ope she weren't too overly excited, Mr. Gryphon. She near knocked me down on the stairs. I was just comin' hup to give you this—" He proffered a sealed envelope. "The boy said hit were hurgent."

Gryf rolled his eyes. "Now what the devil—" He took the note and tore it open.

25 June, 1864, West India Dock, London—

Respectfully beg to inform you the Arcanum *docked 6 p.m., 24 June, Berth 75, now discharging cargo. Captain Grady seriously ill, not expected to recover. I await your instructions.*

> *Yr humble servant*
> *Michael Toomey*
> *Harbormaster's Clerk*

Gryf came to his feet with a strangled oath. For a moment he was unable to summon action through the fear that gripped his throat. Grady, his mind throbbed. Dear God, not Grady.

"Hit can't be bad news, sir?" the valet said, in a tone of worry.

"A cab," Gryf said, bursting out of immobility, "get me a cab. Never mind, I'll find one myself—" He was already halfway out the door, the crumpled note fluttering to the floor behind him. His valet followed quickly, pounding down the stairs in atypical haste.

"I can get one faster, sir!" the man said, brushing past Gryf toward the door. "If you'll manage your own hat and coat . . ." He was gone, leaving Gryf in the hall in a draft from the open door. It was true the manservant could probably hail a cab more quickly, but Gryf's fingers trembled in frustrated haste as he buttoned his coat. He just remembered to grab his top hat and cram it onto his head. He was on the step in time to see a hansom rattle to a stop at the curb.

" 'Ave a care, Mr. Gryphon," the valet said, as Gryf

stumbled on the narrow stairs of the cab. The man-servant held the cab door open for a second longer. "Where you be goin', sir, if I could ask?"

"West India Dock." Gryf had to struggle not to shout.

The valet had a quick conference with the cabbie in incomprehensible cockney accents. " 'E'll take you as far as Fenchurch Street, sir. The rail goes from there straight to Blackwall. Hit's the fastest way."

"Thank you," Gryf said. Somewhere in the frightened turmoil in his mind, he realized that the valet was truly concerned.

"Hit's noffink, sir. You take care, Mr. Gryphon. You do take care." The man motioned to the driver with a sharp chirrup, and the cab swung into jolting motion.

Chapter 8

$\mathcal{S}$he was there, in Berth 75, her tall masts as familiar to Gryf in the forest of other ships as his own face in a mirror. The weedy, tarred odor of the docks pervaded his senses, the smell of home, the sounds of home, the universal bustle of a busy port, this one bigger and busier than any on earth. In his tailored city clothes, Gryf was an object of jeering admiration, but he ignored the calls, striding blindly through the organized chaos of barrels and stevedores and stray dogs, dodging a shower of coal from an unloading collier by instinct.

The *Arcanum* presented a lull in the tumult: her cargo discharged, she lay quietly waiting when she should have been swarming with the activity of preparation for another voyage. The thrift ingrained in his subconscious by hard years of struggle made him momentarily regret the money that ticked away with each minute spent idle on the dock. He shook off the thought, not caring. All he wanted was to see Grady, alive and irascible and complaining about the delay, discounting the note as a figment of some dockworker's drunken illusions.

Gryf bounded up the ladder, announcing his arrival

with a shout. He headed for the cabin, and a tall, dusky figure arose from the shadows of the companionway.

"Captain," the massive Negro said, his cultivated accent at odds with the savage tattoo on his cheek and his canine teeth sharpened to vicious points.

"Mahzu!" Gryf exclaimed in relief. The deserted ship had thrown him into panic, but the sight of the big African was reassuring. Mahzu was one of Gryf's original crew, one of the strange assortment of men that Grady had gathered on the east coast of Africa so long ago. The truth of Mahzu's past was as misty as Gryf's: the man never spoke of who or what he had been, but he made good use of the intimidating combination of tribal tattoos and educated speech. Curious bystanders and suspicious customs agents thought twice before they passed Mahzu to peer into the *Arcanum*'s dark holds.

"Where's Grady?" Gryf demanded. His fear of the answer rendered the question harsh and abrupt.

"Below, Captain."

There was something in the black man's emotionless response that conveyed much more than the simple words. Gryf felt his heart turn.

"No," he said. "Dear God—"

The sailor's head moved, the faintest shake. "Go on, sir. He asked for you."

Gryf spun on his heel and clambered down the companionway. He was at Grady's cabin door in one stride, slamming it open and coming up short at the sight of a man in dark clothes, standing over the bunk with a prayer book in his hands.

"Get out," Gryf said softly, and moved toward the berth.

The stranger looked up at him. He nodded briefly and murmured, "Amen" as he turned away to leave. The moment the door closed Gryf turned to the still form on the berth, heard the slow, painful breathing that meant Grady was still alive.

In the watery light from the porthole, Grady's face was hollow and chalky beneath his ragged beard, ashen except for two burning spots of color over his cheekbones. Gryf fell to his knees, grasping the mate's clammy hands, intertwining his fingers with Grady's and squeezing, willing his own life into the lifeless form beneath him.

"Grady," he whispered, bending over the limp body and pressing their tangled fists to his mouth. "It's Gryphon . . . it's Gryphon, Grady. I've come."

There was no answer, no sign of awareness. Only the sound of rasping breath in a silence that seemed eternal. It was unreal, impossible that this was happening. Grady was sick. He was sick, he wasn't dying. He couldn't be dying.

Gryf stared down into the frighteningly still face, clenching his teeth in a fierce and silent prayer. He thought of years, of good luck and bad, and in every memory was Grady. He thought of loyalty and courage, and felt his own hopeless lack of it, holding on to his friend with every straining fiber of his being. For minutes, for hours, he had no idea how long he knelt there and begged God for each labored breath.

But Grady's shallow sighs became weaker, and the two bright spots of color in his cheeks began to fade. Every breath came shorter, farther apart, rattling in his throat.

"No," Gryf moaned, feeling the life drain out of his friend beneath his hands. "Don't leave me, Grady. Grady, I need you . . . oh, God, I need you. Please . . ."

The faint rise and fall of the mate's chest faltered. The wheezing sound diminished, became inaudible. Gryf held his breath—waiting, praying, willing . . .

A minute passed, and then two; endless silence while Grady lay unnaturally still beneath him.

Gryf squeezed his eyes shut. His head bowed, leaning on Grady's still-warm hands, and his mouth strained open in a soundless cry of denial as he pressed Grady's limp palm against his face.

Someone moved behind him; a hand laid on his shoulder, light, but firm in its message. Gryf held his cheek to Grady's hands, going numb, feeling life turn into darkness. A vast emptiness filled him, an ache beyond words. He moved mindlessly, letting Grady's fingers slip from his grasp as he rose. Behind him, the other's hand closed on his arm.

" 'Twas his heart, lad," the little man said kindly. "It just—gave out on him."

Gryf looked at him, seeing nothing.

"I'm Dr. Stebbins. We'll need to write a certificate."

Gryf nodded dumbly. He could not speak. It was as if his insides had been torn from him, leaving hollow desolation where once there had been life. He went to the door and opened it, not looking back at the motionless figure on the berth.

Outside the cabin he stood for a moment, stared blankly around him. His mind was muddled, as if someone had asked him a question for which there was no answer. Or a thousand answers, none of which made sense. Finally he moved on, walking in silence, the hollow sound of his footsteps as empty as his soul.

It was one thing to follow her heart, Tess found, and quite another to announce her intentions to do so. She sat in the library for a long time after Gryf left, gazing out at the point where he had disappeared into the green depths of the park.

After his gallant offer—or grudging surrender, Tess

corrected herself with an indulgent smile—she had held out her hands and presented herself for another kiss. Of course, mere civility had required him to comply. He had done so with a complete lack of graciousness, as if the act galled him, but as soon as he touched her, the sullenness vanished. Impulsively, his arms enfolded her, and he claimed her mouth with the gentle, swift intensity that she had seen once before, that first night in Brazil, in the wild gray depths of his eyes by candlelight.

It was that kiss that reassured her, that permeated her like a golden mist and banished all lingering doubt. When he left her, she hugged the memory to herself like a miser with a secret horde of treasure, doling out bits and moments of remembered passion to sustain her through the trying day. "I love you," he had said, and when Anne came complaining of her cousin's practical but inelegant stitchery, Tess closed her eyes and remembered. "I won't let you," he had said, and when Aunt Katherine scolded Tess for hesitating over Stephen Eliot, she thought of Gryf's stubborn face and smiled. "I'll marry you," he had said, and the promise wrapped around her: an invisible comfort, a loving embrace, a bulwark against all unkindness.

She sat down after lunch to write a note to Mr. Eliot, asking him to call on her the next day. She sent another, to poor Mr. Bottomshaw, for the day after that. After considerable thought, she decided to wait to tell her family the pleasant news, since they would undoubtedly not consider it at all pleasant. Tomorrow she would find the courage to face them. She knew it was cowardice, but she nourished a small, wistful hope that Gryf would be there with her for the first revelation.

She spent the afternoon in the little conservatory her father had built in the rose garden behind Morrow House. There, in the hot, sweet air, she hummed to her-

self and pollinated orchids, taking careful notes on
color and form. She came across an old notebook of her
father's, stored away and forgotten in an unlocked
metal box under one of the benches. Eleven years old,
that meticulous, boxy handwriting. She bit her lip and
smiled sadly, reading an entry which described the
lovely yellow Aerides hybrid he had named Lady Sarah,
after her mother.

You loved her, Papa, Tess mused. I know you did.

Lady Sarah had been as fair as Tess was dark, a
laughing sprite, a living image of the fairies from Tess's
nursery tales. There had been tragedy in her mother's
life, miscarriages and scarlet fever and tiny graves in the
churchyard in West Sussex, but she had never shown
those hurts to her only surviving daughter. All Tess remembered of her mother was a mischievous giggle, and
the affectionate way she had listened to her husband
when he waxed eloquent over the sex life of dung bee-
tles at the dinner table.

That was love. Laughter and camaraderie, heads bent
together over a newfound bud on a favorite plant or
hands locked in silent comfort . . . that was what Tess
wanted. And with an inner certainty, she knew that neither Mr. Bottomshaw, nor Stephen Eliot, nor any of the
other London gentlemen would give it to her. She had
promised her father to marry well . . . but what did
"well" mean? Did it mean a title, did it mean blue blood
and money? She had assumed so, when he had been
pressing her. But she had misunderstood. He had
wanted her to be happy, that she knew from the depths
of her heart. He would have wanted her to love, and be
loved in return. If he had urged her to accept a man of
wealth, it would have been for her own protection,
rather than for the money alone. The Lord knew, Tess

had learned to live without luxury. Her father would have understood that it made no difference to her.

Happiness. Love. Freedom. She had almost forgotten what those things felt like in the time she had spent under her aunt's supervision.

Only with Gryf did the words become real again.

She carefully replaced the notebook, content in her reasoning, sure that if her father had been there, he would have given his blessing. And her mother . . . there was never a moment's doubt in Tess's mind that her mother would have laughed and hugged her daughter and wished her every happiness that life could offer. An incurable romantic, Lady Sarah, and through the layers of rationality that the earl had instilled, Tess knew that she shared the fault.

"Good afternoon," said a lilting voice, and Tess jumped, scattering a little golden pile of pollen that had taken her twenty minutes to collect.

She turned and frowned at the visitor, saying "Good afternoon" in a voice that was chilly enough to tell Louisa Grant-Hastings that the intrusion was not welcome.

"Larice said you were out here alone."

"Yes," Tess agreed. "As you can see."

"I thought perhaps you might like some company."

"It isn't at all necessary for you to trouble yourself, Miss Grant-Hastings. I'm quite busy just now."

"Oh, it's no trouble at all. You see, I have been looking for a chance to speak with you privately."

"Have you?" Tess dropped her cotton-tipped applicator and turned a cold look on her visitor. "To tell me more prevarications?"

The arrow hit its mark. Louisa reddened, and lowered her eyelashes. "I had wished to apologize for that."

"I am not prepared to accept an apology, Miss Grant-Hastings. I beg you will go away."

"You must listen to me," Louisa said, in a very different voice. Her white-gloved hands clenched. "You must. I beg you. There is an explanation . . ."

"Of course." Tess gathered her equipment in a neat pile and prepared to leave. "There always is, isn't there?"

As she tried to brush past, Louisa caught her arm. "Lady Collier, please!" There was a little catch in her voice that Tess thought very convincing. "You don't understand."

Tess stopped, and looked down at the other girl's distressed face. "I understand that you told me a complete fabrication about yourself and your cousin. He has never 'declared himself' to you, as you tried to make me believe."

"Is that what he said to you?" The hand let up its insistent pressure, and Louisa turned away. "I should have expected it."

Tess had been stepping toward the door; at this, she stopped and whirled in indignation. "Are you trying now to say that it is he who lied to me?"

Louisa's face was hidden; she put a hand to her mouth, covering a barely audible sob as she sank down in her daffodil-yellow crinoline onto a dirty workbench. Tess frowned at that, realizing that the fastidious Miss Grant-Hastings was indeed upset. The other girl's slender shoulders shook, and she fumbled in her reticule, drawing out a handkerchief and pressing it to her lips. "Oh, I am so ashamed," she whispered. "I cannot bear it! I only c-come to you, Lady Collier, to save you from the s-same folly!"

"What are you saying?" Tess demanded sharply.

Louisa looked up, her face reddened with very real

tears. "I *have* lied to you, Lady Collier, I have, but it was only my shame that made me do it. It is all lies, all ruin, and oh—I wish that I had never seen him!"

"Seen who?" Tess's voice was slightly less firm.

"That man—that vile man who has passed as my cousin!"

"Gryphon Everett? What do you mean, 'passed'—"

"I mean that he is *not* my cousin, Lady Collier!" Louisa cried. "He is an impostor, and I and my family have helped him in his dreadful schemes, and now I see that I must pay for it! I only wish that you may escape the same fate, or worse!"

"Not your cousin—" Tess repeated numbly. "I don't understand. Who is he, then?"

Louisa covered her eyes and shook her head. "I do not know! He came to us with a letter, from my Papa's dear friend Abraham Taylor, asking that we take him in as one of our family. It was for *your* sake, Lady Collier! Mr. Taylor thought he was protecting you! He thought that he was sending that—that man to watch over you until you married."

"Protecting me? Protecting me from what?"

"From fortune hunters." Louisa gave a peculiar little sob, almost a laugh. "He couldn't have known he was setting a fox to guard the henhouse."

"Fortune hunters!" Tess said incredulously. "What nonsense! I'm not a newborn babe. I don't believe Mr. Taylor arranged for any such thing as protecting me from fortune hunters—and if he had, why wouldn't I have known about it?"

Louisa sniffed. "It was to be a secret. I don't know why . . . perhaps Mr. Taylor was afraid it would upset you, or make you feel distrusted. Here, I know you don't believe me; I have no right to expect it. But for your own sake, Lady Collier—look at this!" She rummaged again in her reticule, and drew out a single, much-folded piece of paper.

In shocked silence, Tess spread the document flat. It appeared to be a letter, couched in legal prose: "In anticipation of services rendered, including, but not limited to: investigation of the financial and moral attributes of any man who might request the hand in marriage of Lady Terese Elizabeth Collier, sole surviving child of Robert Edwin Collier, the late Earl of Morrow, and encouragement of a relationship of trust between Captain Gryphon Frost and Lady Collier, for the purpose of advising Lady Collier on her prospective marriage; I, Abraham Taylor, agree to disburse to Gryphon Frost the certain sums specified below on the dates specified below. This agreement is accepted on the condition that Lady Collier is unaware of the contracted services throughout the period during which such services may take place, and will terminate at such time as Lady Collier is no longer a *femme seule*."

Mr. Taylor's bold signature was familiar to Tess, and Captain Frost's accurate hand was recognizable, too, from the letters to her father. The amounts specified as payment were enough to make Tess catch her breath. An instant picture flashed into her mind, a vision of Gryf, in the park, willingly discussing with her the merits of her suitors. Her heart sank as she remembered. He had seemed to know all of them quite well for a man who was supposedly new to London, a fact which had escaped her before. And his name was *not* Everett, it was Frost—or was it? Did she really know anything certain about him at all? She looked down at Louisa in confusion.

"I had to see you, Lady Collier!" Louisa sobbed. "He told me not to; he threatened me! I was in fear for my life—you cannot imagine what it is like, to find that a man who has seemed so kind, so gentle, is a monster! He has ruined me, Lady Collier, with his lying words of love. He *did* declare himself to me, he did! I didn't lie about that. And now because I believed him, because I was a foolish, stupid maid, I am forever disgraced."

Tess could only stare helplessly at the other girl. Louisa met the look with brimming eyes, and suddenly slid off the bench, onto her knees in the dirt at Tess's feet, clutching at the folds of her skirt. "Oh, you don't understand, do you—poor, innocent lamb! You don't know to what depths a woman can be brought! I am going to bear his child, Lady Tess. *That* is my shame!" She turned her face aside. "I listened to his words of love and thought to be his wife, and instead, he has made me his whore!"

Tess stepped back in horror at Louisa's words and at her debased position on her knees. Louisa collapsed into a sobbing heap. "Oh, you despise me now! I knew you would. I hoped to the last that he would marry me—I told you we were childhood sweethearts, that was my only lie, and it was to cover up my sin! But he never meant to marry me—it's you—your money—that he wants! I did not listen; I never suspected that he was making you fall in love with him as I had! When I found out he was meeting you in the park, I tried to stop him. I begged him to take away my shame and honor me; just this morning I went to him to beg again . . ." She choked, and pressed the kerchief to her eyes. "He laughed at me. He said that you had consented to have him, and that he would be as big a fool as I if he were to forgo the opportunity. Oh, Lady Tess, forgive me! Forgive me, but I could not let you marry him in innocence!"

All capacity for words deserted Tess. The conservatory suddenly seemed suffocatingly hot. The image of

Gryf that Louisa painted seemed impossible, but there
the once-proud lady lay, on the ground at Tess's feet, in
a paroxysm of tears that could not be feigned. And the
contract—his friendship, his caring, the time he had
spent with her—all for money! Not because he loved
her, or even liked her; he must think her the biggest fool
alive, the way she had fallen for his act. She had made
it easy; she had thrown herself at him, had practically
asked him to marry her. And the way he had hesitated—
had that been false, too? Tess felt nausea rise in her
throat. Oh, God, had it all been a lie? Had he kissed
Tess so sweetly, so passionately, knowing that Louisa
would bear his child?

Tess looked down at Louisa, a miserable heap, still
weeping on the floor. Tess tried to pity the other girl; she
tried to summon a Christian forgiveness, but all that
came was an overwhelming disgust, a revulsion against
that picture of sordid sin and repentance. She could not
relate it to Gryf, or herself; there was nothing in common between this horrible moment and those happy
mornings in the park. But the contract . . . he had lied;
he had lied to her, not once, but many times. Crushing
the document in her hand, she ran to the door of the
conservatory, stopping to look back only once. Louisa
had raised her head, one hand extended, as if in suppli-
cation. The sight sickened Tess. She could not speak: she
shook her head and fled into the cooler, thinner, outside
air, tearing her sleeve on the thorn of a rose as she stumbled toward the garden gate.

Gryf stood across the street from the Corinthian
grandeur of Morrow House, beneath the heavy railings
of Hyde Park, while the rattling morning traffic of Park
Lane passed unseen and unheard in front of him. It had
been two days since he had stood there last, and it

seemed to have been two centuries. He felt that much older; he was dead inside, numb, with a deadness he recognized as shock. It would wear off: the pain would come. He knew it, and he had wandered here, like a wounded animal, like a lost child, to look for comfort where he had no right to find it.

That other morning, he had gone away from this house cursing himself and his own insanity. In a moment of criminal weakness, he had made a promise when he had less than nothing to give, and then he had compounded the disaster by telling Louisa. If the news was not all over Mayfair by now, then Louisa had been kidnapped and gagged by cutthroats.

In the one tiny living part of him, the small space where he still could think and feel, he was glad of that folly. It made the promise irrevocable. It gave him Dutch courage, when his own was locked up somewhere with the rest of his soul. He needed Tess, needed her like a drowning man needs a floating limb. He wanted to see her, to touch her, to feel her body, so strong and graceful, to taste the warm honey of her lips. She was the one focus in an empty world. She was alive, and by some miracle of crazy circumstance, she belonged to him.

He would tell her everything, he had decided. Who he was; what his life had been. She would never believe him; what rational person would believe him? And yet he hoped. She had said that she loved him. Twice.

He crossed the street, dodging an omnibus, and mounted the steps of Morrow House. A butler answered the door: the same skeptical face that had greeted Gryf before. He had been left waiting on the stoop that time; now he was allowed into the hall, a small promotion. Would Lady Collier consent to see him? The butler vanished and returned. She would. If the gentleman would care to wait in the library?

It was a long wait. The living part of his mind paced; his body remained still, heart pounding. When she came finally into the room, he took an involuntary step toward her.

She was beautiful, dressed in a deep-pink gown with a tiny white bow at her creamy throat. Her face was pale, paler than seemed natural. She did not smile. He thought perhaps she was angry with him. He could not bear the thought, and went to her where she stood still by the door. He touched her cheek. "I'm sorry," he said. "I couldn't come sooner."

Her blue-green eyes looked into his for a brief, intense moment, then away. He wanted to kiss her; he would have, but still she did not smile. She did not speak. Her face was strained; white lines marked the corners of her full lips. He waited, at the edge of a precipice, with a dawning awareness that the ground beneath him was crumbling.

"I love you," he said, a desperate pebble thrown into the silence.

She made a move, a tiny shudder, and stepped around him. Her wide skirt brushed his leg as he turned, then the contact was gone, and she stood on the other side of the room with a look that warned him not to follow.

"I have seen Louisa," she said.

For a moment he did not understand her. Everything was different. Wrong. The hot blood his heart pumped made him dizzy. He wanted to sit down. Then it hit him, what she meant. What Louisa would have said.

And he blundered out with the worst possible response. "She's lying," he said. "She's lying."

He saw in an instant it was wrong. Her eyes, those eyes like the sea, became solid ice.

She thrust out a paper. "Is Louisa lying about this?"

He looked at her, silent. The paper shook a little in

her outstretched hand. When she perceived that he would not take the document, she unfolded it jerkily and began to read. "In anticipation of services rendered . . ."

He listened. Her voice was almost natural; it only trembled when she came to the part about "trust." He could hear the angry tears, but she did not shed them. She finished, after repeating the promised sums with special emphasis, and raised her chin proudly.

"Have you seen this contract before?" she asked, in a voice like a high court judge. Like a hangman.

"Yes." It came out a hoarse whisper.

"Is this your signature?"

"Yes."

"Your name is not Everett?"

He had a wild thought of telling her the truth. It vanished into the abyss where it belonged. He said, "No."

"You are not Louisa's cousin?"

"Please . . ." he began, but her white face stopped him. He dropped the hand that he had raised. "No. You must know that I'm not."

"I know it now." He saw her lower lip quiver dangerously. She looked down quickly and back up, the ice lady again. "Can you still say that it is Louisa who has lied?"

He hesitated, afraid. He was not thinking well; it seemed that half his mind was still shrouded in the coffin where they had laid Grady. He would make a mistake. He would say the wrong thing, and so he said nothing.

"You cannot," she said, when the silence had stretched to unbearable proportions. "It is you who have lied to me. And you have ruined Louisa."

A dull ache spread over him. "No."

"What proof do you have?" she cried. "Can you tell me anything—anything that I can believe?"

He spread his hands helplessly. "What do you want?"

"I want you to tell me that this paper is false! I want you to say that you didn't act my friend for money— that you haven't pursued me for my fortune! I want you to say—to say— Oh, God, say anything—but don't stand there as if your only friend has just died!"

The sound that came out of his throat had no meaning. It might have been a laugh, if it had been made by a corpse. She chose to interpret it that way, consigning him to the dead with her wide, accusing eyes.

"I hate you," she said. "I despise you."

He hated himself. He despised himself. There was some fault, some fatal flaw in him that made her believe those things. He could not prove to her that the money meant nothing, that he had signed that contract almost against his own will, because he could not refuse it, because it was a way to be near her when he had no other hope. Proof . . . what proof could there be? Only trust, only love, and for the lack of it he stood there with the last flame of life dwindling away inside of him. He would have gone down on his knees—he felt he must, but some vestige of pride held him up. It would make no difference. She had made her decision.

"Have you nothing more to say?" she asked, very cold.

I love you, his mind answered.

His lips did not move.

She waited. To give her credit, she waited a very long time. At last, she said, "I have accepted Mr. Eliot's proposal. Whatever was said between you and me is— forgotten. I hope that is understood?"

It did not hurt him. He was already dead inside. "I understand."

"Then you will go now." She bit her lower lip. "I wish never to see you again."

There was a peculiar little catch in her voice on the

last word. Gryf gazed at her. He had a terrible premonition that he was going to cry. He swallowed, tried to speak, and found that he could not. Instead he turned and left her, walked across the carpet, noting its greens and blues and faded gray with a dreamlike clarity. He came to the closed door and stopped. The carved wood was dark; it blurred a little in front of his eyes, becoming a black pit instead of a door. He reached out and opened it, stepped into nothing, and closed the barrier very gently and carefully behind him.

Midnight. It was that, at least, or later. The ship was not visible through the riverfront darkness. Gryf had moved her off the dock and out onto the river itself, to a cheaper mooring in Blackwall Reach. She was loaded, ready for sea again, with another of the cargoes that Taylor had arranged.

On the stinking shore, the overturned dinghy Gryf had left in the charge of a tavern potboy was slimy with dew and river scum. He staggered a little as he heaved the boat upright on the slick stones of the causeway: he was extremely drunk, in body if not in mind. He launched the small craft by reflex alone. The flickering lights of the tavern receded swiftly; the tide had just turned, and current ruled the river. In the clear, moonless darkness, everything appeared to rush past. Gryf pulled at one of the sculls, turning himself in a dizzy panorama, searching in the murk to orient himself.

The dark river was alive with tiny lights, lanterns at the bows and mastheads of bulky shadows. The wind blew against the current and ruffled the reflections, bringing the creak of wooden blocks, the rhythmic squeaking groan of anchor chains. Nothing seemed familiar. Up and down the river, the lights and the sounds were the same, without form or distinction.

Gryf found himself suddenly among moored ships, much sooner than he had expected. The dinghy struck a mooring chain with a jarring thump and spun slowly away.

He began a twisting tour of the moorings, peering through the darkness at the outline of each silent ship. The wind had changed—or he had lost his direction. He rowed for the next lantern, and the next. The names and dark shapes began to run together. Again and again he drifted down upon a mooring chain and peered up at the figurehead. Some of the names seemed familiar—or were they the same ones he had just passed? He unshipped the oars and drifted, wiping sweat from his mouth with one hand. A musty taste of blood stained his tongue, and he looked down at his palms, at his hands that had gone soft and now bled from forgotten work. There was no pain. Just a dull ache, like the numbness inside of him.

The last lantern eased past him, lighting an unfamiliar bow. Beyond was darkness. He was lost.

It did not seem to matter. He let the dinghy glide on the current aimlessly. A steam paddler made its splashing way down the channel, recognizable first by its noise and then by the red engine glow and ghostly fall of water, like two white wings on either side. He slowly became aware that he was in its path. He stared impassively at the steamer as the slow, black river carried it toward him. He was tired. Tired of thinking. Tired of feeling. The water was dark and cool, the throb of an engine and the splash of paddles warm and close, like a steady heartbeat pumping lifeblood. It seemed easy, to wait there in the steamer's path as she bore down on him. To not fight anymore; to not be afraid, or lonely, or hurt. To forget. It seemed so very easy to let go . . .

The steamer was almost upon him. His dinghy rose

on a wave, swept inward toward the rusty wall of freeboard, and scraped brutally along the side of the larger
vessel. The unshipped oars jerked free of his hands,
swung forward and back as the dinghy bucked wildly.
The sound of the paddles grew to a roar, and they rose
above him like a demonic waterfall out of the darkness.
At the sight of the towering paddlewheel, a shot of pure
physical terror lanced through Gryf. He scrambled for an
oar. He broke it free and shoved mightily, fending off
from the steamer, fending again, and backing water with
frantic strength amid the white, roiling wake. The dinghy
reeled, tossed like a piece of driftwood, and the great paddle passed within six inches of his stern. The wheel was
slowing rapidly, and Gryf fought the weakening suction
that would have drawn him under seconds earlier. The
paddle creaked to a stop, and a deafening whistle and
roar filled the night as the wheeler blew off steam.

As the whistling scream died away, he could hear
pounding feet and agitated shouts, calling for a life
buoy. He looked up the tall iron side of the steamer and
cupped his hands around his mouth. "Ahoy there.
Belay! I'm afloat!"

The feet pounded down the deck, and in the steamer's
lights he could see heads pop out over the railing. "In
the muckin' wherry?" someone called. "Damme, you
still alive?"

"Aye." Gryf pulled back a little from the steamer as
she lay to, moving slightly with the current. "See to
your course." He wiped water from his face with one
sleeve. "The blame is mine."

"Sweet Jesus, man, you come right athwart 'er! We
like to cut you in two!"

"That I know," Gryf said ruefully. Several inches of
water sloshed about over his boots in the bottom of the
boat.

"Aye," a deeper voice added, " 't were not for the bow light o' that Aberdeen clipper over there off the point, I'd be 'alfway to Wool'ich and you'd be at the bottom, and none to tell the tale. I sees you in the water there, lying across the line o' her light. What kind o' fool you be, governor? You don't say you didn't 'ear us comin', now?"

Gryf looked the way the man pointed, and saw the single light that burned there. With a sudden mental start, the vague chart in his head reversed, and the confusing pieces fell into place. He had been drifting lost, but now with a blinding clarity he knew where he was. He did not have to see the outline of the ship by the point to identify her raking masts and the elegant sweep of her deck. He knew her, every line and curve.

He looked back up at the deck of the steamer. "I've had a drop or two." It was the only explanation he could think of. "I'm sober now."

"Blest if you ain't, arter such a scare!" A gruff concern colored the voice. "Can you get yourself off this river, governor?"

"Aye. That's my ship, by the point."

"Is it now? Would you be an officer, by the sound o' you?"

Gryf hesitated, and then said, "Captain."

There was a short guffaw. "None other, then? You'd best 'ave one o' your boys take you next time, sir, if you be planning on liftin' a pint." The steamer captain's voice paused, and then he said, almost shyly, "You'll be needin' a tug on that beauty sometime, sir?"

"I will," Gryf answered promptly.

"You'll not 'old it against the good *Rose* when that time comes?"

"I shall count it heavily in her favor. The tide turns at five . . . can she be here then?"

"Oh, aye, sir, that she can! She'll 'ave that pretty bird at Gravesend 'fore the day's out."

Gryf manned his oars. "Five, then." He did not ask what the *Rose* would charge for a tow. He owed her.

"Steady on, Captain." Another hearty laugh drifted out over the water as the steam blew again. "Never say die, sir, as long as there's a shot in the locker!"

The words made Gryf stop his rowing. He watched as the steamer charged her boilers. The big, slow paddles began to turn, and she swung again into the stream. Her lights passed on, down the river, and winked out around the point. The river was silent again, only the sound of a barking dog on the far shore, and the faint squeak of one of the *Arcanum*'s spars on the light wind.

Never say die.

He began to pull for his ship . . . for the ship that had saved his life with her steady light. She materialized out of the darkness, solid and real, patiently waiting, the one love that had not deserted him. His life came down to that: that as long as he was alive, he would have her. And when she went down, he would go too.

Never say die.

It was something Grady would have told him.

Chapter 9

*I*t was spring again.

The thought of it made Tess cry. She cried often now . . . silently, without emotion, as if the tears were the slow upwelling of blood from a wound.

In the dark gallery, in the fingers of sunlight that crept under the doors, she could just see the malevolent, pale stares of the huge portraits of Ashland's ancestors as she huddled in a corner and wept. Only in that one corner of the hated room could she sleep, because whatever portrait had hung above it once had been removed, leaving only an outline against the faded wall. Only in that one corner had Stephen not had a bizarre story to tell, a sick fancy to act out, a new and brutal way to punish her for what he had failed to accomplish himself. Until she was a proper wife, until she would do what pleased him and no longer fought, he would see that she suffered the consequences.

"Lady Tess," Mr. Taylor said gently, bringing her back to present reality, to the library at Morrow House instead of Ashland's gallery. She slid too easily into the dreams—the mental scars had not healed as quickly as the chilblains on her hands and feet, the reddened swelling from too many winter weeks without a bed, without even a blanket, in a room so cold that she had to break the ice in the basin before she could drink and wash herself.

She smiled wanly at Mr. Taylor, still half-surprised to see him there, so familiar, so matter-of-fact, a part of the everyday world that had faded almost to unreality during the nightmare of her marriage to Stephen Eliot. She looked down at the stack of papers he had placed before her and said, "It seems you've thought of everything."

He stood up, his whiskered face troubled, and came to lay a hand on her shoulder. "I wish you would come home with me."

Tess looked out the window at the budding trees. April. The world's inexorable clockwork had brought the season round again, in spite of everything. She said, "I can't. I'm sorry."

"What will I tell Mrs. Taylor?"

"Tell her . . ." Tess stopped, blinked. "Give her all my love. Tell her that I have to find him."

"Frost." It was a statement, not a question.

Tess nodded.

"And if you can't?"

"Then I'll come to you. I have to try."

He made no answer. It was a discussion they had had before, in the weeks since he had arrived from Brazil. Ever since he had broken down the ornate door of the gallery at Ashland and found her huddled where Stephen had locked her, Mr. Taylor had barely let her from his sight. That day, the shaft of light through the splintering door had nearly blinded her, but the sound of his voice, bellowing rage and disbelief, had been like a miracle. He had carried her out, taken her away from the darkness into the light and the air. After six months of torment, he had set her free. And he had come because Gryf had sent him.

Her gaze wandered about the room. There Gryf had been once, and there, and there . . . there he had knelt and said that he loved her; there he had stood and endured her accusations and abuse, without protest, with mute patience, and she had not understood. Had not known that women as foul as Louisa Grant-Hastings existed, until all of London was abuzz with the news of Lord Falken's bastard and how much the duke had paid Louisa to take herself off for good. Had not realized that there was more than one kind of honesty, until she learned from her guardian that Gryf had not taken a penny of his earnings for trying to protect Tess, because he felt that he had failed his trust. Had not known—had never even imagined—that monsters lived in the form of men . . .

Until Stephen had come to her room on their wedding night.

She had been frightened anyway that first night at Ashland, miserably nervous and unhappy, all of her fine resolutions to be a good wife lost in the first clear apprehension of the irrevocable commitment she had made. She sat in her silky gown at the dressing table in the great, ancient bedchamber and thought—not of Stephen—but of Gryf. She tried not to. She tried to concentrate on Stephen, to make herself recall his quick, cynical wit, the unerring courtesy and deference he had always shown her, the way he guided her through the shoals of Fashionable Society when she would have floundered on her own. He had made it clear that he would protect her and revere her, and she had tried to imagine his promises were something more than a cage in which to keep a pretty bird. But it was useless. As she sat there at her mirror, married before God and man, another face rose in her mind's eye, and she knew that she would never be truly faithful to her husband in her heart.

It was that conviction that kept her sane through all that followed. She had never loved Stephen, never from the start, and so there had been something else to cling to when the facade of normality cracked, and revealed the madness beneath.

It had begun with the child, the little boy who crept to her door that night and stood behind her staring timidly. She turned from the mirror in surprise. He did not speak, and Tess took a moment to find her own voice before she managed a small smile and said, "Hullo. Who are you?"

He put a finger in his mouth, not answering. She looked at his flowing white gown and large gray eyes in puzzlement. "Are you lost?"

He hesitated a moment, and then shook his head.

"What's your name?" Tess asked.

"Sammy, mum."

The words were no more than a whisper, accompanied by an apprehensive flick of the large eyes, as if the child expected some punishment for daring to speak. Tess smiled again, to reassure him, but received no smile in return.

"Where's your mother, Sammy? She'll be wanting you in bed at this hour."

Tess had half-expected him to look chagrined, for she had decided he must be some servant's child on a nocturnal adventure. Having only arrived that afternoon, she barely knew the staff at Ashland, but what else could he be, dressed in nightclothes as he was? He only shrugged at the question, and sucked a little harder on his finger.

She pressed her lips together in doubt, and reached to ring for the maid. Her movement caused him to start, and the sleeve of his gown fell a little, revealing deep red welts on his wrist. Tess frowned, recognizing inflammation beneath the scabbed skin. "Sammy," she said gently, careful not to frighten him, "you've hurt your arm."

He stared at her warily.

"Come here," she said.

He came readily enough, with a puppetlike obedience. She took his hand, and felt him tense beneath her touch. "I won't hurt," she promised. "Just let me look. Oh, dear, Sammy, however did you manage this?"

He bent his bright, blond head and looked down at his wrist, as if it puzzled him as much as it did her. He looked up again, about to speak, and then his eyes fastened on the mirror behind her, widening. Tess automatically followed his gaze.

She gagged on a stifled scream.

Behind her, reflected in the glass, stood a man. Her fingers dug into Sammy's arm as she stared at the apparition—all black it was, except for the white hood that floated like a death's-head above the shadows. For one suspended moment terror clutched her: she could not move, could not even think, and then she lunged for the bellpull, yanking it madly. No sound accompanied the summons, for the bell itself would be ringing somewhere far belowstairs, but she continued to tug at it with frantic strength, expecting the intruder to flee at the sight of a sounded alarm.

He did not. He simply stood, watching her. She gave off pulling at the bell and whirled to her feet, shoving Sammy behind her as she faced the hooded figure. "What do you want?" she demanded. "Leave here at once."

The eye slits in the hood seemed to regard her with unblinking, silent menace. She choked back dry panic and felt at the dresser behind her, pulling open the drawer. "I have a gun," she lied. "I know how to use it."

The specter took a step. Tess's heart jammed her throat. "No closer." Her hand closed around a brush in the drawer, and she drew it upward, behind her gown, so that the handle thrust out of the filmy material. "I'll shoot to kill."

"Boy," the figure whispered, a harsh sound that sent a chill of horror down her spine. "Come here."

Unbelievably, Sammy disengaged himself from Tess's grip and in docile compliance approached the dark silhouette. She almost called out to stop him, but something in his solemn little face made her hold back the protest. She said, desperately, "You have no right to be here. My husband is coming."

An eerie laugh issued from the white hood. "I have the right."

Tess fingered the hairbrush, unable to take her eyes from the blank visage. Awful stories of victims found with their throats slit seized her imagination. Her legs wanted to collapse under her. For God's sake, where were the servants—why hadn't they answered her call? As Sammy went to stand before the apparition, the intruder reached out with one black-gloved hand and touched a shining blond lock, sliding it through dark fingers with a leisure that was at once tender and yet dreadful.

Tess watched. She swallowed. The gesture, the sibilant voice, some combination of height and weight and outline . . .

"Stephen?" Her own voice was a faint croak.

The blank mask looked up, stared at her.

"What—what is the meaning of this?"

His silence was more ominous than words. She was certain it was Stephen. Her mind struggled to make some sense of the masquerade, of the nameless fear that squeezed her chest in the face of that opaque countenance. Perhaps it was a joke—some obscure nuptial custom whose meaning was beyond her. She did not like it. "Stephen," she said shakily, "I wish you would explain. You frighten me with this—costume."

He moved suddenly, startling her. He crossed the room and came close, so close that she instinctively backed against the dresser. He caught her chin in one hand and forced her to look up into the featureless mask. Tess tried to wrench away, not expecting such strength. His fingers hurt her; she stood still and faced him, trying to see his eyes behind the hood. She was beginning to understand that he *wanted* to frighten her. "Let go of me," she said, as firmly as she could.

He did. She leaned back against the table. His gloved hands came up and took her by the shoulders, his fingers sliding inside the high collar of her gown and pulling downward with a movement too quick to evade. The buttons popped; he pushed the silk down far enough to reveal her pale shoulders. Tess flushed with shame and fear and anger. His intentions were clear enough now.

She waited, determined to be a dutiful wife. This was part of it. She had to comply. But the mask, the gloves, the child—it was all too threatening and strange. The black slits stared at her like a serpent's eyes; she felt hysteria bubbling up uncontrollably. At last, just when she thought she must break and run, he turned away from her with a move that was clearly disgust.

Tess slumped a little. In her relief, she forgot Sammy momentarily, but his muffled whimper caught her attention, and she looked up to see the boy shrink before Stephen's eerie gaze. The pinch of anxiety on his small features stunned her—it was more than a child's natural reaction to that fearsome figure. It was anticipation, a numb, haunted certainty that strengthened as Stephen drew closer—and then suddenly, aghast, Tess knew what was going to happen.

". . . annulment," Mr. Taylor's voice droned. Tess opened her eyes, realizing she had squeezed them shut on the memory as she stared down at the papers. She drew a shaky breath.

Mr. Taylor paused. "Would you like to rest? We can finish this tomorrow."

"No," she said quickly. "No. Let's finish as soon as possible."

He nodded, and went on in the unperturbed way that he used with her, as if it were all a simple matter of business instead of a long, slow walk out of Hell. "This is the doctor's certificate; it states that you have been examined and that your marriage was unconsummated. We'll want to keep this, in view of Mr. Eliot's adverse position concerning the annulment, to forestall any future efforts to reverse the church's decision."

Adverse position. How lifeless such legal terms were, how well they smoothed over and concealed the fury, the threats and counterthreats. Stephen had not let her go without a fight, but he was wary of scandal. An annulment, quiet and quick, was the price to keep his foul pleasures off the pages of *The Times*.

Tess did not care. She was afraid of Stephen still; any thoughts of trying to protect his other victims had long since vanished in the dark eternity locked in the gallery. The tears began again as she thought of Sammy. She had not seen him since that night. For all those black months it had been only Stephen, and a manservant who had come to bring her food enough to stay alive. The servant was almost as terrifying as Stephen himself. He came only when it was too dim to see him and he never spoke. He watched her: she could feel his eyes on her in the dark. Often she had woken from a fitful sleep and seen the dull orange spark of his cheroot illuminate his bearded chin as he stood with insolent leisure against the door that she knew she could not pass.

"You're certain you do not want your family notified?" Mr. Taylor asked. "I'm afraid they will be concerned for your whereabouts."

Tess set her jaw. "They haven't shown any concern yet," she said. She tried to keep the pain from her voice, but still it quavered with the ache of betrayal. "They never even asked Stephen where I was. I don't want anyone to know. I couldn't b—bear the questions."

Mr. Taylor cleared his throat. "I believe we've done enough for the day," he said gently. "It was only to make you aware—there's no need for you to deal with these documents personally. I've tried to make every possible arrangement."

"Thank you." The words were hopelessly inadequate. She pressed her handkerchief against her mouth and said them again.

He only nodded, and cleared his throat again, gruffly.

Tess tried to bring her tears under control, succeeding only partially. "Have you taken care of . . . the other matter?"

He hesitated. "I've opened an account. The money is in it. I cannot do more, not knowing—"

"I'll find him," Tess said, with quick obstinance. She twisted the handkerchief. "I will."

"And when you do?"

She looked up. "I'll ask him to forgive me."

He pulled at his whiskers and regarded her steadily. "Lady Tess, you're not yourself yet. Perhaps you should wait—let your emotions settle. I want you to be happy, and I don't see how such a course can bring you anything but grief."

"Like marriage to the admirable Stephen Eliot?" Bitterness lent a sting to the words.

"Of course not. But I would not want you to mistake gratitude for love."

She shook her head. "You don't understand."

"No," he sighed. "I'm afraid I understand too well. You think you love Frost. Perhaps you do. But the man who came to me in Brazil did not appear to return the sentiment. At all." He frowned at her. "Lady Tess—please reconsider."

Tess lowered her eyes. Mr. Taylor had been grimly honest in his assessment of Gryf's attitude toward her. But she clung to the fact that he had gone all the way to Pará to inform her guardian of her folly, in terms strong enough to persuade Mr. Taylor to leave his ailing wife and sail to England with all speed. If not for Gryf, she would still be trapped in Stephen's web. The story of illness her husband had put about would have spun into a permanent disability. She would have died there, locked away, while the few people who ever thought of her would have shaken their heads and murmured, "A tragedy . . . so young."

After a long moment, Mr. Taylor said, "I see that you are bent on it."

She nodded.

"Then let me conduct the search. The kind of places—" He stopped, looked embarrassed. "I'm afraid your Captain Frost does not normally move in the finest circles."

Tess felt a tiny, incongruous smile tug at the corners of her mouth. "I'm aware of that."

He frowned, with a severity that did not quite reach his kindly eyes. "This goes against all my instincts of what is proper, Lady Tess."

She let the smile magnify. "I believe you like him as much as I do."

"I do not," he responded promptly. "I'm certain he is a complete rogue."

"A scoundrel," she agreed.

"He isn't worth the ground you walk upon. Your position, your fortune, your breeding . . ."

"Will you find him for me?"

He clasped his hands behind his back and sighed. "I shall try, my lady. On my honor, I shall try."

Gryf lounged back in the wooden booth, tapping a slow rhythm with his fist on the scarred table. The sour-sweet smell of stale wine and smoke permeated the close air, even though in the day outside the pastel plasterwork of Lisbon gleamed in the August sun. Across the table, his companion watched him through narrowed eyes. Gryf glanced up from the frowning contemplation of his hand and said, "I can do better," in a mixture of French and English designed to confound the Portuguese squealer whom he knew to be sitting in the booth behind them.

"Very doubtful." The answer was pure French, bizarrely cultivated for the present place and time. Through the beard and the rough-weather clothes and the knife at his belt, the man's soft hands and stiff posture fairly screamed that he was not a seaman. The get-up annoyed Gryf—did the precious monsieur actually think he was fooling someone? Everybody in the place had spotted him instantly, and the farce drew unwelcome attention to Gryf's presence. The Frenchman added, "We are willing to mount twelve nine-pound cannon—"

"That should frighten the U.S.S. *Rhode Island,*" Gryf said dryly.

"We do not anticipate that you will take on an American warship, sir."

"Good. Because I don't intend to, *mon ami*."

The other sat back. "You are afraid."

"Damn right," Gryf said, in the Queen's good English.

"We came to you because we had been told otherwise."

Gryf gave him a sidelong glance and went back to the slow syncopation of his fist and his knuckles on the table, a rhythm which he was well-aware drove the Frenchman crazy. After a long pause, the man said, "*Ainsi soit-il*. Fifty percent."

Gryf smiled and shook his head no and flirted with the tavern girl who came to lay down another two tins of dark ale, which his companion paid for. Gryf's lack of interest in the proposal was not entirely unfeigned— he had little desire to become a privateer and less to do it at someone else's behest. But he was broke. Worse than broke. The loss of two masts in a storm off the Straits had eaten up far more than eight months of meager profits, though he couldn't take that problem to the ship chandler's agent or the yardmaster and expect much sympathy when his receipts were already twice overdue. A writ to attach his ship was already in progress. Without adequate stores, he was stuck in Portugal, and the prospects there, over or under the table, were grim. One part of him wanted to lean over and shout, "I'm not a damned pirate" in this turnip-sucker's face, while the rest, the part that counted reason and advantage and cold cash, angled to make a deal that would be worth selling what little was left of his soul. He tried to crush that faint voice, the last thin thread that reminded him he was becoming what he had always hated. Survival was all that counted now. Survival, and holding on to his ship. It was really no different than when Grady had been there, except that it was lonelier.

Just as the Frenchman was preparing to speak again, a new arrival caused heads to turn in the murky depths of the room. The figure that appeared in the doorway was worth looking at: the heavy flannel breeches, nailed boots, and canvas gaiters were absurdly out of place in this domain, not to mention in the warmth of a Portuguese afternoon. The newcomer was smallish, his cheeks pink with heat as he doffed a canvas hat to reveal a pale bald head. He squinted about the room like a mole come to light, and accosted the giggling tavern girl with unmistakably British formality. Gryf's smile faded into mild astonishment as he heard the man ask clearly for "Frost."

The girl directed him with a wave and smirk. All hope of privacy was lost when he approached the table and introduced himself in English, quite loudly, as, "Miles Sydney, sir. Your servant."

The agitated look on monsieur's face was compensation enough to Gryf for the unwanted attention. "Great pleasure, Mr. Sydney," he said mildly. "What may I do for you?"

"I would like to discuss the possibility of chartering your ship," Mr. Sydney announced.

Gryf raised his eyebrows, then nodded toward the Frenchman's bench. "It seems the line forms over there."

"Oh, me," said Mr. Sydney. "Are you not available?"

"What is it you want to ship?"

"Myself. And a colleague of mine."

"Just passengers?"

"Not precisely." His face took on an enthusiastic glow as he leaned forward to explain. "I understand you have experience in conveying naturalists and their specimens, Captain Frost. That's why I looked you up, and a devil of a time I've had finding you, if I may say so. My colleague and I are botanists, you see, and we have been fortunate enough to gain the support of an excellent sponsor to make collections in the South Seas. It would be a voyage of at least eighteen months—hopefully more, if we have some success."

"Naturalists," Gryf repeated, and a sudden and unwanted image came into his mind. He rejected it viciously. "I've never transported naturalists."

"Oh, yes—well, perhaps not on a collecting trip such as this, but I saw the condition of the Earl of Morrow's specimens when they arrived at the Botanical Gardens. In splendid shape, they were, and I said to my colleague—Thomas Cartwright, you know, perhaps you've heard of him—I said to Tom, '*That's* the kind of fellow who would devote himself to our cause.' We too often find, I'm afraid, that the true value of our specimens is not fully appreciated by the maritime community. But you, sir—I took one look at those *Cecropia* saplings, and I knew you understood."

Gryf's shoulders tensed at the mention of Morrow.

"Mr. Sydney," the Frenchman said impatiently, "I doubt you can pay the terms of Captain Frost."

The little man turned. "Ah, are you his agent, then? But the pay is very good, let me assure you. And we will provide all supplies and ship's stores."

"He isn't my agent," Gryf said shortly. He gave Mr. Sydney a level stare. "I need eight thousand pounds before I can get her off the mooring."

"Oh, yes, quite understandable, Captain. And a little more—say, another two thousand, to tide you over until midway in the voyage? I'm certain we can come to an agreement."

Gryf looked at the Frenchman. "I think you and I have finished our business. *Pour jamais.*"

The man flushed beneath his fabricated beard. He took a breath. "Seventy-five percent, Captain."

Gryf shook his head. Very slowly and softly, he said, "I'm not a pirate. For any price." And felt a great weight lift off his chest.

"Well, well," said Mr. Sydney affably. "Of course you aren't, dear boy. May I sit down? Yes, yes, good day, sir."

Sydney turned out to be much less a fool than he had initially appeared. By the time the *Arcanum* was provisioned and anchored at Le Havre, Gryf was convinced that the little man was not a fool at all. Beneath the fussy amiability beat the heart of a miser—salt beef came for half the going price, or not at all, and bullocks and sheep and poultry for the cabin cost no more than the rum and Spanish limes. All these miracles of frugality were accomplished through long sessions of mutual hand-wringing between Sydney and the chandlers, with frequent appeal made to Gryf as to the sad inevitability of not making this voyage at all. The one point in which Sydney had shown himself generous was in the fee promised to Gryf. That expense, Sydney assured Gryf, was well worth it, since the botanist placed complete confidence in the good captain's concern and affection for the specimens-to-be.

They waited two weeks in Le Havre for Thomas Cartwright. Every day, Sydney promised that his colleague was "on his way, but he's rather preoccupied, you know, and may have forgotten the date." Gryf put his crew on leave and entertained himself prowling the booksellers' shops, having budgeted a miniscule portion of the money which hadn't gone to paying debts for books. The rest he placed in the ship's safe, and sometimes in the middle of the night when he dreamed of pirates and Frenchmen and nine-pound guns, he would wake and get up and go look, to make sure that the coins were still there.

The price he paid for that feeling of security was remembering. The thought of Tess haunted him, brought to vivid life each time Sydney spoke lovingly of his specimens or insisted on some special arrangements for their protection. Gryf tried to banish it. A year ago he had thrust her out of his mind with savage determination, twisting his bitter hurt into fury to keep her out. But now the memories came back in an aching flood: her face, her voice, the feel of her in his arms. He remembered her laugh, rich and vibrant, and the imaginary echo made his own life seem bleak in its emptiness.

He missed her. God, he missed her. He had to drive himself to remember that fate had taken its ordained course, and left him wiser. He should have learned, long ago, that loving was the ultimate weakness. They were lost to him now—everyone he had cared for in his childish need. He would never allow himself to be that vulnerable again.

But in his loneliness, he thought of her still. She crept into his mind so softly that it sometimes seemed that she was there, with him, instead of a hundred miles away in another man's arms. Standing by the rail on a paling summer eve, he could picture her: her dark hair ruffled by the gentle breeze, her slender hands resting on the polished wood. He tormented himself with the image, calling up every lovely detail and then tearing the picture apart, replacing beauty with ugliness and spite. She had chosen Stephen, and Gryf would never forgive her for that. Anyone else—anyone—he might have been able to bear, but Stephen Eliot . . .

No. He hated her, with a passionate, jealous malevolence. Of all his ghosts, she was the one that obsessed him beyond endurance, in his dreams and his heart, like a wound that festered and would not mend.

It was a relief when Thomas Cartwright finally ar-

rived one morning while Gryf was ashore. He returned
to the ship to find Sydney bustling about supervising the
storage of a quantity of trunks and boxes. The little
botanist was in a fever of excitement, taking time only
to grab Gryf's arm and say, "He's come, he's come—
now we shall be on our way! I've put him in that second
cabin, Captain, I hope you won't mind. The other is full
of books. Tom is a trifle—indisposed. I think the Channel crossing didn't agree with him, and then that trip
out here from the dock in such a dreadful little boat—
well, I wouldn't want to put a shine on the matter, but
I fear poor Tom is not at all a sailor. I don't imagine we
shall see him out of his cabin soon."

Gryf saw no point in mentioning that "the second
cabin"—the steward's—had been the one he'd been
using himself. He had slept in it after Grady's death, because it was one of the few places on the ship that held
no vivid memories. But for the price Sydney and his
friend Tom were paying, Gryf was happy to sleep anywhere. He found his kit laid neatly on the saloon table
and moved it into the captain's suite without comment.

He dispatched Mahzu to round up the crew. By afternoon, they were straggling back and sobering up, and
Gryf counted each one of the eight anxiously, for the
crimps were always on the hunt for unwary prey. If a
sailor stumbled into the wrong house, his first sip of
drink would be the last he took on dry land for a while,
for he'd wake up in the wet forecastle of some strange
ship with nothing to show for his former voyage but a
headache and an empty pocket. Six of Gryf's crew were
aboard by nightfall, but Mahzu and old Gaffer remained missing, and Gryf sat up in the moonless darkness on deck and waited, impatient and worried.

Near midnight, the sound of oars made him leap up
and go to the rail, peering down at the splash of an

approaching boat. At Mahzu's low hail, Gryf let out a breath of relief.

"Gaffer?" he asked softly.

"They nearly got him, Captain," Mahzu said from the dinghy. "There was a fight. He's badly hurt."

Gryf cursed under his breath. "Where is he?"

"Here, sir. The doctor said not to move him, but I didn't think you'd want to leave him ashore."

"Hold there. I'll get help."

He roused the others. While they maneuvered the injured Gaffer aboard, Mahzu gave Gryf a description of the sailor's condition, which was not promising. The broken ribs and arm weren't fatal, but they would make Gaffer useless for this trip.

Gryf listened, and then grimaced. "We can't sail short-handed. Lord, old Gaffer of all of them—I can't believe he'd let himself get tangled up in that kind of business."

"I don't think he did, Captain."

Gryf glanced up. "No?"

"He was in a leaving shop—a fair enough place, sir. They came in and took him. Over two other younger ones, and better money."

That news put an entirely new complexion on the matter. "It's my hide they're after, then."

"The crimp sent a message. He's got a man to replace Gaffer. The price is a hundred today and two hundred tomorrow, sir."

It was an old battle between Gryf and the crimps. They had their trade, and they didn't like a captain who generated enough loyalty in his crew to make the seamen turn down the inflated offers of new berths. Gryf wanted to be gone now as much as Sydney, but he did not dare sail short a working man.

"Cap'n," one of the men whispered. "We got company, sir, two points for'ard o' the port beam."

"Ah, damn." Gryf reached for his pistol. He too could see the faint rippling wake of the longboat that bore down on them. "Hail, 'em, and bid them keep their distance."

That was done, but the boat came silently on. Gryf took aim, and placed a shot across her bow. The splash of oars abruptly ceased.

There was a pause, and then a voice roared, *"Capitaine!"* Gryf did not answer.

"Your new man is here," the disembodied voice continued. "The one you asked for. One hundred francs, and another fifty for the trouble of bringing him out to you."

"I asked for no one, *sangsue,*" Gryf spat.

A hoarse chuckle carried over the water. "How do you say that in English—'sucker of blood'? I will drink your blood, *Capitaine,* if you provoke me. One hundred fifty francs."

"We weigh anchor in the morning."

"With seven men? I think not. I think you will be shipping an expensive crew this trip."

The crimp obviously thought that Gryf would be looking for triple the number of men he had now, not just one more man. There would be no going back into Le Havre now for recruiting, not with this shark in control of the docks. After a long moment, Gryf said, "A hundred francs."

Another laugh. "You are going to make me angry, *Capitaine.*"

"One hundred," Gryf said stubbornly. He did not care about fifty francs one way or the other, but he did not want to appear too eager.

"Bon. He is coming aboard. The next one will be three hundred."

"Extortion," Gryf growled, for effect. He could just

make out the flutter of a telltale hanging from one of the furled sails, a sign that the breeze was rising. The moon would not be up for another hour. He drew a mental chart of the harbor entrance, and made a decision. "The money's in the safe. You'll have to wait."

"Oh, I am a patient man," said the crimp. "Very patient."

Gryf handed the pistol to Mahzu, and murmured low instructions in his ear. Before Gryf had reached the companionway, silent figures, almost invisible in the darkness, were on their way up the ratlines. He pounded loudly down the stairs, fumbled to unlock the safe in the murk, and emptied the coins out of one of the bags. He turned, making his way to the sideboard in the saloon by feel, and loaded the empty bag with tin tableware, testing the bundle for the satisfying chink of metal when he dropped it. Scooping it up again, he slipped back up the stairs and strode out onto the deck.

"*Sangsue,*" he sneered, leaning over the rail. "I want the man first."

"Do you think I will cheat you, *Capitaine?* No, I want us to have a long and happy friendship. We will call this fine sailor your first token of my good will." There was an order, and the longboat came alongside. Mahzu kept the pistol at the ready as a figure climbed awkwardly onto the deck amid curses and pushing hands. From the way he staggered, Gryf suspected the newcomer had never set foot on a ship before. He groaned inwardly.

"What do you think, my friend?" the crimp called from the longboat. "Worth a hundred francs, yes? A thousand!"

"Worth what I'm paying," Gryf said, and tossed the bag of tin down into the longboat. At the same moment, Mahzu bellowed his orders, and with a booming crack, the sails bloomed white against the black sky, high up, and the crimp's shout was lost in the bang and flutter as the crew slid down and manned the sheets and the stay-sails.

It took the crimp even longer to grasp the situation than Gryf had anticipated, and the first gunshot rang out well after the ship's bow began to swing under strain of the slip rope aft and the force of the backed headsails. The pistol shots sank into an unfeeling wooden hull.

"Let's go aft!" Gryf shouted. With a pause and a shudder, she bounded free. The sails filled. Like a great bird startled into flight, the *Arcanum* gathered silent way. As the wind laid her over, she seemed to dip and curtsy. He could almost imagine that he heard her laughing as she left the longboat and its crew behind, wasting ammunition on a target that rapidly drew out of range on the brisk night wind from the east.

Chapter 10

$\mathcal{A}$ week out of Le Havre, Gryf stood next to the binnacle, watching for the twentieth time as the new man, Stark, missed his order to loose the fore royal. The man was strong as an ox, and smart enough at backtalk, but he seemed deaf and dumb up there in the foretop. Only after the main royal was already sheeted home and hoisted did it appear to occur to him to throw off the gaskets and drop the bunt, so that the ship staggered awkwardly as the loosed sail caught the wind a moment too late for smooth trimming. Stark couldn't have timed it better if he had meant to foul things up.

Gryf would have kept his patience if Stark had shown the least desire to cooperate. But the man was too old to start at sea—past forty at the least, with his salt-and-pepper beard, and he seemed to take instructions as an insult, unable to overcome the notion that just because the crimp had promised Stark a berth as steward, he should actually assume that position. Gryf had no use for a steward, but he had a crying need for a warm body in the foretop. Even though the *Arcanum*'s blocks and running rigging had been changed and changed again over the years to make her work as light as possible, there was a minimum crew below which Gryf dared not drop. In fair weather, she could sail with a crew of six by rotating through the watches, but in another storm like the one off Gibraltar he would need every manjack aboard. So they drilled, for Stark's sake, and Gryf figured the man would appreciate it when he found himself at the top of a swaying mast in a howling gale as they rounded Cape Horn on some wild night in November.

Passing an order to Mahzu, Gryf gave up on exercises for the day. He was about to go below when Mr. Sydney appeared in the companionway.

"Ah, Captain," the botanist said, reaching into the inner pocket of his coat, "I'm glad to have come across you before I forget again—I had a letter which I was requested to pass along."

Gryf looked at his passenger in surprise. "To me?"

"Oh, yes—" He glanced down at the letter in his hand. "Captain Gryphon Frost. That is you, is it not? I should be distressed to find that it wasn't, at this late hour."

As always, it was impossible to see anything but guileless concern on the little man's face, but Gryf knew by now when he was being roasted. He took the offered packet. "I'm only curious about who would have given you a letter for me."

"Oh, as to that—" The botanist paused, making an ineffectual attempt to smooth a sparse strand of hair across his bald pate in the stiff breeze. "Lady Tess, of course."

Gryf stopped in the motion of breaking the seal.

"The late earl's daughter," Sydney added, with a helpful smile as he scanned Gryf's shocked face. "You remember her well, I expect. She's sponsoring this expedition, God bless her."

"Sponsoring . . ." Gryf looked down at the letter in his hand as if it were a snake. He said, faintly, "Do you mean—paying for it?"

"Yes, indeed. And most generous she has been, don't you agree? She specifically suggested that we take passage with you." Sydney beamed at Gryf, and patted his arm. "Well, well, I have done my duty. I believe I'll wait on dinner below."

Gryf was unable to find his voice. He watched Sydney disappear down the hatch, and then walked to the stern rail to stare blindly out at the horizon.

Tess.

The money that had saved him, had bought back his ship and his self-esteem; the money that lay now in the safe below . . .

All hers.

It was like a heavy blow to the jaw. It left him blank. Reeling. He looked down at the blue water that rushed past and felt physically sick.

How could she . . . She took his pride and his soul and his dreams—hadn't that been enough? He had hated her, ached for her, shut her out of his mind with merciless determination. And now Mrs. Eliot found time in her busy day to pull him from ruin with a flick of her little finger. She wrote him a letter.

He crackled the paper in his fist. What would she say? That she was happy? That Stephen Eliot was a fine husband? It had been over a year—there might be a child. Gryf would have laughed, if he had been able to breathe. An heir. He might open this missive and find that there was a new heir to Ashland.

And what difference would it make? He was purchased and paid for now. Bought . . . for ten thousand pounds and a letter.

Shame flooded him, and excruciating anger. He

wished he had taken the Frenchman's offer—better a second-class pirate than her charity case. Better crushed beneath a falling mast. Better dead. It burned his fingers, that letter. It burned his heart down to cinders. He flung the thing violently away, watched it arch and then fall, and disappear in the white wash of the *Arcanum*'s wake.

"Captain."

Gryf turned at Mahzu's address. The mate stood below the break of the deck, in the traditional place of petition for an audience with the captain. It was not a custom normally followed on the *Arcanum*, since her captain spent almost as much time on the foredeck or in the tops as the other men, but Gryf understood the gesture when he saw the solid figure of Stark standing behind the African.

"Well?" Gryf snapped, not in any mood to listen to the newcomer's grievances.

"It's Stark here, sir. He's asked to speak to you."

"Concerning what?"

Even Mahzu looked a little disconcerted at the chill in Gryf's voice. "Concerning his duties, sir."

"I thought you ought to know," Stark added quickly, "that my talents is being wasted—"

"Your talents." Gryf's words cut across the other man's. "What talents, Stark? Scraping chain cable? Picking oakum? Maybe you've noticed the standing rigging needs to be tarred down."

Stark appeared to miss the threat. Mahzu didn't, but he made no comment, only looked at Stark with a resigned expression that clearly stated, "Give a man enough rope . . ."

"I don't know about all that," Stark said, a little impatiently, "but I've experience in service, sir."

"Ah." Gryf smiled coldly, finding an outlet for the

helpless rage that ate at him. "Waiting at table, pouring wine . . . that sort of thing?"

"Yes, sir. Exactly, sir. I expect, with you and the passengers and all, and there being no service in the cabin, that you would want to use me there."

"Do I understand that you're volunteering for the position of steward?"

"Yes, sir!" Stark said enthusiastically.

"Really! And you'll take that on for no more pay than a common seaman?"

"Course I will, sir."

Gryf looked at Mahzu. "He's starboard watch?"

"Aye, sir," Mahzu supplied.

"All right, Stark. When the starbolins go below, you come on duty as steward and stay till the next watch."

"This evening, sir?"

"Of course this evening."

"But sir—" Stark looked slightly discomposed. "I've been workin' since dawn, sir."

"I suppose you'll have to get used to that. It's bound to be a problem, for a man taking round-the-clock duty."

"I don't know as I understand your meaning, sir."

"No?" Gryf asked with a deadly mildness. "You don't see how that might wear a man out? To stand duty on deck with the starboard watch, and then take port watch as steward? After a few days, I think lack of sleep will be the least of your worries, Stark, for God knows when you'll find the time to eat."

Stark looked satisfactorily shaken as the truth dawned on him. He rallied as Gryf started to turn away, and said indignantly, "I hardly think that's fair, sir—I only thought, being as how you had a lady of quality on board, that you might be in need of my particular assistance."

Gryf stopped, glancing back in exasperation. "If we have any ladies of any description at all on board, then you know more about it than I do, Stark."

For a split second, the man's dark face held startlement. Then his broad features took on a sly look. "I don't know as I don't then, Captain. I guess I'd ask that cracked old cock with the queer hat about it, if I was you, sir."

From the corner of his eye Gryf saw Mahzu stiffen, and fought down the same reaction in himself. The snide assurance, the self-important grin . . . He realized Stark was sure that he was speaking out of some clear knowledge beyond Gryf's own. "I'll see Stark in the cabin at eight bells, Mr. Mahzu. Keep him busy until then." Gryf started to jerk his head in dismissal, and then stopped, and added, for the pure relish of hazing Stark, "Oh, and Mr. Mahzu—throw half of that fancy tobacco Stark brought along overboard. From now on, he won't have time to smoke those stinking Burma cheroots."

The tiny cabin where Tess confined herself, impersonating the seasick Thomas Cartwright, had grown exceedingly dull. At first, she had been content to sit and smile and listen to the familiar slap of waves against the hull as the *Arcanum* rocked along. Sometimes she recognized Gryf's voice, muffled, shouting orders on deck as the ship tacked out of the English Channel and into the open sea. Sometimes she heard him in the saloon, talking to Mr. Sydney, and she pictured them poring over charts, the one head a tawny-gold and the other balding, bent together in conference to decide where in the whole, wonderful, wide, free world they might take her.

It mattered not at all. Mr. Sydney, that dear little man who had faithfully stayed at home for years and cared for the plants and animals her father had sent back, deserved his day of adventure. He was almost beside himself with joy—each time he brought a tray of food to her cabin he had to sit down with her as she ate and rhapsodize about his gratitude and pleasure with a sincerity that was impossible to resist. They had been lucky: it had only taken Mr. Taylor four months to locate the *Arcanum* in dry dock in Portugal. Tess tried not to imagine too often the magnitude of the storm which had put the ship there, for when she did, a cold mixture of fear and relief crept into her belly. What little Tess had seen of the *Arcanum*'s deck bore the scars: fresh wood and paint that clearly outlined the repair of smashed bulwarks and gaping holes in the planking.

Mr. Taylor was gone now, back to Brazil and his ailing wife, thinking he had left Tess in capable and conservative hands with Mr. Sydney. Tess had not been about to disabuse her trustee of this pleasant notion, and so she had never mentioned that she and her father's curator had been cohorts in crime since Tess had learned to walk. Together, they had perpetrated uncounted escapes from the schoolroom and other dull places, and never been caught out once. Mr. Sydney had fallen in at once with Tess's plan of impersonation.

He brought her food, and seemed to think that no one noticed anything unusual about Thomas Cartwright's weak stomach that consumed three square meals a day. But Tess was restless, longing to see Gryf, not just to hear him; wanting to tell him so much that seemed impossible to explain. She had considered a hundred ways of confronting him and discarded them all. One was too abrupt, another too ridiculous—what was she to say? "Oh, good day, sir, I was just taking a stroll and happened upon your ship in the middle of the Atlantic." The original plan had been to reveal herself just out of port, but with each passing mile, she had lost her courage, becoming more and more sure that she would not be welcome, that Mr. Taylor had been right, that Gryf could only despise her for the things that she had done and said.

It was out of that cowardice that she had decided to write the letter. She'd spent three days over it, writing and revising. She ended up with a missive that was far too long and said almost nothing of what she wanted, but at least it held the facts—she was here on the ship, she had been wrong, and knew it now to her sorrow; her marriage to Stephen Eliot was dissolved as if it had never existed . . . and she loved Gryf, even if he could never forgive her and love her again in return.

The last sentence about never forgiving she had added after some debate and polishing. It was true, of course, but she wasn't above milking the last degree of remorse from the situation, in hopes it might salve his wounded pride. In fact, she rather thought that she wasn't above anything that could work to bring him back to her. Masquerading as one Thomas Cartwright, renowned and seasick botanist, had only been a way to keep Gryf from retreating from her before she had a chance to explain. Once he knew the truth, she vowed, she would not press him.

Well . . . maybe she would a little . . . perhaps she ought not to make that vow just yet.

She frowned at the two gowns she had laid out. Mr. Sydney had passed along the letter. At any time now, Gryf would read it. Might already have read it. The thought made her heart leap uncomfortably. She forced herself to look at the gowns, one sapphire-blue, the other a deep-wine, and try to make a decision. She wanted to look her best. She had a fear, deep and only half-admitted, that her time with Stephen had somehow changed her: that in place of a young woman there was now a haunted, hollow-eyed wraith, that her face still showed what it had shown the first time she had looked in a mirror after Mr. Taylor had brought her out of Ashland. She looked anxiously in the glass above the little washstand in the cabin. She was pale still, and her eyes looked too large, but as she thought of Gryf and the coming reunion, bright color spread up from the ruffled neckline of her camisole and touched her cheeks.

The sound of booted feet on the companionway stairs made her turn with a start. Mr. Sydney had come back down into the saloon ten minutes ago—that could only be Gryf, and to judge from the staccato pounding, he was in a hurry. Her hand flew to her mouth, pressing back sudden panic.

Mr. Sydney's voice gave a congenial greeting, muffled through the door. Tess bit her finger, listening for an answer, but her heart was pumping too loudly for her to discern the exchange. Then Gryf said, quite clearly and coldly, "I think it's time I met your colleague, Sydney."

He had read the letter, then. Tess gulped in excitement and distress. Mr. Sydney kept his calm, as Tess had known he would. She knew she could count on her old friend, but the hardness in Gryf's tone did not bode well for her fate.

She heard Mr. Sydney answer with an amiable ramble, something to do with his colleague being on the mend, and out soon, no doubt about it. Then, before she could summon the coordination to dive under a blanket and cower there, which was what she wanted very much to do, Gryf uttered an impatient oath and crossed directly to her cabin.

She just had time to scoop up one of the gowns and clutch it to her as the door flung open. She sat down on the berth, hard, because her legs refused to hold her up.

She stared at his feet, unable to look him in the face for fear of what she would see.

Silence. Her pulse was so erratic that she thought she might faint. She noticed with absurd attention that the hem of his trousers needed mending. A thick strand of her hair fell free of its loose knot; she ducked her head, and brushed it quickly back off her bare shoulder.

Slowly, when he did not speak, she lifted her eyes. For so long she had imagined this moment, for so many lonely, dark hours tried to call up his face in her mind. To see him now, real and solid before her, but without a glimmer of welcome, even of recognition on his familiar, sunburned features . . .

To her utter dismay, she began to cry.

Her tears were the key that released Gryf from paralysis. From the moment when Stark had made his crazy assertion, Gryf had half-known, half-guessed; but until seeing her, sitting there with her pale shoulders huddled as if she expected him to strike her, he had not let the awareness surface in his conscious mind.

Now, it seemed to him impossible that he had not known. How could he have not seen it? The ruse was so simple, so damnably obvious—even Stark had recognized it. Gryf hated her, for looking so slight and frightened, for calling up with callous ease the feelings he had locked away behind doors of solid iron. He did not want her to cry, or to tell him why she was here; he did not want to know what Stephen Eliot had done that had set her to flight. She had made that bed for herself—if she could no longer lie in it, then she'd have to look elsewhere for sympathy. She could go anywhere to escape her husband, for all Gryf cared. Anywhere but to him.

He focused on the gown laid out on the berth next to her, so that he did not have to look at the soft curve of her neck, or the white, slender fingers pressed to her mouth. "I wouldn't unpack," he said harshly. "We'll be running into Tenerife tomorrow. I expect you can find another ship there."

She made a little noise, barely audible, and he found himself looking at her again. She seemed smaller than he remembered; softer, more vulnerable. Why did she have to cry, damn her? Why did she have to sit there with her damned sea-green eyes and her damned bare shoulders and her damned soft hair all loose and half-tumbled down? Stephen Eliot's wife—Gryf took a step back and slammed the door and stood, staring at it.

After a long moment, Sydney said calmly, "You seem a little put out, dear boy."

Gryf spun around and glared at the botanist. "What did you expect? That I'd enjoy being made to look like a cawker in front of a bloody green hand who hasn't got the hayseed out of his hair?"

"Oh, well, no, we hadn't any notion of that in particular. We hoped that you would be pleasantly surprised."

"Lord," Gryf muttered. "Surprised."

The disgust in his voice carried well through the closed door and Tess paused in her hurry to dress. She choked back another sob, and wiped her eyes with the back of her hand. She struggled into the blue gown and twisted her hair into a tight knot, wincing at the prick of a pin as she shoved it into the unruly mass. With another ungentle swipe at her eyes, she took a deep breath and opened the door.

They looked toward her, one face placid, the other grim. Mr. Sydney smiled congenially, and then said, "Did I understand, Captain, that you intend to put Her Ladyship ashore at Tenerife?"

"Both of you," Gryf said. "The deal is off."

Tess could not quite bring herself to look straight at

him. She looked instead at Mr. Sydney, who sat imperturbably at the cabin table, where he had spread his notebooks. The little man frowned and rubbed the side of his nose. "Oh dear. I believe that will present a problem," he said thoughtfully.

"Whatever problems it presents are yours. I've got my own, thanks."

"I'm afraid this *will* be one of your problems, Captain," Mr. Sydney said mildly. "You see, if we must find another ship for our expedition, then there is the matter of Her Ladyship's ten thousand pounds."

Tess had to glance at Gryf then. His expression did not change, but she saw the dull red flush of blood rise in his face.

He turned away, went into the captain's suite, and reemerged a minute later with two canvas bags that clattered with a metallic thump when he tossed them on the table. "Two thousand," he said. "You'll have a voucher for the rest."

There was a silence. Tess stared at the floor.

"I don't know that a voucher will get us around the Horn," Mr. Sydney said quietly.

"Two thousand will."

"Yes . . . quite true. I always have thought that we were paying you a fraction too much, Captain."

"What do you want?" There was just the trace of unevenness in Gryf's voice. "Thank you?" He looked suddenly at Tess, and his mouth twisted. "My humble gratitude, Your Ladyship. You'll get your money back."

"Will she?" Mr. Sydney put on an apologetic frown. "I'm afraid I'd have to advise Her Ladyship that you haven't a good reputation for paying on tick, Captain. I'd think she would have to look on it as a loan, and consider the collateral. Do you have some equity to cover that large a sum?"

Tess knew she should stop Mr. Sydney. The eight thousand pounds was long gone, in repairing the ship. She didn't begrudge the money; she had given it gladly—would have given a hundred thousand without a second thought if Gryf had needed it. But he was going to put them ashore. He was going to leave her and go away and she'd never see him again in her entire, long, miserable life.

He was still looking at her, not at Mr. Sydney. "I haven't got any equity," he said in a low voice.

Except my ship, was the rest of that sentence, and it hung in the air, unsaid.

"My lady," Mr. Sydney said, "are you content to take his word then?"

She swallowed. She tried to be noble. She tried to envision leaving the ship, absolving the meaningless debt. It would set Gryf free of her forever, as he so clearly wanted to be. She tried to imagine that parting . . . and found the limits of her courage.

"No," she whispered. "I'm not."

His face lost its sullen color, going white beneath the tan. Tess almost withered under his look of blazing hatred. It was more than she had bargained for: far more. His mouth worked, as if he could not find words foul enough to express his loathing for her. After a moment of savage silence, he turned on his heel and pounded up the stairs.

Tess felt her shoulders sag. She had her way, but she had lost. He would never forgive her for holding him by force.

Never.

She began to dream of Stephen after that. Not every night, but often. They sailed within view of the Canary Islands, of Tenerife, and passed on. No one said anything about it. She came out of her cabin now; there seemed no reason to isolate herself any longer, although she often wished there were when she crossed paths with Gryf and had to endure his stony indifference. She should have tried to avoid him, she knew, as he tried to avoid her, but seeing him was a need, like food and drink. She could not help herself. To watch him on deck was her bittersweet pleasure, for there he was in his element, equally at ease whether plotting course and giving orders, or at work mending chafing gear in the rigging like any common seaman.

The *Arcanum* was different from the ship Tess remembered. The reduction in crew was glaringly obvious, as was Gryf's functioning as a working part of it. There were signs of surface wear, weathered paint and green tarnish where before there had been bright white trim and shining brass. Tess slowly came to realize that this was how the ship had always run, for the crew—most of them familiar to her from that other time—were well-versed in their shorthanded functioning.

Only the dreams marred the routine into which Tess fell as the weeks passed and the ship ran before the steady trade winds down the coast of Africa. After a time, the first shock of Gryf's brutal rejection wore into a duller pain. In spite of it, she found moments of pleasure in the voyage. She had Mr. Sydney for company, and though Gryf would not speak to or even look at her, he was nearby, and she found that strangely comforting. She could observe him all she pleased.

One morning six weeks out, Tess followed an unsuspecting Mr. Sydney on deck into the hot equatorial sunlight. She had secreted a bar of soap in her skirts, ready to participate in the fun. Even forewarned, she let out a cry of laughing surprise at the monstrous Neptune awaiting them, a huge, seaweed-covered figure with a makeshift trident. Mr. Mahzu gave an impressive roar from beneath his oakum beard, showing his sharp teeth and gesturing to his cohorts, who grabbed the hapless Mr. Sydney and started to work. The ship was hove to, stopped almost dead in the water, dipping and prancing as if she, too, anticipated the ceremony. Mr. Sydney was stripped of his coat and shirt, although he was allowed to keep his trousers on Tess's account, and thoroughly soaped down.

Before his dunking, the victim was presented with a huge tin mug of some awful-looking concoction which smelled of rum and bilge water. Mr. Sydney declared himself game to become a true Son of Neptune, but just as he lifted the vessel to his trembling lips, there was a flip and a splash within the cup. He jumped, tossing the mug away with a yell, and green bilge water and a large, unhappy crab sailed out over Tess's skirt. She shrieked, leaping back, and the crab dashed wildly away, fastening with determination on Neptune's bare black toe and waving its other claw in defiance.

The ensuing commotion left Tess holding her head between her hands, collapsed in gales of laughter. She leaned against the companionway hatch, too weak with mirth to stand, as the chase ranged over the entire quarterdeck, even involving Gryf, who had been standing aloof at the helm. On being unceremoniously flung from Neptune's toe, the crab made a mad dash for the steering box and Gryf's equally vulnerable feet. He abandoned his dignity, heaving himself on top of the sturdy, four-legged box, where his feet dangled just out of crab-reach. Neptune's trident worried the harassed crustacean from beneath the steering gear, and Tess squealed and gathered her skirts, retreating partway down the hatch. The crab was surrounded, threatened by an assortment of belaying pins and buckets, but it made a last, desperate bid for freedom, skittering crazily between dancing feet until it found a hawsehole and disappeared into the sea.

Tess looked up from the scene of triumphant exit, her face still flushed with breathless merriment. She had expected to confront the bedraggled figure of Mr. Sydney, but instead, it was Gryf who stood behind her. His face had a strange expression—there was laughter fading from his eyes, but just for a moment the shared glance held something else: an unguarded emotion, a hunger, as if the laughter were more pain than pleasure.

Tess parted her lips. Before words could form he was turning away, the armor reassumed, his shield in place. As if she did not exist he strode off, taking the quarterdeck steps in one bound, and disappeared beyond the lifeboats and the deckhouse.

She dreamed that night, again, this one more vivid than all the rest. It began in the gallery, as they all did, in that dark place she hated, and the essence of it was waiting: a formless, endless dread of what might come. She could see the door, hear footsteps; she pressed herself whimpering against the wall, as if she could make herself smaller and smaller and disappear. The door opened with a long, low groan, and she looked toward the sound, trying to see through the blackness. Her eyes seemed glued shut; her limbs twitched with the need to flee. Then she dreamed she was running, but her legs moved so slowly, like molasses. What slipped through the door, what stalked her when she could not see, came ever closer; faceless, cold, reaching out to touch her.

She screamed, and the sound of her own voice almost woke her. Someone—something—touched her still, pressed chilly, suffocating fingers down over her mouth and nose and then was gone as she struggled awake and screamed again. All around was a blackness as dark as the dream. She knew he was there, was sure of it, even as her mind tried to tell her she was awake. Something moved in the dark, and she cried out. She shrank back, sobbing in fear and confusion, struggling to escape— and then he spoke her name, a familiar voice, not Stephen's, but another far more welcome and beloved . . .

Gryf took her in his arms, held her close, stilling her trembling. Tess drew in a shaking breath and clung to him, hardly believing yet that this was the reality and that other place had been the dream. "Oh, God, I thought he was here—" Her voice squeaked on a sob. "I thought—"

His grip tightened. "Shhh," he hushed her. "Don't think of it. There's no one here."

Tess turned her face into his solid shoulder, her tears wetting his skin. "But I felt him. He touched me. It seemed so real . . ."

"It was a dream." He brushed her hair with his lips, stroked his hand down her arm. "A bad dream."

The thump of bare feet on the stairs outside the open cabin door made her stiffen and clutch at his arm.

"Captain?" asked a worried voice out of the darkness. "In the name of God, what—"

"All's well, Mahzu," Gryf said quietly. "Carry on, mister, full and by."

There was the slightest hesitation, and then, "Aye, aye, sir," as the mate retreated. Through her tears, Tess slowly became aware that the heat of Gryf's embrace came from the contact of bare skin: her own light, sleeveless gown made but a thin barrier between them. She knew she should pull away, but she did not. The dream-fear faded beneath the soft, rhythmic stroke of his hand.

After a moment, he said, "Do you smell smoke?"

She lifted her head, instinctively grasping his arm again. "Smoke?" A fire aboard ship would be a holocaust.

"Tobacco," he said, in immediate reassurance. She felt his head turn, and he took in a deep breath.

Tess sniffed. "I smell tar . . ."

He cleared his throat self-consciously. "That's probably me. Sorry."

"It's all right." She bit her lip, and then said timidly, "I rather like it."

She felt his reaction, a slight tensing of his arm around her waist, and wished she could take back the words. He let go of her, as she had known he would. "Can you go back to sleep now?" His disembodied voice was gruff.

She wanted to say no. Her arm and shoulder felt cool where his touch had been. "Gryf—" she ventured. "I'm sorry. About the money, I mean."

He stood up, a sudden movement. She could just see his outline, in the faint light from the porthole.

"I know it upset you," she added. "I couldn't help myself—I was so afraid you would make me go back."

He was silent for a long moment. When he spoke, his voice was oddly husky. "I wouldn't make you go back, Tess."

"Oh—" Her own voice trembled, a little upward break of emotion. "I've been such a fool—if only you could forgive me for—"

"Don't." He cut across her tumbled regrets. "Tess, I—give me time. Please. I'm not ready for this yet."

She sniffed miserably. "I'm sorry."

"Go to sleep," he said, and she heard him move toward the door.

"Gryf?" His leaving seemed an unbearable loss. "Do you really have to go?"

He made a strange sound, a strained, unhappy chuckle. "Oh, yes. I have to. Sleep, now . . . just go to sleep. Stephen's far away. He can't hurt you anymore." He opened the door and stepped outside, not answering her muffled good-night. It sounded to him like a child's, forlorn and small. He shut the door, and then leaned on it, his teeth clenched, his hands strained into painful fists to keep him from flinging the door back and gathering her into his arms again. The cool wood was smooth, like her skin. He pressed his forehead against it, *hard,* to remind himself of who he was, and who she was. He tried to dredge up the barricading anger, the precious insulation of hate, and failed utterly. It was gone, all gone, washed away by the tremulous little voice and the way her fingers closed on his arm. By the way she had not corrected him when he had spoken Stephen's name—the source of nightmares, the memory that made her awaken screaming. The man she fled from, to the other side of the earth.

Gryf took a shuddering breath. God, why hadn't he spared her that? How had he managed to fail so completely to protect her? Send her back to Eliot . . . he could not. Never. But the alternative was torture: to see her, to hear her, to know that she belonged to a man of Eliot's stamp and Gryf had no right to touch her.

With a vast and terrible effort, he forced his hands to relax. His fingers slid slowly down the varnished door. He checked to make sure it was latched, and padded up the ladder.

Chapter 11

𝒯he island was at first no more than a cluster of clouds rising out of the sea, a deeper blue on the azure horizon. As the ship neared, the shadow below the clouds took on substance: olive and moss, hills and valleys, a tangible reality beneath the drifting bank of white. They were finally approaching Tahiti. Gryf stood at the helm and blessed the sight with heartfelt fervor.

Tess was on the quarterdeck, leaning over the rail beside Sydney as the ship rounded Point Venus and stood in toward the entrance to the harbor at Papeete. The day was fair, a crystal hue, and the light wind carried snatches of her voice to Gryf as she pointed excitedly to familiar landmarks. She had abandoned petticoats after they had entered the warm Pacific; her skirt billowed and swung in the breeze, now plastered against her, outlining the curve of her hips, now floating away in a tantalizing puff that threatened to reveal much more. She was barefoot, and his heated imagination made him certain that along with the petticoats she had discarded every other undergarment, leaving nothing on but the thin blue poplin skirt and light cotton blouse.

The idea made his hands sweat. He took a firmer grip

on the helm, tried to take one on himself, too, before he ran aground with fourteen miles of sea room between Tahiti and Moorea. For five months he had been like this, having lost his illusions and become, as Grady had once predicted, a rutting goat: lusting after another man's wife until he had given up all hope of ever feeling stable or sane again. He moved in a kind of mad suspension, dreaming every moment of taking her, of feeling that soft warmth beneath him, of her mouth, her hair . . . while his body went through the rote motions of work and command. Years of practice made functioning possible, though he was certain that every man of his old crew knew that the captain was half out of his mind. It was in the way they looked at him, and the way they carefully did not look at Tess.

If he could just get away from her, he had thought—but no, one hundred sixty feet of waterline might as well have been a ten by ten prison cell, for all he could try to avoid her. And then, after that night in her cabin at the equator, she had begun to seek him out, feeling safe to do so, he supposed, because he had promised not to send her back.

There was no sign of mistreatment about her. She seemed the same on the surface: a little quieter, a little older than the shy, saucy beauty she had been. If anything, in his eyes she had grown more lovely, because in that bleak time after Grady's death Gryf had managed to convince himself that her face and figure had faults, that she was not special or unique, and in seeing her again all those hopeful disparagements had been shamed into pale extinction by reality.

But it haunted him, what Eliot might have done. She showed no sign, but she suffered nightmares, and Gryf's hunger for her was tangled with misery and guilt and another, stronger emotion whose nature frightened him.

It went deeper than desire, right to the center of his being. He knew he could not survive another loss like the ones that had come before. So he covered that feeling, crushed it down, buried it in hot, animal frustration, which was an agony he thought that he might live through, if he did not have to live through it too long.

Several of the islanders' canoes had put out through the break in the reef, their single sails fluttering a gay welcome as they made for the *Arcanum*. Amid much cheerful hallooing a pilot came on board for the short trip through the pass, and Gryf was not really surprised when Tess took up an enthusiastic exchange of greetings with the dusky Tahitians still in the canoes. As far as he could tell, she conversed with them in the island tongue, and whatever she had to say caused a high level of excitement. The man who had come on board, a huge, herculean sort with the countenance of a pleased puppy dog, gave her a bear hug before he made his way to Gryf and took the helm with a friendly grin.

Gryf had enough pride in his ship to forget Tess for the moment and concentrate on getting the *Arcanum* through the reef and to anchor smartly. The pilot spoke a little English, at least to the extent of nautical terminology, and like all the Kanaka sailors Gryf had ever encountered, knew his way around a ship. He and Gryf fell into easy rapport, and under the islander's direction the clipper rolled through the channel and into the quieter waters of the bay. The crew were all at work, readying the chain, hauling in the topsails; at Gryf's order, letting go the anchor. As soon as she was well at rest, Mahzu sent all hands aloft to furl the topsails. Gryf went forward to watch the operation with a critical eye. The *Arcanum* was not the only vessel in Papeete's harbor, and Gryf wanted the furl of her sails to equal or better those of her numerous rivals. That much he owed his ship, that she was as neat and seamanlike as any other, even if her paint was not as fresh.

It was the Tahitian pilot's shout that made Gryf look aft. Tess and Mr. Sydney had left the rail and were strolling toward the companionway, Tess chattering animatedly. She stopped and turned at the sharp cry, as Gryf had, and a split second after, a deafening, metallic clang reverberated across the deck. Both Tess and Sydney jumped reflexively and looked around, but Gryf did not wait for them to discover what he had already seen. He was running aft, up onto the quarterdeck, half-blind with rage. "*Stark!*" he bellowed, his voice almost cracking under the force of his emotion. "Lay below, you bloody son of a bitch!"

Stark came down from the mizzen top like a landlubber, using the ratlines as a ladder instead of sliding down a stay. He was talking, fast, a running denial that cut off short as he hit the deck and Gryf seized him by the collar. It was all Gryf could do in his fury to keep himself from strangling the man; instead, he dragged Stark to the spot where Tess had been about to step; the spot where the wickedly sharp point of a marlinespike dropped from sixty feet above was buried three inches deep in the decking.

"Do you see that?" Gryf snarled. "Do you see that, you murdering bastard?" Stark stammered into blaming his shipmate on the yard, and Gryf backhanded him hard, sending him stumbling against the companionway hatch. "Do you think I'm a fool? Don't you give me your damn excuses—" Stark came upright and raised a hand, as if to strike back, and Gryf hit him again, a blow to the jaw that took Stark down for good. It was an effort for Gryf to stop at that.

He stood back, breathing hard, and tensed when Stark lurched to his feet again. But the man only wiped the blood from his swelling lip and muttered, glancing around at the crew that had gathered in a threatening circle, "It was an accident."

"Bring up your chest, Stark," Gryf snapped. "And clear off. I've had the use of your questionable services long enough."

From the deck a few feet away, Tess concealed her relief at the order. The incident had happened so quickly that she hardly thought of her own safety, but the way Gryf had exploded into violence left her more shaken than the sight of the spike buried point-down in the deck. Never had she seen him like that—the unexpectedness of it was frightening, and yet underneath her shock was another response, one that she was ashamed to admit even to herself. It was gratification: simple, selfish satisfaction to see him so affected by her peril, and to see the steward, whose very presence inexplicably made her skin creep, turned off without ceremony.

She did not speak of it, for Gryf's face was hard and closed when he glanced at her as the crew broke up. Knowing it was traditional among sailors for the victim to make light of any close brush with disaster, she simply took Mr. Sydney's arm and continued on her way below, where she busied herself with last-minute preparations to disembark.

For weeks, Gryf had cherished the idea of losing himself in the waterfront grogshops of Papeete. He wanted release: he wanted noise and liquor and dance-hall women, and he wouldn't have turned down a serious brawl. What he got instead was a formal dinner, followed by a fancy-dress ball.

He stood in the midst of the crowd, a resurrection of Mr. Everett: waistcoated, white-tied, and desperate. He had tried to decline the invitation, but the notorious hospitality of the island routed his best efforts. It would have required a will of iron—or a broken leg—to defeat the combined pleas of Tess and her friend Mahina Fraser. He wished now he had arranged for just such a disabling accident. Anything would have been less painful than the prolonged purgatory of this occasion.

The party bore little resemblance to any London affair. Its setting was Montcalm, a spacious Jamaican-style mansion at the head of the Atimaono Valley, a fitting residence for one William Stewart, the latest darling of French-Tahitian society. The locals seemed under the impression that Stewart was high ton; Gryf knew better, though he saw no need to say so. Having been introduced, he and Stewart duly pretended they had never laid eyes on one another before, although Gryf remembered the handsome, black-bearded adventurer well enough from a year spent in his pay running contraband spirits out of Australia. How Stewart had managed to transform himself from small-time smuggler into wealthy owner of Terre Eugenie, the newest and largest plantation in Tahiti, was a mystery Gryf felt no inclination at all to solve. Knowing Stewart, he thought it might not stand up to close scrutiny under the law.

Stewart's ball was a colorful amalgam of Tahitian gaiety and French pomp, with a dash of British hauteur and American energy to spice the mix. Not to be outdone by the European wives in their shoulderless gowns and crinolines, the Tahitian ladies added fresh flowers to the continental fashions: flowers in crowns on their coiled black hair, flowers behind their ears, flowers draped around their slim necks to set off amber skin. Tess, too, wore a tiara of pearl-white tuberose, and a hibiscus behind one ear. Her hair, as dark as any Tahitian's, seemed as rich as ebony set against her creamy skin and the poppy-red gown which dipped to a deep V from her bared shoulders, revealing pale cleavage between crimson bands of gathered net. It was the dress of a full-grown woman, no debutante. It reminded him—it fairly shouted at him—that she was married, and so entitled to be insanely provocative.

As her escort, he was obliged to dance with her. He barely made it through the ordeal. The fragrance of tuberose was like strong wine; it blurred his senses, obscured his balance, led him on to reckless flights of imagination—that she was his, that he could kiss the inviting curve of her lips, the tender nape of her neck; that he could slip his hands beneath the red flower and the scarlet gown and bring her hair cascading down over her naked breasts. The music stopped, and for a moment he could not even speak. She smiled up at him, all innocence and pleasure, so that he had to look intently at the fat wife of a French official before he could make his tongue form the simple thanks that was required.

He led her off the dance floor, and left her with her friend, young Mrs. Fraser. The two of them fell immediately into a giggling conversation in Tahitian. Mrs. Fraser spared him a sly, doe-eyed glance, and introduced him to another young native socialite, who proceeded, in a gentle, determined fashion, to bully him out onto the veranda and make overtures which he could not have bettered on the waterfront.

She was very pretty, this Mamua, modestly dressed in what appeared to be a long-sleeved pink nightgown. He did not think she was above sixteen. She spoke French and told him ribald jokes, the punchlines delivered with such a smiling ingenuity that he could not help but laugh. But he did not want her, a discovery which unnerved him. He danced with her and ate with her; he even kissed her, when she made it clear that he had no other choice. He thought perhaps he really had lost control of his reason. Five months at sea—five months of constant frustration, and then landfall in this most legendary of romantic isles . . . and he did not want what he was so graciously and blatantly offered.

He told himself it was her age. He told himself it was her innocence. He told himself it was her lack of it. When he had exhausted all possible excuses, he told himself he was indeed crazy, and had been since he had first seen a pair of amused blue-green eyes beneath a dripping sou'wester.

The owner of those eyes appeared to be enjoying herself immensely at the moment. Tess was more animated than he had ever seen her at a ball. Her face was flushed and sparkling; she danced nearly every dance, and she smiled dazzlingly at the British naval captain who guided her most often onto the floor. She took no notice of Gryf after that initial dance, though he could not keep his eyes from the flash of her scarlet grown as she sailed about the dance floor.

Mamua caught him watching, and gave him a reassuring pat. "Come with me," she said. "You make yourself ill over her."

On this observation, delivered with the utmost authority by a Tahitian schoolgirl, Gryf decided it was high time he did leave. Tess and Mr. Sydney were to be guests of the Frasers for the length of their stay in Tahiti, so Gryf had no obligation to escort her home. He doubted she would even notice he was gone.

He let Mamua lead him out the front door, exchanging a nod of mutual neutrality with William Stewart. Stewart had Madame de la Roncière, the *commissaire's wife*, firmly on his arm. It was clearly not the time for friendly reminiscence.

Gryf turned his mind to Mamua. He was determined

to discover some polite way to coax this precocious *vahine* back into the nursery where she belonged. After that, he planned to find the nearest cliff, and cast himself off to the sharks.

Over the epauletted shoulder of Captain Bush, Tess had a hard time keeping track of Gryf, but she noticed when that nubile little cousin of Mahina's coaxed him out onto the shadowy privacy of the veranda. Tess also saw them dancing; and watched the Tahitian girl with him at the refreshment table, offering him bits of pineapple and cake from her graceful brown fingers. When they began to drift toward the door, Tess's determined vitality faltered in spite of her best efforts.

She had some vague hope that she was mistaken in their intention, but when they stopped to take leave of the host, that cheerful illusion vanished. On the strength of all she had learned in London, Tess managed to hide her wretchedness long enough to finish the dance, and then she went straight to Mahina and said she was exhausted.

Mahina gave Tess a searching look, and then left to gather Mr. Fraser and call for the carriage. Tess had been overjoyed to see her friend again, but it was strange to find that the girl who had been so wild and carefree almost a decade before was now the wife of an English merchant and the mother of three. She looked hardly any older, her figure unmarred and her face still smooth. She still laughed just as much, showing white teeth against sun-darkened skin, and her dark eyes still danced with mirth. In all, it was a change in name only, as far as Tess could see. Mr. Fraser, an older, bearded man, hardly seemed to pay her any mind beyond an indulgent smile and a shake of his head as she tried to detach him from his group of business associates.

So Tess and Mahina went home by themselves. As soon as Hina had clucked to the horse and started them on their way, she turned, and said, "You and this captain—did you fight?"

Tess looked at her friend in surprise. "Do you mean Captain Bush? Of course not."

Hina made a face, just like when they had been children together. "Captain Bush," she said scornfully. "He's nothing. I don't know why you danced with him so much. You let Mamua steal the other without even trying."

Tess felt herself blushing in the cool night air. "I don't know what you mean."

"Hah. You haven't changed. Remember when you fell in love with Tavi, and Ana Dodd took him away from under your nose? They got married, after you and your father left, and now Ana is the mistress of one of the Queen's guards. Tavi divorced her. He says sleeping with her was like sleeping with a fighting cock—just feathers and claws and crowing."

This little discourse brought back vividly all the miseries of Tess's first serious venture into romance, at the age of fourteen. She had lost out to the more wanton Ana, because puppy love in Tahiti was a bit more than just stolen kisses behind the barn, and her father had managed to arrange an expedition to another island before Tess could receive clear instructions on just what was required to lure the swaggering young Tavi into her camp.

"Your captain," Hina went on wisely, "he's just what Mamua wants. She thinks he is *purotu roa*. She'll start feeding him papayas and rubbing his back, and pretty soon you won't even have a way to get off this island, because he'll desert his ship and stay."

The idea that Hina's cousin thought Gryf "very handsome" was not comforting to Tess, nor was the picture of his idyllic future in Mamua's generous arms. She dropped her pretense of unconcern and said in a small voice, "But what can I do? He hates me."

Hina turned an unbelieving glance in Tess's direction. "Hates you! All he did was stare at you!"

"Did he?"

"What makes you think he hates you?"

"Well—" Tess searched for an explanation. "He owes me money, in a way. It makes him angry. And there are . . . some other things."

Hina shook her head. "Money. Does he drink?"

"No. Not really."

"Does he keep some other woman?"

"I-I don't think so."

"Then what did he need your money for?"

"To repair his ship."

"Oh." Hina sounded puzzled. "Why don't you just tell him to keep the money?"

"It wouldn't help. It's like—oh, as if I had given him a gift. And he doesn't have anything as good to give back."

"I see." The principle of reciprocal generosity was something the Tahitian girl understood clearly. "He was very foolish, then, to ask for more than he could return."

"He didn't ask for it," Tess admitted slowly. "I tricked him into taking it."

"Tete!" Hina used Tess's Tahitian name in a scandalized voice. "That was very bad! No wonder he's angry. And you said there was more besides? What else?"

Tess bit her lip. "I said that I would marry him, and then I—changed my mind."

Hina clucked disapprovingly. "And now you've changed it back again? You have; I could tell as soon as

I saw you with him. And yet you treat him as if he were some lowborn. Your captain has a proper pride in his lineage, and that's why he's angry with you."

The fact that Hina spoke from the strictures of Polynesian rather than European culture did not make her any less correct in her assessment. Tess bowed her head. "I suppose so. But it's too late now to change it."

Hina shook her head sadly, as if in agreement, and then suddenly broke into a laugh. "No—I don't think it is! He may be angry, and I don't really blame him, but he still wants you. He looked at you all the time, like a hungry dog. Poor man, that's probably why he went off with Mamua, to prove you haven't gotten the better of him!"

"Do you think so?" Tess brightened a little, but not much.

"It could be. And you don't want Mamua to steal him, do you? Like Ana stole Tavi? No, you don't want to make that mistake again. You have to give this captain back his *mana*. If you're going to beat Mamua, you'll have to think like a Tahitian instead of an old missionary."

"Well," Tess said doubtfully, "how?"

"Oh, don't worry. You have a Tahitian on your side. I'm already thinking of a plan!"

It was a week after the *Arcanum*'s arrival in Tahiti when Hina presented her plan to Tess. Though the scheme was based on Hina's eminently Polynesian interpretation of the order of things, it seemed to Tess to make considerable sense. The plan was twofold: first, to restore Gryf's *mana*, which she understood to be a sort of mystical combination of pride, power, and influence, and secondly, to enable him to repay her "gift" with something of equal value.

Step number one would require a clear-cut declaration on Tess's part that she respected and loved him. Tess had protested at first that she had already told him so, in her letter, but Hina discounted his rejection as only the first in a series, the length of which would be determined by Gryf's own assessment of just how much he had to forgive.

The second step caused Hina a bit more difficulty. Her eyes widened when Tess told her the magnitude of the money paid to repair the *Arcanum* and retire Gryf's other debts. Tess saw herself fall a little further in the island girl's estimation for placing such an impossible burden on Gryf's personal prestige. But like a true friend, Hina rallied. After considerable thought, she decided on the only possible nonmonetary gift of equivalent value.

Gryf would have to save Tess's life.

Tess faltered a little at this announcement. She was prepared to go a long way, but she wasn't sure she was prepared to stake her life on Gryf's inclination to save it, especially since she was fairly certain that he would not see the connection between the rescue and the money he supposedly owed her. On the other hand, she well-remembered his reaction to Stark's dropping the marlinespike. Hina recognized the little smile of pleasure that crept onto Tess's face as she recalled the incident.

"You think it will be enough!" Hina exclaimed cheerfully. They were sitting in the shade of a cluster of coconut palms on a Sunday afternoon, watching her children play in the lagoon. "So do I. Now—we only have to arrange the thing."

"Yes! Without getting me killed, thank you! Just how do you propose to manage that?"

"We'll have to trick him, of course," Hina said. "I was thinking, maybe you could be stranded on Miti Popoa'a, and he could find you."

Miti Popoa'a was the tiny atoll some twenty miles south of Tahiti where Tess and Mahina had spent many happy adolescent days. "How is that saving my life?" Tess demanded. "It's a perfectly safe place."

"We know that. Does your captain know that? Suppose you had no food."

"I'd catch fish."

"Suppose you ran out of water."

"I'd break coconuts."

Hina giggled. "You're awfully hard to kill. Suppose there was a big storm."

"I'd wish I were somewhere else, but I could live through it. Besides, why would I go to Miti Popoa'a, and how would he know to come and save me?"

Hina was silent for a moment, deep in thought. Then she said, "We need to get rid of Mr. Sydney. You say to him, walk across the center of the island—"

"Hina! Not by himself. It took Papa and me a week."

"I'll find someone to go with him. He'll be happy; you know he will—all those plants up there in the mountains. Anyway, then you pack up some things and I take you to Miti Popoa'a and leave you there. Then I come back and go to your captain and tell him you're lost. It would be best, I think, if we waited until after a storm. I'll let him look around for a little while, and then I'll remember that you said something about going to Popoa'a to do some collecting. He'll do the rest."

"What if he doesn't?"

"Well, you'll just have to drink coconut milk for a few days! But he'll go. I'm sure of it."

"I don't know—"

"Tete!" Hina said severely. "Don't forget Mamua!"

Tess squinted out at the bright water of Papeete's harbor, where the *Arcanum* rested quietly at anchor. Each morning, Tess had looked anxiously to see that the ship was still there. There was activity on her decks, as there had been every day, but it was apparently no more than a good cleanup and new coat of paint. Tess wondered if Gryf was aboard, or ashore having his back massaged by Mamua. The image was enough. Tess turned to Hina and said, "All right. I suppose it can't hurt to try."

The proper moment to put Hina's plan into execution came much sooner than Tess expected. For two weeks, she saw little of Gryf, for her time was spent with Mr. Sydney making methodical collections of flowering beach plants. Although it was the season for heavy rains, the weather had been pleasant and drier than usual. She was awakened early one morning at the Frasers' house by the sound of a rising breeze, and went immediately to her bedroom window, as she always did, to look down the hill past the roofs and neat coral-dust streets of the town out over Papeete's harbor.

It was just past dawn. She had to search a moment to pick the *Arcanum* out of the blue-gray background, and caught her breath as she saw the clipper's tall masts, their rake unmistakable among more mundane craft, moving in a slow, stately progression past the other anchored ships. Fear leaped in her. He was leaving! She turned away from the window to grab her peignoir, with a half-formed idea of racing down to the waterfront to stop him, when a stronger gust of wind blew in the open window, raising the curtains and knocking over a little vase.

She paused, realizing that the wind was not the steady northeast trade, but out of the west. She ran to the window again, and saw what the early morning dullness had obscured: the sky was overcast, and the ragged leaves of palm trees fluttered and rotated in odd directions. Tess was enough of a sailor to recognize those signals. A storm was coming, and from a direction which left the northwest-facing harbor at Papeete largely unprotected.

Now that she took the time to look, other ships showed obvious signs of preparations to get under way. The *Arcanum* was halfway to the reef entrance, under tow by hardworking figures in the quarter boat, one of the first of several vessels that were struggling against the brisk wind toward the safety of the open sea. Tess watched as the clipper approached the break in the reef, where the growing storm swell began to overpower the efforts of the men at the oars.

Just when it seemed to Tess that the *Arcanum* was about to run upon the reef and be broken to bits, the headsails and topsails broke free. She came smartly about onto the port tack, ninety degrees from her former heading, and lay on enough sail to carry her to freedom, clearing the northern point of the reef with room to spare.

From her vantage point, Tess clapped her hands in solitary appreciation of that neat piece of seamanship. Then she turned and dressed hurriedly, and skipped downstairs to find Hina.

Chapter 12

*T*he *Arcanum* returned to Papeete's harbor five days after she had been chased out by the storm. She could have come back much sooner; the weather had not lasted more than two days, but Gryf had spent the last three sailing aimlessly among the Leeward Islands, telling himself all the reasons why he shouldn't go back and asking himself why the hell he still wanted to. The decision was finally made when the lookout raised Tahiti on the horizon, and Gryf pretended not to wake up from a nap in the shade of the foreword deckhouse. When he finally opened his eyes, they were close enough to the island to make it seem ridiculous to turn back out to sea.

They were barely at anchor before a high-pitched hail reached him, and he turned to find Tess's friend Mahina Fraser climbing aboard from an outrigger canoe.

"*Capitaine,*" she greeted him in breathless French. "You've been so long coming back, I was despairing of you!"

He looked beyond her, expecting Tess, but the island girl was alone.

"You must come," she went on, not giving him time to answer. "You must help me. Tete has disappeared!"

He frowned at her. "Tete—"

"Oh, yes—Lady Tess," she said impatiently. "We call her Tete. Captain, she is gone! She didn't come back after the storm."

It took him a full second to comprehend what Mahina was saying, and then cold fear flooded his veins. "Have you looked?" he asked, and realized the stupidity of the question as soon as he said it. "I mean— where would she have gone?"

"Anywhere," Mahina cried, with an expansive wave of her hand. "The beach, the mountains— She sent Mr. Sydney across the top, and he hasn't come back either, but he had two guides with him. Tete went off on her own. Oh, Captain, you must help me find her. I tried to go to the police, but they're French—no good at all to search the island."

He pictured Tess, alone and hurt in some remote valley, or worse . . . His mind balked, not willing to follow that thought. He swallowed the panic that rose in his throat, fought it down, trying to think. "Where was she supposed to go?" he demanded. "Has anyone seen her at all?"

Seventy-two hours later, he was still asking the same question, and still receiving the same answer: silence, and an eloquent shrug. As Mahina had predicted, the local authorities were unconcerned—they wanted to attribute the disappearance to a lovers' quarrel, and asked Gryf several times if he had beaten his wife so that she had run away. On learning that Tess wasn't his wife, they lost interest entirely, and told him to find another mistress, that there would be any number of willing parties on the island. He gave up on the police. He and Mahina organized their own search, with his pitifully small pool of manpower, and spread out over the island.

After three fruitless days and nights, he was sitting on the rough stump of an old palm in some village whose name he could not pronounce. Across from him, the white spire of a church glistened amid the lush greenery, and a pig rustled and snorted softly in the underbrush. Mahina was nearby, carrying on a lengthy conversation with an old man mending fish nets. Gryf understood not a word of it, but he knew it would be futile, as they all had been. One by one, his crew had come back, reporting nothing. No sign, no glimpse, no single lead. For eight days Tess had been lost.

Eight days.

His imagination had supplied abundant possibilities of what might have happened. Everywhere he looked in this gentle paradise he saw dangers. There were cliffs to fall from, surf to drown in, places so remote and unfrequented that a twisted ankle could mean slow starvation. There were sharks, and deserters from ships, men who recognized no law or decency; mutineers, slavers, murderers . . .

He stood up suddenly, and walked across the small clearing, up the steps and into the church. The interior was cool and sweet-smelling, last Sunday's flowers still fragrant on the altar. He sat down, gazing aimlessly at the white-washed coral walls and dark wood. It was silent in the church, except for the sound of the gentle wind and a faint echo of Mahina's clear voice outside. After a minute, he slid off the bench onto his knees on the rude plank floor. He buried his face in his arms and did something he had not done in fifteen years. He began to pray.

It wasn't an orthodox prayer. It wasn't even addressed to God, except as a kind of despairing hope that there was someone who might listen, who might answer, who would take in trade his feeble promises and give him back her life. I'll do anything, he prayed. Only let her be alive. Let her not be dead or hurt or afraid.

For a long time he prayed. Everything faded before the intensity of his plea. He did not know Mahina had come into the church until she touched his shoulder.

"Rifone," she said softly, her tongue slurring his name into islander's syllables. "Do not worry. You will find her."

He looked up, and got off his knees self-consciously. She smiled at him as he rose, a peculiar little smile, and said, "I think Tete is very lucky that you care so much."

He ignored that, not knowing how to answer. "Did you learn anything?"

"Yes." Her brown eyes remained steadily on his.

"What?" he demanded, when she did not go on. He could not tell from her expression if the news were good or bad. Good, he told himself. It had to be good. But there was something very strange about the way she looked at him.

"The old man—he loaned her a canoe a week ago. He said she hasn't brought it back."

"A week—" Gryf's hand tightened on the back of the pew. "After the storm?"

She hesitated, and then said, in a stifled voice, "No. Before."

He felt the blood drain out of his face. "Does he know where she went?"

Mahina frowned at the floor, and he felt her reluctance to speak like a knife in his belly. "Please—" he said unsteadily. "Just tell me."

She sighed, and flung her dark hair back, facing him with a level stare. "He says she was going to Miti Popoa'a. It's an atoll, to the south. It isn't far—maybe twenty miles."

"Someone went with her, then."

"No."

"No! You're telling me she went off on a twenty-mile voyage in an outrigger canoe by herself just before a storm? I can't believe she could even sail one of those things across the harbor, much less twenty miles on the open ocean."

"Why not?" Mahina sounded almost defensive. "I do. And maybe she didn't realize a storm was coming."

"Didn't realize— Good God," he snapped, driven to anger by his dismay. "She may be foolish, but she isn't that stupid. Are you sure this old man was telling the truth?"

"Of course!" she cried. "Why would he make that up? What you don't know, Rifone, is that Miti Popoa'a is a—a cursed place! If she wanted to go there, she'd have to go alone. No one would take her. She might be there right now, stranded, with no food or water!"

"But why the devil would she go somewhere like that?"

"Oh, she said often that she wanted to collect there. In fact—yes, I remember now! She said she wanted a special flower that her father told her was there. It only blooms after the rains. Yes, yes, that would explain why she went before the storm! I'm sure that's where she is, Rifone. I'm certain of it!"

There was something forced about Mahina's enthusiasm. Gryf thought perhaps she was trying to raise his spirits by overstating the case; it was something the kindhearted island girl would do.

"You must go and get her," Mahina said, taking his arm and urging him outside and down the steps. "The old man said she took water and food, but just enough for a few days. She's stranded—otherwise, she surely would have come back by now."

"If she ever made it in the first place," Gryf said dully.

With each added detail of information, it became harder to deny the possibility that she had gone. His mind chased after horrors again: sharks, the storm surge . . . Lord, it must have been running twenty feet or more at the height. He said, "It'll be tomorrow before we can get there, by the time I find the crew and get back to the ship."

"Oh, no," Mahina exclaimed. "You can't go in your ship. There's no anchorage, and you'd never get your boat in. They say it's hard even for a canoe to get through the reef. I said no one would go there, but it isn't quite true. The old man—his grandfather was the priest who had the temple there—I think, if we offered him enough, he would take you."

Gryf glaced at the leathery Tahitian, who sat calmly mending his nets in the shade with a cockeyed garland of flowers and leaves around his forehead. "No doubt," Gryf said dryly. "How much is enough?"

"Five francs."

"I guess you've already discussed it with him?"

"Oh, yes. I knew you would want to go."

He hesitated. He didn't want to; not really. He didn't want to arrive at this atoll and find that Tess wasn't there, because then the weight of dread that hung over him, that he had fought off for three days, would descend. He would be out of places to look. But he was out of places anyway. He turned to Mahina. "Tell him he's got his five francs. Tell him I want to go now."

Miti Popoa'a was a familiar place to Tess. The white sand and shady groves of coconut within the calm, clear waters of the lagoon had been a special hideout for her and Mahina as adolescents. The lagoon was large, but the island itself was so tiny that few Tahitians bothered with it, preferring instead the bigger groups of atolls to the north for recreational grounds.

Tess had set up camp in the central part of the island, where abundant shrubs provided some protection from the constant breeze. After the storm, rain showers had been frequent, and she had added a layer of palm fronds to the little canvas tent, which kept the interior completely dry. She caught rainwater in a tin tub, and had enough dried fish, bananas, and breadfruit to last a good while. At first, she ate well, having nothing to do but wait and cook for herself and wander along the sparkling beach. After a week, she was looking at the whole situation differently. She began to ration her fish and, using the net and hooks she had brought, to wade in the lagoon looking for more. The skills she had learned so many years before were slow to return. She caught an eel, after considerable effort, and later a few small schooling fish in the net.

The activity, at least, kept her mind off the fact that no one was coming to find her. Or it did until midafternoon, when she had worn herself out wading in the lagoon with her skirt hiked up to her waist, and the sun drove her into the shade of the coconut grove. She had long since decided that this escapade was among the stupidest she had ever tried, and only hoped that Hina would come back for her before she really was reduced to coconut milk and minnows, for it was clear that Gryf wasn't coming.

She dried her feet and put her stockings and boots back on, then spent an hour cleaning and cutting up the eel into a marinade of wine vinegar. Afterward, she sat gloomily in the shade near the edge of the beach, feeling like Robinson Crusoe and wondering if she would ever see civilization again. She tried to keep a lookout, but tired muscles, the steady murmur of the surf out on the reef, and the rustle of palms lulled her into sleep.

She wakened to a shout and scrambled to her feet,

looking wildly up and down the beach. Some fifty yards down the stretch of sand, she saw the fluttering sail of a single canoe. Two male figures, both naked from the waist up, splashed over the side and ran the outrigger onto the beach. One she did not recognize, but Gryf's blaze of golden hair was unmistakable.

Tess froze. Instead of elation, she felt a surge of panic. Her first thought was to run back into the bushes and hide. But he had already seen her. He abandoned the canoe and the other man and ran toward her, up the beach, his bare feet slipping in the deep sand. She stood rooted to the spot, too petrified to appear relieved.

He came near her and stopped, breathing hard, looking at her as if she were some apparition come to life. Tess stared back helplessly. He said, "You goddamned little fool!" and pulled her roughly into his arms.

He held her so tightly that her ribs hurt. Tess leaned against him, returning the embrace in a confusion of joy and guilt. She had not thought— She had not really expected— Oh, it was awful, to have tricked him so, and yet . . . She pressed her cheek against his chest, too happy to castigate herself further.

He loosened his hold finally, not quite letting go of her, and said, "You're all right?"

Tess nodded shyly, unable to bring herself to raise her eyes above the level of his throat. She could see his pulse, beating steadily beneath the tanned skin. She had a strong urge to touch her tongue to the scattered grains of sand that clung there.

He half-turned, looking back down the beach toward the canoe, and exclaimed suddenly, "What the deuce— *Wait!*"

It was his shipboard bellow, and the volume made Tess jump backward. Beyond him she saw the outrigger, afloat again, turn under the guidance of the native's paddle and head back toward the fringing reef. The light craft was already almost beyond earshot, but at Gryf's shout the man waved and called something in Tahitian.

"That bastard," Gryf said in a voice of profound disbelief. "He's leaving!"

Tess cleared her throat. "He said he was coming back."

"Coming back—Where's he going?"

"Back to Tahiti, I think."

"What?"

"He said he would come back tomorrow," she answered quickly, turning away before her nervousness betrayed her. Now—now he'll get angry, she thought. And she was right.

"Tomorrow!" he cried, grabbing her arm before she could get away. "What the hell is wrong with today?"

"Um . . ." The story of superstitious curses that she and Hina had concocted seemed ridiculous now that Tess was faced with quoting it. "I don't know. Perhaps he misunderstood what you wanted."

"He couldn't have. I never said a word to that old witch doctor. Your friend Mahina did all the . . ." His voice trailed off. He looked at Tess: a sudden, probing stare. "How did you get here?"

She took a breath, and said, too fast, "In a canoe."

"Where is it?"

She pulled her arm away. "The storm. It—washed the canoe off the beach." She was not a good liar. Even to herself, it sounded weak.

He evidently thought so, too. He narrowed his eyes suspiciously. "Why didn't you pull it up high enough?"

"It was too heavy."

An excellent explanation, she thought. Unfortunately, it came out with no more authority than the earlier one.

He chewed his cheek, and looked at the horizon. After a long minute, he said in a careless tone, "I suppose the flowers were blooming, after the rain."

Tess frowned. "The flowers?"

"Did you collect many?" He looked at her intently. "I'd be interested to see them."

"I didn't collect any—" She stopped suddenly, aware of the tightening of his mouth, "—flowers," she finished lamely.

"You didn't."

Tess shifted uncomfortably beneath his scrutiny. "Well—" she said, in hasty explanation. "The conditions—haven't been very good. For collecting."

"I don't believe you," he said.

Tess swallowed.

"You set me up," he went on, in a dangerously level tone. "This is all some crazy scheme, isn't it? She knew you were here all along. She let me think—do you know what I thought?" His voice rose. "Do you have any idea what it's like, to spend three days—seventy-two hours—on your feet searching every square inch of one small island? Dear God, Tess, do you know what it's like to come to the end of that island and realize there's nowhere else to look?"

She did not raise her eyes. She couldn't. And in her silence she knew she condemned herself.

"Damn you!" he shouted. "What is this, some new way to squeeze me? Where's the percentage? Do you think there's more money in it?" His voice was shaking with rage. "Maybe Sydney's Grand Tour wasn't enough—Mahina Fraser thinks she ought to have a piece of my hide, too, right? Well, I've got news for you, Tess. There isn't any more. You've got it all. You've got my ship, you've got me so damned deep in debt I'll never get out, you've got me acting like a madman because I thought you'd been eaten alive by a pack of sharks—Jesus, you've got my *mind*; I sit there on that ship and I think about you; day and night, I think about—" He stopped. The look he gave her would have seared metal.

She bowed her head. It was a dressing-down that she deserved. She was sorry, sorry . . . and immeasurably glad. He thought about her. The idea was a heady antidote to remorse. After a moment, she asked in a small voice, "Are you hungry?"

"No," he said coldly.

"I caught an eel."

"An eel." If she had caught an old shoe, he could not have sounded more disgusted. "How the devil did you catch an eel?"

She looked up through her lashes. "It wasn't easy."

"I hate fish."

She managed not to smile. She said softly, "There's enough for two."

By the time Tess finished washing the tin dinner plates it was nearly dark. She fussed about the campsite, trying to control the nervous flutter of her fingers as she stored the cooking utensils. A splatter of large raindrops began to fall, hissing in the coals. Gryf cursed, and Tess hid a smile, thanking nature for falling in so well with her scheme. She gathered her kit and ducked inside the shelter, leaving him to make the inevitable decision by himself.

It was not until the rain was a downpour that he made it. The rustling of the carefully stocked palm fronds which covered her tent had become a roar before his streaming figure appeared at the open end of the hut. He knelt there, looking so sodden and out of temper in the wan light of her oil lamp that she wanted to laugh. Instead, she wordlessly handed him a towel. He rubbed vigorously at his hair and face, ran the towel across his bare chest, and looked down with disgust at the puddle of water that formed beneath his dripping trousers.

It was impossible to speak over the noise of the rain. Tess indicated the area she had cleared and padded with a blanket and a length of worn-out canvas cloth. With the gear she had stacked about, the shelter was just large enough for two people to lie down full length. He moved onto the canvas and sat, not looking at her.

When he was settled in the center of another accumulating pool, Tess began to put The Plan into effect. She sat back on her own blankets and turned the lamp down to a mere flicker. In the half-light, she leaned to unbutton her sturdy boots and slowly pulled them off, setting them aside. Her white-stockinged toes peeked from beneath the heavy skirt; she contemplated them a moment, and then summoned all her courage. Her heart beat faster at her own daring as she inched the skirt upward, all the way to the garter just below her knee. She slid the stocking from her leg, careful to leave a generous length of ivory-smooth skin exposed to the lamplight.

From his puddle, Gryf was close enough to touch the slender, bare calf she revealed. His fist clenched on a fold of wet cloth. With baleful fascination, he watched as she removed the other stocking and stretched her graceful legs before she curled them beneath her. The folds of her skirt fell randomly, leaving two pale, soft feet free to his gaze. He realized he was holding his breath.

Gryf didn't buy the innocent shyness in her lowered face for a minute. She was out to torture him. As she loosened pins and shook her dark hair into a shimmering fall, he made himself close his eyes. When he opened them again, he looked deliberately away at the canvas that lined the interior of the hut, but even there she haunted him, for her shadow fell across the expanse. She was brushing her hair, and with every rhythmic move of her shadow arm, his mind's eye saw the sensual stroke as clearly as if he ran his fingers through the silken fall himself.

The beat of the rain lessened. Gryf continued to stare at her shadow, which was almost still after she had laid the brush aside. In silhouette, her head was bent. As suddenly as it had begun, the rain stopped, leaving only the quick, musical drip of water off the leaves.

His gaze slid inexorably back to the coy gleam of exposed skin beneath her skirt. Her toes curled and uncurled. At the movement—so small, so artless—he was seized by a violent desire, a fury; weeks and months of frustration crystallized into a single moment. He sat frozen, trembling, the need to touch her clamped like a vise onto his throat. He was afraid to move. Afraid to breathe. He heard her rustle among her toiletries. She sighed, a soft, preoccupied sound, like a child or a puppy settling down to sleep. With a sudden twist he turned away and flung himself down and prayed for self-control.

The quick movement startled Tess. She had seen him watching her, the telltale lowering of his eyelids, the way his jaw tightened. She should have been pleased: it was what she had intended. Instead, an apprehensive excitement welled up in her. She forgot what The Plan had called for next. Hina's careful instructions, so clear and simple seemed to have flown completely out of Tess's head. She was supposed to make him kiss her, and then . . . what?

"Gryf?" Her voice was tentative, softly husky from nervousness and distress. "Are you going to sleep?"

He grunted, and did not turn. She saw the long muscles in his back twitch. Though he lay still, tension lined the whole length of his body, as if he might spring up and leave at the slightest provocation.

"Please." Her fingertips grazed his shoulder. "Could we talk?"

"Go to the devil," he said hoarsely.

Tess wet her lips. It wasn't working right at all. Her best chance, and she was failing even before she began. Perhaps she wasn't bold enough—in his irritation at being stranded on the island, he might not even have noticed her overtures. Obviously, the situation required more forceful measures. She spread her fingers across his damp, smooth shoulder and ran her hand with a slow deliberation down his back.

He moved, startling her again, so that she leaned instinctively to restrain him from leaving. The gesture was unnecessary. He rolled onto his back and gripped the dark cascade of loosened hair that had fallen across his chest, glaring up at her. "What is it you want from me?"

Tess parted her lips, could think of nothing to say. She was awkward suddenly, embarrassed: did he really not know?

He curled his fist in her hair. Without thinking, Tess leaned away, resisting the confinement and the prickling pain. His eyes narrowed. He released his grip with a suddenness that made her rock backward a little. "So talk."

She could not meet his eyes. "All I want—" Her throat closed. She felt foolish and helpless, and when he moved as if to turn away from her again, she reached for his hand and grasped it. In desperation, she blurted,

"I want you to love me. I— That's it. I wanted to tell you."

For a long moment, he was utterly still. Her heart seemed to fill her ears with its pounding, waiting for him to answer.

"Love you," he repeated, and there was a baffled note in his voice, as if he had never heard the words before.

Mortification stung her cheeks. Stupidity—how could she have been such a mooncalf as to tell him that way? She looked down miserably and compounded foolishness with folly by interlacing her fingers with his. "Please," she whispered. She brushed his callused palm with her thumb, felt him trembling.

The feathered touch sent a renewed rash of heat through Gryf, and along with it came the suspicion that had wavered momentarily with his astonishment. "I don't believe you," he said gruffly, praying to God that she would release him and go away. The thread of control was stretched impossibly taut; it seemed that he would die of it, ripped apart into a thousand tiny pieces by the strain. "What of Eliot?"

A shadow touched her face. Guilt, he thought, and hated Stephen Eliot with an all-consuming hate. She sat back, trying to withdraw her hand. Gryf closed his fingers over hers, so hard that she drew in a soft, hissing breath. She tore her hand away, began to speak in a choked voice. "Stephen and I—"

"No." A sudden, perverse panic overcame him at what she was about to say. He half-rose to take her by the shoulders. "I don't want to know." He pressed her down, buried his face in the midnight tumult of her hair. "Forget Stephen. Forget him." The words were harsh against the smooth skin of her throat. The feel of her, the supple strength, her body . . . he was lost. "I'll love you—Tess—ah God, yes, I'll make love to you if you want me."

He found her lips, kissed her, an assault that was long and fierce because he could not bear to end it. She was soft under him, the cotton of her blouse scratchy dry against his chest. He let his weight bear down, not believing, not sure if this was real, all his dreams, a thousand nights of wanting, holding her while his hands ran over her arms and up again to her breasts and face, defining her shape, her living contours. She moved— resistance or acquiescence; he was beyond caring. The rain began again, rising to a white roar like the blood that sang in his ears. It deafened him, the noise: the blood and the rain. It defied all caution. He needed her, wanted her, knew himself willing and glad to burn to smoking ash in possessing her.

Tess sank beneath him, bewildered and pliant, unable at first to comprehend the sudden change in circumstances. Her hands fluttered, and then found the hard muscles of his arms and fastened there of their own will. His kiss hurt her—it had hurt before, she remembered, but it was a welcome pain. She opened to it, to the pressure of him, the wonderful suffocating weight.

He dragged his mouth from hers, and Tess gulped air, nursing her bruised lower lip with her tongue. His warm breath touched her, grazed the soreness, then moved lower. She had no time to summon reason or resistance. His searching mouth found her nipple. The touch made her gasp; it was unexpected, frighteningly intimate . . . her simple scheme became suddenly warped, twisted, expanding into something new and completely out of her control. He suckled, wetting the rough cotton, tugging at her gently and then leaving the peak to kiss the soft underside of the swell created by his upward pressing hand.

Tess reached for him, encountering damp curls and heated skin, not knowing if she meant to make him stop or urge him on. His hands slid downward, caressing her hips through the heavy skirt, and back up, working the lower button on her blouse. She felt wicked and eager—too weak—oh sweet Heaven, she was weak. It was too hard to listen to the voice of warning in her head, too easy to submit as his fingers moved upward; his mouth nuzzled an ever-wider opening, and then his tongue seared her naked skin as he dragged the tails free of her skirt.

He sat back suddenly on his knees, and the touch of night air on her breasts made her stiffen. She would have pulled her gaping blouse together, but he reached to stop her, his fingers closing hard on her wrists. The sound of the rain filled the space around and between them, obliterating words. She relaxed her arms, and he let go, slowly, as if she could not be trusted. There was no smile on his face, no trace of love. The lamplight was failing: in the dim, rain-scented shelter he might have been a vision—her sullen angel, glittering dully against the shadows.

He took her hands and raised her as if she had no strength of her own. Indeed, she had none: it had vanished in the realization that they had passed far beyond mere flirtation and teasing. He touched her now as if he owned her. She let her head fall back as his fingers circled her waist beneath the opened blouse and moved upward. His thumbs curved under her breasts. He took their rounded weight in his palms and bent toward them, gliding his tongue over one pink, excited tip. Tess groaned, a vibration in her throat that was lost in the thunder of the rain. The blouse slid from her shoulders, falling in a heap around her hands.

It was like a dream, a pagan ritual, as he pleasured

her in slow motion and silence. She felt his hardness, his tension—the desire that was so compellingly clear in the bulging contours of his wet trousers. Her own passion was a spreading heat, a softening between her thighs. She pressed his head between her hands, drew him up, kissing him with the same fierce eagerness he had shown to her. She welcomed his exploring tongue, met it with her own, searching, enlacing, until suddenly he pushed her down with an animal growl.

He drew back, onto his side, peeled off the damp trousers with quick, rumbling movements. Tess watched him in wonder; he was all tan and gold, leonine, stretching full length against her, his manhood a taut pressure on her thigh. He kissed her breasts, freed her hands from the tangle of blouse, loosened her skirt, and came to his knees again to lift her and rid her of the imprisoning folds. His ministrations were immeasurably gentle; she felt very young, humble and yet wild, willing to trust and be guided. Happiness flooded her as he slid his hands over her body, claiming each uncovered curve. He knew. He understood at last. She was to be his, now and forever.

She turned to him as he lay again beside her, flung her arms around his neck and buried her face in his shoulder. Oh, it had been so long that she'd waited, so achingly long. She squeezed her eyes shut on the tears, not wanting him to see. His hands cupped her buttocks, pulled her to him, fusing their bodies together. When he shifted and rose above her, her legs spread easily. She arched upward, seeking the other half of herself, ready to yield him everything.

And then . . . oh, it hurt, but she bit her lip and closed her eyes, holding herself unflinching beneath the first hard thrust. He conquered the constriction, no gentleness anymore, no hesitation, and she was glad, for beyond the pain was something else, a part of the hurt and yet more: his filling her, the joining, a joy that deepened with each driving stroke. His breath was hoarse and loud against her ear, louder even than the rain. He hung a little way above her, supported on his elbows. Tess wanted to kiss him; she threw her head back, and touched her lips and tongue to his throat, the only part of him she could reach. At the contact, he gripped her shoulders convulsively. He moved against her with a shuddering thrust—harder, deeper than any before, his fingers digging cruelly into her skin. For a suspended moment his body trembled, straining . . . once, twice, and then the breath rushed out of him.

He buried his face in her neck. For a long time, Tess lay beneath him quietly, listening to the slow return of his heartbeat and breathing to normal. The lamplight was almost gone, and shadows leaned in around them. Her own heart pumped a glow of well-being into every limb, every finger and toe. She raised one hand and curled it through his hair, playing, smiling to herself as she felt him turn his head slightly to give her access to the warm, damp skin behind his ear. She was sore everywhere, with a wonderful, woman's ache. His weight pressed her down, but she wanted him there. He could stay resting on top of her for all time, if he would. But he wouldn't, of course. As if in answer to the thought, he shifted and slid to one side, taking her in his arms. She nestled naturally into his shoulder as he turned on his back. The rain made talk useless—just as well, for what more was there to say? She was his; she loved him. That was all there was to the world. That, and the rain, and his body pressed against hers in the close, wet darkness.

Chapter 13

*G*ryf dreamed about his family. Old dreams—good dreams, not the nightmares. He was warm again, and safe; his mother scolded him for inconsequences, and kissed his forehead in forgiving. His younger sister cried over a skinned knee in the dusty street, then smiled, a chubby, tearstained smile, and ran away giggling with the ragged wild flower he picked to comfort her. He dreamed of his father, of his own bed in the cool evening—and there was a question between them, some answer he needed, a test, a broken promise . . . his father's face was grave. Honor, he said. Never forget it. All else is nothing if honor is lost.

And the boy in the dream answered: I'll never forget, Papa. Never . . .

Gryf came awake with a soft start. All black around him, but the dream warmth was still there. Smooth skin curved against his chest and he felt the flowery tickle of loose hair beneath his nose. The rain had stopped; in the silence he could hear Tess's even breathing, feel the rise and fall of her breasts against his side. It seemed more miraculous than the dreams. He lifted his free arm and stroked her hair, without really meaning to wake her.

She sighed, and snuggled closer. A memory of Eliot, of what she was, drifted into conscious thought. Gryf banished it. Later. Later he would deal with that. For now . . . she was here, and already he was hard with wanting her again.

He turned, pulling her against him. She came willingly, with a soft, sleepy sound of pleasure. In the dark he could see nothing, but his hands and his body found sensation enough. He ran his palm down the curve of her slim waist and lovely swell of her hip. Her hair was like silk where it lay across his arm. His fingers drifted downward, tenderly searching the soft skin of her inner thigh, where her smoothness was marked with evidence of their lovemaking. Desire shafted through him at the discovery. The patches of drying moisture seemed a silent message, an assurance. She had wanted him, too. In the heat of his passion, he had not waited to know.

He raised himself on his elbow and leaned to find her lips. He kissed her gently, wanting to compensate for that earlier heedlessness. She was awake now; her hands came up to answer with a caress of their own. She traced the outline of his ear, a touch that made him groan and deepen the kiss, then draw away to run his tongue down the salty-sweet curve of her throat. In his temporary blindness, she seemed more beautiful to him than even touch and taste and sound and scent—all beautiful. He slid his leg between hers, moving half on top of her, his shaft pressed in delicious agony against the satin of her skin.

He wanted to prolong the torture this time. He began a slow exploration with his lips, lingering in the hollow between her breasts while his hands drifted upward. He murmured her name, and felt the faint shudder as she sighed in response. He found her breast with lips and hands, and drew the stiffened peak into his mouth with an eager tug. Her body tightened; her legs moved, twining with his. The smooth slide of her skin against his manhood nearly overcame him; he went suddenly still, struggling to master the urge to drive himself into her instantly.

She gave him no time to summon control. Her hands drifted down his back and spread over his taut buttocks. He pressed downward with a moan of guilty delight, unable to resist the coaxing message in her fingers. Slowly, without conscious volition, his hardness slipped into the warm, inviting recess. He trembled on the verge of thrusting, his breath ragged, his lips grazing the tip of her excited nipple. He bent, circling the swelling peak with his tongue.

Her legs parted then, on a sound of feral pleasure that came from deep in her throat. Gryf held back still, playing and sucking hungrily, reveling in the way she writhed beneath him. He shook with the anticipation, with the torment of her movements that just barely took him in and then retreated, driving him to a wild peak of frustrated lust. Her soft, panting moans increased, her hands kneaded him until he thought that he must burst from the strain of waiting. And then she bent her knees, and drew her legs up around him, pressing him downward.

His body reacted before thought: he plunged into her, burying himself. He felt her flinch and then arch beneath him, heard her low, plaintive cries: his name, and please, and oh . . . oh my— She clung to him, rose hard and awkwardly. A savage joy surged in him, to feel her anxious, unpracticed seeking. He could give her that, at least: the certain knowledge of what her questing body needed. He slid his arms beneath her, taking control of her movement and matching it to his. She responded with a whimper of excitement, meeting his rough kiss greedily, taking him in, straining upward to each thrust with a trembling violence. He prolonged them for her, hard and deep, and then he couldn't hold back any longer: she was urging him on with her hands and her rhythm and he couldn't wait; he had to move, had to answer, had to drive her on until his groan became a sharp cry and he crushed her to him—a momentary, mindless ecstasy—and he let the world blow apart around them.

It was over far sooner than he had wished, a total defeat of his plan to spin out the pleasure. But when he moved to release her from his weight, she held him back and made him stay, clinging as if she was afraid that he might disappear. He nuzzled at the tender skin below her ear, his own satisfaction heightened immeasurably by her voluptuous sigh of contentment. For a long time, he held himself above her, until the sound of her breathing became soft and regular, and his arms could no longer support him. He shifted, very slowly so as not to wake her, and eased himself onto his side.

She made a soft sound and fumbled for his hand, drawing it across her as she turned away and fitted herself into the protective curve of his body. The simple trust of the gesture made him want to squeeze her tightly against him; instead, he brushed his hand across the plump softness of her breast and kissed her shoulder. She sighed again, and pressed back against him for a brief moment before she relaxed.

Sleep took her, but Gryf could not find the same release. He stared into the darkness, feeling the short-lived happiness drain away. Even as he lay in full possession of the sweetest treasure of his life, reality crept in. Everything had changed, and yet nothing had. She was another man's wife.

Stephen Eliot's wife.

The dream came back to Gryf—his father's words about honor. Had that really happened? He could not remember, and the forgetting hurt him more than anything else: to know that it had been that long ago. His father's face was no more than an impression, a vague image of someone tall and quiet. But though his father's features might have faded, in Gryf's mind he was a fortress, a compass point that never varied.

Gryf closed his eyes. The ache that filled him was familiar, a longing that went beyond the physical frustration that had tormented him for months. He thought that he could not stand it again. All his life, all his losses: his family, Grady, Tess; over and over he had let himself love, let himself feel, and then the hurt came, the numbing agony that never healed, but only dulled into the limits of endurance.

He could not love her and bear that again. He would not. Even if she were free, he could not have risked it, would not have had the courage to lay himself open to that kind of pain one more time. And the passion, the desire—she was his in that way if he wanted, he knew that now, but his father stood behind him in the shadows. To take advantage of her flight from Stephen, from the mistake Gryf had not prevented her from making . . . He had no honor anymore, no right to claim it, but he would. In the name of what he had been once, he would find the strength to go away as he should have done long ago, for he could never be near her now and trust himself. He was not what his father had been, not made of that fine, unbending steel. But he could find his own honor. Tomorrow, he would go away.

He lay with his arms around her, gazing ahead in desperate melancholy, as the blackness faded before him.

The first pale gleam of light touched her skin, drawing a soft outline of her body and her hair.

It was dawn. Tomorrow had already come.

Tess blinked, waking to an unfamiliar coolness on her skin. She realized in one quick rush that she was naked, that it was morning, that she was alone. Memory came a moment later, and she sat up to look for Gryf.

The movement caused a twinge of pain, and she glanced down. Smears of darkened blood stained her legs and the blanket beneath her. She blushed, and then shook back her hair with a bubbling laugh. It was true, all true; it hadn't been a dream. He had lain with her and held her—the plan had worked, far better than she could ever have imagined. She belonged to him now, irrevocably.

Shyly, she peeked out of the hut. Gryf was not within view of the campsite. She tiptoed out and filled a basin with fresh rainwater, carried the bowl back and washed herself. She started to dress, but noticed the damp pile of discarded trousers still left in the corner where they had been cast the night before. Another blush heated her cheeks, for the wanton thought which came to her. She hesitated, and then tossed her blouse aside. They were alone—who would ever know?

Abandoning all sense of propriety with a happy giggle, she slipped out of the hut. How strange it felt, the touch of the light morning wind on her body—how delightful. She carefully trod the short path to the beach, where the glare of the sun on the white sand made her squint as she gazed out at the lagoon.

It took her several moments to spot him. He was far out, swimming strongly, in the deep water where the big breakers came rolling over the reef. As she watched, he disappeared beneath the foaming crest of a wave. She tensed instinctively, judging the danger—it was water she would never have dared herself. He reappeared momentarily and was gone. Long minutes passed, and she did not see him again.

Her knees felt weak; she sat down abruptly on the warm sand. Helpless anger filled her. Why had he done that—gone so far out? She bit her lip and tried to tell herself she was foolish. But as she buried her face against her knees she muttered a little prayer, and then called him several unkind names. She waited as long as she could stand before she pushed back the curtain of her hair to look for him again.

If not for the erratic twist of an albatross's flight that caught the corner of her eye, she would not have seen him. He had gone far to the leeward, into calmer water closer to the island. With a relieved cry, she sprang up and ran down the beach, splashing into water up to her thighs and then diving ahead. If he saw her, he gave no sign. Tess fell into the smooth swimming stroke that Hina had taught her so long ago. The water was warm and clear; it stung her sore flesh at first, but the touch was healing. She avoided the coral heads and paid no attention to the dull flash of fish that started away from her.

She caught up with him in a stretch of sandy bottom between the coral. He had stopped swimming, and stood, waist deep, watching her approach. Renewed shyness seized her; she slowed a little distance away and floated, keeping her bare shoulders below the water as she caught her breath. "You scared me," she said, and a little of her worry still colored her voice. "You could drown, out there on the reef."

"Fine." His tone was cold, the look he gave her even colder. "Good riddance."

She spread her arms, riding a swell up and down. The

pleasant assumptions of the morning withered rapidly
beneath his emotionless gaze. She glanced down, frowning at the swaying, crystalline expanse of the lagoon. "I
don't know why you'd say that."

"Why didn't you tell me?"

She looked up again. "Tell you what?"

"Christ." He swung his arm in a jerky move of disgust, sending a spray of water to one side.

"Tell you what?" she repeated, after a moment.

"That you were still a virgin, damn it!"

She bit her lip, tasting salt, taken aback by the vehe-
mence of the accusation. "I did tell you," she said timidly.

"You didn't," he snapped. "Good God, do you think I
would have—" He broke off. "What do you think I am?"

She did not answer that. She was trying to think back,
to remember the letter and how she had phrased it. Impossible, that he could have misinterpreted the meaning.
She said, "I wrote you. About Stephen, and . . . everything."

He simply looked at her, as if she were speaking some
strange and discordant foreign tongue.

"You didn't read it."

Still no answer. He stared with violent disapproval at
a point somewhere near her chin. It dawned on Tess
that if he hadn't read her letter, there were other things
he did not know. She floated helplessly, at a loss as to
how to tell him. As she hesitated, his glance slid downward to where the clear water lapped gently at the swell
of her breasts. Though the frown never left his face,
she saw a muscle tighten in his cheek as he looked
quickly away. The desire, and immediate denial of it,
were plain.

The threat of losing what she had so lately gained
gave her courage. She set her feet down on the yielding
sand and rose, no longer permitting herself to hide in

the questionable concealment of transparent water. "Before you make any judgments about—what happened last night," she said evenly, "I think you should know something."

He kept his eyes determinedly on the far reef, even though the early sun hid nothing of her glistening torso.

"I'm not married," she said.

He looked at her then, all right. As if she were some monstrous, mythical beast, just risen from the sea.

"The vows I took with Stephen were anulled. He never touched me—" She paused, bit her lip. "Not in that way."

Somehow, she had expected him to be glad. Relieved, at least. His stunned expression didn't surprise her, but the slowly dawning fury that replaced it she had not anticipated. In a voice low and trembling, he said, "No. You won't get at me like that. I'm not going to fall for another one of your bloody tricks."

"It's not a trick. It's true."

"Then why are you running away from Eliot, if your marriage was anulled?"

"I'm not running away from him," she said simply. "I wanted to find you."

He blinked, looked confused and angry. "What the hell for? To get your hands on a shabby clipper ship?"

She squinted at the horizon, blue on blue, and then looked back at his face. She hated the strain there, hated being the cause of it once again. "I love you."

That was all she knew to say. To explain everything.

"For God's sake—" he mumbled, and then fell silent, as if further words failed him.

"I know you're angry," she said quickly. "I know you have every right to be. Last night—I didn't plan for that to happen, but I'm glad it did. I'm so glad, because now—"

"Now I tag along with you like some pet lapdog? I'm sorry, Tess, but I'm not that besotted with your charms. I won't be your fancy man."

"No!" she protested. "I didn't mean anything like that. I love you. I thought we—well, I mean, don't you—after last night, want to—"

"What?" he asked painfully. "After last night, what?"

"Won't you marry me?" she whispered, dismayed by his apparent perplexity.

His face changed. The anger faded, replaced by a kind of stupefaction. He seemed struck utterly dumb by the idea. Tess stood for a long time, waiting for him to say yes. It slowly became clear that he would say nothing. The realization seemed to seep into her limbs like melting ice, a horrible disappointment, a wound that caused her chest to ache and made it hard to breathe. When she could not stand his silent answer any longer, she turned away and plunged into the water, swimming hard for the shore. By the time she reached the dry sand there was salt on her cheeks and in her mouth—seawater or tears, she did not know.

Hina was unwilling to accept that the outcome of their scheme had been disaster.

"But he loves you, Tete," she said for the tenth time, as she caught at the skirt that Tess was trying to pack. "I saw him, when he thought you were lost."

"He doesn't." Tess tugged the garment from her friend's hands and threw it into the case. "He had every chance to say so— Believe me, Hina, he doesn't want me. And I'm tired of throwing myself at him."

Tess had been back in Tahiti for one night: a long and sleepless one. The first thing this morning she had gone to the harbor authority to find out which ship would be leaving at the earliest moment. There were none for three days except whalers, but the day after that, a French square-rigged steamer was shipping with a load of island cotton directly for Calais. It was not where she wanted to go, but she really did not know where she wanted to go, except away, and so she had already booked her passage.

"Tete," Hina pleaded. "Don't go. Think of Mr. Sydney—he'll be so sad!"

"I've already talked to him. He's going to stay, as long as he likes, and ship the collections home. I have to go."

Before Hina could resume her solicitations, there was a sound of small feet skipping up the stairs. "Mama," exclaimed the oldest of Hina's little ones, a bright-eyed five-year-old girl. "Moana tane says come. There's a man. He wants Tete."

Tess felt her heart squeeze. It couldn't be . . .

Hina turned on her in triumph. "It must be Rifone. Who else would come looking for you?"

Tess forced herself to go on folding the blouse she had in her hands. "It will be a message from the French captain. I asked him to send me a confirmation of my booking."

Hina snorted. She grabbed a hibiscus flower from the little vase by the window and tucked it behind Tess's ear before propelling her out the door. Tess descended the stairs under the same coercion, and wished that she had resisted when she saw that Hina had been right.

He stood in the open entrance hall, dressed in a dark morning coat and neat neckcloth, looking as if he might have just stepped off a London carriage except for the windblown bronze of his hair. He had in one hand a bouquet of flowers, red and white and pale yellow. He did not smile when he saw her.

Tess stopped at the foot of the stairs. Hina rushed past and gave him an impulsive hug, reaching up to kiss his cheek. "I knew you would come," she said softly.

He endured the embrace, looking all the time at Tess. Hina stepped back, and Tess was hardly aware of it when the island girl collected her daughter and slipped away. Tess kept gazing at the flowers, fear and a crazy hope warring in her breast.

"Sydney told me you were leaving," he said.

She nodded.

"I came—" He stopped, cleared his throat. He held out the flowers. "Do you want these?"

The offering was not particularly graceful. She looked up at him, into serious, silver-gray eyes, and for a moment she could have thrown herself down and begged him to ask her to stay. Then pride returned. She said, "That wasn't necessary." But she stepped forward and took them anyway. Her hand touched his in the transfer. He caught at it, holding her from retreat.

"Marry me," he said.

Tess froze. His fingers closed around hers. His grip was warm and strong, and held her fast.

For some outrageous reason, she could not speak. Perhaps it was her shock, or the sudden way her breath failed. Perhaps it was the bubble of pure joy that welled up and blocked her throat. She felt the flowers sliding from her hands; he caught them, a sudden, easy move, a contrast to his awkward proposal.

She ducked her head, and mumbled at the floor the only word she could manage to say.

"Yes."

They were married in an English ceremony by a French minister in a Tahitian church. They could have had their choice of any other combination they might have liked, but to Tess, the little chapel and the simple decoration were perfect. The church was full, not only with Hina and her family and Mr. Sydney and the *Arcanum*'s crew, but with a crowd of well-wishing islanders who were thrilled to have a party on short notice. Tess stood before them in a flowing waistless robe of white taffeta, loaned to her by Hina, and had not the least regret for the elegant satin gown and massive train she had worn in that other, ill-fated ceremony. This was her real wedding. The other had been no more than a troubled dream.

She listened to the *pasteur*'s voice, and could not help a blink of surprise when she heard him intone in lilting accents, "I, Gryphon Arthur Meridon . . ."

Gryf repeated the name, without the slightest hesitation. She looked up at him, and lost the thread of her curiosity in the wonder of seeing him there, taking a vow to love and cherish her for all the rest of their lives. His name was unimportant. Under any name, she would love him. She repeated her own vows with wholehearted sincerity.

But the question came back to mind that evening, after all the guests and nonguests had wandered away, full of roast pig and the Frasers' gin. Hina had thoughtfully arranged a trip for herself, her children, and Mr. Sydney to visit relatives on Moorea after the party, and Mr. Fraser was absent for several days, as usual, on some business of his own. Tess and Gryf had the two-story thatch-roofed house in Papeete to themselves.

As they walked up the porch steps, Tess said tentatively, "So now I am Mrs. Meriton."

He gave her an ironic look. "Spelled with a *d*." He held open the door. "Meridon."

She had no desire to mention Stephen, or anything to do with him, but the coincidence was startling. She tried to think of an oblique way to approach the question, and finally asked timidly, "Did you know that was the family name of the marquesses of Ashland?"

"Yes."

The shortness of that answer warned her off the subject, but as she stepped inside she turned, and asked lightly, "Surely you're not related to them?"

It was growing dark. In the dim light in the hall his eyes were unreadable. "In a way."

"I see," she said, and was certain that she did. A natural son . . . it explained a lot of things. He stood stiffly, a little distance away. She put out her hand and took his, wanting him to know that it made no difference at all. "I love you," she said.

He pulled his hand free. "Will you be all right here by yourself?"

"By myself?"

"I'm going out."

"Going out! Going out where?"

"Tess," he said flatly. "It's been a long day. We'll talk about it in the morning."

"But—"

"Good night." He was already out the door. He turned before he closed it. "I'll come back before morning. I promise."

Tess was left standing in shock inside the hall. A moment later, she recovered enough to throw open the door, but he had already vanished in the growing dusk. There was no one in the empty, coral-dust street but a small group of children playing at French bowls and a dog that trotted in and out among the thick overhanging trees.

She called his name. One child looked up, and waved. There was no other answer. Numbly, she stepped back inside and let the door fall closed. Going out? She could not imagine . . . Where was he going? The promise to be back before morning was more disturbing than reassuring. Why should he have left her at all?

She twisted her hands together and went slowly upstairs, changing rather sadly into the pretty light gown and peignoir that had been another present from Mahina. Tess did not really believe he would be gone long, so she sat in a chair near the window and read by the light of an oil lamp, a book of French love poems that she had planned to give him. She did not take down her hair, but left the creamy white flowers in it. She read through every poem, and when she came to the end, she turned the lamp down to nothing and remained by the window, staring out into the tropical night.

After the clock downstairs struck midnight, she began to get angry. By the time it was one, she was furious. She stood up and began to pace the dark room, asking herself over and over where he could have gone, and why, and how he could be so heartless as to leave her on such a night. In the two days since he had come and proposed, she had hardly seen him at all. Hina had thrown herself into making all the wedding arrangements. All Tess had known of it was that he was so anxious to have the ceremony as soon as possible that he'd obtained a special license, an impatience which had flattered her enormously. So why now had he said good-night and left her in the hall, as if they were little more than strangers?

She fumed over it, and entertained herself for some time in thinking up cutting responses for when he came back and tried to apologize. Just let him try to apologize! Then she sat down and began to be afraid, and by two o'clock, she was certain he had been knifed and robbed on the waterfront. It was when she was deep in the throes of that agitation that she noticed the red spark in the shadows below her window.

She stopped her pacing, and peered down at the tiny light. It glowed brighter, and then faded, and then in a moment it grew brighter again, illuminating a pale mouth and bearded chin. Her hands tightened on the windowsill. Memory clutched at her, the dreadful recollection of another place—another darkness, and someone watching.

She fought back a whimper of panic. It was a *gendarme,* perhaps, making his rounds. It was some sailor, stopped for a smoke and a last swig from his bottle on the way to the beach. She shrank to the side of the window, holding back the curtain. The red spark made an arc downward, winking out. She waited. A minute went by, then two, as she strained to hear whether the figure was walking away. White spots swam before her eyes as she tried to see into the shadows.

After an infinity of silence, with only the sound of rustling leaves and the distant low murmur of the surf to break the quiet, she almost convinced herself that the loiterer was gone. But she stayed by the window, wishing mightily that Gryf had not left her there alone. Every tiny noise in the house seemed loud.

The clock downstairs struck half past two, and she jumped at the first hollow peal of its chimes. Oh— where was Gryf? Why had he left her? She pulled her robe tightly around her and crept to the stairs.

At the top of them she stopped. It seemed very dark below. She almost went back to get the lamp. After a moment, she carefully placed a slipper on the top step, avoiding the creaky spot she knew would be in the middle. She took another step, and another, slipping down in silence. It was as if her feet knew something that her mind refused to accept. She was not alone in this house. With a certainty that came from no rational reason at all, she knew she was not alone.

At the foot of the stairs, she turned back toward the kitchen, hardly allowing herself to breathe as she slipped along. She stopped just outside the door, and leaned forward, then dug her fingernails hard into her palms to keep herself from screaming.

Inside the kitchen, the quivering glow of a match illuminated a man's silhouette, throwing his long shadow across the floor. He was facing away from her, bent over the kitchen hutch. She stood there long enough to see the flash of metal as he eased something from the drawer. That was enough. She did not wait to see what it was. She broke and ran, down the hall and out the front door, and did not stop running until she had pounded down the hill above the harbor and reached the empty streets of the waterfront.

The *Arcanum* lay only a few hundred feet from the beach. Tess could see the ship, a dark, unlit outline against the starshine on the water. She trotted up and down the cool sand, looking for some way to reach the ship, but there were no boats small enough for her to handle on the beach. She threw a nervous look over her shoulder at the town, and imagined that she saw the shadow of a figure emerging from behind a nearby warehouse. The vision galvanized her: she kicked off her slippers and took off her robe, rolling it into a bundle. Holding it above her head, she waded into the black water. It wasn't cold; it felt warmer than the fresh night air. The nightgown floated out around her and tangled in her legs, so she worked it off her shoulders and left it to wash up on the beach, a slightly whiter shape within the small white waves that broke regularly on the shore. Naked, holding her head and the robe above water, she slid into the bay and stroked for the ship.

By the time she reached it, both arms were exhausted. She floated, trying to rest, while she stared in dismay at the curving wall of freeboard. The deck might as well have been a thousand feet up, for all she could reach it.

She touched the hull beneath the waterline with her feet, and jerked back instinctively from the slimy tendrils of algae that covered the surface. She called out, softly at first, then louder, and received no answer. Slowly, she worked her way around the side, held on to the chain cable beneath the sharp spear of the bowsprit to rest, and then went on. With profound relief, she spotted a dinghy on the other side, tied up to the boarding ladder. Reaching it seemed to take the last of her strength; she tossed her robe inside and held on to the gunwale, breathing hard.

Getting herself into the dinghy without overturning it was the most difficult problem of all. After several abortive tries, accompanied by enough splashing to wake the entire French garrison, the little boat happened to drift over close to the main hull. That time, when she put her weight on the dinghy's side and it tilted, instead of threatening to turn over, the dinghy's gunwale caught under the boarding ladder. She heaved herself upward on trembling arms, and managed to flounder into the boat before it broke free.

She rested again, and then struggled into the robe, for the night air was chilly on her wet skin. The dinghy provided an easy platform from which to mount the boarding ladder, and in a moment, she was on deck. She turned and tried to pull the boarding ladder up after her. When she couldn't manage, she dropped it overboard, ruthless in her fear that the intruder might somehow have followed her. The ladder hit the water with a loud, splashing plop, sank, and then surfaced again, drifting slowly away.

Chapter 14

*T*he ship was dark and absolutely quiet, no sign of any watch, though Tess called up and down in a soft voice. She could see fairly well, enough to find the steps up onto the quarterdeck and then the companionway hatch. Her dark-adjusted eyes picked out the dim glow from below; she made her way down the steps and saw that the light glimmered from the captain's cabin.

She shivered in her damp robe, and peered timidly around the part-open door.

Gryf was there, stretched out on the horsehair couch in the day room, his blond head propped against the locker that served as an armrest. The oil lamp on the wall burned a low, steady flame, but he was sound asleep. She said his name. He didn't wake, only took a longer, deeper breath. She slipped across the cabin and touched the sun-browned hand that dangled over the side of the upholstered berth.

"Gryf," she murmured, and sat down on the edge of the couch. It was impossible to be angry with him as he lay there with his stiff white shirt unbuttoned and his feet bare below the formal trousers he had worn for their wedding. She leaned over and whispered again, directly into his ear.

He drew in another deep breath, and his eyes flickered open. From her closer position, she could smell the sweet, heavy odor of rum, an unspoken explanation of why it took him so long to focus on her. When he did, instead of the rebuff she half-expected, his face broke into a lazy smile.

Tess felt an answering smile tug at the corners of her mouth. Her hero, she thought wryly. It was fortunate she had managed to escape her intruder by herself, for clearly Gryf would have been no help. He seemed to have trouble just keeping his eyes open. He lifted his head, and dropped it back onto the locker with a thump that appeared to knock some awareness into his brain, for his eyes flew open and he gave her a hurt look, as if she were somehow responsible. He levered himself onto his elbows. "How did you get here?" His mumble was rather more lucid than she had expected.

"Why did you leave me?" she countered.

He sat up, elevated one knee, and propped an arm across it, lowering his forehead into the makeshift support. "God, I'm drunk." He rolled his head sideways to peer at her. "You're not supposed to be here."

"Neither are you."

He considered that for a moment. Then he asked, "Why are you wet?"

"I couldn't find a boat."

He groaned, and turned his face down again. "You're crazy."

"Well," she said. "Maybe I am. But I didn't leave you on our wedding night."

"Go away, will you?" His voice was muffled. "Leave me alone."

Tess pressed her lips together. "No. Someone was going to murder me back there."

"Murder you," he repeated into the crook of his arm.

"There was someone in the Frasers' house. I found him in the kitchen. I think he was looking for a knife. Maybe he was a thief."

"A knife thief."

Somehow, safe here on the ship, with Gryf's hard thigh pressed comfortingly against her hip, the episode had lost much of its terror. "Well—" she said apologetically. "He was looking in a drawer in the kitchen hutch."

"Possibly a spoon thief," Gryf suggested thickly.

Tess frowned. "I suppose it might have been Moana tane. He lives behind the house. If he needed something, he wouldn't have wanted to disturb us—" She glanced at Gryf sheepishly. He did not look up, but he had angled his head a little to the side. Tess followed his gaze, and saw that her peignoir had fallen partially open, revealing a smooth expanse of skin above her knee.

"I think you'd better go," he muttered.

She set her jaw stubbornly. "Why? I don't understand you."

"I don't want you here, Tess."

"But I'm your wife—"

"Fine. That's what you were after, wasn't it? You're my wife. Now go away."

She looked at him, nonplussed. Then she covered his hand with her own. "I didn't just want your name."

"Well." He moved his hand. "That's about all I've got. And I don't even have that, most of the time."

There was a rawness in his voice, beneath the sarcasm. Tess wanted to reach out and embrace him, to hold him and tell him it did not matter. But she was learning. All this was pride, the same thing that had held them apart from the beginning. Her money, her position, all of her advantages: there was no way to make up the difference on the surface. Simple words would not suffice, but she knew where his weakness lay. She hadn't spent a month in the islands without absorbing a thing or two about how a woman could communicate with a man.

Think like a Tahitian, Hina had said.

Tess rose, careless of how the peignoir fell open, and reached up as if to tuck back her hair. As she raised her arms, she knew the damp silk clung to her skin, molding the material to the curve of her breasts. She knew it because that was where his gaze traveled before he tore it away and looked up at her face. She smiled into his frowning eyes, and pulled at the comb that held up her hair. A soft tangle of flowered tresses fell across her shoulders.

"Tess—"

She stood before him, smoothing her hair against her skin. She drew a thick lock across her mouth, taking in a deep breath of the sweet scent. "You really want me to go?" she whispered.

He said nothing, only looked at her. She sank down beside him again, taking his lack of answer as permission, and leaned over to make a trail of her fingers down the center of his back. In the process, her lips came close to his ear, and she murmured, "I'd like to stay."

She slipped her hand beneath the loose tails of his shirt and then made the same journey back up, caressing the curved muscles beneath his skin. He slowly turned his head, and his breath warmed her shoulder. The heady smell of rum clung to him; his eyelids lowered as he surveyed the shadowed hollow where the peignoir gaped open between her breasts. She let her hand drift along his jaw and trace the outline of his mouth.

"Do you want me to leave?" she asked again, a smile playing on her lips as he leaned a little toward her. "I can still leave."

He reached up; she felt his fingers, hot and callused at

the pulse of her throat. They slid downward, snagging the edge of the robe. "No." His voice was husky. "I want you to take this off."

The low command sent a chill of excitement through her. She dipped her shoulder, so that the garment fell free under the weight of his hand. He slid his fingers over her other shoulder, and the fabric came with them. He pressed his lips against her skin. "Beautiful," he murmured. "You're beautiful."

"All yours," she said lightly. "Would you like me to rub your back?"

He smiled, the same, slow, lazy smile he had shown when he first opened his eyes and saw her. "No." His hand moved beneath the peignoir, cupped her breast. He added, in a drink-slurred voice, "Rather keep you where I can see you."

She teased. "I thought you didn't want me here."

"Did I say that?" He brushed the robe aside. It slid from her onto the floor. "I was lying. Must have been . . . lying." The last word was muffled against her throat. She shivered as he touched his tongue to the tender hollow. Almost unconsciously, she curled her legs up onto the berth. He caught her arms, pulling her with him as he lay back. His chin was scratchy with day-old beard; the tickling touch elicited a bubble of delight.

"Laughing?" he growled against her skin. "We don't let ladies laugh at the captain on this ship."

That brought forth a clear-cut giggle. His arm came up and caught her around the waist. Tess shrieked as she felt herself roll, and then he was on top of her, kissing her chin and her shoulders and everywhere he could reach while his hands sought out her breasts. "Mutiny," he accused between kisses. "You know what that means."

Tess arched a little beneath the delicious coaxing of his fingers. "The . . . the plank?" she added breathlessly.

He shook his head in disgust. "Waste of a good lady."
He ran his tongue around her mouth, leaving the sweet
taste of rum on her parted lips. "We have more refined
tortures."

He nuzzled her throat and shifted downward, following the path of his hands. When he reached the soft,
pink-tipped mounds of her breasts he paused and gazed
at her. "The only trouble is," he said hoarsely, "it's the
captain who's being tortured. Why'm I dressed, when
you're so ravish—ravishish—" He stumbled over the
word, and finally settled for "—indecent?"

"Because you're completely foxed," she said frankly.
"I doubt you could manage your own buttons."

He gave her a half-lidded grin. "Three sheets in the
wind. Royals and foremast gone to smash. Buttons . . .
are in your watch, mister. Pardon me." He planted a
kiss between her breasts. "Madam."

His inebriated good humor was irresistible. As he
hiked himself up, he stole a series of nips and kisses, and
then lay back expectantly on the couch, with his hands
behind his neck and his hair falling over his forehead,
for all the world like some pickled pasha surveying his
harem. His gray eyes gleamed silver; the smooth contours of his chest and ribs seemed to beckon to her to
reach out and push the starched shirt aside. She had a
moment's hesitation, some belated thought of maidenly
modesty, but his whimsical smile banished all shyness.
He was her husband. The wonder of it filled her with
warm eagerness.

She went to work, rising to her knees on the couch. It
was strangely exciting to take the initiative; to see him
submit to her ministrations as if anything she might do
would please him. She made him sit up long enough to
remove the shirt, and then pushed him back, reveling in
a slow exploration of him; his sun-blackened shoulders,

the hard bone and muscle beneath, the paler, softer skin inside his arms. She traced the same trail with her lips, tasting heat and the faint tang of perspiration. Her tongue grazed his nipple in passing; he groaned, arching, and tangled his hand in her hair to pull her closer.

The discovery of that pleasure point was the beginning of an exhilaratingly sensual mapping project. She found that the tip of her tongue in the hollow at the base of his throat could make his pulse jump. She learned that a pattern drawn by her fingertips on his pectoral muscles made him close his eyes and flex his arms. That same pattern, extended downward to free the buttons on his trousers, made his breath come harsh and faster.

She paused after the buttons, not sure of what to do next, but he did not wait for further experiments. He drew her up and kissed her, his tongue delving deep into her mouth. His hands were occupied; she felt him move awkwardly beneath her, and then her thighs touched bare skin. He broke the kiss and slid his open palms down over her hips, guiding her over him.

He was hot, his skin satiny damp in the cool sea air. Her knees and hands rested on the slick, tight-woven upholstery as she knelt across him, enclosing them both in the dark curtain of her hair. He drew her hips down, pressing himself upward, and she bit her lower lip as she encountered his hardness. It was still surprising, still intimidatingly masculine, but now she saw his face, too. The strain there, the anticipation and controlled desire as he gazed at her lips and waited for her to respond to the steady pressure of his hands was intoxicating. She eased herself downward. He tilted his head back. "Oh, God," he breathed, "Tess." She took him into her, deep, reveling in the penetration. It no longer hurt; it was all pleasure, and her lips curled in the same savage smile as his.

He pulled her forward, drawing his knees up behind her. His mouth found her offered breast, his tongue stroked the taut nipple. She arched, gasping. She moved against him again and again as he tugged and sucked. His hands helped her and encouraged her: she rocked, and a sound began to rise in her own throat, a panting, wordless moan. What she had felt with him before had been good, but this was more, far more; this was a growing frenzy that clutched the very center of her being, that made every sensation unbearably vivid. When his mouth opened as if to take in more of her swelling breast she whimpered and trembled and arched to let him. When he drew back and thrust upward, she felt as if she might explode.

His fingers dug into her waist and he pushed her down, rolling on top. She relaxed her legs, opening to his urgent mounting. The feel of him ignited her. He carried her upward until she could no longer think, no longer exist except as part of him; until she could not hold back the wild cry that grew and grew and finally burst from her . . . a breathless, helpless echo of his own.

For a full minute afterward she lay dizzy, hardly able to take in enough air. He sagged on top of her, equally short of breath, then with an incoherent mumble lifted himself just enough to slide away. He kissed her ear, spread his hand in her hair, and turned her head so that he could kiss her mouth. Then he fell asleep, with his lips still brushing her skin.

Tess smiled, and smoothed a lock of burnished hair from his temple. She, too, drifted off, on a sea of love and security, and the pungent scent of fermented cane.

There were awakened by a loud hail. Tess jerked spasmodically at the unexpected shout, which seemed to come from just outside the cabin, and her movement elicited a sleepy moan from Gryf. The hail came again, and he opened bleary eyes. "Aye," he croaked, and shut them.

Tess sat up, blinking in the clear light that poured through the open porthole. She shook his shoulder, leaned over and kissed his ear. "Company coming aboard, Captain."

He said something that sounded like, "Uhhrrug."

A vigorous thumping on the hull somewhere just forward of the cabin brought him finally to an upright position. Tess stood, giving him room. He shook his tousled head and pulled his open palms down his face, then looked up and saw her through his fingers. "Oh," he said. "The devil."

Tess grinned. "Good morning."

He turned at more insistent shouting from outside, then heaved himself to his feet. He looked none too stable as he hunted up his duck trousers.

"Would you like me to go for you?" Tess asked, as he tottered a little pulling them on.

He gave her a leveling glare. "You stay here. You don't have any clothes."

"Yes, sir," she said meekly and sat down. It was quite entertaining to gaze at his golden, muscular back and shoulders as he dressed. She particularly liked the way his trousers hung low-slung on his hips, with a little line of untanned skin that peeked above the waist. He did not bother with shirt or boots, but swung out the door barefooted. She noticed with a smile that he let it bounce closed, and then a moment later came back and turned the latch from the outside to secure it.

She was examining the salt-stiffened peignoir for wearability when he returned. He slammed the door behind him as he entered, not even glancing at her. "Somebody stole the bloody ladder," he fumed. He yanked open a locker and pulled out a clean shirt. "Why the deuce can't they pick on somebody who can afford it?"

Tess sat down on the bed and held her robe to her mouth.

"Who would want a boarding ladder, I ask you?" He threw the shirt toward her. "Put that on. I don't know why they didn't take the dinghy and the anchor buoy while they were at it. Damnation. Haven't you a skirt left on board somewhere?"

She shook her head, not trusting herself to speak.

"What's wrong with you?" he demanded, flashing a look at her reddened face.

"I threw it overboard," she said in a stifled voice.

"Your skirt?"

Tess burst into helpless giggles. "I'm s-sorry. The ladder. I threw it overboard. I didn't mean to! Bu-but I thought he was after me—the thief, you know. I thought he had a knife."

"Tess," he said dangerously, "I have the mother of a headache."

"I'm awfully sorry!" she cried. "I'll get you another ladder." She stood up and pulled on the shirt. Its long tails came nearly to her knees. As she looked down to button it, her hair fell into her eyes. She brushed it back. "It will be a wedding present. You didn't stay long enough for me to give you the one I already had."

She glanced up, and saw that his expression had softened a little. "Here." He came closer, reaching out to roll up one of the dangling shirt sleeves. His touch was gentle. She held out the other arm when he had finished. "You were really frightened," he said quietly. "Last night, when you came out here."

"Until I found you," she admitted. "I can't think why I was so silly, but—oh, I did panic there for a little while. I saw someone underneath my window. Someone just standing there, smoking. It must have been a sailor, or something like that, but it—I suppose it reminded me of . . ."

"Never mind." He smoothed back a strand of her hair. "I'm sorry I left you there alone. I shouldn't have."

"Well," she said tartly, "that's true."

He glanced up at her at that, a flash of smoky-gray. There was a troubled expression in his eyes, but he moved away without answering. When he turned to close the locker door, she followed him, and put her arms around his waist, pressing her cheek against his back. "I love you," she said, by way of apologizing.

He stood still, his hand upon the open door. She felt him take a deep breath. "Don't do this, Tess," he said. "It just makes things harder."

She kissed the taut skin across his spine. "What things?"

He pulled her hands carefully away from him and turned. "You were planning to take passage on the French steamer."

"I was," she said, and smiled. "Not anymore."

"Take it."

The smile faded. "What do you mean?"

He moved abruptly, knocking the locker shut and facing the blank wood. "It would be best if you went home."

"Home," she echoed. "I don't understand."

"I can't live with you," he said to the wall. "I won't."

She stared at his back.

"I'll give you the marriage papers. You can say that you're widowed, if you like. You don't have to use my name, if you don't want to, but I thought—if there was a child, I thought—"

He seemed to lose the thread of his words. He broke

away and went to the safe on the opposite wall, unlocked it. "I want you to take this." He crossed to her again and pressed something small and cold into her hand. "It's a man's, I know. It's—I couldn't think of anything else. It's what I have, Tess. There's nothing else to give you."

In a kind of waking dream, she opened her hand and looked at the emerald signet ring lying there. She said in a small voice, "You're not sending me away?"

"Don't you understand?" he asked painfully. "I can't give you anything."

"Your love," she cried. "That's all I want. That's all I ever wanted."

His face tightened. In the silence that followed she heard the thud of feet on the deck above, felt a stray breath of wind from the port lift a strand of her hair.

"You don't love me?" she whispered.

Gryf felt his heart twist. God, how was he to answer that? To love her—it would be the ultimate folly. He could not put a name to the turmoil of emotion inside him, the confusing mixture of fear and desperate need, but he was certain that he could not, he *must* not let himself love her. Even he was not so much a fool. With love came grief, and he had had enough of it. He could not bear to open his heart to that again. He had to send her away, for he knew with every fiber of his being that if he kept her with him he was lost.

In a low voice, he answered, "No."

She blinked, trying to straighten the cabin that had gone dizzily distorted in her vision. "Then why—"

"I married you because I had to."

"Had to . . ." The ring cut into her pawn from the force with which she squeezed her hand. "Had to."

He lowered his eyes. "There was no choice. For your sake."

She felt suddenly that her legs would not hold her. She made the two steps to the berth, and sat down, struggling to hang on to some semblance of calm. When she looked up, her words were quick, almost defiant. "Last night you loved me."

He turned away at that, refusing to meet her fierce look. "I don't say I don't . . . desire you. God knows—" He made a choked sound, deep in his throat, and clenched his fists. "Sometimes I've thought I'd die of it. I tried to fight that, but you just kept pushing. You just wouldn't go away."

"I didn't want to go away. I don't want to go now. I won't!"

"It doesn't matter. If you won't go, then I will."

"I don't understand," she said brokenly. "You loved me once. Before Stephen."

He shot her a frown, as if she had delivered an unfair blow. "No. I never did. I was crazy then; I was trying to be—trying to do something I should never have tried. I wish you hadn't gone to Eliot, but you were right to send me packing. You should have left it there. I wish to God you had."

She covered her mouth with her fingers to stifle a sob. "Oh—if I hurt you then one-tenth as much as you are hurting me now, I wish I had never been born."

"I'm sorry." It was a groan. "That isn't what I want—to hurt you. I've tried to remedy the hurt I've already done the best way that I can. Beyond that—there's no more I have to offer."

She stared up at him through a bright haze. In a tiny voice, she asked, "Do you want to be divorced, then?"

He hesitated. After a long time he said, "I don't ask for that. If it's your choice . . ."

"It's not," she said quickly.

"It might be for the best. You deserve more than this.

You could remarry. I don't know how long it would take to prove desertion, but—"

"Desertion!"

He looked at her. When he spoke, his words were soft, almost gentle. "That would be grounds enough, Tess. Even in England."

She gave a half-hysterical little laugh. "I see. You are deserting me. That would certainly remedy whatever hurt has been done." Her bitterness echoed in the small confines of the cabin. "Perhaps you had better leave first, so no one could say it was the other way round, and I had deserted you instead."

He looked away again, but not before she saw the pain in his eyes. In a breath she was on her feet and reaching for him. "Gryf," she pleaded. "You can't mean this. You may not love me now; I've been stupid and foolish and I've made you angry, I know. But I'll make it up. I promise—we'll be happy. Only give me time to show you. You could grow to love me again—you might." She clasped both hands around one of his. "Won't you even try?"

He jerked his arm away. "It isn't a matter of trying." He strode to the door and stopped, his face stony. "I can't love you. I can't stay near you. I'm not—capable of it. If you don't understand that, if you can't live with it, divorce me." His eyes found hers, winter-cold, and then dropped. "I'm leaving now. I'll send Mahina with some clothes for you. The steamer sails this afternoon."

The door closed on his back, and she stared numbly after him.

Gryf stood at the bar in one of Papeete's more genteel saloons, drawing aimless circles in the dew that dripped off the side of his beer mug.

He glanced up as William Stewart bade a hearty

good-day to his French friends and made his way back to where Gryf was waiting to resume their interrupted rendezvous. With a flash of his black-Irish grin, Stewart beckoned Gryf to a table.

"I understand congratulations are in order," Stewart said, and raised his glass. "To matrimony—and other enterprises."

Gryf nodded and drank. The insinuation wasn't worth being offended over, and he wanted Stewart's good will if he could get it.

"Shall we have a bit of a gam, old friend?" Stewart sat back and pulled at his black beard, fixing Gryf with a sharp eye. "I confess to some curiosity about your need for employment. I'd have thought the newly wedded husband of a British peeress wouldn't be interested in work."

Gryf looked at his beer, then out the open door where the sunset made deep, dancing shadows of the bushy oleanders that lined the street. He rubbed the slick side of the mug. "You'd be wrong."

"So—she took her money with her when she sailed off yesterday in tears?"

Gryf set his jaw, glanced up at Stewart's face without answering.

Stewart shrugged and smiled. "It's not a large island. Everyone knows. High romance. I understand you even performed a gallant rescue of the lady from a desert atoll. Neatly done, I'd say. Very neatly done. I can't fathom what went wrong."

Here, in Stewart's town, drinking on Stewart's money, Gryf felt it would be impolitic to give the man the facer he was asking for. Instead he said flatly, "Do you know of any work?"

"Oh, I do indeed. I'm just trying to discern how much you need it."

"I need it."

Stewart smiled. "You're not driving yourself much of a bargain."

"We'll work it out. I figure there isn't much competition in my class, either."

"True enough. What is she? I've forgotten—five hundred tons, at the least."

"Five twenty-seven."

"What's her draft?"

"Seventeen eight, fully loaded."

Stewart sighed. "I suppose it would be a whale in a fish pond to put her in the interisland trade. I'm locked out of the Tuamotus, between Mr. Brander and Mr. Hort and your friend Mr. Fraser."

"It wouldn't pay," Gryf said mildly. This was all a game, he knew. The idea of the *Arcanum* competing with the little schooners that sailed among the islands was ridiculous. "She could make round trip to Sydney with a load of cotton in two months. San Francisco in four."

Stewart pulled a pipe from his pocket and began to fill it. "There's already a regular line to Frisco."

"What's their price?"

"A hundred and twenty francs per ton."

"I'll beat that. I'll also beat them getting there."

Stewart smiled. "Ah, yes, I remember. The eager boy. And you'll do it too, if recollection serves."

"You know I will."

"Unfortunately, shipping cotton isn't really my problem. The difficulty is in finding someone to pick the bloody stuff." He scowled at the match as he lit his pipe. "Here we are," he said, between puffs, "record prices on cotton for at least as long as the American war lasts; the perfect location for growing long-grained, sea-island variety—choicest of the choice—and my overseers come to me every day saying they haven't enough men. Would you be interested in some well-financed black-birding? Say, with my brother James in the Marquesas?"

Gryf frowned. He had no taste at all for transporting human cargo.

"An attack of morality, old friend?" Stewart asked. "But no—you've always been an upright fellow, haven't you? I thought perhaps you'd changed, hearing of your—shall we say, 'advantageous,' marriage? Have you finished your beer? Come—let's walk down to see the *Imperial commissaire*. La Roncière is a notorious nobleman. I'm sure he'll be delighted to meet the newest member of the leisure class." Stewart winked. "After all, he was delighted to meet me."

As they stepped out into the twilight shadows of the street, Stewart knocked his newly lit pipe clean on the porch rail, a cavalier waste of tobacco that told Gryf more about the man's current finances than any balance sheet could have. They had not gone five yards from the bar when Gryf caught another whiff of smoke. He looked around the empty street in passing. A bird called through the tangle of jessamine and hibiscus, and the sound ended on a peculiar sharp click. He stopped. The next moment, he was on the ground, half on top of Stewart, scraping his palms with the force of the dive as the quiet neighborhood echoed to the explosive report of a single gunshot.

Stewart swore, regaining wit and wind, and heaved upward. They both scrambled for cover, no need to talk, no need to question the reflex shove that had taken Stewart down with Gryf. They made the bushes and crouched there, the derringer in Stewart's hand as ready as Gryf's own revolver.

No second shot followed. A pair of hefty Tahitian

musclemen appeared from nowhere, and Stewart laid a hand on Gryf's arm as his finger tensed on the trigger. Stewart whistled, and the islanders looked around. They both slipped into the thicket that lined the street and were gone before the first startled bystanders poked their heads out of the saloon and the shop next door.

Gryf couldn't prevent a jerk of surprise when one of the huge Tahitians materialized silently from the foliage right next to him, but he managed to keep himself from firing. Stewart and the islander held a brief, low conversation, and then the Tahitian moved off again. After another minute, Stewart cast Gryf a glance and jerked his head. Gryf put away his gun, dusted himself off, and followed the other man as he stepped brazenly into the street.

"So you see," Stewart said conversationally, making a show of handing the derringer to Gryf. "It would hardly do for bird hunting, but I imagine it would inflict considerable damage at two paces even in an untrained hand. If I were you, sir, I'd have that lovely new wife of yours carry one at all times."

Gryf examined the tiny, pearl-handed gun, and then handed it back with a wry smile. "As it happens, my wife is probably a better shot than I am. I'll let her pick her own firearms."

With a nod and tip of the hat to the few curious onlookers, Stewart resumed their leisurely stroll down the street. "I think we'll postpone our visit to the palace," he said quietly. "You're interested in the news my two friends might bring back?"

"I'm interested."

"Good. Good." He looked sideways at Gryf with piercing black eyes. "Let me thank you for your prompt action. Did you see anything?"

Gryf shrugged. "I heard the hammer."

"You must have a fine survival sense, my friend. An excellent sense. I can't persuade you into the Marquesas scheme?"

Gryf let silence communicate his reluctance. There was a new tone in Stewart's voice, a tone that augured a better offer. The unthinking instinct that had made Gryf carry Stewart down with him as he hit the rocky street might prove a lucky break.

Stewart nodded. "I thought not." He stopped at the corner they had just reached. Scattered lamps had begun to glow through the clear dusk, lighting the interiors of houses and a few shops. "You know my warehouse— Tahiti Cotton and Coffee, near the intersection of Rue Brea and Rivoli? Wait there. I shall be along in an hour."

Gryf obeyed that offhand order, more because he hoped to ship a load of Stewart's cotton than because he wanted to know who was taking potshots at the man. He found his way through the evening depths into the center of town, past the pretty little spired cathedral, and into the commercial district along the quay. The French *gendarmes* kept good order in this town, and the sound of laughter from the few sailors' haunts did not extend past the long fingers of light that poured out their open doors and windows. The streets were almost empty.

He leaned against the rough plank wall of the warehouse and examined his palms, scraped raw at the base by pulverized coral. He did not care; the stinging annoyance was more than worthwhile if it bought him a way off this island. He wanted to be back at sea. He wanted to be moving. He wanted to forget the sight of the French ship steaming out of the entrance to Papeete's harbor.

He was, he thought, a coward. He made things hard

for himself. Slave trading and deflowering virgins should have been right in his line: the whole Pacific to hide in and no questions asked. But he was afraid to lay awake at night. He needed his sleep—God knew, he needed his sleep. To stare into the dark and see Louisa Grant-Hastings, dishonored and desperate, and know that he had done the same to Tess was beyond his power to endure.

So he had been stupid again, out of his cowardice. The best thing would have been to clear off entirely, no strings. The next best was what he had tried, which was to give her the paper protection of a name—his name, not worth much, except that she could put a Mrs. in front of it if she pleased. He had gotten that far, and then his resolution had failed him. When he asked her to marry him, when he saw the joy on her face, his callous speech about conditions and reservations had simply died in his throat. Instead of a quick, cauterizing cruelty, he had let her imagine that things were not what they were, and so in the end had hurt her more.

She would understand eventually. Why he had forced her to go. It was all so impossible—she had to see that—in a way that went far beyond their outward differences. She was so full of life, so ready to love and be loved; while he was ice inside on his better days, and suicidal on his worst. He could not cope with that kind of emotion anymore. He wanted at least to stay alive, and he was somehow sure that to remain near Tess would kill him. It almost had, once. He didn't need a second lesson.

Gryf straightened as the sound of footsteps echoed along the dark street. Stewart appeared out of the obscurity of shadow. He gave Gryf one brief, intense look, and then unlocked the door, saying nothing. Behind him, the two Tahitian stalwarts supported a battered-looking figure between them. Gryf couldn't make out the prisoner's face, but he saw enough to tell that Stewart's brand of interrogation probably hadn't made the fellow any prettier.

Stewart fumbled inside and turned up a lamp, beckoning to Gryf to sit down on a makeshift chair of cotton bales. The cavernous interior smelled of overripe bananas and dust. There was still no word spoken, which made Gryf uneasy; he looked around as the *mutoi* hauled their man inside. In the dim yellow light, Gryf finally saw the culprit's swollen and purpling face.

It was Stark.

Gryf whistled softly. "Is this your man?"

"I believe you two are acquainted?"

"I ran him off my ship," Gryf said, and looked toward Stewart. The man's eyes were very black and alert in the lamplight. "I hope you don't take that to mean I've anything to do with this incident."

Stewart leaned against a wooden desk scattered with ledgers and bills. He said, in a very level voice, "I am afraid you do, old friend." He picked up a lead pencil and began to toy with it. "I am much afraid that you do. It appears that your marriage has brought you into the line of fire."

Gryf stiffened, and stared at his companion.

Stewart smiled regretfully. "I dislike to be the bringer of bad news, but it seems this fellow has been hired to murder your lady wife."

Chapter 15

$\mathcal{D}$over fog hung at the hotel windows and dripped down the panes. It had been the same in Calais, a raw, rough sea that had delayed Tess's Channel passage for two days. She was no longer a sailor: the heave and throw of close cabins had made life a misery for three months, and when she had finally come ashore she found that she was no longer a landsman, either. The solid ground was as sickening in its unfamiliar stability as the lurch of the decks had been, and she had the constant and unpleasant impression that the chair she was sitting in was slowly pulling away from the nearby table.

This seasickness had taken her by surprise some few weeks out from Papeete, and it had not abated since. If not for a sympathetic fellow passenger, a retired whaling captain's wife, Tess thought she might well not have survived the voyage. But with persistent suggestions for Tess to "take a bit o' duff" or "a little lime" or "hove down" for a rest, that estimable lady had been—in her own words—a windward anchor for a sad and storm-tossed vessel.

At first, even the realization of what was causing the

unfamiliar illness had not raised Tess from her depression. But under the care of the captain's wife, she had gradually regained the will, if not the desire, to eat. She must eat, the good lady explained. It was Tess's duty to the new life growing inside of her to stuff herself with vegetables and fruit, even though the very sight of a potato came to be unnerving.

So Tess had eaten, and somehow lived through the coldest storms around the Horn, the hottest equatorial doldrums, and the fiercest Atlantic hurricane that she ever remembered from all of her travels. She had wept every day from wretchedness, but it was not the weeping of grief or defeat. With each awful pitch and roll of the ship, she became more angry, and more determined that she *would* survive, if only to spite the man who had seen fit to put her through this torture alone.

She frowned out the window of the hotel onto the foggy quay. At midday, all the gas lamps were lit; the dark bulks of carriages rattled slowly along the shining street. She had asked the manservant to arrange a ticket for her on the London rail: it was ten o'clock, the train left at half-past, and she still sat in her robe and tried to stomach the sausage and egg that had long since gone cold on her breakfast plate. The captain's wife had promised this illness would eventually disappear, but there was no sign yet of that happy day. She wished abruptly for coconut milk, the fresh, clear, tangy juice that had no resemblance to the rancid white stuff found in the nuts that traveled as far as England. The wish brought a vivid picture of Tahiti, and she began to cry again.

A light tap on her door made her sit up and wipe at her face. She called for the maid to enter, ready to be rid of the sight of congealing grease on her untouched plate. But the girl only cracked the door and said softly,

"Your husband, mum. He's come for you. He's waitin' in the private sittin' room downstairs."

Tess leaped to her feet, and regretted the move as soon as she had made it. She sat back down quickly, her arm across her stomach, and drew a steadying breath. "My husband—" The gulp of air did not clear the dizziness from her brain. "Oh, my. In a moment—tell him I'll be down in just a moment!" As if he might grow impatient with a few minutes' delay after so many months. She did not stop to think of anything else; she fought back the nausea and dressed, glancing in the mirror and cursing her haggard looks.

There was no overt sign yet of her pregnancy, but she surely appeared to have been ill. She fingered the signet ring, hung on a chain the whaler's wife had bought for her in Valparaiso. She had worn it inside her dress, but now she pulled it proudly free. She had forgiven everything, in the first instant of hearing that he had come for her.

Down the steep steps, she heard male voices, and the firm staccato of the proprietress. They stopped speaking the moment Tess appeared, and the trio in the entryway looked at her: two constables and the landlady. Tess gave them a quick and uncertain smile; she knew very well that the mistress disapproved of her for traveling alone, and now there was something in the woman's expression which seemed smugly satisfied. Tess said questioningly, "My husband—?" and then trailed off, unsure what name Gryf would be using.

The mistress bobbed her head. "His Lordship's in the parlor, my lady."

Tess blinked at the newly formal address, but she was too agitated to pause. She did not even knock at the parlor door; her damp and trembling fingers slipped on the porcelain doorknob and then finally made it move. She stepped inside.

Before she could distinguish anyone in the dim recesses of the room, he said, "My darling."

She froze.

It was not the voice she had expected to hear.

"Now—why did you run away, love?" he added in a gentle tone. "You've put us all in a state."

"Stephen," she whispered. Only the door held her up under the combined impact of shock and fear. She clung to the knob, her spine rigid, and her other arm came up in instinctive protection to her waist.

He stepped forward from a place near the darkened grate. "Dearest. You must come home now."

She let go of the door. She tried to speak, to tell him not to be absurd, but the smiling welcome beneath those familiar ice-blue eyes was terrifying. She took a step backward. "Leave me alone."

"You know I can't do that," he said, as if it were the most reasonable of statements. He walked toward her. "You must come home with me. Think of the children."

"Are you mad?" She was shaking with the need to turn and flee. "Don't you dare touch me. There are officers of the law here."

"Yes, of course there are, love. But you mustn't be afraid. I only brought them along as a precaution." He reached out as if to take her hand. "They understand how sensitive your nerves can be."

Tess whirled away, too late to avoid his fingers closing on her wrist. "Let go of me!"

He did, and she stumbled backward, turning to the policemen. "Has he told you he's my husband?" she cried. "It isn't true!"

The two men looked uncomfortable. Stephen had followed her into the entryway. "Gentlemen," he said softly, "please understand. She isn't well. Darling—"

"No!" Tess jerked away again as he put his hands on

her shoulders. She gulped for breath and reason. "I'm not your darling. I'm not your wife. That's over, Stephen, and this charade won't change it!"

The landlady's face was pinched with disapproval. Stephen looked at her sadly. "My good woman, I apologize. She has done this before."

"No matter, my lord. You take her home now, to her little ones where she belongs."

"He's lying!" Tess cried, reading complete agreement on all the faces before her. "I haven't any children! The marriage was anulled—" She rounded on Stephen. "I'm married now, but not to you!"

He shook his head. "My love, must you do this to me again and again? There is no Gryphon Meridon. You are not Mrs. Meridon, you are Mrs. Eliot. This fancy of yours—I know you cannot help yourself. I want to help you. Come now, and don't make this so painful." He glanced at the landlady. "Perhaps you will have someone ready her things."

"Nooo!" Tess wailed, routed to complete panic by his unaccountable knowledge of whom she had married. "I won't go with you!" She felt the stair at her back, but there was no escape there. Stephen, with his calm, awful smile, reached for her again. She darted around him and made a dash for the front door.

A large hand caught her arm, one of the constables. She cried out, and began to struggle in earnest. "He's not my husband—he has no right! Let me go— Oh God, please let me go!"

The man's fingers tightened painfully, but he sounded sympathetic as he mumbled, "Now, now, ma'am, don't take a fret. Nobody's going to hurt you."

"He will! He'll lock me in." She tried to wrench away, and then threw herself toward the man, going down on her knees with her cheek against the rough wool of his trousers. "He'll lock me in the dark. You can't believe him, you can't—please listen. The marriage was anulled. There are no children. It's all a lie, a lie. Please!"

"Oh, Tess. My dearest love," Stephen said, and she knew the grief in his voice would doom her.

She covered her face and shrieked, "Don't listen to him!"

"God bless you, little mum." The constable raised her by the shoulders. She looked up into his ruddy face, sobbing, and almost succumbed to the fatherly concern there. Then the cunning of fear saved her. She put out her hands to the man, as if accepting his protection. When he loosened his hold on her in response, she tore herself free. She rushed for the door and flung it open, stumbling out onto the dew-slick walk. A passerby halted in surprise and she went headlong into him, knocking him entirely off his feet. The sound of shouting spurred her, but encumbering skirts and wet pavement made running perilous. It was so foggy—if only she could vanish into the fog . . .

She tripped, went down on one knee, and scrambled up again. She heard pounding feet close behind her. A cab rattled by; she darted out into the street as it passed, waving at the startled horse that pulled an omnibus going the opposite direction. The horse shied; the driver shouted and she sprang onto the landing, trying to push her way onto the moving bus. The conductor gave her a hand, but when he asked for two pence and received only a wild look, he suddenly seemed to become aware of the pursuit. The bus was already grinding to a halt under the loud demands of the two constables. Tess jumped off, far beyond rational thought, and fell hard onto the pavement. Before she could rise, conductor, constables, and several passengers had converged to prevent her.

Gasping for breath, she let them haul her to her feet. Her hair was streaming down her face, her skirt was torn. She stood with her head lowered and fought the need to retch. Then she heard him: Stephen, quietly issuing instructions. The hated voice tapped her last reserve of terrified strength. She began to kick and scream, fighting every inch of progress toward a waiting carriage, so that they had to lift her bodily, three hefty men who swore as she scratched and bit. She saw Stephen, standing by the open carriage door with a look of sorrow. "Liar!" she howled at him. "Let me go! You can't—" She braced her feet against the steps and struggled. It was dark inside the carriage; dark, but they threw her inside as if she were a bag of flour. Her head hit the sharp edge of the opposite handle and for a moment hot agony sparked through her brain. Then Stephen was inside, and the door slammed shut. She lay on the floor at his feet and curled herself into a ball, clutching her head as the carriage rocked into motion.

The sounds of the crowd that had gathered receded, except for the shrill cries of street urchins who chased the vehicle for a little way, hurling incoherent insults. Then even they dropped behind, and there was only the growl of the wheels on the stone and Tess's muffled sobbing.

"I shall have to record the names of those fellows," Stephen said calmly. "Should I ever need witness you're truly a madwoman."

Tess made no answer. She was hanging on to consciousness by a thread. Her knees and her hands throbbed, and the bouncing of the hard floor made her teeth rattle. Her empty stomach heaved. She turned her face into her arms, swallowing bile.

"Get up," he said. "You're making yourself quite disgusting."

The tone of voice was one she knew. She would disobey it at her peril. She raised herself onto trembling arms. As she did, the ring swung free on its chain and hit softly against her breast. She clutched at it. Suddenly, she was glad of the darkness in the carriage. With a sharp yank, she pulled at the chain, disguising the move by shoving herself upward into the seat opposite Stephen. The tiny gold links dug into her skin and then snapped at the clasp. The ring fell free into her palm.

She held on to the cool metal, unable to think where to conceal it, or even why it seemed so imperative that she should. But the need to concentrate helped: her head began to clear. The place where she had struck the door handle ached and stung, but that helped, too. It made her angry. It made her remember that she was not helpless. She was no longer in Stephen's legal power. This was an abduction, a criminal act, and nothing less.

Stephen had taken her by surprise once. His actions after their wedding had been so unexpected and unbelievable that she had not understood soon enough to save herself. But she knew him now. She had to keep her wits about her. They were not at Ashland—there would be chances to escape. She bit her lip and held on to the ring.

"Are you prepared to be rational now?" he asked through the stuffy murk of the closed coach.

She took a deep breath. "Yes." She could see just enough to tell that he was looking at her. "Why, Stephen?" She kept her voice as steady as she could. "Why have you done this?"

"Because you've made yourself an embarrassment to me. And it's clear you intend to make yourself more of one if I don't take you in hand."

"An embarrassment."

"I should tell you," he said, "that for all intents and purposes the annulment has been overturned."

"That's impossible."

"My dear, don't delude yourself. It is entirely possible. The incident has been erased and forgotten by those few who ever knew of it."

"But Mr. Taylor—"

"I'll see to Taylor. He won't trouble us further."

The statement was made with perfect equanimity, as if he spoke of nothing more than exterminating a rat. Tess felt a renewed burst of panic. "What are you planning?"

He did not answer. A stray glimmer of light through the shade lit his pale eyes as he looked at her. Tess was suddenly afraid—far more afraid than she had yet been. She could not bring herself to ask again. It was something Stephen would try to do, she told herself, undermine her confidence with half-answers and insinuations. She put a false boldness into her voice as she asked, "How did you know where to find me?"

"I had a telegram. From Calais. A message that arrived on the same ship as yourself. You did me the favor of pursuing the obvious course of crossing to Dover, and the local constables were helpful in searching the town. No one sympathizes with a runaway wife, I fear."

"The same ship—" Tess couldn't conceal her astonishment. "A message from whom?"

"A servant of mine. One Robert Stark."

For a moment the name meant nothing, and then the memory burst upon her: the glow of a cheroot in the gallery at Ashland, and that same glow beneath her window in Tahiti. The smell of smoke . . . she started to speak, lost her voice, and found it again, just barely. "My God, Stephen—"

Once again, he held his silence, but she could not explain away the implication this time. She remembered the dream of cold hands on her mouth; she remembered the marlinespike. She remembered the flash of metal in the quivering light of a match. An embarrassment, Stephen had said. She had become an embarrassment to him.

Her eyes began to water. She blinked. "What are you going to do?"

"That depends. I'm not pleased with your escapades. I want them stopped."

She said, a little too unevenly, "You can't hurt me, Stephen. You can't just let me disappear like before. My husband—"

"Your husband." He leaned forward abruptly and gripped her elbow, dragging her half off the seat toward him. "Yes, Stark informed me of this 'husband' of yours. Just what is it you and this tramp sea captain had planned, my lady? Do you think to frighten me with a name?"

Tess clutched the ring, trying not to drop it under the painful pressure of his fingers. It had long puzzled her, that ring, for it was not a mistress's bauble as she had first assumed. It bore the engraved seal of Ashland: no rightful property of an illegitimate son.

"I never thought to do anything to you," she said between her teeth. "Except never see you again."

He let her go. "Then why come back?" he hissed. "Why flaunt yourself under the name of a boy who died sixteen years ago? There's no gain to be had in that kind of farce. My dear cousin Gryphon was hacked to pieces with the rest of 'em, and all the world knows it."

She almost exclaimed: "Cousin!"

Almost.

The story of the attack that had slaughtered the Meridons of Ashland was common knowledge. It had been related to Tess with relish by Larice. That children had died, Tess had known. That a boy named Gryphon Meridon had been among them, she had not. She held on to the ring and kept her mouth squeezed shut, thinking madly.

Stephen said, "What did you hope to accomplish?"

"I . . . nothing. Just to . . . embarrass you, as you said." She added quickly, "His real name is Frost, I think."

"And you actually went through a marriage ceremony with this vermin? I suppose you slept with him." The words were twisted with disgust.

"I'm his wife in truth," she said, in a voice low with rage. "And it becomes you ill to speak of vermin, Stephen."

"Wife in truth . . ." He leaned back on the seat. "You're his widow now. Stark had at least the wit to stay and take care of that for me."

Tess stiffened. "You're lying." Stephen could have no more news than she if his information had indeed come on the same ship. Gryf had been alive when she sailed. He could take care of himself. She clenched her hands together over the ring and prayed that he could take care of himself.

"Only speculating on the odds. If Stark fails, I surely won't, should your precious captain come after you."

She said sharply, "You needn't worry about that. He doesn't want me. He sent me away."

"Were you such a failure, then? After one night of being a 'wife in truth'?" Stephen laughed dryly. "Well, never mind. You know my tastes lie in other quarters."

"I hate you," she whispered.

He moved suddenly in the dark, and in a moment he caught her, though she fought to get away. He twisted her arm behind her and forced her down onto the floor at his feet. "Do you hate me?" he asked softly. He stroked her throat between his thumb and forefinger, and then gently closed his hand over her windpipe. "Good. I want that. I want you to fear me, Mrs. Eliot." His grip grew stronger, cutting off her air. "I want you to beg."

She knew better than to struggle. As his fingers tightened on her throat she rasped, "Please."

His hold relaxed infinitesimally: the old game. "But I'm not pleased," he murmured. The pressure on her neck increased again. "Not at all."

"Please . . ." She had to force the words out against the choking strength. "Please . . . don't . . ."

This time the compression did not abate. "I'm not pleased," he repeated. Between the brutal pain at her throat and his grip on her arm she felt awareness slipping. Her lungs swelled, demanding air. Her hand had lost feeling; she was sure the ring had fallen free. She jerked convulsively, and the vise tightened. The darkness pressed in. "Don't kill me!" she gasped. "Please—"

He let her go.

She slumped sideways, swallowing air that burned her bruised windpipe. As sense returned to her aching head she stayed silently on the floor, awaiting permission to do otherwise. Furtively, she felt one hand with the other, locating the ring amid the tingling of her blood-starved fingers.

She rested her head against the jolting comfort of the padded seat and prayed for strength. Her greatest fear was for the child. She did not think Stephen would actually murder her, except perhaps by accident. But if he locked her up and starved her as he had before . . .

Stephen said nothing more, having made his point. Tess closed her eyes. She was determined to get free. She was burning with it. But she had to rest now. When her chance came she had to be ready and able to move.

The *Arcanum* made Papeete to Calais in eighty-seven days. The French steamer had taken eighty-nine, but

she'd had four days' head start. Gryf missed Tess by
forty-eight hours.

It might as well have been forty-eight years.

Tracing her to Dover was easy. Finding the hotel
where she'd stayed was easy. There was absolutely no
question there that they remembered the woman who
had registered as Mrs. Meridon. They remembered her
well, and were only too pleased to tell Gryf the story of
how she had left.

So he had come inexorably to this: standing in the
rain in the dark outside of the gates of Ashland Court.
He had developed a kind of fatalism, a resignation like
the stolid misery of the wet and patient hack that stood
beside him. He was afraid, but it was a fear that had
gone so deep that it seemed almost academic. It wasn't
courage that had brought him here. It was simply the
mind making the body move, and doing what had to be
done.

He did not look beyond the goal of finding Tess. To
see her safe and out of Stephen's hands was all Gryf allowed himself to hope. The other things: the guilt, the
longing, the desolation his life had become since their
parting—those he consigned to the same place as his
fear for her. He could not afford to think of them, not
if he wanted to keep his wits and his sanity. Nothing
had changed; he still knew his weakness, knew how
achingly easy it would be to fall back into the deadly
snare of passion and need. He could not let himself
imagine a future. With or without her. Either way promised bitter pain.

But a quick move was necessary. Stark had made it
clear in Tahiti that Eliot meant to be rid of Tess. Dinner
with a talkative pubkeeper in the tiny village near Ashland had confirmed the reason: everyone "knew" that
the young mistress was quite mad. She had tried to set

fire to the house; she had pretended to cut off her fingers; she had threatened Mr. Eliot's man with a long-handled carving knife. She'd been locked up for safety, and finally taken away a year ago to an asylum in France.

As far as Gryf could tell, the only thing everyone didn't know was that there was no Mrs. Eliot anymore. An annulment was never mentioned.

A few more questions revealed that yes, the house was open. Mr. Eliot was at his home; he'd come back from the city just the day before. Old Jack Harper had driven him down from the station at Alton. Alone? The pubkeeper was sure of it. There wasn't room in Jack's dogcart for three. Yes, Eliot was well-enough as a landlord—not friendly, but fair. He'd turned off most of the servants when his wife took ill in the head, but his agent had found them all proper places elsewhere. Still, Eliot was a strange fish. Just look in his eyes, and a fellow could tell that. The man was too cool by half. Wouldn't gamble that he hadn't driven his poor bride mad. Those eyes, y'know. And she had been a pretty thing, too, though the tenants only saw her that once, when he first brought her home.

Gryf listened to the gossip about Eliot and his wife amid the wood and the casks and the cordial bottles, and then made his way out into the thunderstorm despite the exhortations of the pubkeeper that it would surely be over soon, if Gryf would just stay for another round. The man was right; by the time Gryf stood outside Ashland's closed gates the rain had begun to abate. The gatehouse was empty. In the moonlight that came and went he saw only the road that curved up through the trees beyond the iron fancywork. He turned the horse back the way they had come and unfastened its bridle, looped the reins into a tight bundle and secured them beneath the cantle of the saddle, so that the poor beast wouldn't entangle itself in some bush as it made its way home. He gave the animal a sharp slap on the rump, and the horse responded with a look which seemed to say that Gryf had only added further insult to the injury of going for a ride on such a night. Then it heaved a sigh, broke into a trot, and disappeared into the shadows of the lane.

The wall was probably ten feet high, streaked gray and black by moisture. Even with its smooth surface, it looked more negotiable than the spiked iron gate. Gryf ranged along it a short distance until he found a suitable tree.

Half a lifetime spent in the rigging of a clipper had given him some practice at climbing things. A tight frock coat and an even more annoying waistcoat didn't help: he heard a seam rip at his shoulder as he swung himself up. The rough bark bit into his hands, and his hat—which he never remembered he was wearing until too late—fell off at the first opportunity. He didn't trust the branch that hung out over the wall to hold him, so he wedged his foot against the trunk and leaned, reaching for the top of the wall. His hand scraped over the slashing edge of broken glass. He snatched it back with an oath, sucking furiously at the side of his palm.

The cut was deep. After hanging a moment with his mouth full of blood and the fingers of his other hand slipping on the wet, ragged bark, he gave up on staunching the flow and levered himself higher, so that he could catch the wall with his feet as he dropped. His boots hit the glass-embedded top; he balanced for a moment, feeling shards press into the soles of his feet even through the leather, and then kicked free. He landed, slipped, and caught himself before he went face-first on the slick grass.

The rain had stopped, though thunder still moaned a sepulchral warning somewhere ahead of him. He pressed his fingers over the stinging wound until he had some notion that the bleeding had stopped. In the dark it was hard to tell. He wiped both hands on the grass, and started up the long drive to the house.

Outlined against the lightning-lit clouds, Ashland Court looked like something conjured in the mind of Edgar Allan Poe. The house was old, in its beginnings a Norman keep with a round tower that was now the only symmetrical thing about the place. Gryf knew its history: an addition in the time of Henry III and another in the reign of Elizabeth, a major renovation a century ago that had not come near to changing the facade to a tame Palladian elegance, and then another folly, perpetrated by Gryf's great-grandmother—a wing which made an earnest attempt at being a Greek temple. It should have been ridiculous, that house, but now as once before it seemed to Gryf a magnificent sprawl, and it galled him to come for a second time as nothing but a beggar to the door.

With that thought in mind he made some attempt to straighten his neckcloth before he rang the bell. With entirely another thought in mind he checked his revolver. He had no real plan; instinct would have to carry him. His hand was bleeding again; he could see the dark stain in the glow from the fan light above the door. The bell sounded a single peal in the far depths of the house, and a very long time later, the door cracked open.

An old man peeped around the huge slab of carved wood. His rheumy eyes darted about nervously, searching the shadows on the stoop. Gryf felt a twinge of pity for the servant's apprehension. He dredged a name from childhood stories that his father had told him. "Badger?" he asked softly. "Mr. Badger?"

The old man seemed to start, and looked half-behind him in apparent confusion. Then he turned back, and pulled the big door ajar. Dim light poured over Gryf.

Mr. Badger's watery old eyes widened. "My lor—" he croaked. The half-word seemed to be too much for him; he stared at Gryf and said no more, though his mouth worked spasmodically. His seamy hand covered his left breast: for a moment, Gryf thought the man would collapse in a pale heap upon the marble floor.

"I'm sorry," Gryf said quickly. "I didn't mean to frighten you. It's late, I know—"

"My lord," Badger repeated, and now there was a note of wonder in his voice. He still stared very hard at Gryf.

"May I come in?" Gryf asked, after a moment.

The ancient blinked, and seemed to come to his senses. He ducked his bald head and shuffled backward, pulling the door open. "To be sure, my lord. Come in, come in; what am I thinking? I've grown to an old fool." As Gryf stepped through the door, he felt a distinct and exploratory pluck at his damp sleeve. He turned questioningly, and the butler ducked his head again. "An old fool," he repeated. "You'll forgive me. You've lost your hat again, I see. No matter. I know you'll say you've more where that one come from. So proud to see you, sir."

Gryf frowned. He had been prepared for a rebuff, demanding entrance to the house at such an hour. He had not expected to be treated like a familiar guest. He hesitated, looking intently at the butler for some sign of deception, and saw none. Only a stooped old man who stared at the floor as if too frightened to meet Gryf's eyes. Gryf chewed his lip, regretting the dismay he had caused. He said quietly, "Mr. Badger—"

"Oh, sir," the butler said, raising his head. To Gryf's

shock, the wrinkled cheeks were wet with tears. Badger reached out and clasped Gryf's hands with an unexpected strength. "My lord, forgive me. I don't question it. I'm an old man, and when I see what they done to you . . . but it's nothing, 'tis only that I'm glad, for I never thought to look on your face again this side of the grave, and if you've come for me, I'm ready. I've made me peace. I'll go with you and gladly, for I've been lonely these years, and I've a mind to see my good lady again, God rest her."

"Badger—" Gryf said again, helplessly. He glanced toward the stairs, afraid that Eliot or someone else might appear at any moment. When he looked back again at the butler's shining face, it came to Gryf suddenly that Badger's real name was Bridgewater. His father's stories—he recalled one, of how the butler had come to be christened Mr. Badger by a mischievous boy too young to know better. Gryf had forgotten the story, but he remembered the point: no one called the dignified Bridgewater "Mr. Badger" and escaped a whaling. No one except Uncle Alex.

"Good God, you don't think . . ." Gryf stopped, and checked the stairs again. He looked back at the elderly butler's hands, still clenched firmly around his own. "I'm Gryphon," he said softly. "Arthur's son." He squeezed the bony fingers. "No ghost."

At Badger's dubious look, Gryf smiled encouragingly. "I'm bleeding all over you. My father would've skinned me for that."

He felt the old man's hands tremble. Badger gazed up into Gryf's face for one long, searching moment. Instead of showing relief, the butler's wrinkled features crumbled entirely. "Master Gryphon," he said in a quavering voice. "Master Gryphon. Welcome home, then." And he suddenly took Gryf in a hard embrace.

Gryf patted ineffectually at the old man's back as he wept against the bloody shirt, praying that Eliot wouldn't come on them like this. Gryf did not have it in him to push Mr. Badger away. It was stupidity to have admitted his identity, but the elderly servant's joy was somehow worth the risk. Gryf hadn't imagined how good it would feel, to have someone say honestly, "Welcome home."

In the end it was a thought of Badger's own safety that made Gryf disengage himself. The butler stood back and produced an ivory-colored handkerchief. "Your pardon, sir," he mumbled apologetically after he blew his nose. "I'm an old man, I am."

"I need your help," Gryf said. "Badly."

Mr. Badger composed himself a little. "You do look a bit hagged, sir," he agreed. "I'll open a room, and bring up hot water."

"No." Gryf stopped the servant as he was turning away. "Don't bother with that. Where's Eliot?"

Badger hesitated, and looked confused.

"Stephen," Gryf added. "He's here?"

"Mr. Stephen—" The butler licked his thin lips. "He won't be master now, will he? Now you've come home, Lord Gryphon?"

A whole new set of problems opened up before Gryf at that surmise. "Badger," he said fiercely, "I want you to give me your word, your solemn oath, that you will never tell anyone that you've seen or heard of me."

"But my lord—"

"Swear it." Gryf took the old man's arm and squeezed. "And then I want you to go back to your room, and lock yourself in there, and don't come out no matter what you hear. Where's the rest of the staff?"

"There's no one, sir. Save the mute boy what keeps the hounds and the stable at night. The housekeeper's gone to her sister's. Mr. Stephen don't keep staff any-more."

Gryf ran the implications of that through his mind several ways. "All right. You're going to your room?"

"Of course, sir. If you ask."

"I ask. Where's Stephen now?"

"In the tapestry room, my lord."

"Where's that?"

Badger gave Gryf a look of surprise. Gryf reddened. "I've never had a guided tour," he said, a little roughly.

"Upstairs, my lord. I can tell him you're here, if you like."

"*No.*"

The old butler pursed his lips. After a moment, he re-cited the directions in a low voice, while staring at the floor. Then he glanced up. "My lord, it comes to me that you're thinking you're in danger here, in your own home."

Gryf tensed, waiting for the servant to withdraw his earlier loyalty and sound the alarm. But the idea appar-ently did not occur to Mr. Badger. He looked long at Gryf. " 'Tisn't right," was all the old man said. " 'Tisn't what your grandfather wanted."

"Do you swear you've never seen me? No matter what."

Mr. Badger shifted his feet.

"Please," Gryf said. "Do that for me. For my father." If something went wrong—he did not want Badger im-plicated.

A bell sounded shrilly from below. They both jumped.

"That'll be Mr. Stephen, sir. He'll be wondering who come to the door."

"I'll answer it. Go on." Gryf gave the stooped form a slight push in the direction of the kitchen stairs.

"You, sir? 'Tisn't your place, my lord. I—"

"Just go," Gryf said impatiently, allowing a little of his captain's imperative to color his voice. "Do I have your word you never saw me?"

Mr. Badger took a few steps, and then turned. He looked at Gryf unhappily. "I swear, my lord. Because you ask. But I don't like it."

Chapter 16

The tapestry room was mercifully easy to find, on the second floor, directly across from the huge staircase landing. Gryf climbed the stairs alongside his own shadow, cast by candles from inside clear bubble globes set at intervals on the carved rail. His outsized silhouette passed over gilded frames and paintings: men in wigs and women in high, stiff collars, and one that made him stop, in spite of himself—the saintly Titian masterpiece that Gryf had been told of when he was a boy.

He wrenched his mind back to the business at hand as he approached the door at the head of the stairs, hoping to God he had gotten the directions right. With no idea of what Stephen would be doing and no knowledge of the layout of the room, Gryf reckoned his best approach was complete surprise. He cocked his revolver and took hold of the knob, shoving the heavy door wide before he had a chance to listen to his own second thoughts.

The door crashed open with a hollow boom. The effect was everything Gryf could have hoped. Stephen Eliot, dressed in his shirt sleeves, leaped up from an armchair by the fire and turned, exclaiming, "What the—"

Gryf leveled the revolver. "Move away from the bell, Eliot."

Stephen's face lost its look of shock. He seemed to regain his composure instantly. With a quizzically cocked brow, he took two steps to a position just out of reach of the bellpull. "What's this?" he asked softly, his eyes on the gun.

"I want Tess."

A stillness came over Stephen's taut figure. He surveyed Gryf. "Everett, isn't it?" he said slowly. "It's been some time. London, I think . . . the season past."

Gryf stayed silent. Thunder rumbled sullenly in the background, and a stray draft lifted one of the dull-colored tapestries and sent a fluttering ripple along its lower edge. He could see Stephen sorting possibilities in his mind.

"You want my wife," he said after a moment. "I'm afraid I don't take your meaning."

Without lowering the gun, Gryf reached behind him and swung the door shut with a crash as loud as the first. "I understand we're alone here," he said deliberately.

Stephen's blue eyes flicked with faint contempt over Gryf's figure. "Have you shot all the staff, then? Rather messy business, by the looks of it."

Gryf suppressed a spark of admiration for Stephen's calm. He could have used some of that sangfroid himself. His hand was steady, but he had an irritating urge to look down to see if his palm was bleeding again. He fought down the panicky thought that the old butler's actions had all been an elaborate charade and the local blues would be arriving shortly. Stephen's self-possession was doing exactly what it was meant to do:

subtly shifting the balance of power. "Eliot," Gryf said, "tell me where she is."

"My wife?" Stephen inclined his head curiously. "I remember now—you were one of the spurned suitors. Perhaps you should have made a pair after all. It appears that you're both lunatics."

"Oh, yes," Gryf agreed. "Completely mad." He raised the revolver and fired at the mirror above the fireplace. Glass exploded over Stephen's head and came down in a waterfall of silver shards onto the mantel. "But serious," he added with a slight smile.

Stephen had jumped when the gun went off. He turned back toward the shattered mirror. "So I see." He looked ruefully at Gryf. "Before you take it upon yourself to redecorate the entire room in this manner, let me tell you that my wife is in France, in an asylum."

"No games, Eliot. She's not in France. And she isn't your wife anymore."

For a split second, Stephen's urbanity cracked. His face lost a shade of color. Gryf fingered the trigger under the other man's probing stare.

"God in Heaven," Stephen murmured. "I see now."

Gryf took a step forward. His boot grated on shards of glass. "Where is she?"

"You're Meridon." The tone in Eliot's voice was dead certain. "How the devil did I ever mistake it?"

It was disconcerting to be identified with such speed. Gryf had hoped to edge around the truth, to reveal it when it might do him the most good.

"Cousin," Stephen said, and held out his hand. "By God, it's good to see you. We all thought—"

"I know what you thought," Gryf snapped. "I'm not here for a family reunion. Let's understand each other, Eliot—Robert Stark is in the custody of the military governor in Tahiti. I put him there."

Eliot had completely regained his self-possession. "Did you?" he said thoughtfully. "And now you've come after your new wife. Do you love her, Cousin? Or was your marriage just part of some obscure plan to dispossess me?"

Gryf didn't bother to answer that.

"I hope all this unpleasantness isn't for the purpose of putting me out," Stephen added. "You could have managed much more sensibly, you know. Just come back and prove who you are, and I would gladly stand aside. I don't know why you've waited so long."

But the small, cold smile in Stephen's eyes said he knew exactly why. Gryf said skeptically, "Of course. It wouldn't bother you at all to give up Ashland."

"Naturally, it would. But if you have some proof of who you are, I wouldn't have much choice, would I?"

"You seem to have convinced yourself who I am easily enough."

Stephen shrugged. "I can see certain . . . resemblances between you and Lord Alexander. Ill-considered impetuosity, for one thing. But I'm afraid my childhood recollections would hardly hold up in a court of chancery, should I choose to submit them to examination. Which wouldn't really be in my self-interest, now that I think of it."

"You might give your self-interest a little more thought," Gryf said. "I have ample proof to make things uncomfortable for you."

"Then it's to be blackmail merely?"

"Call it a trade. I want Tess."

"Tess. I should have thought she was still amusing herself with man-eating flowers in equatorial Africa or some such place."

"At the hotel in Dover they told me differently."

"Ah." Stephen looked down, his hands clasped behind his back, and flipped a shard of mirror over with his foot. "You do have a talent for ferreting out unpleasant details. Assuming I can produce her, then—what do I receive in return?"

Gryf waggled the gun. "Besides not having a bullet put through your head?"

A ghostly flicker of lightning at the window punctuated the words, and a roll of thunder followed.

"That wouldn't be a clever move," Stephen said calmly as the rumble died away. "If you really want to find her."

Gryf wanted to believe that Stephen meant she was still alive. But it was too easy to imagine himself in the other man's position, staring down the barrel of a gun and looking for ways to gain time. Stephen would deal, whether he had anything to deal with or not.

Just as Gryf was about to do.

"I'll give you Ashland's signet," he said. "And then I'll disappear for good."

Stephen looked up abruptly from the floor, and Gryf blessed himself as an extraordinarily lucky bastard. It had been a wild chance, that Tess had not handed the ring over to Stephen, but Eliot's expression of surprise was not feigned.

"The signet," Stephen echoed. He smiled faintly. "You do know how to make a trade, Cousin. You have it with you?"

"Do you have Lady Tess with you?" Gryf responded dryly.

"She's belowstairs, actually. In the cellars."

Gryf's heart leaped, but he kept his face emotionless. He stood back from the door and jerked his head. "Let's go."

Stephen made a move, not toward the door, but toward the small table where he had been sitting. Gryf stepped forward in quick reaction and Stephen froze. "The lamp, Cousin," he said, looking sideways at Gryf. "We'll need to take the lamp."

There was no gas at Ashland; the ancient house was lit by candles or oil. Gryf didn't trust Stephen with any possible weapon, even a lamp, but there was little choice. To carry the light himself, along with his heavy revolver, was just as precarious. He gave Stephen a brief nod. "Left hand. Just keep your right where I can see it."

Stephen obeyed. He lifted the lamp and preceded Gryf out, ignoring the threatening gun with aristocratic panache. The man was well-suited to be master of Ashland, Gryf thought, and the notion carried a strange lack of resentment. He himself felt like what Eliot had called him once, a rustic yokel, following his cousin down the magnificent staircase and through the vaulted entry into rooms and corridors he could not have imagined in his craziest dreams of richness. He did not even know what they were for, these bare, stately halls of statuary and gilded plasterwork that gleamed in the moving light of the lamp. His muddy boots set up an echo on floors laid in fabulous patterns of colored marble, and when they passed into a long gallery with high, shuttered windows all along one side, he instinctively avoided stepping on the red and gold carpet.

Stephen stopped suddenly in the gallery, and looked back at Gryf. "Our ancestors," Eliot said, raising the lamp so that dark portraits leaped out from the damask-covered walls.

Gryf glanced at them and back at Eliot suspiciously.

Stephen smiled. "You aren't interested?"

"Not at the moment."

"That's the late marquess." He pointed at one of the portraits in spite of Gryf's words. "Your grandfather.

Lord Alexander's portrait hung next to it." Stephen paused as a wild, silent glimmer from outside spread a crazy geometry of light across the walls. He added in a peculiar voice, "I had him taken down."

A cracking burst of thunder overhead made Gryf start. It echoed down the hall.

"Are you afraid of storms?" Stephen said, and his tone was again strange. Almost gentle.

"No," Gryf said.

"I am." Stephen stared at the blank place on the wall. "Especially here. She used to bring me here, and tell me stories about the pictures."

Gryf frowned at his cousin. "Who?" he asked, after a moment.

Stephen looked at him, and then back at the portraits. "You wouldn't remember, would you? No . . . I always heard about you, out there in India. I used to dream about it. What it would be like. Warm, I thought. When it was so damned cold in here and she wouldn't let me have a fire or a candle, I used to think about India. I used to hate you, because I knew you must be warm."

Gryf shifted his feet, caught between impatience and unease. "What are you talking about?"

"Childhood," Stephen said cryptically. "At Ashland."

There was something so set in his expression as he stared at the paintings that Gryf found himself peering through the murk too, as if expecting to see one of those poised figures step down from its canvas in the fitful balefire. He asked, half against his own will, "Who told you stories?"

Stephen was silent for a long moment. Then he said, "Mary. The nursemaid. She used to lock me in here."

"Lock you in . . ." Gryf was startled. "Why?"

"I suppose I was a bad little boy," Stephen said lightly. But there was a bitterness beneath the words. He held out his hand, palm upward, and even in the lamp-light Gryf could see the old scar tissue there. "She rather favored scalding my hand over a candle flame for lesser offenses."

"You're joking."

Stephen smiled slightly. "No, Cousin. I don't consider it a joking matter."

"I can't believe my grandfather—"

"Your grandfather didn't give a pin for an Eliot. He lived and breathed for Lord Alex." Stephen's voice softened. "We all did. When he was here . . . it was different. He took me riding once or twice."

Suddenly Gryf saw it all too clearly, the picture Stephen painted, of a lonely boy in a house like this. It made him angry to understand so easily, because he had always thought of Stephen Eliot as the enemy, as the man who had taken what should have been Gryf's own, and now . . . now a completely insane notion took him: that they might have been friends; that somewhere, somebody had failed them both and brought them to this. He stood there with his gun aimed at the only flesh and blood family he had left and hated whoever had made Eliot what he was; whoever had made a twisted man of a lonely boy. That was who Gryf would have killed, and gladly.

He said, "Move on, Eliot. I don't see us making any progress toward the cellar."

Stephen inclined his head, the aristocrat again, and went ahead as if he were doing no more than giving a visitor a tour of the house.

There was a door at the end of the gallery; he opened it, and led the way into another marble hall and through an ornate, narrow arch. He turned, as if to go left, and kept turning . . . too far. Gryf had the thought and the reaction at the same time, an instant late, as the lamp tilted. He jerked back from the crash of glass and flame that exploded at his feet and ran fluidly across the opening. A yard-high wall of burning oil sprang to life. Gryf cursed viciously, caught behind it. Before he had even looked up, Eliot was gone. Stephen had picked his spot well; passages went off in the dark in three directions beyond the arch, and the fiery liquid was oozing across the stone floor toward an upholstered bench beneath a hanging banner. Gryf tore off his coat and threw it down; struggled out of his waistcoat and added that, and when the last of the flames were smothered he was left in sudden, utter darkness.

He fumbled his gun back into his hand and held his breath, listening. The low growl of thunder obscured sound, but there might have been footsteps somewhere ahead. He moved backward, with one hand on the wall, unwilling to chase Stephen into the dark.

Gryf had not the faintest idea where he was. Damn Ashland for its confusion of rooms and corridors; he would have gone straight for the cellars if he'd known how. As it was, he could not even find his way back to the entrance hall.

Staying close to the windows, where lightning gave intermittent illumination, he edged along until he came to a recess. Instead of a door, it held a statue: he nearly lost an eye on the outstretched marble hand. Around the other side, he slid his palm along the wall and encountered a doorknob. That surprised and then elated him; from what he had seen in the light of Stephen's lamp, every public entry in Ashland was a grand one, with a full foot's width of carved frame. This had to be some servant's passage: a private shortcut to the kitchen and cellars. It opened silently outward beneath his touch.

A breath of cool, musty air emanated from the ob-

scurity behind the door. He waited for another flash of
lightning. When it came, he made out a rough stone
wall, and just beside the door, a small wooden pedestal,
complete with candles, a blackened brass snuff and a tin
box that would be certain to hold matches. He opened
the box and extracted one, silently blessing the efficient
lamplighters of Ashland as a sharp scratch against the
stone brought forth the familiar flare of blue light.

Armed with a lit candle and two extras stuffed into
his waistband, he took a guess at a direction. The corridor, hardly wider than his shoulders, ran the length of
the room he had been in and then intersected a broader
hall. He headed left at random. At intervals steep stairs
led off the passage, up, and so he did not investigate
them. He was trying to second-guess Stephen, no easy
task, and the only conclusion Gryf could come to was
that he needed to find Tess and get out in a hurry.

Inside the stone corridor no lightning penetrated, but
the low-timbred thunder seemed to make a continual
echoing roll. It rose to a dull boom at one point, almost
as if another door had slammed shut, and he stopped.
The candle sputtered and went out in a gentle rush of
air that swept past.

Gryf turned his head. He pressed against the cold
stone, staring into nothing in both directions. After a
moment, the unmistakable click of footsteps punctuated
the thunder, but he could not make out the direction.
The sound seemed to come from all around him.

He froze, straining his ears to locate the source. The
sound grew louder, closer, and still more confused with
echoes. Gryf tensed, and drew a great breath of air into
his lungs.

"Eliot," he shouted, and the word reverberated off
the walls and ceilings and floors, as directionless as the
footsteps, he hoped. While it still rolled through the cor-

ridor the response came: a flash of light to Gryf's left, and the simultaneous report of gunfire that mingled with the echo and created a crescendo of sound in the hollow space.

Gryf scrambled. The shot answered one question, anyway: Stephen was armed now, and he had murder on his mind. Gryf ran, away from the light, one hand out to find the next side passage. He came to it and threw himself up the stairs, cracking his knee on the cold stone as another shot rang within the walls. An involuntary yelp escaped him. That sound too carried, weirdly loud in the strange acoustics of the corridor. He crouched on the stairs, rubbing his knee, and listened as the noise died away. Then there was silence, no footsteps, no voice. Only the dull rumble of thunder. He waited.

And waited longer.

And then he began to moan.

It was a fairly good imitation of a wounded man, but the damned echoes garbled it. He stopped and listened, then started again. Over his own voice he heard a soft footfall. He drew the trigger of his revolver back. Another footfall, and another: measured, suspicious. He left off moaning and set up a slow, ragged pant. The footsteps paused. Gryf made his breath uneven, a gurgling vibration in his throat; a death rattle. One last squeaky gasp, and he went silent.

Half a minute later, Stephen took the bait. Gryf counted the footsteps . . . seven, eight, nine . . . *close.*

He fired into absolute blackness.

Missed.

He threw himself down the stairs after the shadow he had seen in the split second of detonation, and fired once again in that direction, too wildly to do anything but keep Stephen on the run. Gryf himself went with all

speed the opposite way—he hoped it was the opposite
way—careering between the walls in the dark until he
smashed face-first into solid stone.

He staggered back, knocked half-silly by the impact.
Some angel of mercy kept him from triggering his gun
and killing himself in the ricochet. He put his hand over
his face and bent double. God, it felt like his jaw was
broken, his nose and all his teeth, too. He probed them
carefully: they were solid, except for a stabbing agony
that went through his jaw when he moved it in one direction.

The corridor was silent again. He might have hit
Stephen; there was a decent chance he had, in that last
unaimed shot within the confined space. But he wasn't
going back to find out—too easy to figure Eliot might
try the same fake that Gryf had. He felt the walls beside
him, looking for another side passage.

"Merid-don-n-n . . ." The name was just discernible
in the hissing echoes. Gryf jerked around and plastered
himself against the wall. The sibilant vibration came
again. "Wrong-g-g w-w-way . . ."

It was late information. Eliot's gun cracked again,
deafening echo and yellow fire, and Gryf flung himself
down. As the sound died away he began crawling out of
the dead end on his belly, quiet, as quiet as he could, an
awkward scramble to keep his boots from dragging on
the ringing stone. It wasn't far to the stairs he had just
left. He had a headache from trying to see in the blackness; couldn't even tell if his eyes were open or shut. He
didn't fire, for fear of giving away his location, and it
was either that same fear or lack of ammunition that
kept Stephen's gun silent.

Nose to the floor, Gryf inched forward. He could not
tell how far or fast, or from what distance Eliot's voice
had come. Gryf was terrified that his exploring hand

would encounter Stephen's ankle instead of the staircase. The thought of dying at Eliot's feet in the godforsaken dust and dark made Gryf sick to his stomach, and the pain that pierced his jaw with every move didn't help settle it. A cobweb spread light, sticky fingers across his face. He held his breath.

It was like something out of a penny-dreadful weekly, lying there struggling not to sneeze and reveal himself. He rolled to one side in silent convulsions, and his boot heel scraped loudly across the floor.

It was enough. The hall resounded with Stephen's shot. Gryf saw—actually saw—the blue-white spark where the bullet hit the floor a foot in front of his face. He started back with his eyes squeezed shut as chips of stone spattered his chest and neck like hot pinpricks.

So much for Stephen being out of ammunition. Gryf wiped the cobweb off his nose.

"Mer-idon-idon-n-n" came the echo again, and right after it, another shot. Gryf didn't see where that one hit: he was cowering with his arms over his head and waiting for the bullet or its ricochet to plow into him. After a moment, he resumed his crawl for the stairs, keeping himself in the dirty space against the wall for what poor safety that afforded in the narrow corridor. The cut on his palm ached. His jaw was killing him, and he was furious with himself for ending up as target practice in the dark.

One more shot exploded, bringing the echoes to thundering life. He went still, instinctive paralysis, and then forced himself to scramble fast under cover of the noise. Miraculously, his searching hand found a rough-hewn corner. He heaved himself forward onto his knees as the echoes died away. How many shots was that? Five? Six? Six, he thought, the limit of a revolver without reloading, but he wasn't willing to stake his life on his ability to count under fire. He crept up the bottom step. Just as he pulled his foot up into the stairwell, light flickered and then blazed in the corridor.

It seemed incredibly bright to his dark-adjusted eyes. Every crack and hollow in the stone walls sprang to pinpoint clarity and then just as quickly disappeared. The dark closed in again like a coffin. It took Gryf a moment to realize what had happened.

The son of a bitch had struck a match.

Just soon enough to see an empty hall. If he had lit it a second earlier, he would have seen an easy mark.

Gryf pressed his fist over his mouth to stifle a hard exhalation. Once he was in the side passage, his situation was radically improved. He had options again: go up or wait in the ample cover of the stairway. He didn't want to kill Stephen. He really didn't want to, for a few logical reasons and a whole slew of stupidly emotional ones. Stephen, on the other hand, had shown no sign of any such scruples, and he also had logical reasons for wanting Gryf dead.

The afterimage on the back of Gryf's eyelids from the brief flash of light faded slowly. He heard nothing from Stephen. After a long time, the silence began to prey on Gryf's nerves. He thought of a hundred ruses Stephen might be planning, and the one that stuck in his mind was an idea that Stephen might have stolen out of the warren of corridors and was even now in the process of locking all the doors from the outside. Gryfs conscious mind told him there was no way Stephen had had the time, but his instincts quailed in panic at the prospect.

He began to crawl up the stairs, stopping between each one to listen. Then when he reached the top a new possibility occurred to him: Stephen knew the house; knew which stairwell Gryf had to have taken. Stephen might be waiting when Gryf opened the door.

He rubbed his injured jaw. Stephen might be behind the door. He also might be waiting in the corridor below. Gryf chose the more pleasant of alternatives: escaping the musty dark. He leaned back against the wall and reached to ease the door open.

The room beyond was just as dark, except when lit by the storm outside the heavily draped windows. Gryf peered carefully around the corner. In a moment's flash, he saw a huge, empty bed and the shine of an oval mirror above a dressing table. He pulled out one of the candles still in his waist band and tossed it into the room. It landed and bounced with a dull thud on the thin carpet. Nothing else moved. He edged out into the opening.

Another burst of lightning made him jump. It illuminated the room, making him a clear target, but no attack followed. Satisfied that he was alone, he crossed to the main door and opened it a crack.

There, at last, was steady light: the soft glow of bubble globes on a stairway. It was a mirror image of the one he had come up to the tapestry room. Only the portraits were different. He slipped out, keeping to the shadows behind a bronze bust on a pedestal, and stood for a moment, contemplating how best to negotiate the lighted stairs in safety. As he hesitated, a latch clicked nearby. Gryf shrank back, his heart pounding, and then grinned.

Incredible, God-given, imbecilic luck. Stephen Eliot let himself quietly into the hall. Gryf watched from behind the pedestal as Stephen scanned the wide landing. When the other man crossed to the head of the stairs, Gryf cocked his revolver.

"Eliot."

Stephen whirled. He should have frozen; that was what Gryf had expected. That was what any sane man would have done, but Stephen's gun swung upward—an unmistakable threat—and Gryf reacted. The revolver jerked in his hand in crashing recoil; he saw the crystal globe at the stairhead burst; he saw Stephen stumble and fall against the rail and take another globe down with him. The upper hall went dark and Gryf heard the heavy, rolling thump of Stephen's body on the stairs, another crash of glass, and the light from the last lamp winked out.

Gryf stood in the dark, trembling. He cursed himself; he cursed Stephen and Tess and the whole blasted world. After a moment he went to the head of the stairs and waited for the next flash of lightning to illuminate what he had done.

It came, and revealed Stephen's twisted body on the cold marble below. His gun glittered evilly on a step a few feet above him. Gryf bit down on his tongue, welcoming the sharp pain in his jaw. It helped him collect his wits. He went down the stairs to his cousin.

He knelt beside Stephen's prone form in the dark and felt for a pulse. It was there, erratic. Gryf looked for a wound and found none, but it was so dark . . . he could only discern Stephen's shallow, bubbling breath by leaning close to listen. He felt a slick wetness on the unconscious man's face. Gryf touched his finger to his tongue. Blood. From Stephen's mouth or nose, Gryf couldn't tell.

"Damn," he said softly. "God damn you for a fool, Cousin. Why the devil did you try to fire?"

For answer, there was nothing.

Gryf rose. With that kind of wound—little blood except from the nose and mouth—there wasn't much to be done now. He had better find Tess and get out. He felt his way around the stairs and along the wall, then remembered the last candle and the matches he had saved. His hands were not quite steady as he lit the wick.

It took him a long time to find the cellars, even with the candle. He searched for a stairway down, and came to the empty servants' quarters: kitchen and laundry and scullery. He was aided, rather ridiculously, by carefully lettered signs which identified not only a whole long row of brass bells, but each and every room in the service area. He avoided the housekeeper's and butler's rooms, and found at last a larder with an unmarked wooden door.

It wasn't locked, as he had feared it might be. It came open with a loud squeak. He stepped inside and shut the door behind him, holding the candle high.

A dirt-floored, brick-lined tunnel, just high enough for him to stand straight, stretched a short way ahead of him, and ended in a cross-tunnel that went an indefinite distance both ways into the dark. He stood at the intersection and quietly called Tess's name.

A rustle came in response, and he saw the red eye of a rat far off ahead. He called again, louder, awakening echoes that were duller and softer than those in the narrow, stone corridors above. He moved down the cross-tunnel the way the rat had gone, stopping to duck through each low, arched doorway and check the tiny storerooms. All he found were bins of onions and turnips, and wheels of cheese, and in one room, two great glass-fronted cabinets in which ornate silver tableware reflected his candle flame. He came to the end of the tunnel and another short passage to a door that led back into the house.

Retracing his steps, he started down the other branch. A slow dread, begun when he had seen Stephen's body at the bottom of the stairs, crept from Gryf's belly into his throat. He called Tess's name again, and hated the silence that followed. She wasn't here. He knew in his heart that she wasn't here. In this end of the tunnel, the storeroom doors were all closed, each perforated by a small, barred window. Within, tall wine racks stood, casting spectral shadows as he walked among them.

"Tess," he said loudly.

Something rattled.

He stood stock-still, listening, and repeated her name. The rattle came again, insistent. It was not in the room he was in. He shouted in elation, and flung himself back out the door, almost dropping the candle in his haste. He turned left, the way he had not been yet, and—

It was like being hit in the back with a brick bat. The impact threw him forward; he was aware of dirt in his mouth and the sound of explosion simultaneously. For a disorganized moment he could not focus, could not breathe, recognizing only a peculiar dull burning just below his ribs and a far more immediate agony in his jaw.

A vertical line formed before his eyes, a strange texture of light and dark, and he realized slowly that it was the floor. He tried to lift his head, but his muscles seemed to disobey him and he only ground his face a little in the dirt. There was something hard beneath his outstretched hand: his gun, and with that insight came the stunned understanding that he had been shot.

Like a difficult puzzle, his numbed mind put together the pieces. Stephen. Stephen wasn't dead. Stephen was here, now, his shoes visible in the range of Gryf's vision, making the shadows dance dizzily with the light he had just ignited. Gryf realized abruptly that he ought to be afraid; that he was flat on his belly with a killer behind him; and just as suddenly he *was* afraid: he was sweating, crying, stomach-twisting *scared,* and his hand closed on the gun, and his limbs obeyed him, and he made it as far as turning half-over before Stephen shot him again.

The bullet knocked Gryf onto his back, a paralyzing blow to his left shoulder. With a peculiar clarity he knew that he had at least taken Stephen by surprise, for the other man to miss his heart at such close range. There was black around the edges of Gryf's vision, but he could see Eliot's face well enough. Stephen was wiping at it with his shirt sleeve, white linen that came away spotted with red, and from the far-distant place where Gryf seemed to be he saw another drop of blood well from Stephen's nostril.

A nosebleed.

Oh, God, a nosebleed.

Gryf wanted to laugh, for the way he had mistaken a bloody nose for a mortal wound. He would have, except he could feel a warm dampness spreading across his own abdomen, and his jaw hurt and his arm wouldn't work. There was blood there, too, pooling and trickling down into his armpit. He looked up dully as Stephen came near. The revolver was aimed at Gryf's head.

"I'm sorry," Stephen said, and he actually sounded like he was telling the truth. "If it's any comfort, Cousin . . . you'll be going to join your wife."

Gryf hardly heard the words, but somewhere in the back of his brain they had an instant effect on his body. He moved. His leg caught Stephen's ankle, and a tearing wrench went through his belly as he heaved. Stephen yelled and fired, but he was already toppling, arms outspread and flailing for balance, and Gryf pulled his trigger without any reasoned notion of what he was doing. His eyes were squeezed shut. He felt the jarring thud of Stephen's body beside him and had no thought of anything except that Stephen had said that Tess was dead.

Stephen lay still, and Gryf lay gasping as the shock

wore off and the pain came, and it was like scarlet-hot spikes driven through his gut and his shoulder and pinning him to the ground. He tried to get up, twice, and the third time struggled onto his knees. He stood shakily, leaning hard against the wall. There was blood all over his shirt and his hands. It welled stickily between his fingers; it wouldn't stop, and he gave up trying to stanch it.

He took a step, and his quivering legs folded. His good shoulder slid down the rough brick wall. Oh, Tess, he thought miserably. Oh, Tess.

The dirt floor came up to meet him. He did not care. He was thirsty; his vision came and went; sometimes he saw the arched bricks of the tunnel in the light of the lamp Stephen had lit, and sometimes all he saw was an infinite blue, like the ocean. After a while, even those were gone, and everything was black, and all he knew was that he was breathing, because he could hear it, and he hurt in his heart and his body, and he wanted to be numb in both. He wanted to die, and he wasn't dying. Or he was, but it was taking so long . . . Why was it taking so long? And dear God, why did it have to hurt so much?

Chapter 17

*T*ess looked up from her sewing at the sound of a cart's wheels in the farmyard below her window. She levered herself to her feet, and the unborn child kicked in agitation at the move—a sensation which had become familiar in the three months since Stephen had brought her here. Outside, the weak sunlight of September lit the chilly purple moors, empty as far as she could see in all directions except for the stone and slate farmhouse itself.

Before the donkey ambled to a halt, a dark-haired girl leaped off the cart, ignoring her mother's laughing command. Tess smiled. She had become almost fond of her gentle jailers, especially twelve-year-old Janey, who wanted so much to learn to read. Tess could see that the girl had found new material; she was clutching a much-folded newspaper, and with her skirt hiked up to show her boots she was headed as fast as her skinny legs could take her up to Tess.

Over the passing summer and fall, Tess had become resigned to life in the farmhouse. She knew things could have been far worse. Her attempts to escape from Stephen on the dreadful trip north—once when he bundled her from the carriage into a private railway car, and once when the train was stopped at a transfer point—had been defeated. Then he had brought her here and left her.

That was the last she had seen of him.

She had only a general notion of where she was. In Scotland, certainly: it had taken her weeks to make sense of the heavy dialect of the crofter family who kept watch on her. She had learned, mostly from the little girl, that the family had been evicted from their tiny cottage on one of the great highland estates to make way for sheep. They were pathetically grateful to Stephen for the abundant food and ample farmhouse he had provided. It was compensation almost unbelievably generous for the small trouble of keeping Tess, and she soon found that they would hear nothing against him. She also found that they never let her out of their sight. She had the freedom of the farmyard, but if she made any move to go farther, she found her way blocked by the huge husband, who urged her back with an apologetic smile and promises of a treat for dinner, as if she were a guest too welcome to be allowed to leave.

At first, she had lived in terror of Stephen's return. But when he did not come, and her body grew heavier and more unwieldy, she began to lose the driving desire to escape. There seemed to be plenty of money for food, for Janey and her mother had gone off twice in the cart and returned with flour and cheese and honey, and there were three pigs and a milk-goat in the yard. The crofter's wife was anxious for Tess to be well-cared-for, and had even offered cloth and assistance in making gowns for the coming baby. In all, it was a benevolent incarceration, for the family seemed to think of Tess as a kind of good-luck piece, to be cherished rather than neglected. The only real signs of imprisonment were the bars on her bedroom door and windows.

The pounding of Janey's feet on the stairs was followed by a hesitation, and Tess could almost see the young girl on the other side of the door suddenly recalling her manners. There was a polite knock. When Tess answered, Janey forgot her temporary decorum and waved the paper with proud enthusiasm. "Look ye, wha the grocer gie us! It's nae sae auld—yon weekie past, nae moor. Wi' ye read ut, missie?"

"Immediately!" Tess laughed, as glad as Janey to have news of the outside world. "Let's go down, so your parents can hear, too."

Janey put a trusting hand in Tess's and laid a cheek on her arm. "I love ye, missie."

Tess squeezed the small hand. She was rapidly coming to love Janey, too. What a pleasure it would be to have her own little girl!

In the kitchen, the family gathered around Tess at the big table, Janey's mother hastily finished putting away the goods from town, and then insisted that Tess must have a cup of tea with honey first. Tess accepted that, and spread the folded paper flat on the table.

She glanced down, ready to begin at the date, but her eye was drawn immediately to the bold black letters beneath. She choked on a swallow of tea.

"Good God," she said, and set the cup down before her trembling fingers dropped it.

"Eliot Case Decided," the headline proclaimed. "Mysterious Murderer Sentenced To Hang." Tess caught up the paper and devoured the smaller print.

"The trial for murder at the Winchester Summer Assizes in the tragic case of Mr. Stephen Eliot of Ashland Court, Hamps., has come to a swift conclusion with a verdict of guilty against the accused," the paper said. "Notwithstanding the refusal of the prisoner to cooperate with police, counsel, or bench, to the radical extent of withholding even his name, on the basis of the evidence presented the jury decided that the accused had entered Mr. Eliot's home, in the absence of most of the normal staff, and killed Mr. Eliot in an attempt at theft on the night of 25 June."

She skipped downward. ". . . victim and incapacitated assailant were discovered in cellar . . . prisoner remained insensible for four days . . . given over to the care of . . . considerable experience in the Crimea enabled him successfully to treat the assailant's bullet wounds despite serious loss of blood . . . upon partial recovery and trial, the assailant made no effort to defend his actions or identify himself, but stood silently in the dock throughout the proceedings . . . given the assumed name of John Doe . . ."

And then her widening eyes fastened on another paragraph. "The accused is a young man of good appearance; six feet two inches high; a nobly shaped head; bronze, sun-bleached hair curling at the temples; aquiline features, and a pair of fine gray eyes. His figure is that of an athlete, and his darkened complexion and callused hands have led police to infer an occupation of manual labor, although otherwise he gives much the appearance of a mannered gentleman. His gait and bearing showed him to be in lingering pain. He several times appeared to be faint in the dock, but never lost consciousness or asked to be seated."

A whimper escaped her, a sound of dawning horror. She read every word of the remainder of the article with tremulous concentration. "The only sign of interest or awareness which the prisoner exhibited during the entire inquest and trial was to raise his head and stare most intently at the elderly Mr. Bridgewater when the butler was called as witness. This glowering perusal appeared considerably to disconcert the witness, who mumbled his testimony and contradicted himself concerning the time of discovery of the crime, but since this testimony was not central to the case and Mr. Bridgewater, a man in his ninetieth year, was clearly distressed, he was not examined further.

"In a peculiar sidelight to this strange and unhappy case, Mr. Eliot's wife still has not been located. Local sources indicated that Mrs. Eliot had been placed in an asylum for the insane in France, but her family denies any such placement, and so far police have been unable to determine the lady's whereabouts.

"Still more mysteriously, the wounded man was reported to have spoken clearly of Mrs. Eliot during moments of delirium, using her Christian name, in addition to further ravings which the doctor understood to concern a ring, possibly an emerald of considerable personal or monetary value to the guilty man. There may be some readers who suspect from these circumstances that the motive for murder might have been other than theft, but the good name of the elusive Mrs. Eliot prevents this paper from speculating on such a point."

And then, within a black-walled box at the bottom, the paper said:

"The condemned man will be executed at eight before noon Monday, 17 September, at Winchester Prison."

Tess looked up at the crofter's wife and cried, "What day is it?"

" 'Tis mairkit day, miss," the woman said, her face anxious.

"The date! What's the day of the month?" Tess gave up on the crofter woman's blank confusion, and looked down at the dateline of the paper. Market day—that would be Wednesday . . . if the paper was really only a week old. Or the nineteenth if it was older. Her mind strained to count the time she had been here. Could it already be the nineteenth? It couldn't, pray God it couldn't.

She leaped to her feet, and only after the startled crofter had uprighted the chair she knocked over did she remember her keepers. Janey put out her hand. "Is't sae mortal bad?" she asked apprehensively.

Tess wet her lips. "Mr. Eliot is dead."

The crofter's mouth dropped. "Master Eliot!"

"He was—" She stopped, aware that these people would have no sympathy for the murderer of their benefactor. "There was an accident. See, Janey, here is his name. E-L-I-O-T. Can you read it?"

Janey repeated the letters, and strung them together as Tess had taught her. "Aye, miss, it's him."

"It canna be," her father said in a stunned voice. "It's nae our mannie. It's maun tae be some oother."

Tess had to bite back a frustrated exclamation. To the crofter, news of Stephen's death meant disaster for all newfound hopes. But the man had to be made to accept it, or Tess knew she would not get free until the money Stephen had left ran out. Panic rose in her breast. She pointed at the paper. "Janey, what is that date?"

" 'Tis twenty and five. O' June, missie," Janey said promptly. She had learned all her months well.

"That's the day he was killed. Three months ago." Tess looked at the man. "Have you heard anything from him since?"

The crofter pulled the paper to him and pored helplessly over print that Tess knew was incomprehensible to him. He looked up, and Tess ached for the anxiety in his eyes. "I ken there's been nae word since ye coome, miss. But we've still siller in plenty."

"But you thought he would come back. Didn't he say he would come back before now?"

The man lowered his eyes. "Aye. So he said."

Janey's mother said softly, "Yon laird's been our savin', miss. We waur sairly beset."

Tess turned to the other woman. "I know. I know." She clenched her hands. "And you've been kind to me. But you cannot hold me here longer. The police are looking for me. Please—take me into the town. I'll see that you're taken care of. I promise."

"Dunna go from us, miss," Janey begged.

"But I must," Tess cried. "The silver will run out sometime, and then you'll just need more. Mr. Eliot isn't coming back. I can help you, if you'll just take me." She caught the hands of the crofter's wife. "It's wrong to hold me here against my will: You know it is."

The woman looked down, and then up at her husband. There was shame in her eyes. "Duncan—"

"It isna wrong," the man said stubbornly. "Nae more than we starve, lassie, and bleak winter comin'."

But the crofter's wife had taken Tess's side. "Before the Lord God, Duncan? It dinna fash ye before Him? I ken it do, tho ne'r ye speak of't."

The crofter shuffled his big feet, and looked down at the paper again with a frown. He seemed to Tess like a child caught out at some grave mischief. In a low voice, he mumbled, "Where do we go, then?"

"Come with me!" Tess exclaimed. "I'll take care of you. I promise. I'll buy you your own farm, wherever you like. I can do that. I'm rich. I'm very rich."

There was a long silence. They all looked at the crofter. The man stood up, his head bowed. "We wouldna take aught from ye, miss. We dinna deserve it. But I'll carry ye to town."

On a hard wooden pew in the gloomy chapel of Winchester Prison, Gryf sat staring at his clasped hands. The droning voice from the lectern rose and fell within the cold stone walls. A pause came in the service, a shuffling of feet, and the warder behind Gryf gave him an ungentle shake on the shoulder.

He tightened his jaw against the stab of pain and slid awkwardly onto his knees, hampered by the shackles on his wrists and the soreness of his half-healed wounds. He bowed his head, not in prayer, but because it was expected, and he was indifferent to whatever they wanted him to do.

From behind barred railings, the other prisoners responded to the chaplain in a toneless murmur. When Gryf raised his head they were all looking at him, in his place of display below the lectern, and he simply looked back at them, emotionless, far past feeling or fear at the recital of his own burial service.

When the executioner came the next morning to take Gryf from his cell, there was a cluster of press reporters behind. They, too, all stared at him, as if they expected something. His eyes met the eager glance of one young scribbler. The contact held, and after a moment the boy's cocky expression faltered. Blood rose in his face, and he looked down at his notebook. Another, in a low voice, asked, "Have you repented?" "Are you ready to meet your God?" "Will you not confess?"

Gryf ignored them all, and looked only at the young reporter, at the rosy cheeks of inexperience. The garble of unanswered questions gradually subsided, and suddenly one of the older men pushed the cub forward. "You've got his attention, lad. Ask him something."

The boy was crimson. He stood before Gryf with his head bowed, as if it were he who had committed some atrocious crime. When he raised his face, it was chalk-white. In a failing voice, he asked, "Are you afraid, sir?"

Gryf thought of Tess. His family. Grady. Stephen.

He found a small, painful smile from some hidden place inside him. "No."

The boy bit his lip. He looked as if he might be ill. Gryf felt something, for the first time in many days. A twinge of pity. A thin thread of regret for lost futures. He said softly, "You are."

The boy ducked his head. "I'm sorry, sir." As if he had somehow let Gryf down. He turned, and shoved his way out among the rest, and Gryf did not see him again.

The executioner took Gryf's arm, and pinioned him with gentle efficiency. The reporters fell dutifully back. Gryf and the hangman went forward, out into the crisp daylight. There was a crowd there, huge and drab, and the rumble of conversation became a roar as Gryf appeared. He mounted the scaffold and came to stand in front of the waiting coffin, above the square outline of the trapdoor with the coarse rope dangling next to him.

He looked out over the cheering sea of faces. The morning was beautiful: the trees and the sky, the spire of the cathedral still partially hazed by white mist. A cool taste of autumn touched his cheek. He faced the crowd and blessed old Badger for keeping his secret at the inquest and trial; for sparing Gryf's father's and grandfather's name from this. He had that much, at least. Nothing else.

For he had lied to the young reporter. When Gryf had stepped out into the bright day he had realized it. He was afraid, in the last miserable corner of his soul. He knew too much about dying. He wished he had gone in a storm, or in the heat of some fight—no time to think, then. No time to imagine what might have been. He felt the pain in his heart stirring, like the twinges in his still-raw wounds.

A face rose before his eyes, Tess's face, as bright and beautiful as the day. When the black silk went over his head, blotting out sunlight for the last time, he kept the image there.

The fierce reaction of the crowd faded suddenly as the noose was placed on his neck. In the weird silence, the executioner said quietly to Gryf, "My rope's well-oiled, son. You'll not suffer. God rest you."

Then the hangman left Gryf's side and he was alone in the artificial dark.

The impressive, expectant hush was broken by a cat-call. Another followed. Gryf waited. A long time went by. Every one of his senses seemed to stretch to its limits to drink in the last of life: he could see the tiny pin-pricks of light through the black silk and smell the sharp mustiness of the aniline dye; he could feel the weight of the slipknot resting on his back. The skin of his hands rubbed together with a peculiar sensation of swollen smoothness and his fingers prickled from the tightness of the bonds. At every sound near the platform, he expected it to happen.

He might have saved himself from this, he knew. He could have told his ten-guinea defense counsel who he was; what had really happened, instead of the crazy scenario the prosecution had conjured of a failed attempt to steal the sterling silver. A killing done in the course of a robbery was murder. It mattered not in the eyes of the law if a thief was ambushed and shot in the back. If that burglar killed to save himself, he committed murder by constructive malice.

Gryf hadn't been trying to rob Stephen. But he was a murderer, all the same.

Tess's murderer.

He had sent her away, and now she was gone, and Stephen was gone, and Grady—they were all dead, all passed beyond Gryf's reach, and somehow he himself had gotten left behind. Like the first time, left behind, when he should have perished along with the rest of his family in the sun-washed, clean, salt air.

The moments spun out longer, and still he stood waiting. A murmur of impatience rose from the crowd. He began to feel dizzy. His heart pumped too much blood, in momentary expectation of extinction. Hadn't it been long enough? The black mask made it hard to breathe— a graphic example of how it would feel to strangle. Still nothing happened. In the incredible delay he felt his physical courage dissolving. It seemed to him that whole minutes had passed. Hours. He tried to count heartbeats, got as far as seventy and forgot what came next. He was afraid his knees were going to collapse. Please, he thought. Please. The crowd began to babble. Gryf heard the sound of footsteps on the scaffold.

Surely now . . .

A hand fell on his shoulder, and he staggered, too surprised and witless to maintain his balance. The noose tightened across his throat, but his feet were still under him. "Easy, son," the executioner's mild voice said softly. Strong fingers closed around Gryf's arm. "You've been got off."

It did not penetrate his mind at first. The crowd burst into fearful noise, an incoherent mob sound that rose up around the scaffold like a tangible fog, coming to a shrill crescendo as the hangman lifted the noose from Gryf's neck. The black mask was removed. Gryf blinked. His legs were like jelly. The executioner grinned and jerked his head toward the howling crowd.

"Don't pay no never mind to them," he shouted. "Not a one could've stood up here as long as you have."

He urged Gryf off the trapdoor and took him back to a place near the stairs. A man Gryf had not seen before went forward on the platform and faced the crowd, waiting for the noise to subside. When it did, the newcomer announced in stentorious tones, "Her Majesty has exercised Her Royal Perogative of Mercy. The prisoner's sentence is hereby commuted to penal servitude and imprisonment for life."

The crowd exploded into a frenzy. The executioner and several warders moved forward, surrounding Gryf as he was hustled back into the gaol. He could hear the shouts behind him; he could still hear them when the door of his cell clanged shut. The executioner gave a cheerful farewell. They left Gryf alone.

He was alive.

He looked around at the dark stone walls.

A whole lifetime now, to look at those walls.

He sat down on the stool and put his face in his hands. If he'd had a knife, he would have cut his throat.

After a long time—hours, days, he had little notion—they came and took him from the tiny dark cell that had the moss in the corner and put him in a larger one, long and narrow, with a small barred window at one end and a crank box on a pedestal at the other. There was a plain wooden table, a copy of Sturm's *Reflections on the Works of God,* a chamber pot and a standing gas pipe. That was all. He was told that he would spend his time turning the iron drum of the crank box at twelve hundred revolutions an hour for nine hours a day, six days a week. When he was taken from the cell to the chapel, he would wear a mask with tiny eye slits and a short jacket with a number on the back. He would not see anyone. He would not speak. He would meditate on the magnitude of his crimes. For the rest of his life.

That, they said, was the Queen's Mercy.

His food was changed: no longer greasy broth alone, but occasional meals of meat and vegetables brought by a stark-faced representative of the Evangelical Visiting

Society, the only exception to the rule of solitude. She talked to him about repentance and would not leave until he ate what she had brought. She knelt down by the table and prayed aloud for the soul of God's most base and miserable sinner and left a religious tract as she went out the door. He kept them neatly in a stack, and between the cold that crept through the barred window and the growing pile of blessed pamphlets and the slow healing of his wounds, his days passed into months. Winter came, and gave onto early spring. He avoided all thought of things future or past. He avoided all thought of anything. There was only the squeak of the crank as it turned: mechanical and even. Like breathing.

One morning before dawn, when Gryf was lying awake staring into the dark with his back against the ungiving wall, a warder came rattling down the corridor. With a muffled curse for the recalcitrant lock, he forced open the iron door of Gryf's cell. A youth with a pail of water and a razor shuffled in after.

"Hup wi' you," the warder said, and prodded Gryf's outstretched leg. "The boy's to shave yer for yer trial."

Gryf rose to his feet. At first he thought it was a mistake. By the time he was shackled and taken out into the bitter, early-morning dark, where a jostling crowd stared and hissed at him as he was pushed into the police wagon, he had another theory. He imagined that he had already died, and this was Hell. Like Sisyphus, he was doomed to penance, but instead of a boulder to push to the top of a hill he was required to stand trial for Eliot's murder, over and over, and instead of the boulder rolling down at the top, he would have to endure forever that climb onto the scaffold and the endless wait with the rope around his neck, and then the cell and the crank and the woman with her prayers.

Two warders accompanied him, but when the dark wagon creaked to a halt, they were not at the site of the Winchester Court of Assizes where he had been tried before. They were at the railway station. Another crowd met them there, a larger one, for it was nearly light and all the work traffic had already begun. The hoots of spectators mingled with the rasping huff of the waiting trains. He tripped mounting the steps to the car and the warders lifted him bodily, roughly, shouting over the crowd as if chastening him for stumbling in some effort to get away. Once inside they shoved him down onto a bench so that the shackles tore into his wrists and his back, and then a moment later the train began to pull away from the station.

For a long time he just listened to the sound of the wheels and watched the sun come up over the countryside. The slow awakening of thought in his brain was like the bright morning light in his weakened eyes: painful. They were traveling in an empty car, and the two warders talked between themselves as if Gryf were not there. After some twenty minutes the train began to brake, and he heard a distant voice call "Basingstoke!" over the sound of the wheels.

"Where am I going?" he asked, and his voice was hoarse from long disuse.

The warders broke off their conversation abruptly. After a minute's disconcerted silence, one of them said, "Up to London, then. So mind you watch your manners."

Gryf shifted a little, to ease the bite of the cuffs into his hands. He didn't bother to ask further. He'd learned that it was better not to know. The gray fields and trees touched with pale-green flew past. Suburbs of raw new houses began to appear, row upon row of stuccoed villas, and then those gave way to the gray and black skyline of London: sharp, Gothic spires and smoke from a hundred thousand chimneys. The view was obscured by embankments, and then, like a dark hand, closed over by the city itself.

He should have grown used to the ogling crowds, but the one that met them as the train hissed to a stop at Waterloo Station was almost more than he could face. Before the locomotive had fully halted, there was a rush on the platform, with uniformed bobbies trying to beat the public to the door of Gryf's car. The police won the race, and formed up quickly into a cordon to hold back the surging push. Gryf's escorts looked out the window, and nervously at each other. They pulled Gryf to his feet with unnecessary force: he was already halfway up when they started swearing at him to move. The combined noise of the train and crowd seemed to beat on his ears, and when he stepped to the door, the sound rose to a tremendous roar within the arched vault of the station. He stopped on the stairs, scared out of his wits by the mob that greeted him. It seemed nothing but a roiling blur of color and sound that stretched into obscurity in both directions, with one thin hard-fought alley between the cordons of police.

The warders urged him on; they wanted to run, but something made Gryf set his feet. He was not going to show his fear. He made himself step down from the car slowly; made himself look in the eyes of the screaming crowd behind the police. His escorts' fingers dug viciously into his arms, and suddenly it gave him a cynical pleasure to know that they were as frightened as he was. He looked sideways at one, and grinned.

At that the mob broke into a frenzy, and straining hands reached out between the official lines. He felt them touch him, expected blows, and then realized with a start that they were cheering. The distorted faces behind the police were not screaming curses, but acclamation. He stopped, and turned an astounded look on them.

The warders pushed him on. A windowless carriage pulled by two agitated grays lay ahead, the Black Maria that carried prisoners from the prison to the court. He was shoved into it, and the warders scrambled up behind, pulling the door shut with a bang that could barely be heard over the thunder of the crowd.

The wagon rocked forward.

By fits and starts, they proceeded. He thought several times that the wagon would be overturned. By the time the vigorous thump of the coachman above signaled that they had arrived at wherever they were going, a kind of camaraderie had sprang up between Gryf and his two escorts. To sit in the dimness and hear the noise and feel the carriage shake brought them all near to the breaking point of nerves. The warder who moved to the door at the signal hesitated before drawing the bolt. His fellow gave him a nod, and they both looked at Gryf.

He pasted the fierce grin back on his face. Above the din, he shouted, "Open it," and the warder threw back the inside bolt. Someone had already opened the outer one, and the door swept wide. Gryf crouched down and went first, into the puddle of open space that the bobbies held tenaciously.

He looked around in bewilderment. Above him, instead of the grim wall of the Old Bailey, towered the ornate stone steeples of the new Houses of Parliament. He had no time to stop or ponder; he was hustled the short distance inside by an extra phalanx of police, with his Winchester warders trailing ignominiously. Once within the building, the tumult ceased but he was still given no moment to ask why he was there. The two warders fell behind and were lost as other officers handed him along the halls of state. He wound up finally in a small room, where the police removed his shackles.

A tall, broad-shouldered man with silver hair and a buoyant gait strode in as the bobbies went out. He glanced over Gryf with a critical eye.

"So," he said. "The prisoner."

It might have been a title, so portentously did he utter the word. He appeared to like what he saw, for his handsome face broke into a smile as he held out a huge lion's paw of a hand. "Ruxton Wood," he said. "Your counsel."

The name was ringingly familiar. David Ruxton Wood, Serjeant-at-Law. The Great Defender. Gryf began to understand. He was going to be made into some kind of crusade; another hopeless case, another opportunity for the brilliant barrister to pour out golden oratory in a lost cause.

Gryf looked at the offered hand and set his jaw. "I don't want your counsel."

"Ah." Serjeant Wood changed the offer to a smooth, slight bow. He said, in a perfectly unconcerned voice, "Perhaps you don't. But don't think anyone gives a damn about that, my boy. Here's your valet. Twenty minutes." He reached out and ran a finger along Gryf's jaw. "Make it thirty, and tidy up that shave."

With that, Serjeant Wood left, calling for hot water. Gryf was stripped of the numbered prison garb, with a mutter of disgust from the servant, who pushed Gryf down into the tin tub of lukewarm water that a charwoman had hauled in. Shaving and bathing done, the man took after Gryf's hair with the razor, and then produced a set of morning clothes that Gryf recognized with a shock as his own. Serjeant Wood, now in the black silk robe of a Queen's counsel, returned just as the valet was tying Gryf's neckcloth.

"Splendid," the barrister said smoothly. "One would think your ancestors were nobility, Mr. Doe."

Gryf looked up. He met Serjeant Wood's mild blue eyes, "What is this?" he asked in a low voice.

"This," the Serjeant said, "is an attempt to patch up the royal shambles you seem to have made of your life. Are you quite ready? I'm afraid they'll have to put these handcuffs back on . . . Would you prefer them in front or in back?"

Out again into the long halls, with Serjeant Wood setting an enthusiastic pace, Gryf was carried along in the little knot of police. He had been in Westminster once before, on a morning tour to pass the time one day during that faraway spring spent in London. The halls and corridors were indistinguishable, but when a narrow door was opened quietly for them by a uniformed man-at-arms, Gryf suddenly knew exactly where he was.

The gilded pavilion with its empty throne, the high ceiling and galleries on two sides, the tiers of seats—empty when he had seen them before, and full now with the distinguished company just taking their places—all were unforgettable. And unmistakable.

They had brought him to the House of Lords.

Chapter 18

*I*n the little office where Serjeant Wood had left her, Tess paced. She was supposed to be "resting," an impossibility suggested to her with perfect seriousness by her physician. The solicitors and barristers seemed to have some idea that after being delivered of a fine and healthy boy some four months ago she was liable to collapse at the earliest opportunity.

But there had been no time to collapse. The terror of those days before the execution were still with her: the rush to the capital, the interview with Serjeant Wood, the intolerable strain of waiting for two days to gain an audience with the Queen and the home secretary, when Serjeant Wood would not let Tess speak, but told her story for her, piecemeal, not nearly as much as she would have told herself. She had not slept all night. On the morning of the execution, word had gone out from the home secretary's office by telegraph.

Commuted sentence.

It wasn't enough for Tess, or for Serjeant Wood. He had put Tess's solicitors and his own junior barristers to work. He had hired investigators. He interviewed Tess until she felt like a squeezed fruit: drained of every recollection of the time she had spent with Gryf. From the signet ring and the name of Gryphon Meridon on her marriage license, Serjeant Wood had put together a past. The more he probed it, the more solid it became. Good evidence; *hard* evidence, as the serjeant-at-law began to gloat. By the time Robert Gryphon Meridon came in December, Tess was certain her son was the next heir to Ashland.

Which did not clear his father of a charge of murder.

Tess put her hands to her temples, trying to subdue the headache that raged behind her eyes. He was here; she was going to see him, after all the helpless months of waiting. She had no inkling of his condition or spirit: to the smuggled messages for which she had paid so handsomely, not one response had ever come. She did not even know if they had reached him. Every one had disappeared without a trace into the grim machine of the Queen's "reformed" prison system, that vast, inhuman darkness that swallowed its victims whole and refused to give them up.

The door opened behind her and she whirled. It was one of Serjeant Wood's juniors. He said only, "Come with me, ma'am, if you please. He wants you to hear."

She followed the barrister with a thumping heart, slipping behind him into an unobtrusive spot in the lords' chamber. She pressed herself close against the wall, hoping to attract no notice, for she knew she had no right to be there at all. Her attention was riveted by the opening of the far door.

It was Gryf. He entered escorted by two men-at-arms, walking steadily despite the shackles that bound his hands behind him. He eyes were lowered. He stopped at a touch from one of his guards, and remained there, staring blankly at the floor.

Tess bit her lip. She had tried to prepare herself, but even so . . .

The familiar tan was gone, and his hair was a darker gold, no longer sun-bleached. His cheekbones seemed too prominent and the tailored coat could not hide the unnatural leanness beneath. But mostly—mostly it was the look of vacancy on his face that frightened her. It was as if he were not really there, not even alive, but only a wax figure set to motion, obedient and mindless.

A sergeant at arms stepped forward, crying, "Oyez! Oyez! Oyez!" He thumped his staff on the floor. "Our Sovereign Lord the Queen strictly charges and commands all manner of persons to keep silence upon pain of imprisonment."

A man stood up, magnificent in white shoulder-length wig and scarlet robe. The lord chancellor. From his position in front of the cushioned bench Tess knew as the woolsack, the chancellor announced, "Her Majesty's commission is about to be read. Your Lordships are desired to attend to it in the usual manner."

Stepping forward with the document handed to him by the lord chancellor, a clerk began: "Victoria Regina by the Grace of God of Great Britain, Ireland, and India, Defender of the faith, and so forth, to our right trusty and right well beloved counselor, Lord Chelmsford, Chancellor of Great Britain, Greeting. Know ye that . . ."

Tess could barely follow the convoluted language of the commission: it was full of "wherefores" and "aforesaids," and Gryf's John Doe alias peppered every line. She watched him anxiously, looking for his response to the charges of felony and murder. There was none. He might have been carved of stone. But then another name was mentioned, and suddenly his head came up.

". . . is alleged to be in fact Lord Gryphon Arthur Meridon, the Most Honorable the Sixth Marquess of Ashland," the clerk read solemnly. "We, considering

that justice is an excellent virtue, and being willing that
if said personage of John Doe should be judged by our
present Parliament to be in fact Lord Gryphon Arthur
Meridon, Marquess of Ashland, said personage, of and
for the felony and murder whereof he is indicted, in our
present Parliament, may be heard, examined, sentenced,
and adjudged; and that all other things which are necessary on this occasion may be duly exercised and executed. By the Queen Herself, in her Own Hand."

The sergeant at arms intoned, "God save the Queen."

And Tess saw the first evidence of emotion in Gryf, as
he turned a stare of silent fury on Serjeant Wood.

The intensity of that look astonished and dismayed
her. Relief, hope, gratitude; those reactions Tess would
have understood. She would even have understood no
reaction at all, as a sign of incomprehension. But it was
clear that Gryf had divined exactly what was happening, and his response was pure rage.

She squeezed her hands together in confusion. What
did this mean? Didn't he want to go free? Didn't he
want another chance? As John Doe, Gryf had been tried
by his equals and convicted. But as the marquess of
Ashland—no provincial jury in a circuit court could
claim to judge a peer of the realm. The House of Lords
alone had the right to pass final judgment on one of
their own. If Serjeant Wood could prove it . . .

But Gryf looked far from appreciative. From his con-
temptuous glare and hard-set jaw, it appeared as if the
shackles alone kept him from going for the famous barrister's golden throat.

The lord chancellor said, "Bring the prisoner before
the House."

Between two men-at-arms, Gryf was taken to stand at
the foot of the long table, facing the seated figure of the
lord chancellor. Behind the lord, up the steps beneath

the canopy, the pointed back of the empty throne glittered in silent majesty. Gryf leveled his gaze on that. His mouth was set in stony pride as he ignored the stirring and the interested eyes.

"Are you," the lord chancellor asked, "in fact, Gryphon Arthur Meridon, the present marquess of Ashland?"

Bitterly aware of the chains at his back, Gryf met the dry look of the questioner. The chamber hushed. In the expectant silence, Gryf felt their concealed amusement; the smug anticipation of a jolly laugh at this convicted felon who had the audacity to demand an appeal to the very lords of the realm. He damned Ruxton Wood, and whoever else was behind it. He would rather have stood on the scaffold again than to endure their scorn.

And yet—how could he lie, in the House where his grandfather and great-grandfather and twelve more generations of Meridons had taken their rightful places? Before, it had been different. No one had known. No one could have guessed. It had been an omission to withhold his name, not a lie.

But to stand up now and deny his heritage because he was afraid that they would laugh was cowardice.

"Your Lordship," he said. "I am."

And he waited for the jeers.

They did not come. There was only the subdued stirring again. After a moment, the chancellor said, "I will entertain evidence for the assertion that this man is in fact Lord Gryphon Arthur Meridon, the Most Honorable the Marquess of Ashland."

A white-haired lord, an obvious plant, stood up and asked for permission for Serjeant Wood to speak. It was given. Serjeant Wood did not look at Gryf. He came forward empty-handed, without notes or prompters, and surveyed the packed seats of the House. The lengthening pause he left before he spoke was pure theater, but somehow, even to Gryf, it was magic. It drank in every cough and rustle until Gryf could hear his heart beat in the silence of the chamber. Ruxton Wood addressed his audience with a bearing of such quiet power that it shamed the gilded throne itself.

"My lords," he said, in a soft voice that yet carried to the height and breadth of the room. "In rising to the task which it now becomes my duty to perform, I feel a heavy responsibility. If I fail, the consequences of my failure are simple. Simple unto death, or—perhaps worse—to a lifetime spent in hopeless incarceration and waste behind the bleak walls of prison." He scanned the chamber. "I want to tell you a story today, my lords. A story based entirely on external sources, not one kernel of which was provided to me by the prisoner himself. It is a remarkable story, an incredible story . . . a tragic story. But I believe that when you have heard it, and the evidence which supports it, you will have no honorable choice but to agree with me that this man's conviction and imprisonment has been an appalling miscarriage of justice."

At the merest turning of Serjeant Wood's head, a junior barrister leaped forward and handed him a thick volume. The serjeant placed the book on the table, opened it to a ribbon marker, and lifted it again. "Allow me to read to you from a number in the *Naval Chronicle* of 1851. It is a copy of a letter from Captain Nathaniel Eliot to Vice Admiral Sir Colin Shee, dated on board of H.M.S. *Mistral,* 17 December, 1850."

Gryf could have quoted from memory the letter that Wood produced. The official story of the pirate attack on the *Arcturus* made Nathaniel Eliot out to be a hero, and Lord Alexander an arrogant and uncooperative civilian who had deliberately left the protection of Her

Majesty's warship and blundered into disaster. The *Arcturus* had been sighted after the attack, Eliot wrote. Dismasted, with decks already a mass of flame. No survivors. Pursuit of pirate and gallant battle, enemies destroyed to the last man.

Serjeant Wood reached the end of the vivid account and closed the book. He laid it gently down, and looked directly at Gryf.

Gryf stared back fiercely. It was lies, all lies, but if Ruxton Wood thought Gryf was going to stand up now and tell the truth for the benefit of his esteemed counsel, the barrister was far off the mark. Gryf had no intention of prostituting himself and Ashland on the altar of an ambitious criminal counsel's sensationalistic career. Gryf had admitted who he was, but not for Wood's sake. Not for anything, except to live up to the honor of his name in the only way he had left. He wasn't going to beg these robed and powdered lords for mercy. He didn't want their mercy. He didn't want anything, except an end to his misery. Let them hang him. Maybe it would work this time.

The serjeant addressed no word to Gryf, but turned instead and spoke to the gallery. "Sadly, Captain Eliot, who writes with such poignant sensibility about the murder of his relatives, passed away himself, safe at home in his bed, some four years ago, so he cannot be questioned about his account. I have, however, a witness to the events of 8 through 16 December, 1850, aboard H.M.S. *Mistral:* one Colonel Malcolm Jones— at that time lieutenant—of the Royal Marines. Your Lordships will find that he tells a somewhat different story of those dreadful days. With your permission . . ."

Malcolm Jones had a limp and a set of glossy red sideburns streaked with gray. From her corner Tess watched him closely, knowing that Serjeant Wood had used all of his considerable powers of persuasion to drag the shy ex-marine before a full sitting of Parliament. Colonel Jones did not look particularly comfortable to be addressing the House of Lords. He looked, in fact, as if he would rather be storming the heights of Sebastapol.

"Will you tell us," Serjeant Wood asked, "in your own words, what happened aboard the *Mistral* on 15 December, 1850?"

"Yes, sir," Colonel Jones said nervously. "There ain't much to tell, sir, for the morning. The marines stayed belowdecks, mostly. All hands was called in the afternoon watch, and then in about an hour, or just under, Captain Eliot ordered the marines on deck. When I come up, there was another ship, lying close by. She was adrift, it looked to be; hove to and drifting. There was bodies on the deck. The captain sent the first lieutenant and me on board to look for survivors."

The colonel paused then. Serjeant Wood prompted gently, "And what did you find?"

"We found—" Colonel Jones stopped again. He seemed to have trouble speaking for a moment. "We found a massacre, sir. They was butchered. Even the little girls."

Tess saw Gryf close his eyes. He gave no other sign of hearing, but the tiny move was like a shaft to her heart. For the first time, the awful reality of what he must have experienced came fully clear to her. To have lived through that; to have seen his family slaughtered before his eyes, and then be left alone . . . He was there, so close and hurting, and no frustration in her life equaled the helpless longing to rush to him now and smooth the hardened lines of grief from his face.

"All dead?" the serjeant asked. "You found no one alive?"

"We counted thirty bodies, sir."

"Was there any sign of fire?"

"No, sir."

"Did you have time to examine any of the bodies?"

"Not many, sir. I was just startin' that when the lieutenant ordered me off the ship with him. After we captured the pirate, we went back and spent two days searching, but we never did find her again."

"Never found her. Did she sink?"

"Don't know, sir."

"What was the name of the lost ship, Colonel Jones? Did you see her name when you boarded to look for survivors?"

"Oh, yes, sir. Painted beautiful on her bows. She was the *Arcturus,* sir."

Serjeant Wood stood back. "Thank you, Colonel."

There were four more men to testify. Four more times Gryf had to listen to the story, and his mind filled in the details that the others left out. It all came back, from the dark corners of Gryf's memory, a waking nightmare he had tried to bury and never quite succeeded. He stared unseeingly, his ears full of screams and his heart full of a boy's panic, more real than the polished table in front of him. When Serjeant Wood announced that he would call the *Mistral*'s first lieutenant, it seemed only one more phase of the torment. Gryf half-turned, blindly, with some idea that he could not listen to any more; that he had to get away in spite of his hands in chains and the men at his back. They caught him, and turned him again.

He looked up. He blinked. He began to wonder if he had not somehow wandered completely into dreams.

For there, clean and neat and properly dressed, with no sign of the bruises left by two Tahitian bodyguards, was Robert Stark.

And he was saying under oath that he had been the first lieutenant aboard H.M.S. *Mistral* seventeen years ago.

"I had debts," Stark said. "Captain Eliot paid them and took my note."

That was how he explained witnessing the *Mistral*'s falsified logs.

The rest was "orders." It was "orders" that had made him keep a steady course when smoke was sighted and the *Arcturus* had signaled intention to investigate. He'd gone to inform the captain, Stark said, but Eliot had refused to come on deck.

Later, it was "orders" that had caused Stark to set alight two tins of bright varnish in the hold of the *Arcturus*. It was a little more than orders that had made him then betake himself and the marine lieutenant back to the *Mistral* so quickly—at that point, it was worrying for his own skin, in case a can of varnish should have been tipped over by the rolling swell sooner than convenient.

"And what did you expect the burning tins of varnish to do?" Serjeant Wood asked tonelessly.

"I expected them to set fire to the ship. That was what I understood my orders to be."

"Did they do so?"

Stark shrugged.

"Was that a yes or a no, Mr. Stark?"

"Well—" Stark said defensively, and stopped.

"Did you see any smoke?"

"No." Then he added quickly, "but it got dark soon after."

"Was there any light, then? Light as from a fire."

Stark said, "Well—no. But we'd gone off, you see. Far off."

"How far?"

"Oh, ten leagues, at least."

"Thirty miles?"

"Close on."

"Have you ever seen a ship burn at night, Mr. Stark?"

Stark cleared his throat. "No."

"Are you aware that when an empty frigate burned off Blackpool some years ago, it was seen as far away as the Isle of Man—a distance of some sixty miles?"

"No, sir." It was said very low.

"Is it possible the ship didn't burn?"

"I don't know. I suppose—if the tins never fell over."

"Is that likely, given the heavy swell you spoke of?"

"Anything's possible."

"Likely. I asked you if it were likely that neither one of two separate cans of burning varnish tipped over in a disabled ship in a rolling swell?"

"Not likely, no. Not very likely."

"What are the other alternatives for why the ship didn't catch fire from the tins of varnish?"

Stark hesitated a very long time. Then he said, "I can't think of any."

"None, Mr. Stark? Not one single one?"

Stark looked unhappy. He glanced around at the company and then back at Serjeant Wood. "I suppose someone might have put it out."

A soft sound whispered through the chamber. Grady, Gryf thought with an ache.

"Can you think of any other reason why a rolling ship should not be set afire by an open tin of burning oil and resin?"

Stark appeared to be giving the question considerable thought. At length, he said, barely above a whisper, "No."

"Speak up, Mr. Stark. Their Lordships may be interested in your answer."

"No," Stark said. "No, I can't."

"Then if that ship where you left the burning cans seventeen years ago is still afloat and in good condition today, there must have been someone left behind alive on her that day?"

And Stark said, "Yes. There must have been."

The testimony went on and on. The ship was positively identified as the *Arcturus* by the original drawings, the men who had built her, and the discovery of the original figurehead and name boards hidden in a false bulkhead. The handwritten will, signed by Alexander Meridon, naming Gryf as heir, was found to be authentic by no fewer than five respected graphologists. Even Mahzu, with his catlike stride and his tattoos, came to testify and tell how he had joined a crew of two, a man and a twelve-year-old boy, on the western coast of Africa in early 1851.

And finally, old Badger shuffled into the chamber with the aid of a gowned official. Gryf tried not to look at the elderly retainer; but he found his gaze pulled helplessly that way. As Badger took his oath, he met Gryf's eyes and held them with a trembling, determined frown. After a moment, Gryf looked away, knowing this time Badger would tell the truth.

It seemed to come as a surprise to the lord chancellor when the old man who had fumbled and wept his way through the first trial now stood firm and said that he had invited the prisoner into the house himself.

The chancellor said, "Mr. Bridgewater, that is not what you testified on the witness stand earlier."

Old Badger's lip quivered, but he said nothing.

"Mr. Bridgewater, I remind you that you are under oath."

"Yes, Your Lordship," Mr. Badger said. "I'm telling you the truth. I was—I was lying before."

"Mr. Bridgewater," Serjeant Wood said quickly, "you say you were lying in earlier testimony. Exactly what part of your earlier testimony do you now say is false?"

"I said before that I first found him in the cellar in the morning. 'Twasn't true. The night before, the bell rang, and I answered it and asked him to come in."

"But you did not tell the police this?"

"No, sir."

"Mr. Bridgewater, why did you lie to the police?"

"Because when he—when he first come in out of the storm, he asked me to swear to never say that I had seen or heard of him."

"The prisoner asked you to swear to that?"

"Yes, sir." Badger looked at Gryf, and there was pleading in his eyes. Gryf gave his head one tiny shake, forgiving. It wasn't important any longer. There would have been no good in Badger repeating his shaky attempt to perjure himself. Not with Serjeant Wood boring in on his point.

It took all of half a minute to come out.

"Mr. Bridgewater," the tall barrister said, "when you opened the door and saw the prisoner, did you recognize him?"

"I thought so, sir."

"Who did you think he was?"

"Lord Alexander, sir."

The chamber hummed.

"But Lord Alexander has been dead for seventeen years, has he not?"

"Yes, sir."

"How long did you entertain this misconception?"

"Until he told me he wasn't Lord Alex, sir."

"Was there sufficient light to see well?"

"Yes, sir."

"Before he told you he was not Lord Alexander, how

did you account for a man you knew to have been dead for seventeen years standing there before you in the flesh?"

Badger pursed his lips. "You'll think me an old fool, sir."

The advocate's face softened. "Of course not, Mr. Bridgewater. I only want you to tell what you thought. No one here can laugh at you for telling the truth."

"Well, I thought he was a ghost, sir."

"How did you come to that conclusion?"

"He's the image of Lord Alex, sir, and he had blood all over his neckcloth. They said, you know, they always said that the pirates must have slashed his throat, sir. Lord Alex's."

"You've said that the prisoner told you he was not Lord Alexander. Who then did he say he was?"

"He said he was Arthur's son Gryphon."

The counselor gave no sign of hearing the stir in the room. "Did you believe him?"

"Oh, yes, sir."

"But in all this time when no one could determine the identity of the prisoner, you knew who he claimed to be and never mentioned it to the police?"

"Not to anyone, sir. I'd swore not to." And then, as he had in the hall of Ashland Court, Mr. Badger burst into tears. "I never thought he'd let them try to hang him."

The barrister waited a few moments, until Badger recovered a little. Then he said softly, "Do you still believe the prisoner to be Gryphon Meridon, the grandson of the late marquess?"

"Oh, yes, sir! Yes."

"Mr. Bridgewater, am I correct in saying there is a portrait of Lord Alexander at Ashland Court?"

"Yes, sir, there is."

"Where does it hang?"

"In the tapestry room, sir, on the north wall by the door. It used to be in the gallery, but Mr. Eliot took it upstairs after his father died."

"Your Lordship," Serjeant Wood said to the lord chancellor, "I ask permission to bring before the lords the portrait mentioned by this witness. It is a full-length study by Sir George Richmond. Lord Alexander sat for it in December of 1849, when he was thirty years old."

The portrait was carried in covered by a sheet of blue felt, as tall as the men who handled it. Serjeant Wood directed them to stand the picture next to Gryf, where it was in full view of the lord chancellor.

The barrister pulled off the felt.

Gryf couldn't see the portrait, but he could see the face of the chancellor. The venerable white eyebrows went up. He nodded slowly. "I believe you make your point, Serjeant. Have it turned to display to Their Lordships."

The ushers carried the portrait up the short flight of steps in front of the empty throne and faced it full on to the gallery. A ripple of sound went through the room.

The painting was of a young man. Behind him, instead of the usual dog and Greek temple, was the shoulder-high wheel of a ship. In his right hand was a sextant. He leaned easily against the steering box, his blond hair windblown and a daredevil grin on his face.

"Is this the portrait of which you spoke, Mr. Bridgewater? That hung in the tapestry room of Ashland Court?"

"Yes, sir," said Badger. "It is."

Gryf might as well have been looking at himself in a mirror, at the wheel of the *Arcanum/Arcturus.*

Tess could not bring herself to stay in the chamber for the vote. When they dismissed Gryf, she slipped out, on the slim hope that she might be able to speak to him. He had not seen her in the House, she knew. She was nearing the edge of her sanity with wondering what he thought and felt, and how he would greet her. But the armed guards formed a phalanx around him, and by the time Tess had slipped back into the hall, he was gone.

She spent the endless half-hour of waiting in the same office where Serjeant Wood had left her earlier. The barrister did not appear. She wondered if he was with Gryf, and felt another surge of frustration. Gryf needed her. She was his wife—didn't she have a right to be with him now, while the future of both of them hung in the balance? Why didn't he ask for her?

But she knew the answer to that. He had sent her away before because he didn't love her. There was no reason to think he had changed his mind. None. Except— he had come to save her from Stephen. Surely that meant something, that he had risked his life for her sake. She clung to that hope, knowing all the time that it was flimsy. Guilt, anger, duty—there were any number of reasons that might have brought him back to rescue her, and none of them had to do with love.

The same junior barrister came to fetch her for the announcement. She could tell nothing from his bearded young face, and could not bring herself to ask. She stepped quietly into the same place she had held before and watched as they brought Gryf into the room. The dead, uncaring emptiness was in his eyes again. He did not look up as he came to a halt before the lord chancellor.

"My lord," the chancellor said, and paused.

Serjeant Wood, standing near Gryf, cleared his throat meaningfully. Tess distinctly saw one of the guards nudge the side of Gryf's foot. He looked up.

The chancellor gave Gryf a peculiar little smile and

said again, "My lord, your peers and equals have considered the allegation that you are in fact Gryphon Arthur Meridon, Marquess of Ashland. They have likewise considered the evidence, and everything which has been alleged in your favor, and upon the matter their Lordships have unanimously agreed to accept in your person the person of Gryphon Arthur Meridon, the Most Honorable the Marquess of Ashland, with all rights and privileges appertaining thereto."

Tess swallowed hard. She felt her spirits rising, and did not trust the elation. There was still a trial for murder yet to go. Gryf looked completely unmoved by his change of circumstance, even though by that one sentence he was made instantly into one of the wealthiest men in the Empire. It was too much, perhaps. Too hard to comprehend.

The proceedings went inexorably on. A clerk read the indictment against Gryf, and the finding of the Winchester jury. And then the lord chancellor spoke to Gryf again.

"You are brought to this bar to receive your trial upon a charge of murder of Stephen Eliot of Hampshire," the chancellor said. "An accusation, with respect to the crime and the jury who make it, of the most solemn and serious nature."

Tess wrung her hands, and then made herself hide them in her skirt.

"Yet, my lord," the chancellor went on with greatest formality, "you may consider it but as an accusation, for it is a happiness resulting from Your Lordship's birth and the constitution of this country that Your Lordship is now to be tried by your peers in full Parliament."

The chancellor looked very intently at Gryf, as if waiting for a response. None came, and after a moment, he added, "What greater consolation can be suggested to a person in your unhappy circumstances, than to be reminded that you are to be tried by a set of judges whose justice nothing but the whole truth can influence or direct?"

Gryf did not appear at all consoled by these circumlocutions. He looked tired. She wished they would invite him to sit down.

"How plead you now," the chancellor asked. "Guilty or not guilty?"

The ensuing silence stretched into monstrous proportions. Once again, Serjeant Wood stepped into the breach.

"His Lordship pleads not guilty, my lord."

Another man rose. Tess recognized him as the attorney-general. Here would be the prosecution's case.

"Your Lordships," the prosecutor said, "after anxious and careful consideration of the new evidence which has come to light, we have reached the conclusion that there is no case to be submitted to Your Lordships on which we could properly ask you to convict the prisoner. Therefore, we offer no evidence against him."

Tess pressed her hands over her mouth. It was a quick, instinctive move, to keep the cry of joy from bursting from her lips. In that same moment, Gryf looked up.

He saw her.

The shock hit him with a violence that was physical. For a split second his knees failed him. His breath stopped in his chest. Darkness threatened behind his eyes, driving the chamber and the lords and Tess to a pinpoint of light down a long tunnel—far, far away from himself. He had been numb, blessedly numb, and now—

Bright pain arced through him, silent and searing, like the sob that choked his throat. The joy was a kind of agony, a dreadful fear that his brain was playing tricks, that the slender figure half-hidden in the shadows at the corner of the room was no more than the creation of a mind pushed to the breaking point. That he would awake, and find himself again in the dark cell, knowing too well she was gone

But the chains on his hands were real, and the sound of the lord chancellor's voice, speaking words that barely registered. ". . . a statement clarifying for Their Lordships this decision not to prosecute?"

"Your Lordships," the attorney-general said, "the facts in this case are extremely complex. Without taxing your patience, let me say that we are assured that the prisoner entered the premises without intent to commit the felony of robbery or of murder. We are further assured that the victim had sufficient motive to attack the prisoner, that the victim did so, and that the prisoner retreated as far as was possible out of a genuine desire to avoid bloodshed. These facts are substantially consistent with a plea of self-defense, and the counsel for the Crown sees no purpose in pursuing the case longer."

"You will submit a written report of this evidence to Their Lordships?"

"Of course, my lord. Within the week."

The words ran past Gryf like babbling water. As the image of Tess remained real and solid, his fear began to turn to panic. Believing her dead, he had longed for death himself. To find her alive wrenched away even that. One part of him cried out to her in need; the other shrank away, dreading the pain, the possibility of suffering again. He had built himself into a fortress, stone by gray stone, and she had brought it down around him with one blink of her storm-colored eyes.

Tess stared back at him, unable to read his face or the sudden peculiar stiffening of his frame as he met her eyes. The lord chancellor said, addressing the room at large, "Your Lordships have heard that there is no evidence to be submitted on which the prisoner may be properly convicted. I suggest to you that it is your duty to return a verdict of not guilty of the felony and murder whereof the prisoner stands indicted. What say Your Lordships—is the prisoner, Lord Ashland, guilty of the felony and murder whereof he stands indicted, or not guilty?"

It was only a formality. The room rang to the intoned chorus of "not guilty." The lord chancellor turned again to Gryf. "Lord Ashland, the lords have considered the charge of felony and murder which has been brought against you; they have likewise considered the statement of the attorney-general and upon the whole Their Lordships have unanimously found you are not guilty of the felony and murder whereof you stand indicted."

A guard immediately stepped behind Gryf and freed his hands from the shackles.

Gryf did nothing. He simply stood gazing at Tess, his face white. She looked back at him, feeling her cheeks go hot with agitation. She wanted to smile and was afraid to, afraid to see his rigid expression turn to something worse. What thin hopes she had cherished dwindled away to the vanishing point. He did not want her. He wasn't relieved to see her, or even pleased. He was . . . she didn't know what. Angry? Shocked? Disgusted? All of those things might have been in his face, or none of them. The only thing she could positively tell was that the sight of her brought him no happiness.

The sergeant at arms repeated his bawling "Oyez!" three times and announced, "Our Sovereign Lord the Queen does strictly charge and command all manner of persons here present and that here attend, to depart hence in the peace of God and of our said Sovereign

Lord the Queen, for His Grace My Lord Chancellor intends now to dissolve his commission."

The junior who had brought Tess touched her arm again. She had to tear her eyes away and go with him, back to the little room. She sat near the window, staring out. When the door opened behind her, her heart nearly stopped beating.

It was not Gryf. It was Serjeant Wood.

He swept in, in his black robe and wig, grinning. He went immediately to the window and threw open the leaded glass. "Air!" he exclaimed. "Unruly clients give me the vapors. By God, I thought I was going to expire when he wouldn't even plead."

Tess gave a half-hysterical giggle. "Have we won, then?"

Serjeant Wood turned, sending his robes in a whirl around him. "Won! Of course we won, dear girl. *Nolle prosequi*. No case. No case at all of premeditated murder. The Crown had all the same evidence we did—the falsified annulment records; Stark's arrest in Tahiti and his telegram to Eliot; the witnesses who saw Eliot nab you; the fact that Eliot shot our man in the back . . . it's endless. No other sensible construction to be put on it than just what all the papers have been saying: that your husband went to Eliot to demand your whereabouts, and Eliot took his chance to rid himself of an embarrassing detail. The Crown was sunk, as soon as the lords recognized him as Ashland. And that, I must concede, is wholly due to the worthy Mr. Stark. Perhaps we won't make him go back to rot in a French jail after all."

Serjeant Wood winked at Tess.

She smiled nervously, her mind not really focused on the details of some rather hazy legal threats which had been waved over Stark to make him tell the truth after they had extradited him from France. "Where is Gryf?"

"Receiving his accolades. He'll be along; I told Fleeceman to bring him in here."

"Oh," Tess said. She was slowly tearing the lace from a small handkerchief into tiny little shreds.

Serjeant Wood came and stood behind her. He laid one of his great hands on her shoulder. "He won't be all wine and roses, I'm afraid. Not at first."

"He's exhausted, I expect." Tess was trying to be rational. Her voice only shook a small amount.

"Dazed," said the serjeant. "You look exhausted yourself. I'll leave you to peace and quiet for a while."

Tess nodded. She sat alone in the little room for a long time after he had left. The peace and quiet drove her slowly crazy.

And Gryf never came to see her.

Chapter 19

He didn't sleep well in the closed bed curtains of the lord's chamber at Ashland. It was a ritual with Badger, that the old butler always came in and stood until Gryf got into bed, and then pulled the curtains. Suggesting otherwise did no good—apparently Badger could not comprehend so monstrous a change in the scheme of things.

So for the sake of the old man's rest, Gryf had taken to retiring almost as soon as the sun had set. He would lie awake in the suffocating dark of the bed until he could stand it no longer, and then he got up and fought his way out of the clinging curtains and dressed.

Outside was the only place he could bear to be at night. Outside, in the free air under the sky. He walked down to the little lake in its amphitheater of hills and watched the moon rise. He sat on the grass. It was still a wonder, to feel the rough, living texture; still precious after months on cold stone. Far more than all the wealth and status that had suddenly crashed upon him.

There was a certain black humor in it, he thought. To have everything now, when he could not mobilize the slightest trace of feeling in his heart. He should be glad, and instead he was frozen. Unnaturally calm, like the shining, silent surface of the lake. Underneath that sheet of polished steel was something else, dark and frightening, but as long as he did not think of it, as long as he did not question or feel, he was safe.

He forced his mind to the goal he had set for himself, which was to think about the future. To make some plan, sight some course. To look ahead. He could go anywhere. Do anything. Buy whatever he might want.

And he found he wanted nothing.

In all his midnight walks beside this lake in the time since he had been released, he had come down to that. All dreams, all hopes; they seemed to have vanished into air. Even the ship—what point, to outfit her and load her and sail aimlessly about the ocean, when the paltry money she might make was nothing to the sum of his inheritance?

Ironic, it was, to have life lose its point just when it was given back. Ironic—and bitter. Sometimes his insides twisted with the pain of it: that was the surface cracking, the pebble in the smooth and shining lake. What monsters lay beneath he did not want to know.

But they were moving. They threatened him, demanding release and entry into the calm, cold spaces of his soul. He wanted to run from that buried part of himself before it rose up to engulf him.

Where he would go made no difference. He only knew that he could not stay here. Ashland was not really his. He did not want it. All the years he had raged and hated and despaired of his lost heritage—he had not understood. Or perhaps he had, deep down. Perhaps some part of him had always known that what he'd really wanted back were impossibilities—his childhood, his family . . . irreplaceable things. Not a house and a title. Not the money he had coveted so long.

But it was not so easy to shake off his fortune and go back to what he had been. It was not possible simply to walk away. Something had to be done with the estate. Whenever he came to that thought, the monsters started stirring. He trod around them delicately in his mind. Charities, schools, conveyances to the Crown: those were the things he could rationally consider. For nights on end he had come out here and considered them, endlessly, pointlessly, because he had no legal or moral right to give Ashland to a single one.

What he had, instead, was a wife and son.

He leaped up suddenly, and began to walk the shore. The thought of Tess was like touching a lacerated wound. Instant agony. He retreated from it in frantic haste.

The thought of his son was easier to bear. There, he could maintain some distance. The baby was little more than a name on a piece of paper, a theory. When he'd been told he was a father, Gryf had simply stared blankly at Serjeant Wood, with no more emotion than he might have felt at the news that an extra scullery maid had been hired for the kitchen. A baby . . . the idea was impossibly remote. It seemed almost unreal and therefore safe to contemplate. He could even talk about it; had, in fact, held lengthy conversations with his solicitors.

His solicitors. How convenient, he thought wryly, to have solicitors at one's beck and call. They did not even argue with him, as he had thought they might. They only listened gravely to his plans and pointed out, lawyerlike, that it might be politic to consult the boy's mother before Gryf saddled her with sole charge of his son and his estate without appointing a trustee.

But that was what he wanted to avoid at all costs: seeing Tess. At the very thought of it, he had to lock one

fist inside the other and press them to his mouth to still
the trembling. He had thought before that he knew the
full extent of his weakness, but he had not. To let himself love again—a human being, a fragile life that could
be torn from him in an instant—the idea made him sick
with panic. He did not want to see her. He did not want
to speak to her. He wanted to be stone, cold and unfeeling and safe. And he knew that if he met her, he'd be
shattered glass instead.

After a moment, he forced his hands back into his
pockets. Old habits were falling into place: he sought a
way out, some loophole he might slip through and disappear into the protection of anonymity. In the letter
that had come today, he thought he might have found it.
Abraham Taylor had written to say that he had returned
to England after the death of his wife. He was planning
to retire; he would like to discuss with Gryf the transfer
of the trusteeship Taylor still held for Lady Tess to her
husband, which was where the earl had intended for it
to rest. Could a meeting be arranged?

Gryf's course came clear in his mind. He would talk
to Taylor, and decline the trusteeship. That was Gryf's
choice—once again, he had the solicitors' word on it.
Taylor would be forced to appoint someone else. Gryf
had faith in the consul's judgment: Taylor would choose
someone worthy. It was only one more step to place
Ashland, too, in trust and appoint the same trustee.
Taylor himself might even be persuaded to change his
mind and reassume the reponsibility.

Best of all, Gryf could send Taylor to speak to Tess.
Even the solicitors would understand that: an old family
friend and associate. They were all the same breed, Taylor and the solicitors. They could copy great mounds of
documents and sign them to their hearts' content, and

Gryf would be free of walls and bed curtains and the threat of what lay barricaded in his own heart.

Two days later, he was waiting in his grandfather's study, drumming his fingers anxiously on the black and gold writing desk given by Louis XIV to the first marquess, when old Badger shuffled in. "My lord," he announced, and read from a card, "Her British Majesty's Agent and Consul-General to the province of Pará, Abraham Taylor, Esquire."

Gryf knew this routine by now. He stood up, and said, "I'll see him directly."

"Here, my lord?"

"Here."

Taylor was ushered formally in. He looked older, more lined and less ruddy beneath the black whiskers, but he grinned when he took Gryf's hand. "Your Lordship—"

Gryf shook his head. He smiled briefly. "For God's sake, don't call me that. I get enough verbal genuflecting from the bloody butler." He held the consul's hand a moment longer than necessary. "I'm sorry," he said softly, "about Mrs. Taylor."

Taylor looked down. His grip tightened a little. "Thank you." There was a pause, as if he might say more, but then he let go of Gryf's hand and turned away. "It's time for a change for me now, you see. I have a place in Hereford—I thought I might go up there and potter about. I'd like to have things set out properly with you first. The documents are all in order. It's just a matter of a signature."

Gryf spread his fingers and leaned on the writing table. His mouth felt dry, now that he was faced with saying what he intended. "Mr. Taylor—" He glanced down, not quite able to look the consul in the eyes. "I don't want the trusteeship."

Taylor said nothing for a long moment. Then he asked, in a level tone, "You decline it?"

"Yes."

"May I ask why?"

Gryf looked up, affecting a shrug. "Lack of experience." Another silence.

Gryf took a breath, and said, "I'm putting my own assets in trust, too. I thought I would ask you to help me choose a suitable administrator."

Taylor was looking at him in a most peculiar way. Gryf doubled up his fist and tapped it on the table. His nerve was failing already.

Finally, Taylor said, "If you feel unsure of your acumen, I can put you in touch with some excellent advisers to help you administer the trust, though I doubt the need of it, myself. And I certainly don't think another trustee besides yourself would be appropriate for Lady Tess's property, or—if you'll suffer my advice—for your own. You're a young man, with all your faculties. There's no need to put your estate in trust."

"Well," Gryf said, "that's what I'm going to do."

It was hardly a persuasive answer.

"But your responsibilities—"

"Damn my responsibilities." The words were twisted with bitterness. Before Taylor could speak Gryf turned away. "My *responsibilities* nearly got me hung."

He heard the floor creak as Taylor shifted his feet. "I see."

The hell you do, Gryf thought. There was no way to put the explanation into words. No way to say that he was in complete emotional rout, afraid to risk meeting his own wife for fear of smashing the fragile shell of detachment he'd built around himself. He only knew that he could not take over the trust. The very idea raised a film of sweat on his palms.

"I'd have expected better of your grandfather's lineage," Taylor said harshly, after the silence had spun out to awkward lengths.

That hurt. Gryf frowned down at his reflection in the polished ebony. "I know I don't belong here," he said in a low voice. "I'm trying to go away."

"Run away, I think you mean."

Gryf let out a long breath. "Call it what you like, then. It doesn't matter to me."

Taylor clasped his hands behind his back and took a turn the length of the room. Gryf waited. The consul came back to an abrupt halt in front of him.

"I've been at Westpark these two weeks," Taylor said. There was a warning challenge in his tone.

Gryf kept a careful silence. He felt the pulse speed up in his throat.

"Would you like to ask after anyone there?" Taylor inquired with deadly courtesy. "Your wife and son, perhaps?"

"How are my wife and son?" Gryf returned flatly, making it clear he had no interest in the answer.

"Your son is well." Taylor glared at Gryf. "Your wife is miserable."

"This is a pointless conversation."

"Is it? Shall I tell her you said so?"

"Yes!" Gryf snapped. "Tell her that. Tell her I won't take her trust and I won't see her and I don't care if she and her son fall off the face of the Earth and land in Hades. Do you understand that, Taylor? Is that clear enough?"

The consul's face had hardened into a mask of hostility. "Quite clear," he said. "And I shall tell her none of it. I'm sure I couldn't do justice to your invective."

Gryf did not answer. He wanted to throw something. His equilibrium was cracking, dissolving, giving way to things underneath. He made a desperate effort to pull himself together. "I'm sorry," he managed finally. "I didn't—"

His voice failed him again. He turned his face from Taylor and stared at the satin upholstery on the desk chair, burningly aware of the older man's scrutiny.

Taylor spoke, at length, and his voice held a softer note. "Do you know, when first I heard who you really were, it came to me that Lord Morrow had guessed it all along. He knew your grandfather, and your uncle. I understand you greatly resemble them both."

Gryf looked up, suspicious of this sudden reverse of temper. "So I'm told," he said stiffly. "Although people haven't exactly stopped me on the street about it for the last seventeen years."

"People see what they expect to see." Taylor inclined his head thoughtfully. "Most people. But Lord Morrow was a master of accurate and unprejudiced observation. He also had a formidable memory. I think he guessed."

"I think it's highly unlikely."

"Perhaps. In his last instructions to me, he was very insistent to put his daughter in your way."

"The more fool he," Gryf said.

"Not at all." The consul smiled. "Eccentric, I will give you. A fool, no."

"Why are you telling me this?"

Taylor shrugged. "I'm wondering if what Morrow saw in you is really there." He waved his hand slightly toward the window. "*Probitas Fortis*. Isn't that what it says over the front door here?"

Gryf narrowed his eyes. "Believe me," he said slowly, "I have never—ever—stood up to that motto. I haven't even tried."

The older man smiled. "What a liar you are."

There was no answer to that. Taylor nodded, in obvious farewell. He went to the door and stopped. "She deserves better from you, you know."

Gryf took a breath. He had his armor back.

"We don't always get what we deserve," he said softly. "Do we?"

The nursery at Westpark overlooked the eighteenth-century pleasure gardens: the wide promenade and the boxwood maze, with its little crystal and white greenhouse that Tess's father had built in the center, an enchantingly filigreed prize within the reasoned squares and rectangles. Westpark itself was like that, a serene and orderly magnificence, a house of exact proportions, each silvery stone and window and door in its perfect place—but with a surprise at the heart: the round room beneath the huge glass dome at the center of the house, filled with wild trees and flowers; plants her father had collected and Mr. Sydney had cared for, until they were grown to great heights and formed a green canopy that delighted the little parrot Isidora.

From the nursery, Tess could step to the door or the window and see either view: interior or exterior. It was the outside she watched fretfully this morning, her eyes focused on the little slice of drive that was visible as it curved through the far trees on its way to the house.

She was dressed. The baby was dressed. She'd been up since dawn at work on both their toilettes, driving the nurse and the housemaids and her own lady's maid to the same mental distraction she was in herself. She had chosen first a pink gown, then demanded a gray one, and finally settled on a dotted swiss of palest apple-green, with puffed bishop sleeves and a pearl-white sash. It made her look very feminine, she thought. Breakable, like a delicate porcelain. No one could possibly connect her now with the rough-and-tumble girl who slogged through mud on the Amazon and speared eels in Tahiti.

Or so she hoped.

She sat on the windowsill, folding and refolding her hands as she waited. It had been nearly three weeks since Mr. Taylor had returned from Ashland with discouraging reports, and two since Gryf's rigidly formal note, asking if he could call on her to discuss her trust and other matters.

And other matters. That was the phrase that terrified her. She was certain he was going to start divorce proceedings, even though Mr. Taylor assured her that there were no legal grounds on his side. The marriage in Tahiti had been confirmed by the home church, and the confusion Stephen had made of the annulment with his bribes and persuasions had been cleared, to the regret of several defrocked parsons. Tess was being the model wife: staying at home, attending no parties, caring for her child. She had read all the books, and pored over the *Englishwoman's Domestic Magazine* with a vengeance. No detail of what it would require to make her a proper gentleman's lady had escaped notice.

It was all she had known to do. When she had first made the connection between Gryf and the signet ring and the story of the *Arcturus,* it had hardly seemed real. She had clutched at it as a way to save him, when there was no other appeal but to the lords themselves. It was only after, when they had recognized and acquitted him, that she began to understand the full meaning of the change from vagabond captain to sixth marquess.

No longer was there a barrier of rank and wealth between them. In title and inheritance, he was more than her equal. The newspapers in their glee over the amazing tale spared no detail of the lord's balance sheet: income from rail interests, Welsh coal mines, Mayfair and

Westminster ground rents, rich farming estates in Hampshire and Dorset . . . it was every man's dream, to be turned up rich, and the dailies made the most of it. Tess, too, had been overjoyed. Each pound of annual income that the papers listed seemed to her a brick taken down from the wall of pride that separated them. She was patient, thinking he would come to her as soon as he grasped the reality of his fortune.

But he did not.

And in his silence, there was a message. It was some flaw of her own that made him turn away.

Mr. Taylor tapped on the half-opened nursery door. Tess looked up with a start, and then invited him in. She managed a wan smile.

"I've come to say good morning to this godchild of mine," he said affably. He bent over the cradle and dangled his fingers, but his eyes were on Tess. "You look charming, madam."

"Do you think so?" Tess stood up and began to dawdle nervously about the room.

"Very much. Though I could wish for a little more color in your cheeks."

Tess went immediately to a mirror and began to pinch at them.

Mr. Taylor shook his head with a smile. "No, no. I didn't mean it literally, my dear."

"Oh." She glanced at him, and bit her lip. "Do I look so knock-kneed?"

"Panic-stricken," he said gently.

She took a deep breath, and let it out. "This is worse than my first ball." She glanced again out the window. "It's already five past. Do you suppose he'll be very late?"

Mr. Taylor spread his hands. "I can't venture to say."

"Perhaps he won't come at all."

"I shall be after him with a stick, in that case."

She turned a sad smile on him. "I thought you'd already tried that approach."

"Oh, no. He hasn't seen anything of my temper yet. I shall give him this chance to make amends."

Tess looked down at her skirt. She said unhappily, "From what you said of him, I don't think he's coming to make amends."

Mr. Taylor gave the baby one last chuck beneath the chin and straightened. "He can't divorce you, Lady Tess. You must believe that."

"What difference does it make, whether or not he can? It's enough that he wants to."

"There's no indication that a divorce suit is what he wants."

"Oh," she said, on a slightly squeaky note. "He must regret it more than ever, now. Being forced to marry me, when every choice should be open to him."

"Lady Tess," her guardian said soothingly. "He didn't seem to me to be regretful."

"How did he seem, then?" she asked in despair. "What was he like?"

Mr. Taylor frowned slightly, and looked down at the baby, wide-eyed but quiet in his cradle. "I would say . . ." He squinted thoughtfully. "Something like a man who has been sleeping, and is waking up."

Tess said in a small voice, "I don't understand."

"No. It isn't easy to describe." He left the cradle and lowered himself on the windowsill opposite Tess. "It would be as if—but no, you wouldn't have ever seen an infantryman in that state." He paused. "It's a breakdown of nerves. If you pin a man under heavy fire for too long, no way to go forward, no way to go back, no hope of rescue—and then, when he's given himself up for dead, pull him out . . ." He shook his head. "It has its effects. I suspect that your husband isn't quite rational yet."

"And it's my fault. He would never have suffered it, but for me."

"Perhaps." Mr. Taylor raised his eyebrows. "As it turned out, he'd be an ungrateful sod to blame you for what gave him back his inheritance."

"If only I were a better lady," Tess groaned. "He's probably ashamed to have a hedge bird like me for a marchioness. You know what they're saying in the papers?"

"Those letters?" Her guardian snorted. "You haven't given a thought to a bunch of stuffed corsets like that, have you? I give you my oath, your husband hasn't. He doesn't even know the Ladies' Society for Christian Womanhood exists, and he certainly won't care if they decline to admit you to their ranks because you've read Lyell's *Principles of Geology*."

"And Darwin," she reminded him. "They liked that rather less." She pursed her lips. "I suppose it's slightly more decorous to think the Earth is millions of years old than to believe one's ancestors were related to apes."

A tap on the door interrupted. The majordomo said in his quiet voice that Lord Ashland had arrived. Tess felt all the life drain out of her fingers—she had hoped to be prepared, by watching for the carriage. Mr. Taylor looked at her, and then politely took his leave with no further word.

"In the rose drawing room," Tess told the servant. That was part of the private apartments that had been her mother's; the sunny, pleasant room opened directly onto the nursery. Tess had a half-conscious idea that if Gryf saw or heard his child that it might make him want to stay with her. She gave the dozing baby a quick butterfly kiss and went into the drawing room, closing the nursery door behind her. She doubted her son would cry, for though his tantrums could be monumental, they were mercifully seldom, and the head nurse had orders to look in on him every five minutes.

Tess made herself sit still on the divan and wait, but she could not help blindly tracing the outline of one of the huge chintz roses that cascaded across the couch. A light knock sounded at the door, and she clenched her fingers. "Come in."

At first sight of him, her heart sank. He stood just inside where the footman left him, not even looking at her. In that airy summer room, his chill figure in black frock coat and gray trousers was the single dark image. A devil in the garden, with bright hair and ice-cold eyes.

"Good morning," she said, before her voice could fail her.

He looked at her, and then away, as if he could not endure the sight. "Good morning."

A moment's awkward silence followed. Tess fell to tracing the rose again, her hand hidden by the pastel volume of her skirt.

She heard him draw a deep breath. "Thank you for seeing me," he said. "I won't take much of your time."

She glanced up at him in quick anguish, and then made an effort to recover herself. "Will you sit down?" she asked, trying to match the formality of his tone.

He came farther into the room, but not to sit. He stopped by the mantelpiece of carved alabaster, a few yards away from her, and stood stiffly. She saw him rub the fingers of his right hand against his palm, as if he wished he had something to crush in it.

"I wanted to tell you what I've planned," he said without preamble. "About your trust. To see if you approve."

"I'm sure I'll approve anything you think is best," she

said, and was proud of herself for coming up with such a proper wifely gem.

He threw her a sardonic look, the first break in his reserve. She lowered her eyes. Even her best efforts could not seem to match the mold of feminine duty.

"Good," he said flatly. "Then it won't distress you if I ask Mr. Taylor to appoint a trustee other than myself."

She had expected that; Mr. Taylor had warned her. What she dreaded to hear was the reason behind it. She said humbly, and untruthfully, "Of course not."

He took a few more restless steps, with his hands behind his back. She watched him from the corner of her eye. He did not seem to her at all like a man who had been sleeping. He seemed more like a man who had not slept, not for a long time, his face and his movements wooden with strain.

He said, "I'm also placing Ashland in trust, for you and the boy. If you know of a trustee you would like to have appointed, please tell me."

Burning bridges, Tess thought. She couldn't quite manage another pearl of connubial bliss, so she only nodded mutely.

"Do you know of anyone?"

She bent her head and shook it, blinking rapidly.

A long silence ensued. Tess fought the blurring of her eyes. It should not have hurt her; she should have been resigned by now. But still, she had cherished some small hope that he might have changed his mind.

"That's all I have to say, then."

His words were expressionless. Final. For an instant, as she slowly raised her eyes, she caught him looking at her. He turned away to the open window. "No—that isn't quite all." He stared down at the windowsill. "I wanted to thank you. For your—"

His voice broke suddenly, on the smallest upward

crack, and she saw his mouth and jaw grow taut. He did not try to finish the sentence. Once again, he curved his hand into that empty, white-knuckled grip. "Damn," he said softly, to the landscape outside.

She swallowed. After a moment, she asked, "Am I to understand you're leaving Ashland?"

He nodded once, still gazing out the open window.

The marriage manuals had warned, in great capital letters, that a wife was not to interfere in her husband's affairs. But the next question popped out before she could censor it.

"Where will you go?"

He shrugged. "It doesn't matter. Back to the ship, I think."

"You aren't happy at Ashland?"

"No," he said, and looked down at the floor. "No, I haven't been very happy there."

She felt her heart beat faster. She said faintly, "Perhaps you would be happier here."

The stiffening of his shoulders beneath the black coat was obvious. He turned slightly, and met her eyes. "Absolutely not."

"Do you hate me so much?" It was barely a whisper.

He swung back toward the window with a harsh sound. "I don't hate you, Tess."

That was something, at least. She gazed at the straight line of his back. "You don't think we might . . . be a family someday?"

He gripped the window sash. The question went unanswered.

"I'm such a dunderhead." She plucked disconsolately at her skirt. "I wish I knew how to be what you want."

"Tess—" His voice was raw with pain.

She said suddenly, "Would you like to see your son?"

He didn't answer. He just stared out the window, so

that she could not see his face. She rose, interpreting permission from his silence. She went out of the room, shutting the nursery door behind her.

At the soft sound of the latch, Gryf turned back from the window. The moment's respite was godsent: he thought if he had stayed there one more instant he would have thrown himself onto the pavement below, as the only answer to the intolerable pressure inside of him. He wanted to leave, but his feet would not move. He stood rooted to the spot, staring longingly at the door he had entered, like a dying man would stare at the sanctuary he could not reach.

A family. The idea terrified him. He had learned his lesson well and finally: only alone and untouched was he safe. Love was the siren song that he had followed all his life, the veil of enchantment that hid the savage rocks beneath. He had to go, now, before he was ensnared in it again. He had to go, and yet he could not move. When Tess appeared at the door with her bundle, he had not the strength even to turn his face away.

She did not bring the child to him, but went back to her place on the couch and sat down. He could see her shyness, embarrassment, almost, that she tried to hide by bending over the froth of white lace so that two stubby arms brushed her face as they waved in jerky exploration. A cheap trick, he thought fiercely. An appeal on the basest level; emotional blackmail of the lowest kind. He tried to harden his heart to the scene, and almost succeeded. Almost, he found he could walk away from that posed and pretty picture of English domesticity and say that it meant nothing.

And then there was a swift flutter at the open window next to him. Something bright and green plummeted past his shoulder, a tiny parrot, that made one quick, silent circle of the room and came to land on top of Tess's head.

She straightened abruptly, and the bird sidestepped upward with monumental unconcern, leaning over to peer down her forehead as if to see the baby. "Oh!" Tess cried, and shook her head. The bird spread emerald wings and tried to take off at the sudden move, but its claw tangled in the net that held Tess's thick, dark hair. "Isidora!" she wailed, as one whole side of the coiffure came free, tumbling down across her shoulder. The baby began to shriek, and Isidora struggled harder, flapping and hopping frantically to get free of the trap. Tess sprang up from the couch with the baby. In the commotion, Gryf's feet took him forward; he found his son dumped without ceremony into his arms. Tess pressed both hands down over the offending bird, wailing, "Oh, how could you, you stupid beast! Now you've ruined everything!"

Isidora answered with a muffled screech. Tess stamped her foot, and huge tears started in her eyes. She made little sobbing sounds of frustration as Isidora's head popped in and out between her fingers. She worked at the tangled net, and a moment later the bird shot free. It circled the room again and came back, this time to sit on Gryf's shoulder. Tess plopped down on the couch with a knotted fist pressed to her mouth. Her hair had all fallen down now, and her face was screwed into the trembling pout of a thwarted child. The prim picture of motherhood had dissolved into chaos.

In its shambles, Gryf stood with a struggling, bawling bundle in his arms, a lovely and equally distraught female in front of him, and a green parrot nibbling determinedly at his ear.

He closed his eyes. Something in him strained to its ultimate limit. He began, in dumb silence, to cry.

The tears seemed to come out of nowhere, no emotional source or sensation, simply welling up from inside him out of some nameless spring of despair. His breath came quick and harsh; he stared desperately at the ceiling as the moisture crept down his cheeks. It seemed the final betrayal of body over mind. He had made his choice; he had asked for nothing. Only to be left alone. But the tears kept coming, a wordless revelation that he had somehow got it wrong—again—and things were not what he had reckoned.

"Oh, dear," Tess said, over the squalling cries of the baby. She looked up at Gryf with a dawning horror. "Oh, dear—what is it? Let me take him; just a moment—just a moment—oh, don't, please, don't—" She reached for the child and then threw a wild look over her shoulder as she whisked him toward the other room. "Sit down; don't leave; I won't be an instant—"

Gryf did not sit down. He looked at the fireplace, the window, the overstuffed sofa. He listened to the fading cries of the child. His son. His own son. How was that possible, that out of the utter emptiness of his life he had a son . . . and a wife . . . and an importunate green parrot that nuzzled insistently at his ear? That there was laughter still in the world, and beauty; that he was alive to see and hear it . . .

He drew in a shuddering breath. He knew why. He knew how. It was Tess, with her crazy schemes and her blue-emerald eyes; with her animals and her courage and her unconscious grace. He loved her; his happiness flowed from her like lifeblood, the center and the meaning of his whole existence. When she slipped back into the room, he did not even dare look at her. The parrot took wing again, and sailed out the window in a flurry of green. Gryf stood rigid, staring at the floor one last hopeless effort to reconstruct his defenses, to crush all feeling. One last stand against total surrender.

Tess paused at the door. She knew her plan to be a

proper lady had, like all her other plans, ended in abysmal failure. She had apologies on her lips, excuses, and a ready plea that she would learn, if only he would give her time. But the sight of him—

She thought suddenly: this is how he looked on the scaffold. When he knew he was going to die.

It touched a place so near her heart that she responded without thought. She went to him, and took his hand, and pressed it to her cheek. "What is it?" she whispered. "What's wrong?"

His fingers curled around hers. "Oh, God," he said miserably, in a voice so low she could hardly hear it. "I'm afraid."

She kissed his trembling fingers, and stroked them, as she might have soothed a child. "Afraid of what?"

His hand clenched and unclenched over hers, and then he spread it across her cheek. "I thought you were gone." His voice was hollow. "I thought Stephen had killed you."

Tess raised wide eyes.

"I wanted to die—" he said painfully. "I wanted to. I couldn't believe I didn't die." He stroked her skin with his thumb. "In prison—they won't even let you starve yourself in peace. They come and pray over you, until you eat."

"Oh, no," she murmured. "Don't think of it."

"Tess—" His gaze followed the trace of his fingers: her temple, her cheek, her lips. "I can't bear that again."

She shook her head. "No one can take you back to that horrible place. Ever. I won't let them."

He made a little sound, a kind of rasping laugh. "My champion." He stroked a lock of her loosened hair. "It wasn't the place. It was knowing I'd lost you. Believing it."

"But I thought—" She had to struggle to speak. "I thought you didn't want me."

"Oh, Tess—all my life, I've wanted—" His voice seemed to fail him. He turned from her suddenly. "I thought I'd killed you," he said harshly. "By sending you back. It was my fault, my blame; it would never have happened if I hadn't made you go. I should have figured it out, about Stark— Good God, he tried to kill you on our wedding night, and I'd left you there alone. Because I was afraid." His voice was ragged with self-disgust. "Because I didn't want to love you; because you might have hurt me again; you might have sent me away like before, and so I— Oh, Tess, it was impossible; it was hopeless . . . I've always loved you; I can't help myself. It gives me nightmares. If I lose you—" He looked at her with that terrible vulnerability in his eyes. "Oh, God—Oh, God—what if I lose you again?"

For a long moment, Tess said nothing. When she spoke, it was barely a whisper. "You aren't going to lose me."

He took a shuddering breath and shook his head helplessly.

She went forward, caught his hands, brought them up to press against her cheeks. "Never. Do you think I've gone to all this trouble of trying to look like a perfect lady only to be lost?"

He gazed down at her. She waited, her face lifted to his, watching the play of emotion: of doubt and need and fear in his smoky-gray eyes. Her whole world, her whole future, seemed to turn on that suspended look.

He lowered his eyes, to scan the fragile lace collar and delicate appliqued flowers at her throat. "A lady—" he repeated hoarsely. "I think I'd rather you looked indestructible."

"Oh." She peeped up at him modestly. "Well. If that's all. You should have seen me the time I'd just escaped from man-eating piranhas on the Río Negro." She smoothed the lapel of his coat with her fingers. "Or the time I stopped a charging boar in its track with a single shot. Or after I was attacked—"

He kissed her.

"—by a rabid llama. Vicious beasts, those . . ." He kissed her again, his mouth hard and warm and insistent on hers. ". . . llamas . . ." she mumbled gamely. The rest was lost as his arms slid downward to drag her against him and squeeze the breath out of her with his embrace. Tess gave up on her recital and wrapped her arms around his neck, rising on tiptoe to return the pressure. A rush of wings heralded Isidora, who landed on Tess's shoulder and whistled loudly. Gryf reached up and knocked the protesting parrot off, without even lifting his head.

Epilogue

The drifting clouds were touched with late afternoon pink, brushing misty fingers against the ragged peaks that circled the little bay. The ship lay anchored at the center, her teak decks glowing gold in the slanting light. While Mr. Sydney held the outrigger in place, Tess tucked her skirts around her and scrambled up the boarding ladder, met at the top by Mahzu, who gave her a hand across the rail.

A delighted squeal rang across the deck, and Tess turned to smile at her son, who was attempting without success to tumble off his perch of coiled hemp onto the quarterdeck. Her smile broadened as she saw the toddler twist around and hold out his arms with a shrill demand. At the sound, Gryf looked down from his sighting along one of the backstays. His intent expression changed to a grin. He barked a quick order to someone else to supervise the routine work on the standing rigging, and reached out to swing his son up by the arms and mount him on one shoulder.

The baby let out little yelps of pleasure, trying to grab at every rope or fitting that came within reach as Gryf strode across the deck and down the stairs. Tess lifted her arms to take the child, but Mr. Sydney's offering of a brightly colored feather carried the day. Gryf surrendered his crowing son to the little botanist and turned to Tess.

She accepted the substitution with pleasure. He kissed her hair as she leaned gratefully against his bare chest.

"Tired?" he murmured, stroking her cheek.

"Just a bit. We finished the windward side, at last. I'll have to straighten up our notes and start recopying them tonight."

"Not tonight," he said softly. "You're busy tonight."

Tess raised her head. "Am I?"

"Mmm." He nuzzled her ear. "I have plans for you, my lady. Anniversary celebration."

"Our anniversary isn't until next week."

He looked down at her, and traced a finger along her temple with a rueful smile. "How quickly they forget."

Tess frowned. After a moment, her eyes opened wide. "Oh." Her cheeks flooded with color as she realized the event to which he referred. The memory of that night on a deserted atoll made her duck her head to hide a giggle.

He tilted her chin up and kissed her. "You have exactly one minute to greet your son." He let her go and stood back. "After which, my love, prepare yourself to be kidnapped."

Obediently, Tess let the baby tweak her nose, which was all the greeting the toddler could spare between patty-cakes with Mr. Sydney. A short time later, she found herself in the dinghy with Gryf, watching appreciatively as he rowed them ashore with easy strokes. The dinghy came to rest on a beach out of sight of the ship, where crystalline waves lapped up on the silvery sand. Gryf splashed overboard, but when Tess stood and began to loosen her sturdy boots to follow, he caught her up and carried her through the last of the water and across the beach to the trees.

In a lean-to made of palm fronds, he knelt and laid her on the soft blankets that lined the shelter, pushing her down with a demanding kiss. She lifted her arms and answered with her own demand, but he pulled away. "The dinghy," he muttered. "I'll have to beach it." He brushed her forehead with his lips. "Don't move."

In his absence, Tess looked at her surroundings. The little hut was new, fragrant with fresh-cut palm and the scent of flowers that had been strewn generously among the blankets. Just outside, a faint plume of smoke issued from a mound of disturbed sand, and nearby on a bed of banana leaves were a pile of fruit and a bottle of red wine. She tilted her head back and laughed.

"What's for dinner," she teased, as Gryf came back up the beach. "Baked eel?"

He dropped to his knees beside her with a grimace. "Lord, no. I hate fish."

"How could I forget? The sea captain who hates fish."

He cupped a hand behind her neck and drew her to him roughly. "Watch your tongue, mate," he growled in her ear, "or I'll have you for dinner."

"Hmmm." Tess smiled up into his laughing eyes. "A tempting offer."

He traced her earlobe with his lips, and Tess tilted her head back languorously. Her fingers moved to his waistband to loosen the buttons there.

"Uh uh." He brushed her hand away with reluctance. "You need to eat."

Tess sighed, knowing that once he took one of his "health and well-being" notions about her or his son, there was no swaying him. She nestled back to watch in

contentment as he unearthed the bundles of meat and
banana leaves that had been steaming over coals beneath the sand. The prison pallor had long since left his
face, but more importantly to Tess, the haunted expression was gone from his eyes. He laughed now, and
often, and if sometimes at night she was awakened by
the unconscious tightness of his embrace, she had no
complaints. No complaints at all.

After a substantial meal of spicy pork and fruit, she
lay back with her head propped against a convenient
pillow of extra blankets. Gryf sat down at her feet and
began to unbutton her ankle-high boots, pulling off
both shoes and socks. Tess groaned in pleasure as he
rubbed her tired soles with his thumbs. He smiled, sliding his palms up the smooth length of her calves, pushing her skirt along. When he reached her knees, he bent
to kiss the nearest one. "Do you know your legs drive
me crazy?"

She wriggled her toes complacently. "I suspected as
much."

His eyes lowered on a silver gleam. In the tropical
heat, she'd shunned all undergarments along with her
petticoats, and she saw his expression go warm and intent as his palm grazed the tender skin of her inner thigh.

"You're perfect," he said thickly. "So soft." His hands
moved upward and molded to her hips. Tess straightened her legs as he leaned across her. "So fragile."

"Fragile!" She made a face. "Hardly."

"Look." He caught one of her arms and drew it up,
wrapping his hard, tanned fingers around her wrist. Her
skin looked translucently pale against his, an ivory twig
that might snap in his hand. He kissed her open palm.
"Like a flower."

Tess tried to hide the spontaneous smile that sprang to
her lips. "You sound like the besotted Mr. Bottomshaw."

He sighed with dolorous eloquence and began to work at the fastening of her blouse. "It's midsummer moon with me. Hopelessly ensnared by a pretty face." His hands slipped beneath the fabric to her breast. He lowered his mouth and nibbled the curve of her throat. "Among other things."

A sudden shyness washed over her. She put her arms around his neck and said into his shoulder, "Are you really happy with me?"

The delightful play of his fingers stopped. He pushed her down gently and looked into her eyes. "Could you really think I'm not?"

"Well—" She bit her lip. "You weren't given much of a choice. You might have had a proper wife, who would stay home and manage your house and know how to be fashionable and make clever conversation and give balls and things. Someone you could be proud of."

He gazed at her a moment, all the humor gone from his smoky eyes. "I never wanted someone like that," he said slowly.

Tess frowned, rolling a little ball of thread from the blanket in her fingers. "You think so. But you didn't have a chance to find out, did you? You only lived on your own estate for a few months, and I know you didn't care for it much then, but I'm sure in time you would have grown accustomed. You could have taken your seat in Parliament, and become a member of your grandfather's clubs—"

"—and ride to the hounds and go shooting in the country?" he interrupted.

Tess nodded up at him through her eyelashes.

"And drink milk punch," he continued blandly, "and discuss shares, and pay morning calls, and change clothes five times a day, and attend charity routs, and dance with every debutante once—but not twice—and talk to their mothers for a quarter-hour each." His fingers curved again around her breast, and his gaze slid downward. "Instead of which, I have the bad luck to find myself secluded in paradise with the most beautiful woman alive, whom I adore with my whole body and soul . . . and an entire night of lovemaking ahead of me."

She felt herself flushing. "You know what I mean. Your position—Ashland—you don't miss that?"

"No."

The negative was unhesitating. Absolute.

Tess considered it, and then smiled up at him wickedly. "Then can you think of any other ways I might try to fish for compliments?"

He didn't bother to answer that with words, but used his hands and his mouth to deliver the most delicious compliments she could have imagined. Tess leaned back and let him fill her, mind and senses, until there was nothing in her world but his golden warmth. He pressed her eyes closed with kisses, but her fingers found the buttons that had been denied her before, and then the waiting hardness beneath.

He took her slowly, with the patience of knowing they had time. This night and longer. Forever. The sand beneath the blanket gave as she did, molding to the imprint of his body on hers. Her small sounds of pleasure whispered in his ears. He arched to her soft and compelling rhythm; his palms slid down her naked sides and up again as her hips and breasts moved like smooth fire in his hands. "Tess—" he groaned, his muscles knotting. "My love, my love. Oh God, Tess . . ." He strained into her, felt her burst beneath him with a shudder and a sharp cry. Her tremors brought him his own fulfillment, a crimson-hot explosion. It left him limp and gasping.

Afterward he held her close, thinking of possibilities. Another child, perhaps. He smiled into her hair, taking a deep draught of her fragrance. Another child, another life to love and fear for. He was strong enough now. He welcomed the vulnerability for the sake of the joy. That much he had learned: that love was a risk, and to live without risk was to live in a cage darker than any prison cell.

He frowned faintly as he remembered her earlier questioning. He leaned over as they lay together, and kissed the tip of her nose. "What's all this about a proper wife? Do *you* want to go back to England?"

Her blue-green eyes looked into his, wide and luminous. The sunset danced rosy-gold on her skin. "Do you?"

"I don't care." He played with a lock of dark hair. "I want to be with you. It doesn't matter where."

Tess watched him in the fading light, the curve of his cheek, the gleam of lithe muscle beneath his skin. He looked like a pagan stretched beside her, a wild son of nature in copper and bronze. The thought of covering that heathen beauty in civilized starch was more than she could bear.

"Then come with me," she whispered fiercely, as she pulled him down to her mouth. "Come with me, Captain. We've got a whole world to explore."